I0762927

HANS CHRISTIAN
ANDERSEN &
BROTHERS GRIMM

TRANSLATED BY J. H. STICKNEY, EDGAR TAYLOR,
AND MARIAN EDWARDES

Published by Harper Muse, an imprint of HarperCollins Focus LLC, 501 Nelson Place, Nashville, TN 37214, USA.

ISBN 978-1-4003-5573-0 (HC)

HarperCollins Publishers, Macken House, 39/40 Mayor Street Upper, Dublin 1, D01 C9W8, Ireland (https://www.harpercollins.com)

Printed in Vietnam

26 27 28 29 30 31 32 33 34 35 36 37 38 / RRD / 16 15 14 13 12 11 10 9 8 7 6 5 4 3 2 1

These tales are presented as Hans Christian Andersen, Jacob Grimm, and Wilhelm Grimm first wrote them in the nineteenth century. While originally written for children, many are darker and more morally complex than the happier versions found in modern retellings. We encourage you to read and enjoy them with that context in mind.

Hans Christian Andersen was a Danish writer who created some of the world's most famous fairy tales. His stories about ducklings, mermaids, and royalty have made him one of the most popular children's authors of all time.

While written for children, Andersen's stories tackle serious topics like poverty and social inequality. Many of his characters face hardship and cruelty. "The Ugly Duckling" (1843) is believed to reflect Andersen's own challenging childhood experiences.

Andersen gained recognition during his lifetime, and his legacy continues today. His 156 stories across nine volumes have been translated into over 125 languages and adapted into countless ballets, plays, and films.

Grimm's Fairy Tales, originally titled Children's and Household Tales (Kinder- und Hausmärchen), is a famous collection of stories by the Brothers Grimm, Jacob and Wilhelm.

First published in 1812, the first edition featured eighty-six tales written for adults and wasn't necessarily suited for children. It included academic commentary and stories that addressed darker themes, such as death, betrayal, and violence. By altering the content and adding illustrations in later versions, the Grimms succeeded in appealing to a wider audience. Their Kleine Ausgabe ("small edition"), published in 1825, was specifically aimed at children and went through ten editions. By the seventh edition in 1857, their collection grew to include two hundred fairy tales and ten legends.

Grimm's Fairy Tales has endured for over two centuries, captivating readers of all ages. While early versions of the tales were shadowed by hardship and complexity, their enduring charm lies in their ability to transport us to magical worlds, teach moral lessons, and entertain with imaginative twists. Today, the collection remains one of the most treasured literary works of all time.

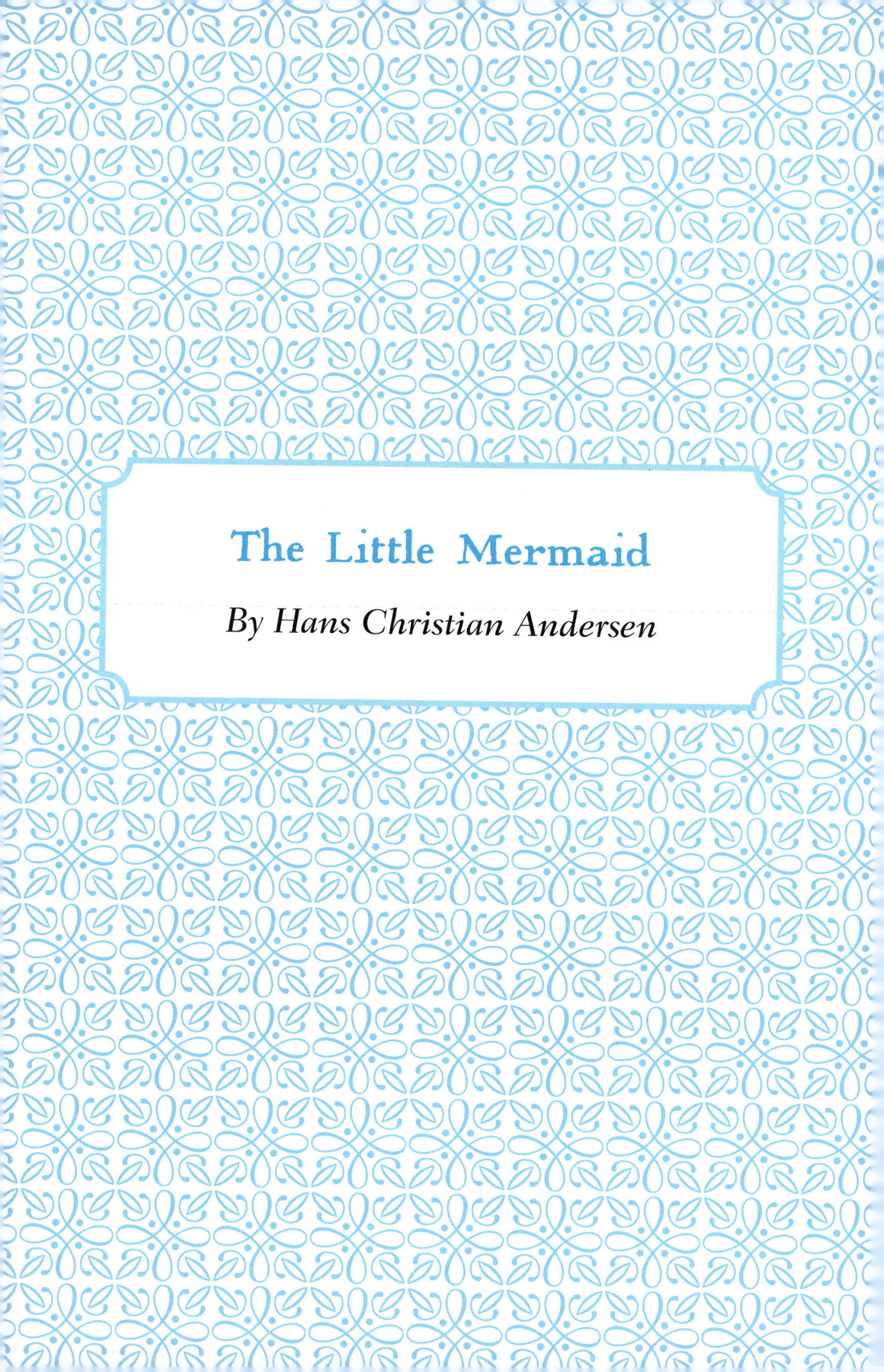

The Little Mermaid

By Hans Christian Andersen

Far out in the ocean, where the water is as blue as the prettiest cornflower, and as clear as crystal, it is very, very deep; so deep, indeed, that no cable could fathom it: many church steeples, piled one upon another, would not reach from the ground beneath to the surface of the water above. There dwell the Sea King and his subjects. We must not imagine that there is nothing at the bottom of the sea but bare yellow sand. No, indeed; the most singular flowers and plants grow there; the leaves and stems of which are so pliant, that the slightest agitation of the water causes them to stir as if they had life. Fishes, both large and small, glide between the branches, as birds fly among the trees here upon land. In the deepest spot of all, stands the castle of the Sea King. Its walls are built of coral, and the long, gothic windows are of the clearest amber. The roof is formed of shells, that open and close as the water flows over them. Their appearance is very beautiful, for in each lies a glittering pearl, which would be fit for the diadem of a queen.

The Sea King had been a widower for many years, and his aged mother kept house for him. She was a very wise woman, and exceedingly proud of her high birth; on that account she wore twelve oysters on her tail; while others, also of high rank, were only allowed to wear six. She was, however, deserving of very great praise, especially for her care of the little sea-princesses, her granddaughters. They were six beautiful children; but the youngest was the prettiest of them all; her skin was as clear and delicate as a rose leaf, and her eyes as blue as the deepest sea; but, like all the others, she had no feet, and her body ended in a fish's tail. All day long they played in the great halls of the castle, or among the living flowers that grew out of the walls. The large amber windows were open, and the fish swam in, just as the swallows fly into our houses when we open the windows, excepting that the fishes swam up to the princesses, ate out of their hands, and allowed themselves to be stroked. Outside the castle there was a beautiful garden, in which grew bright red and dark blue flowers, and blossoms like flames of fire; the fruit glittered like gold, and the leaves and stems waved to and fro continually. The earth itself was the finest sand, but blue as the flame of burning sulphur. Over everything lay a peculiar blue radiance, as if it were surrounded by the air from above, through which the blue sky shone, instead of the dark depths of the sea. In calm weather the sun could be seen, looking like a purple flower, with the light streaming from the calyx. Each of the young princesses had a little plot of ground in the garden, where she might dig and plant as she pleased. One arranged her flowerbed into the form of a whale; another thought it better to make hers like the figure of a little mermaid; but that of the youngest was round like the sun, and contained flowers as red as his rays at sunset.

She was a strange child, quiet and thoughtful; and while her sisters would be delighted with the wonderful things which they obtained from the wrecks of vessels, she cared for nothing but her pretty red flowers, like the sun, excepting a beautiful marble statue. It was the representation of a handsome boy, carved out of pure white stone, which had fallen to the bottom of the sea from a wreck. She planted by the statue a rose-colored weeping willow. It grew splendidly, and very soon hung its fresh branches over the statue, almost down to the blue sands. The shadow had a violet tint, and waved to and fro like the branches; it seemed as if the crown of the tree and the root were at play, and trying to kiss each other. Nothing gave her so much pleasure as to hear about the world above the sea. She made her old grandmother tell her all she knew of the ships and of the towns, the people and the animals. To her it seemed most wonderful and beautiful to hear that the flowers of the land should have fragrance, and not those below the sea; that the trees of the forest should be green; and that the fishes among the trees could sing so sweetly, that it was quite a pleasure to hear them. Her grandmother called the little birds fishes, or she would not have understood her; for she had never seen birds.

"When you have reached your fifteenth year," said the grandmother, "you will have permission to rise up out of the sea, to sit on the rocks in the moonlight, while the great ships are sailing by; and then you will see both forests and towns."

In the following year, one of the sisters would be fifteen: but as each was a year younger than the other, the youngest would have to wait five years before her turn came to rise up from the bottom of the ocean, and see the earth as we do. However, each promised to tell the others what she saw on her first visit, and what she thought the most beautiful; for their grandmother could not tell them enough; there were so many things on which they wanted information. None of them longed so much for her turn to come as the youngest, she who had the longest time to wait, and who was so quiet and thoughtful. Many nights she stood by the open window, looking up through the dark blue water, and watching the fish as they splashed about with their fins and tails. She could see the moon and stars shining faintly; but through the water they looked larger than they do to our eyes. When something like a black cloud passed between her and them, she knew that it was either a whale swimming over her head, or a ship full of human beings, who never imagined that a pretty little mermaid was standing beneath them, holding out her white hands towards the keel of their ship.

As soon as the eldest was fifteen, she was allowed to rise to the surface of the ocean. When she came back, she had hundreds of things to talk about; but the most beautiful, she said, was to lie in the moonlight, on a sandbank, in the quiet sea, near the coast, and to gaze on a large town nearby, where the lights were twinkling like hundreds of stars; to listen to the sounds of the music, the noise of carriages, and the voices of human beings, and then to hear the merry bells peal out from the church steeples; and because she could not go near to all those wonderful things, she longed for them more than ever. Oh, did not the youngest sister listen eagerly to all these descriptions? and afterwards, when she stood at the open window looking up through the dark blue water, she thought of the great city, with all its bustle and noise, and even fancied she could hear the sound of the church bells, down in the depths of the sea.

In another year the second sister received permission to rise to the surface of the water, and to swim about where she pleased. She rose just as the sun was setting, and this, she said, was the most beautiful sight of all. The whole sky looked like gold, while violet and rose-colored clouds, which she could not describe, floated over her; and, still more rapidly than the clouds, flew a large flock of wild swans towards the setting sun, looking like a long white veil across the sea. She also swam towards the sun; but it sunk into the waves, and the rosy tints faded from the clouds and from the sea.

The third sister's turn followed; she was the boldest of them all, and she swam up a broad river that emptied itself into the sea. On the banks she saw green hills covered with beautiful vines; palaces and castles peeped out from amid the proud trees of the forest; she heard the birds singing, and the rays of the sun were so powerful that she was obliged often to dive down under the water to cool her burning face. In a narrow creek she found a whole troop of little human children, quite naked, and sporting about in the water; she wanted to play with them, but they fled in a great fright; and then a little black animal came to the water; it was a dog, but she did not know that, for she had never before seen one. This animal barked at her so terribly that she became frightened, and rushed back to the open sea. But she said she should never forget the beautiful forest, the green hills, and the pretty little children who could swim in the water, although they had not fish's tails.

The fourth sister was more timid; she remained in the midst of the sea, but she said it was quite as beautiful there as nearer the land. She could see for so many miles around her, and the sky above looked like a bell of glass. She had seen the ships, but at such a great distance that they looked like seagulls. The dolphins sported in the waves, and the great whales spouted water from their nostrils till it seemed as if a hundred fountains were playing in every direction.

The fifth sister's birthday occurred in the winter; so when her turn came, she saw what the others had not seen the first time they went up. The sea looked quite green, and large icebergs were floating about, each like a pearl, she said, but larger and loftier than the churches built by men. They were of the most singular shapes, and glittered like diamonds. She had seated herself upon one of the largest, and let the wind play with her long hair, and she remarked that all the ships sailed by rapidly, and steered as far away as they could from the iceberg, as if they were afraid of it. Towards evening, as the sun went down, dark clouds covered the sky, the thunder rolled and the lightning flashed, and the red light glowed on the icebergs as they rocked and tossed on the heaving sea. On all the ships the sails were reefed with fear and trembling, while she sat calmly on the floating iceberg, watching the blue lightning, as it darted its forked flashes into the sea.

When first the sisters had permission to rise to the surface, they were each delighted with the new and beautiful sights they saw; but now, as grown-up girls, they could go when they pleased, and they had become indifferent about it. They wished themselves back again in the water, and after a month had passed they said it was much more beautiful down below, and pleasanter to be at home.

Yet often, in the evening hours, the five sisters would twine their arms round each other, and rise to the surface, in a row. They had more beautiful voices than any human being could have; and before the approach of a storm, and when they expected a ship would be lost, they swam before the vessel, and sang sweetly of the delights to be found in the depths of the sea, and begging the sailors not to fear if they sank to the bottom. But the sailors could not understand the song; they took it for the howling of the storm. And these things were never to be beautiful for them; for if the ship sank, the men were drowned, and their dead bodies alone reached the palace of the Sea King.

When the sisters rose, arm-in-arm, through the water in this way, their youngest sister would stand quite alone, looking after them, ready to cry, only that the mermaids have no tears, and therefore they suffer more. "Oh, were I but fifteen years old," said she: "I know that I shall love the world up there, and all the people who live in it."

At last she reached her fifteenth year. "Well, now, you are grown up," said the old dowager, her grandmother; "so you must let me adorn you like your other sisters"; and she placed a wreath of white lilies in her hair, and every flower leaf was half a pearl. Then the old lady ordered eight great oysters to attach themselves to the tail of the princess to show her high rank.

"But they hurt me so," said the little mermaid.

"Pride must suffer pain," replied the old lady. Oh, how gladly she would have shaken off all this grandeur, and laid aside the heavy wreath! The red flowers in her own garden would have suited her much better, but she could not help herself: so she said, "Farewell," and rose as lightly as a bubble to the surface of the water. The sun had just set as she raised her head above the waves; but the clouds were tinted with crimson and gold, and through the glimmering twilight beamed the evening star in all its beauty. The sea was calm, and the air mild and fresh. A large ship, with three masts, lay becalmed on the water, with only one sail set; for not a breeze stiffed, and the sailors sat idle on deck or amongst the rigging. There was music and song on board; and, as darkness came on, a hundred colored lanterns were lighted, as if the flags of all nations waved in the air. The little mermaid swam close to the cabin windows; and now and then, as the waves lifted her up, she could look in through clear glass windowpanes, and see a number of well-dressed people within. Among them was a young prince, the most beautiful of all, with large black eyes; he was sixteen years of age, and his birthday was being kept with much rejoicing. The sailors were dancing on deck, but when the prince came out of the cabin, more than a hundred rockets rose in the air, making it as bright as day. The little mermaid was so startled that she dived under water; and when she again stretched out her head, it appeared as if all the stars of heaven were falling around her, she had never seen such fireworks before. Great suns spurted fire about, splendid fireflies flew into the blue air, and everything was reflected in the clear, calm sea beneath. The ship itself was so brightly illuminated that all the people, and even the smallest rope, could be distinctly and plainly seen. And how handsome the young prince looked, as he pressed the hands of all present and smiled at them, while the music resounded through the clear night air.

It was very late; yet the little mermaid could not take her eyes from the ship, or from the beautiful prince. The colored lanterns had been extinguished, no more rockets rose in the air, and the cannon had ceased firing; but the sea became restless, and a moaning, grumbling sound could be heard beneath the waves: still the little mermaid remained by the cabin window, rocking up and down on the water, which enabled her to look in. After a while, the sails were quickly unfurled, and the noble ship continued her passage; but soon the waves rose higher, heavy clouds darkened the sky, and lightning appeared in the distance. A dreadful storm was approaching; once more the sails were reefed, and the great ship pursued her flying course over the raging sea. The waves rose mountains high, as if they would have overtopped the mast; but the ship dived like a swan between them, and then rose again on their lofty, foaming crests. To the little mermaid this appeared pleasant sport; not so to the sailors. At length the ship groaned and creaked; the thick planks gave way under the lashing of the sea as it broke over the deck; the mainmast snapped asunder like a reed; the ship lay over on her side; and the water rushed in. The little mermaid now perceived that the crew were in danger; even she herself was obliged to be careful to avoid the beams and planks of the wreck which lay scattered on the water. At one moment it was so pitch dark that she could not see a single object, but a flash of lightning revealed the whole scene; she could see everyone who had been on board excepting the prince; when the ship parted, she had seen him sink into the deep waves, and she was glad, for she thought he would now be with her; and then she remembered that human beings could not live in the water, so that when he got down to her father's palace he would be quite dead. But he must not die. So she swam about among the beams and planks which strewed the surface of the sea, forgetting that they could crush her to pieces. Then she dived deeply under the dark waters, rising and falling with the waves, till at length she managed to reach the young prince, who was fast losing the power of swimming in that stormy sea. His limbs were failing him, his beautiful eyes were closed, and he would have died had not the little mermaid come to his assistance. She held his head above the water, and let the waves drift them where they would.

In the morning the storm had ceased; but of the ship not a single fragment could be seen. The sun rose up red and glowing from the water, and its beams brought back the hue of health to the prince's cheeks; but his eyes remained closed. The mermaid kissed his high, smooth forehead, and stroked back his wet hair; he seemed to her like the marble statue in her little garden, and she kissed him again, and wished that he might live. Presently they came in sight of land; she saw lofty blue mountains, on which the white snow rested as if a flock of swans were lying upon them. Near the coast were beautiful green forests, and close by stood a large building, whether a church or a convent she could not tell. Orange and citron trees grew in the garden, and before the door stood lofty palms. The sea here formed a little bay, in which the water was quite still, but very deep; so she swam with the handsome prince to the beach, which was covered with fine, white sand, and there she laid him in the warm sunshine, taking care to raise his head higher than his body. Then bells sounded in the large white building, and a number of young girls came into the garden. The little mermaid swam out farther from the shore and placed herself between some high rocks that rose out of the water; then she covered her head and neck with the foam of the sea so that her little face might not be seen, and watched to see what would become of the poor prince. She did not wait long before she saw a young girl approach the spot where he lay. She seemed frightened at first, but only for a moment; then she fetched a number of people, and the mermaid saw that the prince came to life again, and smiled upon those who stood round him. But to her he sent no smile; he knew not that she had saved him. This made her very unhappy, and when he was led away into the great building, she dived down sorrowfully into the water, and returned to her father's castle. She had always been silent and thoughtful, and now she was more so than ever. Her sisters asked her what she had seen during her first visit to the surface of the water; but she would tell them nothing. Many an evening and morning did she rise to the place where she had left the prince. She saw the fruits in the garden ripen till they were gathered, the snow on the tops of the mountains melt away; but she never saw the prince, and therefore she returned home, always more sorrowful than before. It was her only comfort to sit in her own little garden, and fling her arm round the beautiful marble statue which was like the prince; but she gave up tending her flowers, and they grew in wild confusion over the paths, twining their long leaves and stems round the branches of the trees, so that the whole place became dark and gloomy. At length she could bear it no longer, and told one of her sisters all about it. Then the others heard the secret, and very soon it became known to two mermaids whose intimate friend happened to know who the prince was. She had also seen the festival on board ship, and she told them where the prince came from, and where his palace stood.

"Come, little sister," said the other princesses; then they entwined their arms and rose up in a long row to the surface of the water, close by the spot where they knew the prince's palace stood. It was built of bright yellow shining stone, with long flights of marble steps, one of which reached quite down to the sea. Splendid gilded cupolas rose over the roof, and between the pillars that surrounded the whole building stood life-like statues of marble. Through the clear crystal of the lofty windows could be seen noble rooms, with costly silk curtains and hangings of tapestry; while the walls were covered with beautiful paintings which were a pleasure to look at. In the centre of the largest saloon a fountain threw its sparkling jets high up into the glass cupola of the ceiling, through which the sun shone down upon the water and upon the beautiful plants growing round the basin of the fountain. Now that she knew where he lived, she spent many an evening and many a night on the water near the palace. She would swim much nearer the shore than any of the others ventured to do; indeed once she went quite up the narrow channel under the marble balcony, which threw a broad shadow on the water. Here she would sit and watch the young prince, who thought himself quite alone in the bright moonlight. She saw him many times of an evening sailing in a pleasant boat, with music playing and flags waving. She peeped out from among the green rushes, and if the wind caught her long silvery-white veil, those who saw it believed it to be a swan, spreading out its wings. On many a night, too, when the fishermen, with their torches, were out at sea, she heard them relate so many good things about the doings of the young prince, that she was glad she had saved his life when he had been tossed about half-dead on the waves. And she remembered that his head had rested on her bosom, and how heartily she had kissed him; but he knew nothing of all this, and could not even dream of her. She grew more and more fond of human beings, and wished more and more to be able to wander about with those whose world seemed to be so much larger than her own. They could fly over the sea in ships, and mount the high hills which were far above the clouds; and the lands they possessed, their woods and their fields, stretched far away beyond the reach of her sight. There was so much that she wished to know, and her sisters were unable to answer all her questions. Then she applied to her old grandmother, who knew all about the upper world, which she very rightly called the lands above the sea.

"If human beings are not drowned," asked the little mermaid, "can they live forever? do they never die as we do here in the sea?"

"Yes," replied the old lady, "they must also die, and their term of life is even shorter than ours. We sometimes live to three hundred years, but when we cease to exist here we only become the foam on the surface of the water, and we have not even a grave down here of those we love. We have not immortal souls, we shall never live again; but, like the green seaweed, when once it has been cut off, we can never flourish more. Human beings, on the contrary, have a soul which lives forever, lives after the body has been turned to dust. It rises up through the clear, pure air beyond the glittering stars. As we rise out of the water, and behold all the land of the earth, so do they rise to unknown and glorious regions which we shall never see."

"Why have not we an immortal soul?" asked the little mermaid mournfully; "I would give gladly all the hundreds of years that I have to live, to be a human being only for one day, and to have the hope of knowing the happiness of that glorious world above the stars."

"You must not think of that," said the old woman; "we feel ourselves to be much happier and much better off than human beings."

"So I shall die," said the little mermaid, "and as the foam of the sea I shall be driven about, never again to hear the music of the waves, or to see the pretty flowers nor the red sun. Is there anything I can do to win an immortal soul?"

"No," said the old woman, "unless a man were to love you so much that you were more to him than his father or mother; and if all his thoughts and all his love were fixed upon you, and the priest placed his right hand in yours, and he promised to be true to you here and hereafter, then his soul would glide into your body and you would obtain a share in the future happiness of mankind. He would give a soul to you and retain his own as well; but this can never happen. Your fish's tail, which amongst us is considered so beautiful, is thought on earth to be quite ugly; they do not know any better, and they think it necessary to have two stout props, which they call legs, in order to be handsome."

Then the little mermaid sighed, and looked sorrowfully at her fish's tail. "Let us be happy," said the old lady, "and dart and spring about during the three hundred years that we have to live, which is really quite long enough; after that we can rest ourselves all the better. This evening we are going to have a court ball."

It is one of those splendid sights which we can never see on earth. The walls and the ceiling of the large ballroom were of thick but transparent crystal. Many hundreds of colossal shells, some of a deep red, others of a grass green, stood on each side in rows, with blue fire in them, which lighted up the whole saloon, and shone through the walls, so that the sea was also illuminated. Innumerable fishes, great and small, swam past the crystal walls; on some of them the scales glowed with a purple brilliancy, and on others they shone like silver and gold. Through the halls flowed a broad stream, and in it danced the mermen and the mermaids to the music of their own sweet singing. No one on earth has such a lovely voice as theirs. The little mermaid sang more sweetly than them all. The whole court applauded her with hands and tails; and for a moment her heart felt quite gay, for she knew she had the loveliest voice of any on earth or in the sea. But she soon thought again of the world above her, for she could not forget the charming prince, nor her sorrow that she had not an immortal soul like his; therefore she crept away silently out of her father's palace, and while everything within was gladness and song, she sat in her own little garden sorrowful and alone. Then she heard the bugle sounding through the water, and thought, "He is certainly sailing above, he on whom my wishes depend, and in whose hands I should like to place the happiness of my life. I will venture all for him, and to win an immortal soul, while my sisters are dancing in my father's palace, I will go to the sea witch, of whom I have always been so much afraid, but she can give me counsel and help."

And then the little mermaid went out from her garden, and took the road to the foaming whirlpools, behind which the sorceress lived. She had never been that way before: neither flowers nor grass grew there; nothing but bare, gray, sandy ground stretched out to the whirlpool, where the water, like foaming millwheels, whirled round everything that it seized, and cast it into the fathomless deep. Through the midst of these crushing whirlpools the little mermaid was obliged to pass, to reach the dominions of the sea witch; and also for a long distance the only road lay right across a quantity of warm, bubbling mire, called by the witch her turfmoor. Beyond this stood her house, in the centre of a strange forest, in which all the trees and flowers were polypi, half animals and half plants; they looked like serpents with a hundred heads growing out of the ground. The branches were long slimy arms, with fingers like flexible worms, moving limb after limb from the root to the top. All that could be reached in the sea they seized upon, and held fast, so that it never escaped from their clutches. The little mermaid was so alarmed at what she saw, that she stood still, and her heart beat with fear, and she was very nearly turning back; but she thought of the prince, and of the human soul for which she longed, and her courage returned. She fastened her long flowing hair round her head, so that the polypi might not seize hold of it. She laid her hands together across her bosom, and then she darted forward as a fish shoots through the water, between the supple arms and fingers of the ugly polypi, which were stretched out on each side of her. She saw that each held in its grasp something it had seized with its numerous little arms, as if they were iron bands. The white skeletons of human beings who had perished at sea, and had sunk down into the deep waters, skeletons of land animals, oars, rudders, and chests of ships were lying tightly grasped by their clinging arms; even a little mermaid, whom they had caught and strangled; and this seemed the most shocking of all to the little princess.

She now came to a space of marshy ground in the wood, where large, fat water snakes were rolling in the mire, and showing their ugly, drab-colored bodies. In the midst of this spot stood a house, built with the bones of shipwrecked human beings. There sat the sea witch, allowing a toad to eat from her mouth, just as people sometimes feed a canary with a piece of sugar. She called the ugly water snakes her little chickens, and allowed them to crawl all over her bosom.

"I know what you want," said the sea witch; "it is very stupid of you, but you shall have your way, and it will bring you to sorrow, my pretty princess. You want to get rid of your fish's tail, and to have two supports instead of it, like human beings on earth, so that the young prince may fall in love with you, and that you may have an immortal soul." And then the witch laughed so loud and disgustingly, that the toad and the snakes fell to the ground, and lay there wriggling about. "You are but just in time," said the witch; "for after sunrise tomorrow I should not be able to help you till the end of another year. I will prepare a draught for you, with which you must swim to land tomorrow before sunrise, and sit down on the shore and drink it. Your tail will then disappear, and shrink up into what mankind calls legs, and you will feel great pain, as if a sword were passing through you. But all who see you will say that you are the prettiest little human being they ever saw. You will still have the same floating gracefulness of movement, and no dancer will ever tread so lightly; but at every step you take it will feel as if you were treading upon sharp knives, and that the blood must flow. If you will bear all this, I will help you."

"Yes, I will," said the little princess in a trembling voice, as she thought of the prince and the immortal soul.

"But think again," said the witch; "for when once your shape has become like a human being, you can no more be a mermaid. You will never return through the water to your sisters, or to your father's palace again; and if you do not win the love of the prince, so that he is willing to forget his father and mother for your sake, and to love you with his whole soul, and allow the priest to join your hands that you may be man and wife, then you will never have an immortal soul. The first morning after he marries another your heart will break, and you will become foam on the crest of the waves."

"I will do it," said the little mermaid, and she became pale as death.

"But I must be paid also," said the witch, "and it is not a trifle that I ask. You have the sweetest voice of any who dwell here in the depths of the sea, and you believe that you will be able to charm the prince with it also, but this voice you must give to me; the best thing you possess will I have for the price of my draught. My own blood must be mixed with it, that it may be as sharp as a two-edged sword."

"But if you take away my voice," said the little mermaid, "what is left for me?"

"Your beautiful form, your graceful walk, and your expressive eyes; surely with these you can enchain a man's heart. Well, have you lost your courage? Put out your little tongue that I may cut it off as my payment; then you shall have the powerful draught."

"It shall be," said the little mermaid.

Then the witch placed her cauldron on the fire, to prepare the magic draught.

"Cleanliness is a good thing," said she, scouring the vessel with snakes, which she had tied together in a large knot; then she pricked herself in the breast, and let the black blood drop into it. The steam that rose formed itself into such horrible shapes that no one could look at them without fear. Every moment the witch threw something else into the vessel, and when it began to boil, the sound was like the weeping of a crocodile. When at last the magic draught was ready, it looked like the clearest water. "There it is for you," said the witch. Then she cut off the mermaid's tongue, so that she became dumb, and would never again speak or sing. "If the polypi should seize hold of you as you return through the wood," said the witch, "throw over them a few drops of the potion, and their fingers will be torn into a thousand pieces." But the little mermaid had no occasion to do this, for the polypi sprang back in terror when they caught sight of the glittering draught, which shone in her hand like a twinkling star.

So she passed quickly through the wood and the marsh, and between the rushing whirlpools. She saw that in her father's palace the torches in the ballroom were extinguished, and all within asleep; but she did not venture to go in to them, for now she was dumb and going to leave them forever, she felt as if her heart would break. She stole into the garden, took a flower from the flowerbeds of each of her sisters, kissed her hand a thousand times towards the palace, and then rose up through the dark blue waters. The sun had not risen when she came in sight of the prince's palace, and approached the beautiful marble steps, but the moon shone clear and bright. Then the little mermaid drank the magic draught, and it seemed as if a two-edged sword went through her delicate body: she fell into a swoon, and lay like one dead. When the sun arose and shone over the sea, she recovered, and felt a sharp pain; but just before her stood the handsome young prince. He fixed his coal-black eyes upon her so earnestly that she cast down her own, and then became aware that her fish's tail was gone, and that she had as pretty a pair of white legs and tiny feet as any little maiden could have; but she had no clothes, so she wrapped herself in her long, thick hair. The prince asked her who she was, and where she came from, and she looked at him mildly and sorrowfully with her deep blue eyes; but she could not speak.

Every step she took was as the witch had said it would be; she felt as if treading upon the points of needles or sharp knives; but she bore it willingly, and stepped as lightly by the prince's side as a soap bubble, so that he and all who saw her wondered at her graceful-swaying movements. She was very soon arrayed in costly robes of silk and muslin, and was the most beautiful creature in the palace; but she was dumb, and could neither speak nor sing.

Beautiful female slaves, dressed in silk and gold, stepped forward and sang before the prince and his royal parents: one sang better than all the others, and the prince clapped his hands and smiled at her. This was great sorrow to the little mermaid; she knew how much more sweetly she herself could sing once, and she thought, "Oh if he could only know that! I have given away my voice forever, to be with him."

The slaves next performed some pretty fairy-like dances, to the sound of beautiful music. Then the little mermaid raised her lovely white arms, stood on the tips of her toes, and glided over the floor, and danced as no one yet had been able to dance. At each moment her beauty became more revealed, and her expressive eyes appealed more directly to the heart than the songs of the slaves. Everyone was enchanted, especially the prince, who called her his little foundling; and she danced again quite readily, to please him, though each time her foot touched the floor it seemed as if she trod on sharp knives.

The prince said she should remain with him always, and she received permission to sleep at his door, on a velvet cushion. He had a page's dress made for her, that she might accompany him on horseback. They rode together through the sweet-scented woods, where the green boughs touched their shoulders, and the little birds sang among the fresh leaves. She climbed with the prince to the tops of high mountains; and although her tender feet bled so that even her steps were marked, she only laughed, and followed him till they could see the clouds beneath them looking like a flock of birds travelling to distant lands. While at the prince's palace, and when all the household were asleep, she would go and sit on the broad marble steps; for it eased her burning feet to bathe them in the cold seawater; and then she thought of all those below in the deep.

Once during the night her sisters came up arm-in-arm, singing sorrowfully, as they floated on the water. She beckoned to them, and then they recognized her, and told her how she had grieved them. After that, they came to the same place every night; and once she saw in the distance her old grandmother, who had not been to the surface of the sea for many years, and the old Sea King, her father, with his crown on his head. They stretched out their hands towards her, but they did not venture so near the land as her sisters did.

As the days passed, she loved the prince more fondly, and he loved her as he would love a little child, but it never came into his head to make her his wife; yet, unless he married her, she could not receive an immortal soul; and, on the morning after his marriage with another, she would dissolve into the foam of the sea.

"Do you not love me the best of them all?" the eyes of the little mermaid seemed to say, when he took her in his arms, and kissed her fair forehead.

"Yes, you are dear to me," said the prince; "for you have the best heart, and you are the most devoted to me; you are like a young maiden whom I once saw, but whom I shall never meet again. I was in a ship that was wrecked, and the waves cast me ashore near a holy temple, where several young maidens performed the service. The youngest of them found me on the shore, and saved my life. I saw her but twice, and she is the only one in the world whom I could love; but you are like her, and you have almost driven her image out of my mind. She belongs to the holy temple, and my good fortune has sent you to me instead of her; and we will never part."

"Ah, he knows not that it was I who saved his life," thought the little mermaid. "I carried him over the sea to the wood where the temple stands: I sat beneath the foam, and watched till the human beings came to help him. I saw the pretty maiden that he loves better than he loves me"; and the mermaid sighed deeply, but she could not shed tears. "He says the maiden belongs to the holy temple, therefore she will never return to the world. They will meet no more: while I am by his side, and see him every day. I will take care of him, and love him, and give up my life for his sake."

Very soon it was said that the prince must marry, and that the beautiful daughter of a neighboring king would be his wife, for a fine ship was being fitted out. Although the prince gave out that he merely intended to pay a visit to the king, it was generally supposed that he really went to see his daughter. A great company were to go with him. The little mermaid smiled, and shook her head. She knew the prince's thoughts better than any of the others.

"I must travel," he had said to her; "I must see this beautiful princess; my parents desire it; but they will not oblige me to bring her home as my bride. I cannot love her; she is not like the beautiful maiden in the temple, whom you resemble. If I were forced to choose a bride, I would rather choose you, my dumb foundling, with those expressive eyes." And then he kissed her rosy mouth, played with her long waving hair, and laid his head on her heart, while she dreamed of human happiness and an immortal soul. "You are not afraid of the sea, my dumb child," said he, as they stood on the deck of the noble ship which was to carry them to the country of the neighboring king. And then he told her of storm and of calm, of strange fishes in the deep beneath them, and of what the divers had seen there; and she smiled at his descriptions, for she knew better than anyone what wonders were at the bottom of the sea.

In the moonlight, when all on board were asleep, excepting the man at the helm, who was steering, she sat on the deck, gazing down through the clear water. She thought she could distinguish her father's castle, and upon it her aged grandmother, with the silver crown on her head, looking through the rushing tide at the keel of the vessel. Then her sisters came up on the waves, and gazed at her mournfully, wringing their white hands. She beckoned to them, and smiled, and wanted to tell them how happy and well off she was; but the cabin boy approached, and when her sisters dived down he thought it was only the foam of the sea which he saw.

The next morning the ship sailed into the harbor of a beautiful town belonging to the king whom the prince was going to visit. The church bells were ringing, and from the high towers sounded a flourish of trumpets; and soldiers, with flying colors and glittering bayonets, lined the rocks through which they passed. Every day was a festival; balls and entertainments followed one another.

But the princess had not yet appeared. People said that she was being brought up and educated in a religious house, where she was learning every royal virtue. At last she came. Then the little mermaid, who was very anxious to see whether she was really beautiful, was obliged to acknowledge that she had never seen a more perfect vision of beauty. Her skin was delicately fair, and beneath her long dark eyelashes her laughing blue eyes shone with truth and purity.

"It was you," said the prince, "who saved my life when I lay dead on the beach," and he folded his blushing bride in his arms. "Oh, I am too happy," said he to the little mermaid; "my fondest hopes are all fulfilled. You will rejoice at my happiness; for your devotion to me is great and sincere."

The little mermaid kissed his hand, and felt as if her heart were already broken. His wedding morning would bring death to her, and she would change into the foam of the sea. All the church bells rung, and the heralds rode about the town proclaiming the betrothal. Perfumed oil was burning in costly silver lamps on every altar. The priests waved the censers, while the bride and bridegroom joined their hands and received the blessing of the bishop. The little mermaid, dressed in silk and gold, held up the bride's train; but her ears heard nothing of the festive music, and her eyes saw not the holy ceremony; she thought of the night of death which was coming to her, and of all she had lost in the world. On the same evening the bride and bridegroom went on board ship; cannons were roaring, flags waving, and in the centre of the ship a costly tent of purple and gold had been erected. It contained elegant couches, for the reception of the bridal pair during the night. The ship, with swelling sails and a favorable wind, glided away smoothly and lightly over the calm sea. When it grew dark a number of colored lamps were lit, and the sailors danced merrily on the deck. The little mermaid could not help thinking of her first rising out of the sea, when she had seen similar festivities and joys; and she joined in the dance, poised herself in the air as a swallow when he pursues his prey, and all present cheered her with wonder. She had never danced so elegantly before. Her tender feet felt as if cut with sharp knives, but she cared not for it; a sharper pang had pierced through her heart. She knew this was the last evening she should ever see the prince, for whom she had forsaken her kindred and her home; she had given up her beautiful voice, and suffered unheard-of pain daily for him, while he knew nothing of it. This was the last evening that she would breathe the same air with him, or gaze on the starry sky and the deep sea; an eternal night, without a thought or a dream, awaited her: she had no soul and now she could never win one. All was joy and gayety on board ship till long after midnight; she laughed and danced with the rest, while the thoughts of death were in her heart. The prince kissed his beautiful bride, while she played with his raven hair, till they went arm-in-arm to rest in the splendid tent. Then all became still on board the ship; the helmsman, alone awake, stood at the helm. The little mermaid leaned her white arms on the edge of the vessel, and looked towards the east for the first blush of morning, for that first ray of dawn that would bring her death. She saw her sisters rising out of the flood: they were as pale as herself; but their long, beautiful hair waved no more in the wind, and had been cut off.

"We have given our hair to the witch," said they, "to obtain help for you, that you may not die tonight. She has given us a knife: here it is, see it is very sharp. Before the sun rises you must plunge it into the heart of the prince; when the warm blood falls upon your feet they will grow together again, and form into a fish's tail, and you will be once more a mermaid, and return to us to live out your three hundred years before you die and change into the salt sea foam. Haste, then; he or you must die before sunrise. Our old grandmother moans so for you, that her white hair is falling off from sorrow, as ours fell under the witch's scissors. Kill the prince and come back; hasten: do you not see the first red streaks in the sky? In a few minutes the sun will rise, and you must die." And then they sighed deeply and mournfully, and sank down beneath the waves.

The little mermaid drew back the crimson curtain of the tent, and beheld the fair bride with her head resting on the prince's breast. She bent down and kissed his fair brow, then looked at the sky on which the rosy dawn grew brighter and brighter; then she glanced at the sharp knife, and again fixed her eyes on the prince, who whispered the name of his bride in his dreams. She was in his thoughts, and the knife trembled in the hand of the little mermaid: then she flung it far away from her into the waves; the water turned red where it fell, and the drops that spurted up looked like blood. She cast one more lingering, half-fainting glance at the prince, and then threw herself from the ship into the sea, and thought her body was dissolving into foam. The sun rose above the waves, and his warm rays fell on the cold foam of the little mermaid, who did not feel as if she were dying. She saw the bright sun, and all around her floated hundreds of transparent beautiful beings; she could see through them the white sails of the ship, and the red clouds in the sky; their speech was melodious, but too ethereal to be heard by mortal ears, as they were also unseen by mortal eyes. The little mermaid perceived that she had a body like theirs, and that she continued to rise higher and higher out of the foam. "Where am I?" asked she, and her voice sounded ethereal, as the voice of those who were with her; no earthly music could imitate it.

"Among the daughters of the air," answered one of them. "A mermaid has not an immortal soul, nor can she obtain one unless she wins the love of a human being. On the power of another hangs her eternal destiny. But the daughters of the air, although they do not possess an immortal soul, can, by their good deeds, procure one for themselves. We fly to warm countries, and cool the sultry air that destroys mankind with the pestilence. We carry the perfume of the flowers to spread health and restoration. After we have striven for three hundred years to all the good in our power, we receive an immortal soul and take part in the happiness of mankind. You, poor little mermaid, have tried with your whole heart to do as we are doing; you have suffered and endured and raised yourself to the spirit-world by your good deeds; and now, by striving for three hundred years in the same way, you may obtain an immortal soul."

The little mermaid lifted her glorified eyes towards the sun, and felt them, for the first time, filling with tears. On the ship, in which she had left the prince, there were life and noise; she saw him and his beautiful bride searching for her; sorrowfully they gazed at the pearly foam, as if they knew she had thrown herself into the waves. Unseen she kissed the forehead of her bride, and fanned the prince, and then mounted with the other children of the air to a rosy cloud that floated through the aether.

"After three hundred years, thus shall we float into the kingdom of heaven," said she. "And we may even get there sooner," whispered one of her companions. "Unseen we can enter the houses of men, where there are children, and for every day on which we find a good child, who is the joy of his parents and deserves their love, our time of probation is shortened. The child does not know, when we fly through the room, that we smile with joy at his good conduct, for we can count one year less of our three hundred years. But when we see a naughty or a wicked child, we shed tears of sorrow, and for every tear a day is added to our time of trial!"

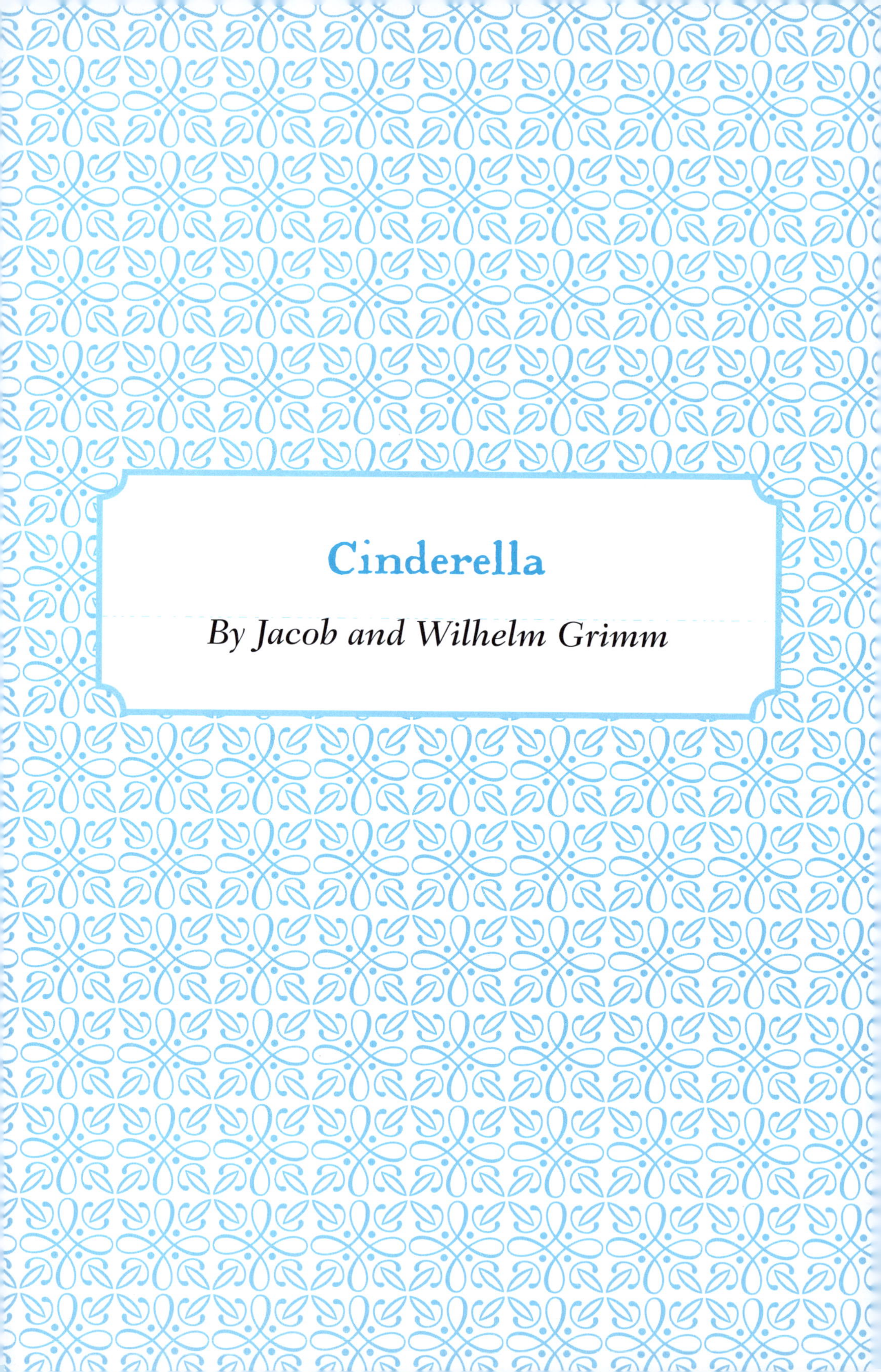

Cinderella

By Jacob and Wilhelm Grimm

The wife of a rich man fell sick; and when she felt that her end drew nigh, she called her only daughter to her bedside, and said, "Always be a good girl, and I will look down from heaven and watch over you." Soon afterwards she shut her eyes and died, and was buried in the garden; and the little girl went every day to her grave and wept, and was always good and kind to all about her. And the snow fell and spread a beautiful white covering over the grave; but by the time the spring came, and the sun had melted it away again, her father had married another wife. This new wife had two daughters of her own, that she brought home with her; they were fair in face but foul at heart, and it was now a sorry time for the poor little girl.

"What does the good-for-nothing want in the parlour?" said they; "they who would eat bread should first earn it; away with the kitchen maid!" Then they took away her fine clothes, and gave her an old grey frock to put on, and laughed at her, and turned her into the kitchen.

There she was forced to do hard work; to rise early before daylight, to bring the water, to make the fire, to cook and to wash. Besides that, the sisters plagued her in all sorts of ways, and laughed at her. In the evening when she was tired, she had no bed to lie down on, but was made to lie by the hearth among the ashes; and as this, of course, made her always dusty and dirty, they called her Cinderella.

It happened once that the father was going to the fair, and asked his wife's daughters what he should bring them.

"Fine clothes," said the first.

"Pearls and diamonds," cried the second.

"Now, child," said he to his own daughter, "what will you have?"

"The first twig, dear father, that brushes against your hat when you turn your face to come homewards," said she.

Then he bought for the first two the fine clothes and pearls and diamonds they had asked for: and on his way home, as he rode through a green copse, a hazel twig brushed against him, and almost pushed off his hat: so he broke it off and brought it away; and when he got home he gave it to his daughter. Then she took it, and went to her mother's grave and planted it there; and cried so much that it was watered with her tears; and there it grew and became a fine tree. Three times every day she went to it and cried; and soon a little bird came and built its nest upon the tree, and talked with her, and watched over her, and brought her whatever she wished for.

Now it happened that the king of that land held a feast, which was to last three days; and out of those who came to it his son was to choose a bride for himself. Cinderella's two sisters were asked to come; so they called her up, and said, "Now, comb our hair, brush our shoes, and tie our sashes for us, for we are going to dance at the king's feast." Then she did as she was told; but when all was done she could not help crying, for she thought to herself, she should so have liked to have gone with them to the ball; and at last she begged her mother very hard to let her go.

"You, Cinderella!" said she; "you who have nothing to wear, no clothes at all, and who cannot even dance—you want to go to the ball? And when she kept on begging, she said at last, to get rid of her, "I will throw this dishful of peas into the ash heap, and if in two hours' time you have picked them all out, you shall go to the feast too."

Then she threw the peas down among the ashes, but the little maiden ran out at the back door into the garden, and cried out:

"Hither, hither, through the sky,
Turtle doves and linnets, fly!
Blackbird, thrush, and chaffinch gay,
Hither, hither, haste away!
One and all come help me, quick!
Haste ye, haste ye!—pick, pick, pick!"

Then first came two white doves, flying in at the kitchen window; next came two turtledoves; and after them came all the little birds under heaven, chirping and fluttering in: and they flew down into the ashes. And the little doves stooped their heads down and set to work, pick, pick, pick; and then the others began to pick, pick, pick: and among them all they soon picked out all the good grain, and put it into a dish but left the ashes. Long before the end of the hour the work was quite done, and all flew out again at the windows.

Then Cinderella brought the dish to her mother, overjoyed at the thought that now she should go to the ball. But the mother said, "No, no, you have no clothes, and cannot dance; you shall not go." And when

Cinderella begged very hard to go, she said, "If you can in one hour's time pick two of those dishes of peas out of the ashes, you shall go too." And thus she thought she should at least get rid of her. So she shook two dishes of peas into the ashes.

But the little maiden went out into the garden at the back of the house, and cried out as before:

"Hither, hither, through the sky,
Turtle-doves and linnets, fly!
Blackbird, thrush, and chaffinch gay,
Hither, hither, haste away!
One and all come help me, quick!
Haste ye, haste ye!—pick, pick, pick!"

Then first came two white doves in at the kitchen window; next came two turtledoves; and after them came all the little birds under heaven, chirping and hopping about. And they flew down into the ashes; and the little doves put their heads down and set to work, pick, pick, pick; and then the others began pick, pick, pick; and they put all the good grain into the dishes, and left all the ashes. Before half an hour's time all was done, and out they flew again. And then Cinderella took the dishes to her mother, rejoicing to think that she should now go to the ball. But her mother said, "It is all of no use, you cannot go; you have no clothes, and cannot dance, and you would only put us to shame": and off she went with her two daughters to the ball.

Now when all were gone, and nobody left at home, Cinderella went sorrowfully and sat down under the hazel tree, and cried out:

"Shake, shake, hazel tree,
Gold and silver over me!"

Then her friend the bird flew out of the tree, and brought a gold and silver dress for her, and slippers of spangled silk; and she put them on, and followed her sisters to the feast. But they did not know her, and thought it must be some strange princess, she looked so fine and beautiful in her rich clothes; and they never once thought of Cinderella, taking it for granted that she was safe at home in the dirt.

The king's son soon came up to her, and took her by the hand and danced with her, and no one else: and he never left her hand; but when anyone else came to ask her to dance, he said, "This lady is dancing with me."

Thus they danced till a late hour of the night; and then she wanted to go home: and the king's son said, "I shall go and take care of you to your home"; for he wanted to see where the beautiful maiden lived. But she slipped away from him, unawares, and ran off towards home; and as the prince followed her, she jumped up into the pigeon house and shut the door. Then he waited till her father came home, and told him that the unknown maiden, who had been at the feast, had hid herself in the pigeon house. But when they had broken open the door they found no one within; and as they came back into the house, Cinderella was lying, as she always did, in her dirty frock by the ashes, and her dim little lamp was burning in the chimney. For she had run as quickly as she could through the pigeon house and on to the hazel tree, and had there taken off her beautiful clothes, and put them beneath the tree, that the bird might carry them away, and had lain down again amid the ashes in her little grey frock.

The next day when the feast was again held, and her father, mother, and sisters were gone, Cinderella went to the hazel tree, and said:

"Shake, shake, hazel tree,
Gold and silver over me!"

And the bird came and brought a still finer dress than the one she had worn the day before. And when she came in it to the ball, everyone wondered at her beauty: but the king's son, who was waiting for her, took her by the hand, and danced with her; and when anyone asked her to dance, he said as before, "This lady is dancing with me."

When night came she wanted to go home; and the king's son followed here as before, that he might see into what house she went: but she sprang away from him all at once into the garden behind her father's house. In this garden stood a fine large pear tree full of ripe fruit; and Cinderella, not knowing where to hide herself, jumped up into it without being seen. Then the king's son lost sight of her, and could not find out where she was gone, but waited till her father came home, and said to him, "The unknown lady who danced with me has slipped away, and I think she must have sprung into the pear tree."

The father thought to himself, "Can it be Cinderella?" So he had an axe brought; and they cut down the tree, but found no one upon it. And when they came back into the kitchen, there lay Cinderella among the ashes; for she had slipped down on the other side of the tree, and carried her beautiful clothes back to the bird at the hazel tree, and then put on her little grey frock.

The third day, when her father and mother and sisters were gone, she went again into the garden, and said:

"Shake, shake, hazel tree,
Gold and silver over me!"

Then her kind friend the bird brought a dress still finer than the former one, and slippers which were all of gold: so that when she came to the feast no one knew what to say, for wonder at her beauty: and the king's son danced with nobody but her; and when anyone else asked her to dance, he said, "This lady is my partner, sir."

When night came she wanted to go home; and the king's son would go with her, and said to himself, "I will not lose her this time"; but, however, she again slipped away from him, though in such a hurry that she dropped her left golden slipper upon the stairs.

The prince took the shoe, and went the next day to the king his father, and said, "I will take for my wife the lady that this golden slipper fits." Then both the sisters were overjoyed to hear it; for they had beautiful feet, and had no doubt that they could wear the golden slipper. The eldest went first into the room where the slipper was, and wanted to try it on, and the mother stood by. But her great toe could not go into it, and the shoe was altogether much too small for her. Then the mother gave her a knife, and said, "Never mind, cut it off; when you are queen you will not care about toes; you will not want to walk." So the silly girl cut off her great toe, and thus squeezed on the shoe, and went to the king's son. Then he took her for his bride, and set her beside him on his horse, and rode away with her homewards.

But on their way home they had to pass by the hazel tree that Cinderella had planted; and on the branch sat a little dove singing:

"Back again! back again! look to the shoe!
The shoe is too small, and not made for you!
Prince! prince! look again for thy bride,
For she's not the true one that sits by thy side."

Then the prince got down and looked at her foot; and he saw, by the blood that streamed from it, what a trick she had played him. So he turned his horse round, and brought the false bride back to her home, and said, "This is not the right bride; let the other sister try and put on the slipper." Then she went into the room and got her foot into the shoe, all but the heel, which was too large. But her mother squeezed it in till the blood came, and took her to the king's son: and he set her as his bride by his side on his horse, and rode away with her.

But when they came to the hazel tree the little dove sat there still, and sang:

"Back again! back again! look to the shoe!
The shoe is too small, and not made for you!
Prince! prince! look again for thy bride,
For she's not the true one that sits by thy side."

Then he looked down, and saw that the blood streamed so much from the shoe, that her white stockings were quite red. So he turned his horse and brought her also back again. "This is not the true bride," said he to the father; "have you no other daughters?"

"No," said he; "there is only a little dirty Cinderella here, the child of my first wife; I am sure she cannot be the bride." The prince told him to send her. But the mother said, "No, no, she is much too dirty; she will not dare to show herself." However, the prince would have her come; and she first washed her face and hands, and then went in and curtsied to him, and he reached her the golden slipper. Then she took her clumsy shoe off her left foot, and put on the golden slipper; and it fitted her as if it had been made for her. And when he drew near and looked at her face he knew her, and said, "This is the right bride." But the mother and both the sisters were frightened, and turned pale with anger as he took Cinderella on his horse, and rode away with her. And when they came to the hazel tree, the white dove sang:

"Home! home! look at the shoe!
Princess! the shoe was made for you!
Prince! prince! take home thy bride,
For she is the true one that sits by thy side!"

And when the dove had done its song, it came flying, and perched upon her right shoulder, and so went home with her.

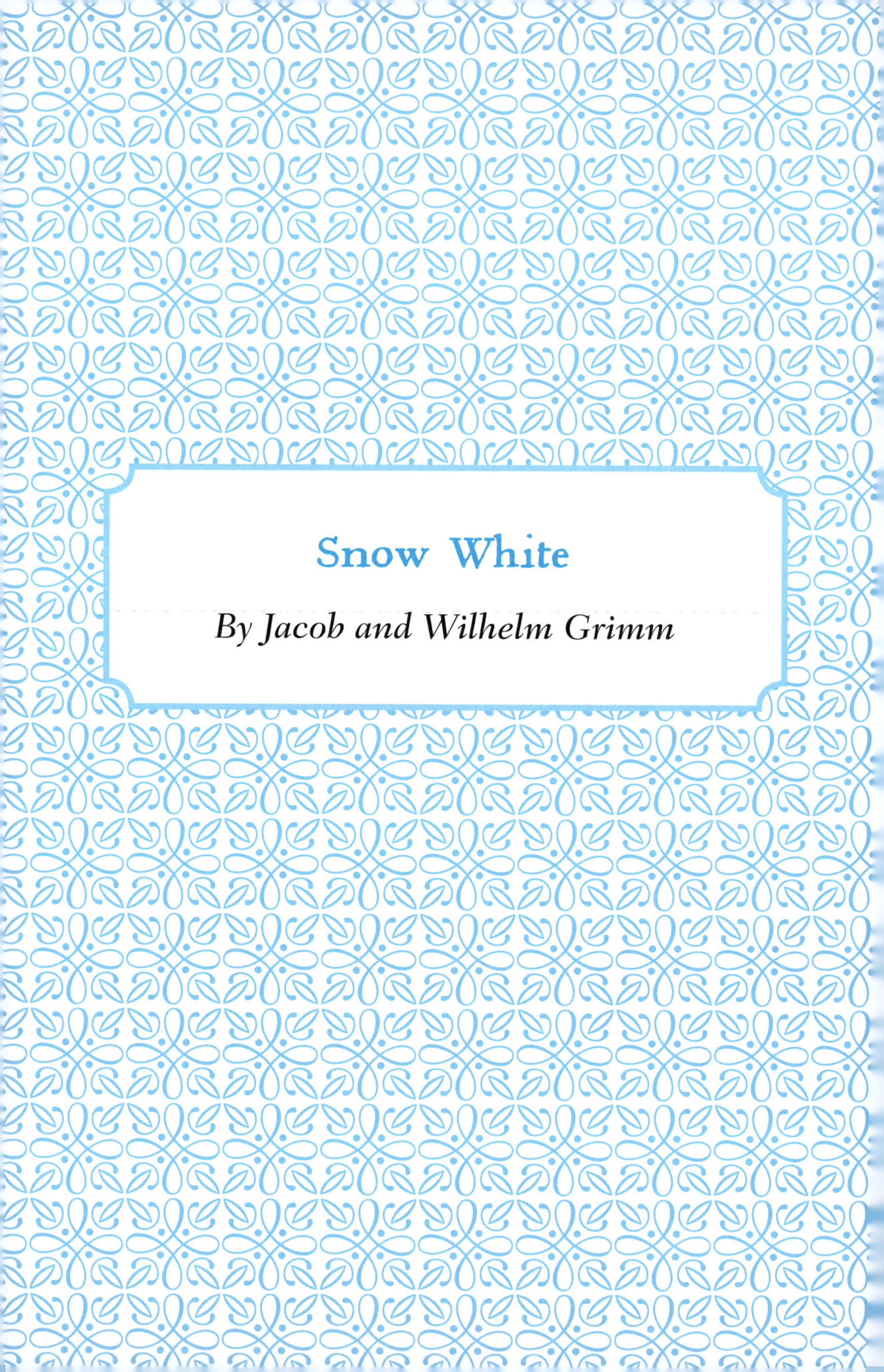

Snow White

By Jacob and Wilhelm Grimm

It was the middle of winter, when the broad flakes of snow were falling around, that the queen of a country many thousand miles off sat working at her window. The frame of the window was made of fine black ebony, and as she sat looking out upon the snow, she pricked her finger, and three drops of blood fell upon it. Then she gazed thoughtfully upon the red drops that sprinkled the white snow, and said, "Would that my little daughter may be as white as that snow, as red as that blood, and as black as this ebony window frame!" And so the little girl really did grow up; her skin was as white as snow, her cheeks as rosy as the blood, and her hair as black as ebony; and she was called Snow White.

But this queen died; and the king soon married another wife, who became queen, and was very beautiful, but so vain that she could not bear to think that anyone could be handsomer than she was. She had a fairy looking glass, to which she used to go, and then she would gaze upon herself in it, and say:

"Tell me, glass, tell me true!
Of all the ladies in the land,
Who is fairest, tell me, who?"

And the glass had always answered:

"Thou, queen, art the fairest in all the land."

But Snow White grew more and more beautiful; and when she was seven years old she was as bright as the day, and fairer than the queen herself. Then the glass one day answered the queen, when she went to look in it as usual:

"Thou, queen, art fair, and beauteous to see,
But Snow White is lovelier far than thee!"

When she heard this she turned pale with rage and envy, and called to one of her servants, and said, "Take Snow White away into the wide wood, that I may never see her any more."

Then the servant led her away; but his heart melted when Snow White begged him to spare her life, and he said, "I will not hurt you, thou pretty child." So he left her by herself; and though he thought it most likely that the wild beasts would tear her in pieces, he felt as if a great weight were taken off his heart when he had made up his mind not to kill her but to leave her to her fate, with the chance of someone finding and saving her.

Then poor Snow White wandered along through the wood in great fear; and the wild beasts roared about her, but none did her any harm. In the evening she came to a cottage among the hills, and went in to rest, for her little feet would carry her no further. Everything was spruce and neat in the cottage: on the table was spread a white cloth, and there were seven little plates, seven little loaves, and seven little glasses with wine in them; and seven knives and forks laid in order; and by the wall stood seven little beds. As she was very hungry, she picked a little piece of each loaf and drank a very little wine out of each glass; and after that she thought she would lie down and rest. So she tried all the little beds; but one was too long, and another was too short, till at last the seventh suited her: and there she laid herself down and went to sleep.

By and by in came the masters of the cottage. Now they were seven little dwarfs, that lived among the mountains, and dug and searched for gold. They lighted up their seven lamps, and saw at once that all was not right. The first said, "Who has been sitting on my stool?"

The second, "Who has been eating off my plate?"

The third, "Who has been picking my bread?"

The fourth, "Who has been meddling with my spoon?"

The fifth, "Who has been handling my fork?"

The sixth, "Who has been cutting with my knife?"

The seventh, "Who has been drinking my wine?"

Then the first looked round and said, "Who has been lying on my bed?" And the rest came running to him, and everyone cried out that somebody had been upon his bed. But the seventh saw Snow White, and called all his brethren to come and see her; and they cried out with wonder and astonishment and brought their lamps to look at her, and said, "Good heavens! what a lovely child she is!" And they were very glad to see her, and took care not to wake her; and the seventh dwarf slept an hour with each of the other dwarfs in turn, till the night was gone.

In the morning Snow White told them all her story; and they pitied her, and said if she would keep all things in order, and cook and wash and knit and spin for them, she might stay where she was, and they would take good care of her. Then they went out all day long to their work, seeking for gold and silver in the mountains: but Snow White was left at home; and they warned her, and said, "The queen will soon find out where you are, so take care and let no one in."

But the queen, now that she thought Snow White was dead, believed that she must be the handsomest lady in the land; and she went to her glass and said:

"Tell me, glass, tell me true!
Of all the ladies in the land,
Who is fairest, tell me, who?"

And the glass answered:

"Thou, queen, art the fairest in all this land:
But over the hills, in the greenwood shade,
Where the seven dwarfs their dwelling have made,
There Snow White is hiding her head; and she
Is lovelier far, O queen! than thee."

Then the queen was very much frightened; for she knew that the glass always spoke the truth, and was sure that the servant had betrayed her. And she could not bear to think that anyone lived who was more beautiful than she was; so she dressed herself up as an old pedlar, and went her way over the hills, to the place where the dwarfs dwelt. Then she knocked at the door, and cried, "Fine wares to sell!"

Snow White looked out at the window, and said, "Good day, good woman! what have you to sell?"

"Good wares, fine wares," said she; "laces and bobbins of all colours."

"I will let the old lady in; she seems to be a very good sort of body," thought Snow White, as she ran down and unbolted the door.

"Bless me!" said the old woman, "how badly your stays are laced! Let me lace them up with one of my nice new laces."

Snow White did not dream of any mischief; so she stood before the old woman; but she set to work so nimbly, and pulled the lace so tight, that Snow White's breath was stopped, and she fell down as if she were dead.

"There's an end to all thy beauty," said the spiteful queen, and went away home.

In the evening the seven dwarfs came home; and I need not say how grieved they were to see their faithful Snow White stretched out upon the ground, as if she was quite dead. However, they lifted her up, and when they found what ailed her, they cut the lace; and in a little time she began to breathe, and very soon came to life again. Then they said, "The old woman was the queen herself; take care another time, and let no one in when we are away."

When the queen got home, she went straight to her glass, and spoke to it as before; but to her great grief it still said:

"Thou, queen, art the fairest in all this land:
But over the hills, in the greenwood shade,
Where the seven dwarfs their dwelling have made,
There Snow White is hiding her head; and she
Is lovelier far, O queen! than thee."

Then the blood ran cold in her heart with spite and malice, to see that Snow White still lived; and she dressed herself up again, but in quite another dress from the one she wore before, and took with her a poisoned comb. When she reached the dwarfs' cottage, she knocked at the door, and cried, "Fine wares to sell!"

But Snow White said, "I dare not let anyone in."

Then the queen said, "Only look at my beautiful combs!" and gave her the poisoned one. And it looked so pretty, that she took it up and put it into her hair to try it; but the moment it touched her head, the poison was so powerful that she fell down senseless. "There you may lie," said the queen, and went her way. But by good luck the dwarfs came in very early that evening; and when they saw Snow White lying on the ground, they thought what had happened, and soon found the poisoned comb. And when they took it away she got well, and told them all that had passed; and they warned her once more not to open the door to anyone.

Meantime the queen went home to her glass, and shook with rage when she read the very same answer as before; and she said, "Snow White shall die, if it cost me my life." So she went by herself into her chamber, and got ready a poisoned apple: the outside looked very rosy and tempting, but whoever tasted it was sure to die. Then she dressed herself up as a peasant's wife, and travelled over the hills to the dwarfs' cottage, and knocked at the door; but Snow White put her head out of the window and said, "I dare not let anyone in, for the dwarfs have told me not."

"Do as you please," said the old woman, "but at any rate take this pretty apple; I will give it you."

"No," said Snow White, "I dare not take it."

"You silly girl!" answered the other, "what are you afraid of? Do you think it is poisoned? Come! do you eat one part, and I will eat the other."

Now the apple was so made up that one side was good, though the other side was poisoned. Then Snow White was much tempted to taste, for the apple looked so very nice; and when she saw the old woman eat, she could wait no longer. But she had scarcely put the piece into her mouth, when she fell down dead upon the ground. "This time nothing will save thee," said the queen; and she went home to her glass, and at last it said:

"Thou, queen, art the fairest of all the fair."

And then her wicked heart was glad, and as happy as such a heart could be.

When evening came, and the dwarfs had gone home, they found Snow White lying on the ground: no breath came from her lips, and they were afraid that she was quite dead. They lifted her up, and combed her hair, and washed her face with wine and water; but all was in vain, for the little girl seemed quite dead. So they laid her down upon a bier, and all seven watched and bewailed her three whole days; and then they thought they would bury her: but her cheeks were still rosy; and her face looked just as it did while she was alive; so they said, "We will never bury her in the cold ground." And they made a coffin of glass, so that they might still look at her, and wrote upon it in golden letters what her name was, and that she was a king's daughter. And the coffin was set among the hills, and one of the dwarfs always sat by it and watched. And the birds of the air came too, and bemoaned Snow White; and first of all came an owl, and then a raven, and at last a dove, and sat by her side.

And thus Snow White lay for a long, long time, and still only looked as though she was asleep; for she was even now as white as snow, and as red as blood, and as black as ebony. At last a prince came and called at the dwarfs' house; and he saw Snow White, and read what was written in golden letters. Then he offered the dwarfs money, and prayed and besought them to let him take her away; but they said, "We will not part with her for all the gold in the world."

At last, however, they had pity on him, and gave him the coffin; but the moment he lifted it up to carry it home with him, the piece of apple fell from between her lips, and Snow White awoke, and said, "Where am I?" And the prince said, "Thou art quite safe with me."

Then he told her all that had happened, and said, "I love you far better than all the world; so come with me to my father's palace, and you shall be my wife." And Snow White consented, and went home with the prince; and everything was got ready with great pomp and splendour for their wedding.

To the feast was asked, among the rest, Snow White's old enemy the queen; and as she was dressing herself in fine rich clothes, she looked in the glass and said:

"Tell me, glass, tell me true!
Of all the ladies in the land,
Who is fairest, tell me, who?"

And the glass answered:

"Thou, lady, art loveliest here, I ween;
But lovelier far is the new-made queen."

When she heard this she started with rage; but her envy and curiosity were so great, that she could not help setting out to see the bride. And when she got there, and saw that it was no other than Snow White, who, as she thought, had been dead a long while, she choked with rage, and fell down and died: but Snow White and the prince lived and reigned happily over that land many, many years; and sometimes they went up into the mountains, and paid a visit to the little dwarfs, who had been so kind to Snow White in her time of need.

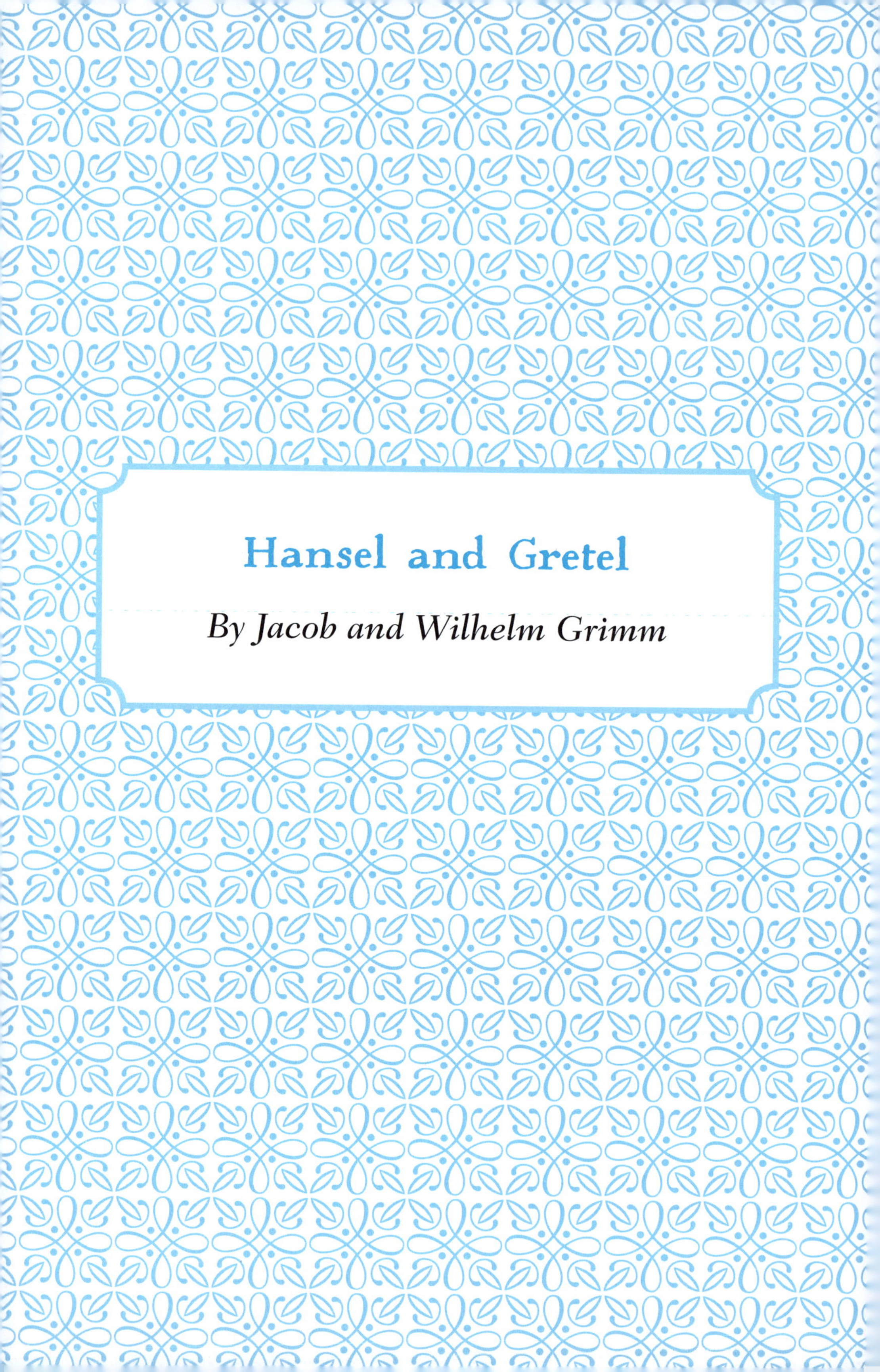
Hansel and Gretel
By Jacob and Wilhelm Grimm

Hard by a great forest dwelt a poor woodcutter with his wife and his two children. The boy was called Hansel and the girl Gretel. He had little to bite and to break, and once when great dearth fell on the land, he could no longer procure even daily bread. Now when he thought over this by night in his bed, and tossed about in his anxiety, he groaned and said to his wife: "What is to become of us? How are we to feed our poor children, when we no longer have anything even for ourselves?"

"I'll tell you what, husband," answered the woman, "early tomorrow morning we will take the children out into the forest to where it is the thickest; there we will light a fire for them, and give each of them one more piece of bread, and then we will go to our work and leave them alone. They will not find the way home again, and we shall be rid of them."

"No, wife," said the man, "I will not do that; how can I bear to leave my children alone in the forest?—the wild animals would soon come and tear them to pieces."

"O, you fool!" said she, "then we must all four die of hunger; you may as well plane the planks for our coffins," and she left him no peace until he consented.

"But I feel very sorry for the poor children, all the same," said the man.

The two children had also not been able to sleep for hunger, and had heard what their stepmother had said to their father. Gretel wept bitter tears, and said to Hansel: "Now all is over with us."

"Be quiet, Gretel," said Hansel, "do not distress yourself, I will soon find a way to help us." And when the old folks had fallen asleep, he got up, put on his little coat, opened the door below, and crept outside. The moon shone brightly, and the white pebbles which lay in front of the house glittered like real silver pennies. Hansel stooped and stuffed the little pocket of his coat with as many as he could get in. Then he went back and said to Gretel: "Be comforted, dear little sister, and sleep in peace, God will not forsake us," and he lay down again in his bed. When day dawned, but before the sun had risen, the woman came and awoke the two children, saying: "Get up, you sluggards! we are going into the forest to fetch wood." She gave each a little piece of bread, and said: "There is something for your dinner, but do not eat it up before then, for you will get nothing else." Gretel took the bread under her apron, as Hansel had the pebbles in his pocket. Then they all set out together on the way to the forest. When they had walked a short time, Hansel stood still and peeped back at the house, and did so again and again. His father said: "Hansel, what are you looking at there and staying behind for? Pay attention, and do not forget how to use your legs."

"Ah, father," said Hansel, "I am looking at my little white cat, which is sitting up on the roof, and wants to say goodbye to me."

The wife said: "Fool, that is not your little cat, that is the morning sun which is shining on the chimneys." Hansel, however, had not been looking back at the cat, but had been constantly throwing one of the white pebble stones out of his pocket on the road.

When they had reached the middle of the forest, the father said: "Now, children, pile up some wood, and I will light a fire that you may not be cold."

Hansel and Gretel gathered brushwood together, as high as a little hill. The brushwood was lighted, and when the flames were burning very high, the woman said: "Now, children, lay yourselves down by the fire and rest, we will go into the forest and cut some wood. When we have done, we will come back and fetch you away."

Hansel and Gretel sat by the fire, and when noon came, each ate a little piece of bread, and as they heard the strokes of the wood axe they believed that their father was near. It was not the axe, however, but a branch which he had fastened to a withered tree which the wind was blowing backwards and forwards. And as they had been sitting such a long time, their eyes closed with fatigue, and they fell fast asleep. When at last they awoke, it was already dark night. Gretel began to cry and said: "How are we to get out of the forest now?"

But Hansel comforted her and said: "Just wait a little, until the moon has risen, and then we will soon find the way." And when the full moon had risen, Hansel took his little sister by the hand, and followed the pebbles which shone like newly coined silver pieces, and showed them the way.

They walked the whole night long, and by break of day came once more to their father's house. They knocked at the door, and when the woman opened it and saw that it was Hansel and Gretel, she said: "You naughty children, why have you slept so long in the forest? We thought you were never coming back at all!" The father, however, rejoiced, for it had cut him to the heart to leave them behind alone.

Not long afterwards, there was once more great dearth throughout the land, and the children heard their mother saying at night to their father: "Everything is eaten again, we have one half loaf left, and that is the end. The children must go, we will take them farther into the wood, so that they will not find their way out again; there is no other means of saving ourselves!" The man's heart was heavy, and he thought: "It would be better for you to share the last mouthful with your children." The woman, however, would listen to nothing that he had to say, but scolded and reproached him. He who says A must say B, likewise, and as he had yielded the first time, he had to do so a second time also.

The children, however, were still awake and had heard the conversation. When the old folks were asleep, Hansel again got up, and wanted to go out and pick up pebbles as he had done before, but the woman had locked the door, and Hansel could not get out. Nevertheless he comforted his little sister, and said: "Do not cry, Gretel, go to sleep quietly, the good God will help us."

Early in the morning came the woman, and took the children out of their beds. Their piece of bread was given to them, but it was still smaller than the time before. On the way into the forest Hansel crumbled his in his pocket, and often stood still and threw a morsel on the ground. "Hansel, why do you stop and look round?" said the father, "go on."

"I am looking back at my little pigeon which is sitting on the roof, and wants to say goodbye to me," answered Hansel.

"Fool!" said the woman, "that is not your little pigeon, that is the morning sun that is shining on the chimney." Hansel, however, little by little, threw all the crumbs on the path.

The woman led the children still deeper into the forest, where they had never in their lives been before. Then a great fire was again made, and the mother said: "Just sit there, you children, and when you are tired you may sleep a little; we are going into the forest to cut wood, and in the evening when we are done, we will come and fetch you away."

When it was noon, Gretel shared her piece of bread with Hansel, who had scattered his by the way. Then they fell asleep and evening passed, but no one came to the poor children. They did not awake until it was dark night, and Hansel comforted his little sister and said: "Just wait, Gretel, until the moon rises, and then we shall see the crumbs of bread which I have strewn about; they will show us our way home again." When the moon came they set out, but they found no crumbs, for the many thousands of birds which fly about in the woods and fields had picked them all up. Hansel said to Gretel: "We shall soon find the way," but they did not find it. They walked the whole night and all the next day too from morning till evening, but they did not get out of the forest, and were very hungry, for they had nothing to eat but two or three berries, which grew on the ground. And as they were so weary that their legs would carry them no longer, they lay down beneath a tree and fell asleep.

It was now three mornings since they had left their father's house. They began to walk again, but they always came deeper into the forest, and if help did not come soon, they must die of hunger and weariness. When it was midday, they saw a beautiful snow white bird sitting on a bough, which sang so delightfully that they stood still and listened to it. And when its song was over, it spread its wings and flew away before them, and they followed it until they reached a little house, on the roof of which it alighted; and when they approached the little house they saw that it was built of bread and covered with cakes, but that the windows were of clear sugar.

"We will set to work on that," said Hansel, "and have a good meal. I will eat a bit of the roof, and you Gretel, can eat some of the window, it will taste sweet."

Hansel reached up above, and broke off a little of the roof to try how it tasted, and Gretel leant against the window and nibbled at the panes. Then a soft voice cried from the parlour:

"Nibble, nibble, gnaw,
Who is nibbling at my little house?"

The children answered:

"The wind, the wind,
The heaven-born wind,"

and went on eating without disturbing themselves. Hansel, who liked the taste of the roof, tore down a great piece of it, and Gretel pushed out the whole of one round windowpane, sat down, and enjoyed herself with it. Suddenly the door opened, and a woman as old as the hills, who supported herself on crutches, came creeping out. Hansel and Gretel were so terribly frightened that they let fall what they had in their hands.

The old woman, however, nodded her head, and said: "Oh, you dear children, who has brought you here? do come in, and stay with me. No harm shall happen to you." She took them both by the hand, and led them into her little house. Then good food was set before them, milk and pancakes, with sugar, apples, and nuts. Afterwards two pretty little beds were covered with clean white linen, and Hansel and Gretel lay down in them, and thought they were in heaven.

The old woman had only pretended to be so kind; she was in reality a wicked witch, who lay in wait for children, and had only built the little house of bread in order to entice them there. When a child fell into her power, she killed it, cooked and ate it, and that was a feast day with her. Witches have red eyes, and cannot see far, but they have a keen scent like the beasts, and are aware when human beings draw near. When Hansel and Gretel came into her neighbourhood, she laughed with malice, and said mockingly: "I have them, they shall not escape me again!" Early in the morning before the children were awake, she was already up, and when she saw both of them sleeping and looking so pretty, with their plump and rosy cheeks, she muttered to herself: "That will be a dainty mouthful!" Then she seized Hansel with her shrivelled hand, carried him into a little stable, and locked him in behind a grated door. Scream as he might, it would not help him. Then she went to Gretel, shook her till she awoke, and cried: "Get up, lazy thing, fetch some water, and cook something good for your brother, he is in the stable outside, and is to be made fat. When he is fat, I will eat him." Gretel began to weep bitterly, but it was all in vain, for she was forced to do what the wicked witch commanded.

And now the best food was cooked for poor Hansel, but Gretel got nothing but crab shells. Every morning the woman crept to the little stable, and cried: "Hansel, stretch out your finger that I may feel if you will soon be fat." Hansel, however, stretched out a little bone to her, and the old woman, who had dim eyes, could not see it, and thought it was Hansel's finger, and was astonished that there was no way of fattening him. When four weeks had gone by, and Hansel still remained thin, she was seized with impatience and would not wait any longer. "Now, then, Gretel," she cried to the girl, "stir yourself, and bring some water. Let Hansel be fat or lean, tomorrow I will kill him, and cook him." Ah, how the poor little sister did lament when she had to fetch the water, and how her tears did flow down her cheeks!

"Dear God, do help us," she cried. "If the wild beasts in the forest had but devoured us, we should at any rate have died together."

"Just keep your noise to yourself," said the old woman, "it won't help you at all."

Early in the morning, Gretel had to go out and hang up the cauldron with the water, and light the fire. "We will bake first," said the old woman, "I have already heated the oven, and kneaded the dough." She pushed poor Gretel out to the oven, from which flames of fire were already darting. "Creep in," said the witch, "and see if it is properly heated, so that we can put the bread in." And once Gretel was inside, she intended to shut the oven and let her bake in it, and then she would eat her, too. But Gretel saw what she had in mind, and said: "I do not know how I am to do it; how do I get in?"

"Silly goose," said the old woman. "The door is big enough; just look, I can get in myself!" and she crept up and thrust her head into the oven. Then Gretel gave her a push that drove her far into it, and shut the iron door, and fastened the bolt. Oh! then she began to howl quite horribly, but Gretel ran away and the godless witch was miserably burnt to death.

Gretel, however, ran like lightning to Hansel, opened his little stable, and cried: "Hansel, we are saved! The old witch is dead!" Then Hansel sprang like a bird from its cage when the door is opened. How they did rejoice and embrace each other, and dance about and kiss each other! And as they had no longer any need to fear her, they went into the witch's house, and in every corner there stood chests full of pearls and jewels. "These are far better than pebbles!" said Hansel, and thrust into his pockets whatever could be got in, and Gretel said: "I, too, will take something home with me," and filled her pinafore full. "But now we must be off," said Hansel, "that we may get out of the witch's forest."

When they had walked for two hours, they came to a great stretch of water. "We cannot cross," said Hansel, "I see no foot-plank, and no bridge."

"And there is also no ferry," answered Gretel, "but a white duck is swimming there: if I ask her, she will help us over." Then she cried:

"Little duck, little duck, dost thou see,
Hansel and Gretel are waiting for thee?
There's never a plank, or bridge in sight,
Take us across on thy back so white."

The duck came to them, and Hansel seated himself on its back, and told his sister to sit by him. "No," replied Gretel, "that will be too heavy for the little duck; she shall take us across, one after the other." The good little duck did so, and when they were once safely across and had walked for a short time, the forest seemed to be more and more familiar to them, and at length they saw from afar their father's house. Then they began to run, rushed into the parlour, and threw themselves round their father's neck. The man had not known one happy hour since he had left the children in the forest; the woman, however, was dead. Gretel emptied her pinafore until pearls and precious stones ran about the room, and Hansel threw one handful after another out of his pocket to add to them. Then all anxiety was at an end, and they lived together in perfect happiness. My tale is done, there runs a mouse; whosoever catches it, may make himself a big fur cap out of it.

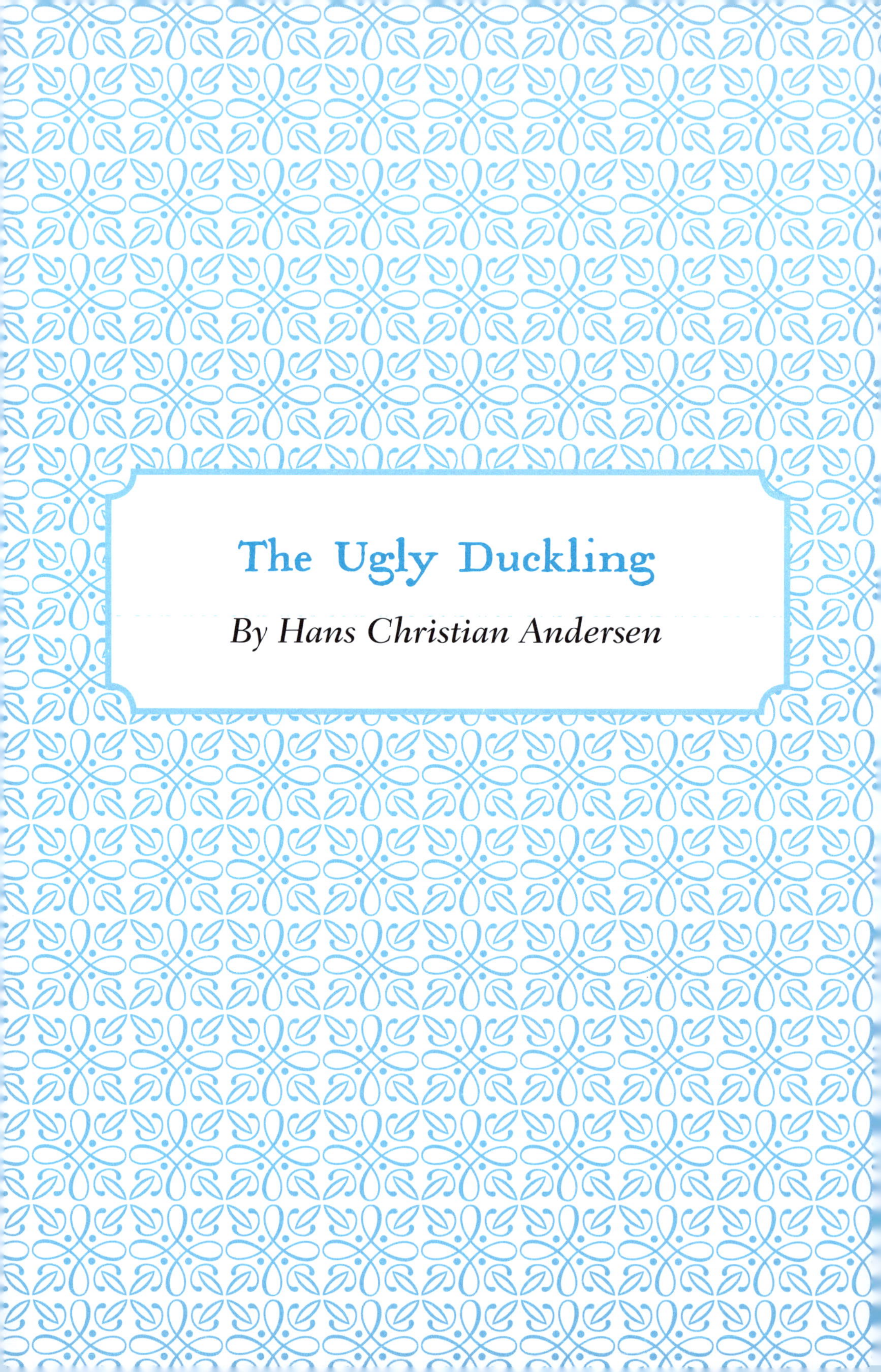

The Ugly Duckling

By Hans Christian Andersen

It was lovely summer weather in the country, and the golden corn, the green oats, and the haystacks piled up in the meadows looked beautiful. The stork walking about on his long red legs chattered in the Egyptian language, which he had learnt from his mother. The cornfields and meadows were surrounded by large forests, in the midst of which were deep pools. It was, indeed, delightful to walk about in the country. In a sunny spot stood a pleasant old farmhouse close by a deep river, and from the house down to the water side grew great burdock leaves, so high, that under the tallest of them a little child could stand upright. The spot was as wild as the centre of a thick wood. In this snug retreat sat a duck on her nest, watching for her young brood to hatch; she was beginning to get tired of her task, for the little ones were a long time coming out of their shells, and she seldom had any visitors. The other ducks liked much better to swim about in the river than to climb the slippery banks, and sit under a burdock leaf, to have a gossip with her. At length one shell cracked, and then another, and from each egg came a living creature that lifted its head and cried, "Peep, peep." "Quack, quack," said the mother, and then they all quacked as well as they could, and looked about them on every side at the large green leaves. Their mother allowed them to look as much as they liked, because green is good for the eyes.

"How large the world is," said the young ducks, when they found how much more room they now had than while they were inside the eggshell.

"Do you imagine this is the whole world?" asked the mother; "Wait till you have seen the garden; it stretches far beyond that to the parson's field, but I have never ventured to such a distance. Are you all out?" she continued, rising; "No, I declare, the largest egg lies there still. I wonder how long this is to last, I am quite tired of it"; and she seated herself again on the nest.

"Well, how are you getting on?" asked an old duck, who paid her a visit.

"One egg is not hatched yet," said the duck, "it will not break. But just look at all the others, are they not the prettiest little ducklings you ever saw? They are the image of their father, who is so unkind, he never comes to see."

"Let me see the egg that will not break," said the duck; "I have no doubt it is a turkey's egg. I was persuaded to hatch some once, and after all my care and trouble with the young ones, they were afraid of the water. I quacked and clucked, but all to no purpose. I could not get them to venture in. Let me look at the egg. Yes, that is a turkey's egg; take my advice, leave it where it is and teach the other children to swim."

"I think I will sit on it a little while longer," said the duck; "as I have sat so long already, a few days will be nothing."

"Please yourself," said the old duck, and she went away.

At last the large egg broke, and a young one crept forth crying, "Peep, peep." It was very large and ugly. The duck stared at it and exclaimed, "It is very large and not at all like the others. I wonder if it really is a turkey. We shall soon find it out, however, when we go to the water. It must go in, if I have to push it myself."

On the next day the weather was delightful, and the sun shone brightly on the green burdock leaves, so the mother duck took her young brood down to the water, and jumped in with a splash. "Quack, quack," cried she, and one after another the little ducklings jumped in. The water closed over their heads, but they came up again in an instant, and swam about quite prettily with their legs paddling under them as easily as possible, and the ugly duckling was also in the water swimming with them.

"Oh," said the mother, "that is not a turkey; how well he uses his legs, and how upright he holds himself! He is my own child, and he is not so very ugly after all if you look at him properly. Quack, quack! come with me now, I will take you into grand society, and introduce you to the farmyard, but you must keep close to me or you may be trodden upon; and, above all, beware of the cat."

When they reached the farmyard, there was a great disturbance. Two families were fighting for an eel's head, which, after all, was carried off by the cat. "See, children, that is the way of the world," said the mother duck, whetting her beak, for she would have liked the eel's head herself. "Come, now, use your legs, and let me see how well you can behave. You must bow your heads prettily to that old duck yonder; she is the highest born of them all, and has Spanish blood, therefore, she is well off. Don't you see she has a red flag tied to her leg, which is something very grand, and a great honor for a duck; it shows that everyone is anxious not to lose her, as she can be recognized both by man and beast. Come, now, don't turn your toes, a well-bred duckling spreads his feet wide apart, just like his father and mother, in this way; now bend your neck, and say 'quack.'"

The ducklings did as they were bid, but the other duck stared, and said, "Look, here comes another brood, as if there were not enough of us already! and what a queer-looking object one of them is; we don't want him here," and then one flew out and bit him in the neck.

"Let him alone," said the mother; "he is not doing any harm."

"Yes, but he is so big and ugly," said the spiteful duck, "and therefore he must be turned out."

"The others are very pretty children," said the old duck, with the rag on her leg, "all but that one; I wish his mother could improve him a little."

"That is impossible, your grace," replied the mother; "he is not pretty; but he has a very good disposition, and swims as well or even better than the others. I think he will grow up pretty, and perhaps be smaller; he has remained too long in the egg, and therefore his figure is not properly formed"; and then she stroked his neck and smoothed the feathers, saying, "It is a drake, and therefore not of so much consequence. I think he will grow up strong, and able to take care of himself."

"The other ducklings are graceful enough," said the old duck. "Now make yourself at home, and if you can find an eel's head, you can bring it to me."

And so they made themselves comfortable; but the poor duckling, who had crept out of his shell last of all, and looked so ugly, was bitten and pushed and made fun of, not only by the ducks, but by all the poultry. "He is too big," they all said, and the turkey cock, who had been born into the world with spurs, and fancied himself really an emperor, puffed himself out like a vessel in full sail, and flew at the duckling, and became quite red in the head with passion, so that the poor little thing did not know where to go, and was quite miserable because he was so ugly and laughed at by the whole farmyard.

So it went on from day to day till it got worse and worse. The poor duckling was driven about by everyone; even his brothers and sisters were unkind to him, and would say, "Ah, you ugly creature, I wish the cat would get you," and his mother said she wished he had never been born. The ducks pecked him, the chickens beat him, and the girl who fed the poultry kicked him with her feet. So at last he ran away, frightening the little birds in the hedge as he flew over the palings.

"They are afraid of me because I am ugly," he said. So he closed his eyes, and flew still farther, until he came out on a large moor, inhabited by wild ducks. Here he remained the whole night, feeling very tired and sorrowful.

In the morning, when the wild ducks rose in the air, they stared at their new comrade. "What sort of a duck are you?" they all said, coming round him.

He bowed to them, and was as polite as he could be, but he did not reply to their question. "You are exceedingly ugly," said the wild ducks, "but that will not matter if you do not want to marry one of our family."

Poor thing! he had no thoughts of marriage; all he wanted was permission to lie among the rushes, and drink some of the water on the moor. After he had been on the moor two days, there came two wild geese, or rather goslings, for they had not been out of the egg long, and were very saucy. "Listen, friend," said one of them to the duckling, "you are so ugly, that we like you very well. Will you go with us, and become a bird of passage? Not far from here is another moor, in which there are some pretty wild geese, all unmarried. It is a chance for you to get a wife; you may be lucky, ugly as you are."

"Pop, pop," sounded in the air, and the two wild geese fell dead among the rushes, and the water was tinged with blood. "Pop, pop," echoed far and wide in the distance, and whole flocks of wild geese rose up from the rushes. The sound continued from every direction, for the sportsmen surrounded the moor, and some were even seated on branches of trees, overlooking the rushes. The blue smoke from the guns rose like clouds over the dark trees, and as it floated away across the water, a number of sporting dogs bounded in among the rushes, which bent beneath them wherever they went. How they terrified the poor duckling! He turned away his head to hide it under his wing, and at the same moment a large terrible dog passed quite near him. His jaws were open, his tongue hung from his mouth, and his eyes glared fearfully. He thrust his nose close to the duckling, showing his sharp teeth, and then, "splash, splash," he went into the water without touching him. "Oh," sighed the duckling, "how thankful I am for being so ugly; even a dog will not bite me." And so he lay quite still, while the shot rattled through the rushes, and gun after gun was fired over him.

It was late in the day before all became quiet, but even then the poor young thing did not dare to move. He waited quietly for several hours, and then, after looking carefully around him, hastened away from the moor as fast as he could. He ran over field and meadow till a storm arose, and he could hardly struggle against it. Towards evening, he reached a poor little cottage that seemed ready to fall, and only remained standing because it could not decide on which side to fall first. The storm continued so violent, that the duckling could go no farther; he sat down by the cottage, and then he noticed that the door was not quite closed in consequence of one of the hinges having given way. There was therefore a narrow opening near the bottom large enough for him to slip through, which he did very quietly, and got a shelter for the night. A woman, a tom cat, and a hen lived in this cottage. The tom cat, whom the mistress called, "My little son," was a great favorite; he could raise his back, and purr, and could even throw out sparks from his fur if it were stroked the wrong way. The hen had very short legs, so she was called "Chickie short legs." She laid good eggs, and her mistress loved her as if she had been her own child. In the morning, the strange visitor was discovered, and the tom cat began to purr, and the hen to cluck.

"What is that noise about?" said the old woman, looking round the room, but her sight was not very good; therefore, when she saw the duckling she thought it must be a fat duck, that had strayed from home. "Oh what a prize!" she exclaimed, "I hope it is not a drake, for then I shall have some duck's eggs. I must wait and see." So the duckling was allowed to remain on trial for three weeks, but there were no eggs.

Now the tom cat was the master of the house, and the hen was mistress, and they always said, "We and the world," for they believed themselves to be half the world, and the better half too. The duckling thought that others might hold a different opinion on the subject, but the hen would not listen to such doubts. "Can you lay eggs?" she asked. "No." "Then have the goodness to hold your tongue." "Can you raise your back, or purr, or throw out sparks?" said the tom cat. "No." "Then you have no right to express an opinion when sensible people are speaking." So the duckling sat in a corner, feeling very low spirited, till the sunshine and the fresh air came into the room through the open door, and then he began to feel such a great longing for a swim on the water, that he could not help telling the hen.

"What an absurd idea," said the hen. "You have nothing else to do, therefore you have foolish fancies. If you could purr or lay eggs, they would pass away."

"But it is so delightful to swim about on the water," said the duckling, "and so refreshing to feel it close over your head, while you dive down to the bottom."

"Delightful, indeed!" said the hen, "why you must be crazy! Ask the cat, he is the cleverest animal I know, ask him how he would like to swim about on the water, or to dive under it, for I will not speak of my own opinion; ask our mistress, the old woman—there is no one in the world more clever than she is. Do you think she would like to swim, or to let the water close over her head?"

"You don't understand me," said the duckling.

"We don't understand you. Who can understand you, I wonder? Do you consider yourself more clever than the cat, or the old woman? I will say nothing of myself. Don't imagine such nonsense, child, and thank your good fortune that you have been received here. Are you not in a warm room, and in society from which you may learn something? But you are a chatterer, and your company is not very agreeable. Believe me, I speak only for your own good. I may tell you unpleasant truths, but that is a proof of my friendship. I advise you, therefore, to lay eggs, and learn to purr as quickly as possible."

"I believe I must go out into the world again," said the duckling.

"Yes, do," said the hen. So the duckling left the cottage, and soon found water on which it could swim and dive, but was avoided by all other animals, because of its ugly appearance. Autumn came, and the leaves in the forest turned to orange and gold. Then, as winter approached, the wind caught them as they fell and whirled them in the cold air. The clouds, heavy with hail and snowflakes, hung low in the sky, and the raven stood on the ferns crying, "Croak, croak." It made one shiver with cold to look at him. All this was very sad for the poor little duckling.

One evening, just as the sun set amid radiant clouds, there came a large flock of beautiful birds out of the bushes. The duckling had never seen any like them before. They were swans, and they curved their graceful necks, while their soft plumage shone with dazzling whiteness. They uttered a singular cry, as they spread their glorious wings and flew away from those cold regions to warmer countries across the sea. As they mounted higher and higher in the air, the ugly little duckling felt quite a strange sensation as he watched them. He whirled himself in the water like a wheel, stretched out his neck towards them, and uttered a cry so strange that it frightened himself. Could he ever forget those beautiful, happy birds? And when at last they were out of his sight, he dived under the water, and rose again almost beside himself with excitement. He knew not the names of these birds, nor where they had flown, but he felt towards them as he had never felt for any other bird in the world. He was not envious of these beautiful creatures, but wished to be as lovely as they. Poor ugly creature, how gladly he would have lived even with the ducks had they only given him encouragement. The winter grew colder and colder; he was obliged to swim about on the water to keep it from freezing, but every night the space on which he swam became smaller and smaller. At length it froze so hard that the ice in the water crackled as he moved, and the duckling had to paddle with his legs as well as he could, to keep the space from closing up. He became exhausted at last, and lay still and helpless, frozen fast in the ice.

Early in the morning, a peasant, who was passing by, saw what had happened. He broke the ice in pieces with his wooden shoe, and carried the duckling home to his wife. The warmth revived the poor little creature; but when the children wanted to play with him, the duckling thought they would do him some harm; so he started up in terror, fluttered into the milk-pan, and splashed the milk about the room. Then the woman clapped her hands, which frightened him still more. He flew first into the butter-cask, then into the meal-tub, and out again. What a condition he was in! The woman screamed, and struck at him with the tongs; the children laughed and screamed, and tumbled over each other, in their efforts to catch him; but luckily he escaped. The door stood open; the poor creature could just manage to slip out among the bushes, and lie down quite exhausted in the newly fallen snow.

It would be very sad, were I to relate all the misery and privations which the poor little duckling endured during the hard winter; but when it had passed, he found himself lying one morning in a moor, amongst the rushes. He felt the warm sun shining, and heard the lark singing, and saw that all around was beautiful spring. Then the young bird felt that his wings were strong, as he flapped them against his sides, and rose high into the air. They bore him onwards, until he found himself in a large garden, before he well knew how it had happened. The apple trees were in full blossom, and the fragrant elders bent their long green branches down to the stream which wound round a smooth lawn. Everything looked beautiful, in the freshness of early spring. From a thicket close by came three beautiful white swans, rustling their feathers, and swimming lightly over the smooth water. The duckling remembered the lovely birds, and felt more strangely unhappy than ever.

"I will fly to those royal birds," he exclaimed, "and they will kill me, because I am so ugly, and dare to approach them; but it does not matter: better be killed by them than pecked by the ducks, beaten by the hens, pushed about by the maiden who feeds the poultry, or starved with hunger in the winter."

Then he flew to the water, and swam towards the beautiful swans. The moment they espied the stranger, they rushed to meet him with outstretched wings.

"Kill me," said the poor bird; and he bent his head down to the surface of the water, and awaited death.

But what did he see in the clear stream below? His own image; no longer a dark, gray bird, ugly and disagreeable to look at, but a graceful and beautiful swan. To be born in a duck's nest, in a farmyard, is of no consequence to a bird, if it is hatched from a swan's egg. He now felt glad at having suffered sorrow and trouble, because it enabled him to enjoy so much better all the pleasure and happiness around him; for the great swans swam round the newcomer, and stroked his neck with their beaks, as a welcome.

Into the garden presently came some little children, and threw bread and cake into the water.

"See," cried the youngest, "there is a new one"; and the rest were delighted, and ran to their father and mother, dancing and clapping their hands, and shouting joyously, "There is another swan come; a new one has arrived."

Then they threw more bread and cake into the water, and said, "The new one is the most beautiful of all; he is so young and pretty." And the old swans bowed their heads before him.

Then he felt quite ashamed, and hid his head under his wing; for he did not know what to do, he was so happy, and yet not at all proud. He had been persecuted and despised for his ugliness, and now he heard them say he was the most beautiful of all the birds. Even the elder tree bent down its bows into the water before him, and the sun shone warm and bright. Then he rustled his feathers, curved his slender neck, and cried joyfully, from the depths of his heart, "I never dreamed of such happiness as this, while I was an ugly duckling."

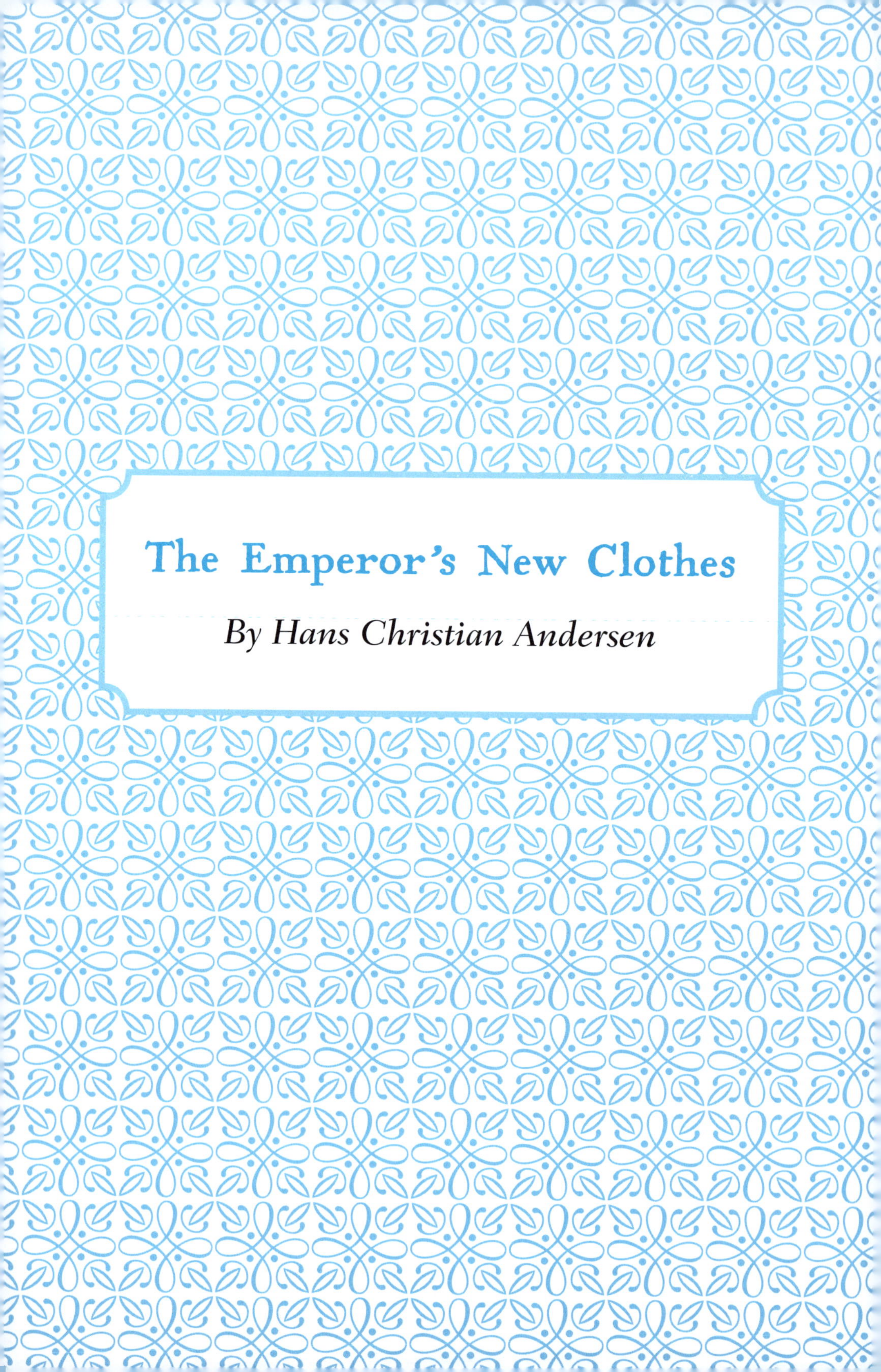

The Emperor's New Clothes

By Hans Christian Andersen

Many, many years ago lived an emperor, who thought so much of new clothes that he spent all his money in order to obtain them; his only ambition was to be always well dressed. He did not care for his soldiers, and the theatre did not amuse him; the only thing, in fact, he thought anything of was to drive out and show a new suit of clothes. He had a coat for every hour of the day; and as one would say of a king, "He is in his cabinet," so one could say of him, "The emperor is in his dressing room."

The great city where he resided was very gay; every day many strangers from all parts of the globe arrived. One day two swindlers came to this city; they made people believe that they were weavers, and declared they could manufacture the finest cloth to be imagined. Their colours and patterns, they said, were not only exceptionally beautiful, but the clothes made of their material possessed the wonderful quality of being invisible to any man who was unfit for his office or unpardonably stupid.

"That must be wonderful cloth," thought the emperor. "If I were to be dressed in a suit made of this cloth I should be able to find out which men in my empire were unfit for their places, and I could distinguish the clever from the stupid. I must have this cloth woven for me without delay." And he gave a large sum of money to the swindlers, in advance, that they should set to work without any loss of time. They set up two looms, and pretended to be very hard at work, but they did nothing whatever on the looms. They asked for the finest silk and the most precious gold cloth; all they got they did away with, and worked at the empty looms till late at night.

"I should very much like to know how they are getting on with the cloth," thought the emperor. But he felt rather uneasy when he remembered that he who was not fit for his office could not see it. Personally, he was of opinion that he had nothing to fear, yet he thought it advisable to send somebody else first to see how matters stood. Everybody in the town knew what a remarkable quality the stuff possessed, and all were anxious to see how bad or stupid their neighbours were.

"I shall send my honest old minister to the weavers," thought the emperor. "He can judge best how the stuff looks, for he is intelligent, and nobody understands his office better than he."

The good old minister went into the room where the swindlers sat before the empty looms. "Heaven preserve us!" he thought, and opened his eyes wide, "I cannot see anything at all," but he did not say so. Both swindlers requested him to come near, and asked him if he did not admire the exquisite pattern and the beautiful colours, pointing to the empty looms. The poor old minister tried his very best, but he could see nothing, for there was nothing to be seen. "Oh dear," he thought, "can I be so stupid? I should never have thought so, and nobody must know it! Is it possible that I am not fit for my office? No, no, I cannot say that I was unable to see the cloth."

"Now, have you got nothing to say?" said one of the swindlers, while he pretended to be busily weaving.

"Oh, it is very pretty, exceedingly beautiful," replied the old minister looking through his glasses. "What a beautiful pattern, what brilliant colours! I shall tell the emperor that I like the cloth very much."

"We are pleased to hear that," said the two weavers, and described to him the colours and explained the curious pattern. The old minister listened attentively, that he might relate to the emperor what they said; and so he did.

Now the swindlers asked for more money, silk, and gold cloth, which they required for weaving. They kept everything for themselves, and not a thread came near the loom, but they continued, as hitherto, to work at the empty looms.

Soon afterwards the emperor sent another honest courtier to the weavers to see how they were getting on, and if the cloth was nearly finished. Like the old minister, he looked and looked but could see nothing, as there was nothing to be seen.

"Is it not a beautiful piece of cloth?" asked the two swindlers, showing and explaining the magnificent pattern, which, however, did not exist.

"I am not stupid," said the man. "It is therefore my good appointment for which I am not fit. It is very strange, but I must not let anyone know it"; and he praised the cloth, which he did not see, and expressed his joy at the beautiful colours and the fine pattern. "It is very excellent," he said to the emperor.

Everybody in the whole town talked about the precious cloth. At last the emperor wished to see it himself, while it was still on the loom. With a number of courtiers, including the two who had already been there, he went to the two clever swindlers, who now worked as hard as they could, but without using any thread.

"Is it not magnificent?" said the two old statesmen who had been there before. "Your Majesty must admire the colours and the pattern." And then they pointed to the empty looms, for they imagined the others could see the cloth.

"What is this?" thought the emperor, "I do not see anything at all. That is terrible! Am I stupid? Am I unfit to be emperor? That would indeed be the most dreadful thing that could happen to me."

"Really," he said, turning to the weavers, "your cloth has our most gracious approval"; and nodding contentedly he looked at the empty loom, for he did not like to say that he saw nothing. All his attendants, who were with him, looked and looked, and although they could not see anything more than the others, they said, like the emperor, "It is very beautiful." And all advised him to wear the new magnificent clothes at a great procession which was soon to take place. "It is magnificent, beautiful, excellent," one heard them say; everybody seemed to be delighted, and the emperor appointed the two swindlers "Imperial Court weavers."

The whole night previous to the day on which the procession was to take place, the swindlers pretended to work, and burned more than sixteen candles. People should see that they were busy to finish the emperor's new suit. They pretended to take the cloth from the loom, and worked about in the air with big scissors, and sewed with needles without thread, and said at last: "The emperor's new suit is ready now."

The emperor and all his barons then came to the hall; the swindlers held their arms up as if they held something in their hands and said: "These are the trousers!" "This is the coat!" and "Here is the cloak!" and so on. "They are all as light as a cobweb, and one must feel as if one had nothing at all upon the body; but that is just the beauty of them."

"Indeed!" said all the courtiers; but they could not see anything, for there was nothing to be seen.

"Does it please your Majesty now to graciously undress," said the swindlers, "that we may assist your Majesty in putting on the new suit before the large looking glass?"

The emperor undressed, and the swindlers pretended to put the new suit upon him, one piece after another; and the emperor looked at himself in the glass from every side.

"How well they look! How well they fit!" said all. "What a beautiful pattern! What fine colours! That is a magnificent suit of clothes!"

The master of the ceremonies announced that the bearers of the canopy, which was to be carried in the procession, were ready.

"I am ready," said the emperor. "Does not my suit fit me marvellously?" Then he turned once more to the looking glass, that people should think he admired his garments.

The chamberlains, who were to carry the train, stretched their hands to the ground as if they lifted up a train, and pretended to hold something in their hands; they did not like people to know that they could not see anything.

The emperor marched in the procession under the beautiful canopy, and all who saw him in the street and out of the windows exclaimed: "Indeed, the emperor's new suit is incomparable! What a long train he has! How well it fits him!" Nobody wished to let others know he saw nothing, for then he would have been unfit for his office or too stupid. Never emperor's clothes were more admired.

"But he has nothing on at all," said a little child at last. "Good heavens! listen to the voice of an innocent child," said the father, and one whispered to the other what the child had said. "But he has nothing on at all," cried at last the whole people. That made a deep impression upon the emperor, for it seemed to him that they were right; but he thought to himself, "Now I must bear up to the end." And the chamberlains walked with still greater dignity, as if they carried the train which did not exist.

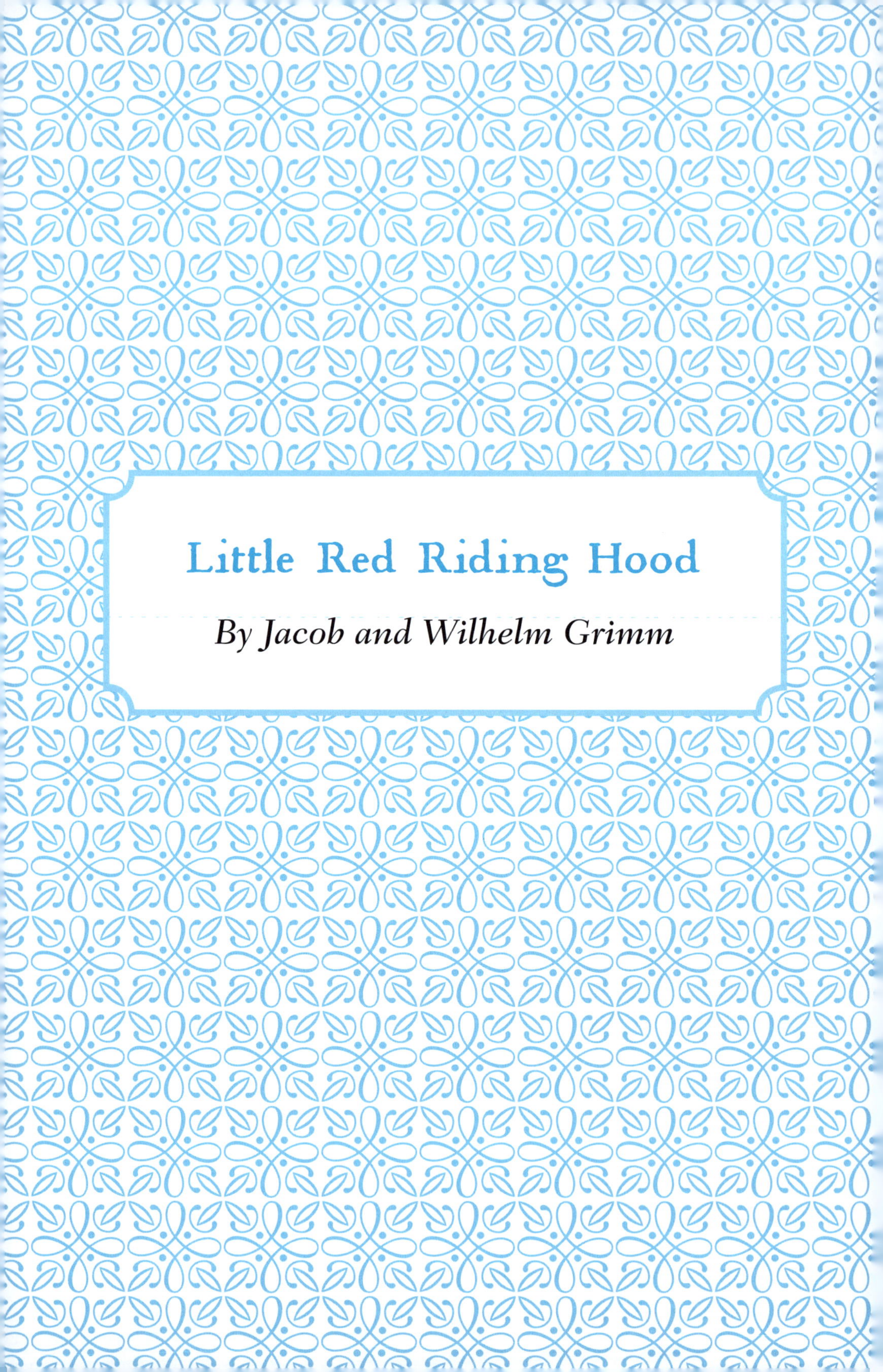

Little Red Riding Hood

By Jacob and Wilhelm Grimm

Once upon a time there was a dear little girl who was loved by everyone who looked at her, but most of all by her grandmother, and there was nothing that she would not have given to the child. Once she gave her a little cap of red velvet, which suited her so well that she would never wear anything else; so she was always called "Little Red Riding Hood."

One day her mother said to her: "Come, Little Red Riding Hood, here is a piece of cake and a bottle of wine; take them to your grandmother, she is ill and weak, and they will do her good. Set out before it gets hot, and when you are going, walk nicely and quietly and do not run off the path, or you may fall and break the bottle, and then your grandmother will get nothing; and when you go into her room, don't forget to say, 'Good morning,' and don't peep into every corner before you do it."

"I will take great care," said Little Red Riding Hood to her mother, and gave her hand on it.

The grandmother lived out in the wood, half a league from the village, and just as Little Red Riding Hood entered the wood, a wolf met her. Little Red Riding Hood did not know what a wicked creature he was, and was not at all afraid of him.

"Good day, Little Red Riding Hood," said he.

"Thank you kindly, wolf."

"Whither away so early, Little Red Riding Hood?"

"To my grandmother's."

"What have you got in your apron?"

"Cake and wine; yesterday was baking day, so poor sick grandmother is to have something good, to make her stronger."

"Where does your grandmother live, Little Red Riding Hood?"

"A good quarter of a league farther on in the wood; her house stands under the three large oak trees, the nut trees are just below; you surely must know it," replied Little Red Riding Hood.

The wolf thought to himself: "What a tender young creature! what a nice plump mouthful—she will be better to eat than the old woman. I must act craftily, so as to catch both." So he walked for a short time by the side of Little Red Riding Hood, and then he said: "See, Little Red Riding Hood, how pretty the flowers are about here—why do you not look round? I believe, too, that you do not hear how sweetly the little birds are singing; you walk gravely along as if you were going to school, while everything else out here in the wood is merry."

Little Red Riding Hood raised her eyes, and when she saw the sunbeams dancing here and there through the trees, and pretty flowers growing everywhere, she thought: "Suppose I take grandmother a fresh nosegay; that would please her too. It is so early in the day that I shall still get there in good time"; and so she ran from the path into the wood to look for flowers. And whenever she had picked one, she fancied that she saw a still prettier one farther on, and ran after it, and so got deeper and deeper into the wood.

Meanwhile the wolf ran straight to the grandmother's house and knocked at the door.

"Who is there?"

"Little Red Riding Hood," replied the wolf. "She is bringing cake and wine; open the door."

"Lift the latch," called out the grandmother, "I am too weak, and cannot get up."

The wolf lifted the latch, the door sprang open, and without saying a word he went straight to the grandmother's bed, and devoured her. Then he put on her clothes, dressed himself in her cap, laid himself in bed, and drew the curtains.

Little Red Riding Hood, however, had been running about picking flowers, and when she had gathered so many that she could carry no more, she remembered her grandmother, and set out on the way to her.

She was surprised to find the cottage door standing open, and when she went into the room, she had such a strange feeling that she said to herself: "Oh dear! how uneasy I feel today, and at other times I like being with grandmother so much." She called out: "Good morning," but received no answer; so she went to the bed and drew back the curtains. There lay her grandmother with her cap pulled far over her face, and looking very strange.

"Oh! grandmother," she said, "what big ears you have!"

"The better to hear you with, my child," was the reply.

"But, grandmother, what big eyes you have!" she said.

"The better to see you with, my dear."

"But, grandmother, what large hands you have!"

"The better to hug you with."

"Oh! but, grandmother, what a terrible big mouth you have!"

"The better to eat you with!"

And scarcely had the wolf said this, than with one bound he was out of bed and swallowed up Little Red Riding Hood.

When the wolf had appeased his appetite, he lay down again in the bed, fell asleep and began to snore very loud. The huntsman was just passing the house, and thought to himself: "How the old woman is snoring! I must just see if she wants anything." So he went into the room, and when he came to the bed, he saw that the wolf was lying in it. "Do I find you here, you old sinner!" said he. "I have long sought you!" Then just as he was going to fire at him, it occurred to him that the wolf might have devoured the grandmother, and that she might still be saved, so he did not fire, but took a pair of scissors, and began to cut open the stomach of the sleeping wolf. When he had made two snips, he saw the little red cap shining, and then he made two snips more, and the little girl sprang out, crying: "Ah, how frightened I have been! How dark it was inside the wolf"; and after that the aged grandmother came out alive also, but scarcely able to breathe. Little Red Riding Hood, however, quickly fetched great stones with which they filled the wolf's belly, and when he awoke, he wanted to run away, but the stones were so heavy that he collapsed at once, and fell dead.

Then all three were delighted. The huntsman drew off the wolf's skin and went home with it; the grandmother ate the cake and drank the wine which Little Red Riding Hood had brought, and revived, but Little Red Riding Hood thought to herself: "As long as I live, I will never by myself leave the path, to run into the wood, when my mother has forbidden me to do so."

It is also related that once when Little Red Riding Hood was again taking cakes to the old grandmother, another wolf spoke to her, and tried to entice her from the path. Little Red Riding Hood, however, was on her guard, and went straight forward on her way, and told her grandmother that she had met the wolf, and that he had said "good morning" to her, but with such a wicked look in his eyes, that if they had not been on the public road she was certain he would have eaten her up. "Well," said the grandmother, "we will shut the door, that he may not come in." Soon afterwards the wolf knocked, and cried: "Open the door, grandmother, I am Little Red Riding Hood, and am bringing you some cakes." But they did not speak, or open the door, so the grey-beard stole twice or thrice round the house, and at last jumped on the roof, intending to wait until Little Red Riding Hood went home in the evening, and then to steal after her and devour her in the darkness. But the grandmother saw what was in his thoughts. In front of the house was a great stone trough, so she said to the child: "Take the pail, Little Red Riding Hood; I made some sausages yesterday, so carry the water in which I boiled them to the trough." Little Red Riding Hood carried until the great trough was quite full. Then the smell of the sausages reached the wolf, and he sniffed and peeped down, and at last stretched out his neck so far that he could no longer keep his footing and began to slip, and slipped down from the roof straight into the great trough, and was drowned. But Little Red Riding Hood went joyously home, and no one ever did anything to harm her again.

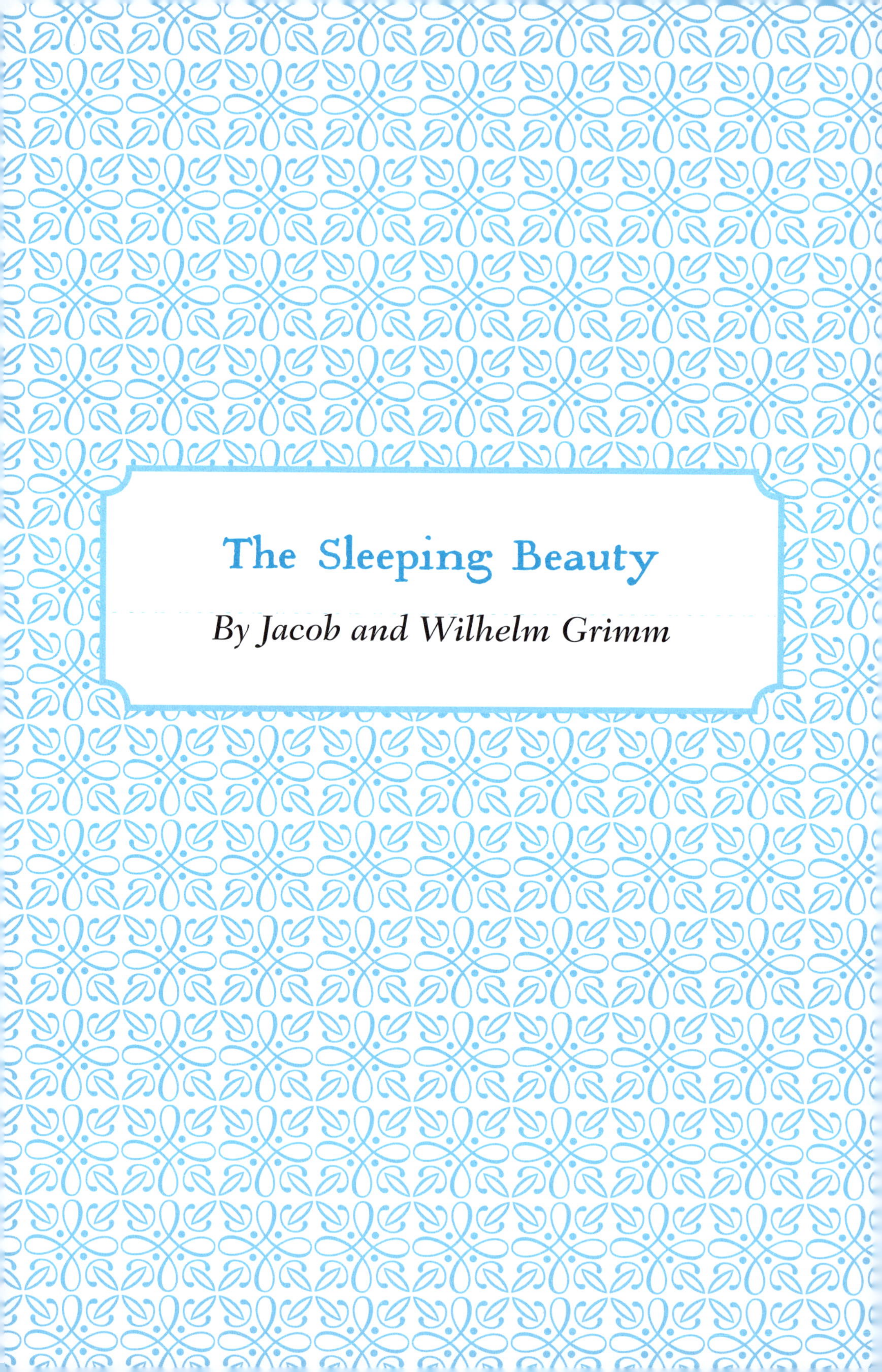

The Sleeping Beauty

By Jacob and Wilhelm Grimm

A king and queen once upon a time reigned in a country a great way off, where there were in those days fairies. Now this king and queen had plenty of money, and plenty of fine clothes to wear, and plenty of good things to eat and drink, and a coach to ride out in every day: but though they had been married many years they had no children, and this grieved them very much indeed. But one day as the queen was walking by the side of the river, at the bottom of the garden, she saw a poor little fish, that had thrown itself out of the water, and lay gasping and nearly dead on the bank. Then the queen took pity on the little fish, and threw it back again into the river; and before it swam away it lifted its head out of the water and said, "I know what your wish is, and it shall be fulfilled, in return for your kindness to me—you will soon have a daughter." What the little fish had foretold soon came to pass; and the queen had a little girl, so very beautiful that the king could not cease looking on it for joy, and said he would hold a great feast and make merry, and show the child to all the land. So he asked his kinsmen, and nobles, and friends, and neighbours. But the queen said, "I will have the fairies also, that they might be kind and good to our little daughter." Now there were thirteen fairies in the kingdom; but as the king and queen had only twelve golden dishes for them to eat out of, they were forced to leave one of the fairies without asking her. So twelve fairies came, each with a high red cap on her head, and red shoes with high heels on her feet, and a long white wand in her hand: and after the feast was over they gathered round in a ring and gave all their best gifts to the little princess. One gave her goodness, another beauty, another riches, and so on till she had all that was good in the world.

Just as eleven of them had done blessing her, a great noise was heard in the courtyard, and word was brought that the thirteenth fairy was come, with a black cap on her head, and black shoes on her feet, and a broomstick in her hand: and presently up she came into the dining hall. Now, as she had not been asked to the feast she was very angry, and scolded the king and queen very much, and set to work to take her revenge. So she cried out, "The king's daughter shall, in her fifteenth year, be wounded by a spindle, and fall down dead." Then the twelfth of the friendly fairies, who had not yet given her gift, came forward, and said that the evil wish must be fulfilled, but that she could soften its mischief; so her gift was, that the king's daughter, when the spindle wounded her, should not really die, but should only fall asleep for a hundred years.

However, the king hoped still to save his dear child altogether from the threatened evil; so he ordered that all the spindles in the kingdom should be bought up and burnt. But all the gifts of the first eleven fairies were in the meantime fulfilled; for the princess was so beautiful, and well behaved, and good, and wise, that everyone who knew her loved her.

It happened that, on the very day she was fifteen years old, the king and queen were not at home, and she was left alone in the palace. So she roved about by herself, and looked at all the rooms and chambers, till at last she came to an old tower, to which there was a narrow staircase ending with a little door. In the door there was a golden key, and when she turned it the door sprang open, and there sat an old lady spinning away very busily. "Why, how now, good mother," said the princess; "what are you doing there?"

"Spinning," said the old lady, and nodded her head, humming a tune, while buzz! went the wheel.

"How prettily that little thing turns round!" said the princess, and took the spindle and began to try and spin. But scarcely had she touched it, before the fairy's prophecy was fulfilled; the spindle wounded her, and she fell down lifeless on the ground.

However, she was not dead, but had only fallen into a deep sleep; and the king and the queen, who had just come home, and all their court, fell asleep too; and the horses slept in the stables, and the dogs in the court, the pigeons on the housetop, and the very flies slept upon the walls. Even the fire on the hearth left off blazing, and went to sleep; the jack stopped, and the spit that was turning about with a goose upon it for the king's dinner stood still; and the cook, who was at that moment pulling the kitchen-boy by the hair to give him a box on the ear for something he had done amiss, let him go, and both fell asleep; the butler, who was slyly tasting the ale, fell asleep with the jug at his lips: and thus everything stood still, and slept soundly.

A large hedge of thorns soon grew round the palace, and every year it became higher and thicker; till at last the old palace was surrounded and hidden, so that not even the roof or the chimneys could be seen. But there went a report through all the land of the beautiful sleeping Briar Rose (for so the king's daughter was called): so that, from time to time, several kings' sons came, and tried to break through the thicket into the palace. This, however, none of them could ever do; for the thorns and bushes laid hold of them, as it were with hands; and there they stuck fast, and died wretchedly.

After many, many years there came a king's son into that land: and an old man told him the story of the thicket of thorns; and how a beautiful palace stood behind it, and how a wonderful princess, called Briar Rose, lay in it asleep, with all her court. He told, too, how he had heard from his grandfather that many, many princes had come, and had tried to break through the thicket, but that they had all stuck fast in it, and died. Then the young prince said, "All this shall not frighten me; I will go and see this Briar Rose." The old man tried to hinder him, but he was bent upon going.

Now that very day the hundred years were ended; and as the prince came to the thicket he saw nothing but beautiful flowering shrubs, through which he went with ease, and they shut in after him as thick as ever. Then he came at last to the palace, and there in the court lay the dogs asleep; and the horses were standing in the stables; and on the roof sat the pigeons fast asleep, with their heads under their wings. And when he came into the palace, the flies were sleeping on the walls; the spit was standing still; the butler had the jug of ale at his lips, going to drink a draught; the maid sat with a fowl in her lap ready to be plucked; and the cook in the kitchen was still holding up her hand, as if she was going to beat the boy.

Then he went on still farther, and all was so still that he could hear every breath he drew; till at last he came to the old tower, and opened the door of the little room in which Briar Rose was; and there she lay, fast asleep on a couch by the window. She looked so beautiful that he could not take his eyes off her, so he stooped down and gave her a kiss. But the moment he kissed her she opened her eyes and awoke, and smiled upon him; and they went out together; and soon the king and queen also awoke, and all the court, and gazed on each other with great wonder. And the horses shook themselves, and the dogs jumped up and barked; the pigeons took their heads from under their wings, and looked about and flew into the fields; the flies on the walls buzzed again; the fire in the kitchen blazed up; round went the jack, and round went the spit, with the goose for the king's dinner upon it; the butler finished his draught of ale; the maid went on plucking the fowl; and the cook gave the boy the box on his ear.

And then the prince and Briar Rose were married, and the wedding feast was given; and they lived happily together all their lives long.

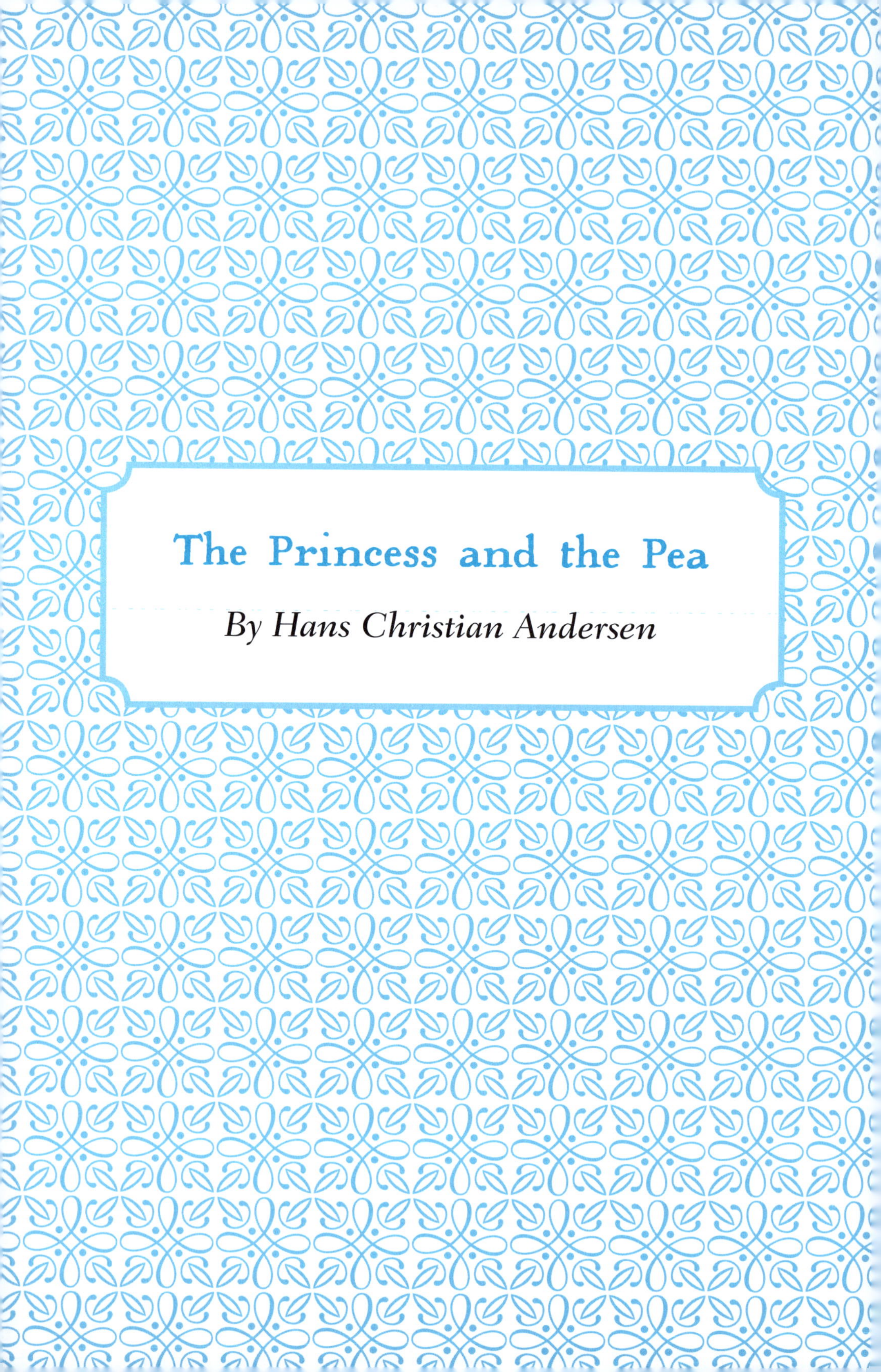

The Princess and the Pea

By Hans Christian Andersen

Once upon a time there was a prince who wanted to marry a princess; but she would have to be a real princess. He travelled all over the world to find one, but nowhere could he get what he wanted. There were princesses enough, but it was difficult to find out whether they were real ones. There was always something about them that was not as it should be. So he came home again and was sad, for he would have liked very much to have a real princess.

One evening a terrible storm came on; there was thunder and lightning, and the rain poured down in torrents. Suddenly a knocking was heard at the city gate, and the old king went to open it.

It was a princess standing out there in front of the gate. But, good gracious! what a sight the rain and the wind had made her look. The water ran down from her hair and clothes; it ran down into the toes of her shoes and out again at the heels. And yet she said that she was a real princess.

"Well, we'll soon find that out," thought the old queen. But she said nothing, went into the bedroom, took all the bedding off the bedstead, and laid a pea on the bottom; then she took twenty mattresses and laid them on the pea, and then twenty eiderdown beds on top of the mattresses.

On this the princess had to lie all night. In the morning she was asked how she had slept.

"Oh, very badly!" said she. "I have scarcely closed my eyes all night. Heaven only knows what was in the bed, but I was lying on something hard, so that I am black and blue all over my body. It's horrible!"

Now they knew that she was a real princess because she had felt the pea right through the twenty mattresses and the twenty eiderdown beds.

Nobody but a real princess could be as sensitive as that.

So the prince took her for his wife, for now he knew that he had a real princess; and the pea was put in the museum, where it may still be seen, if no one has stolen it.

There, that is a true story.

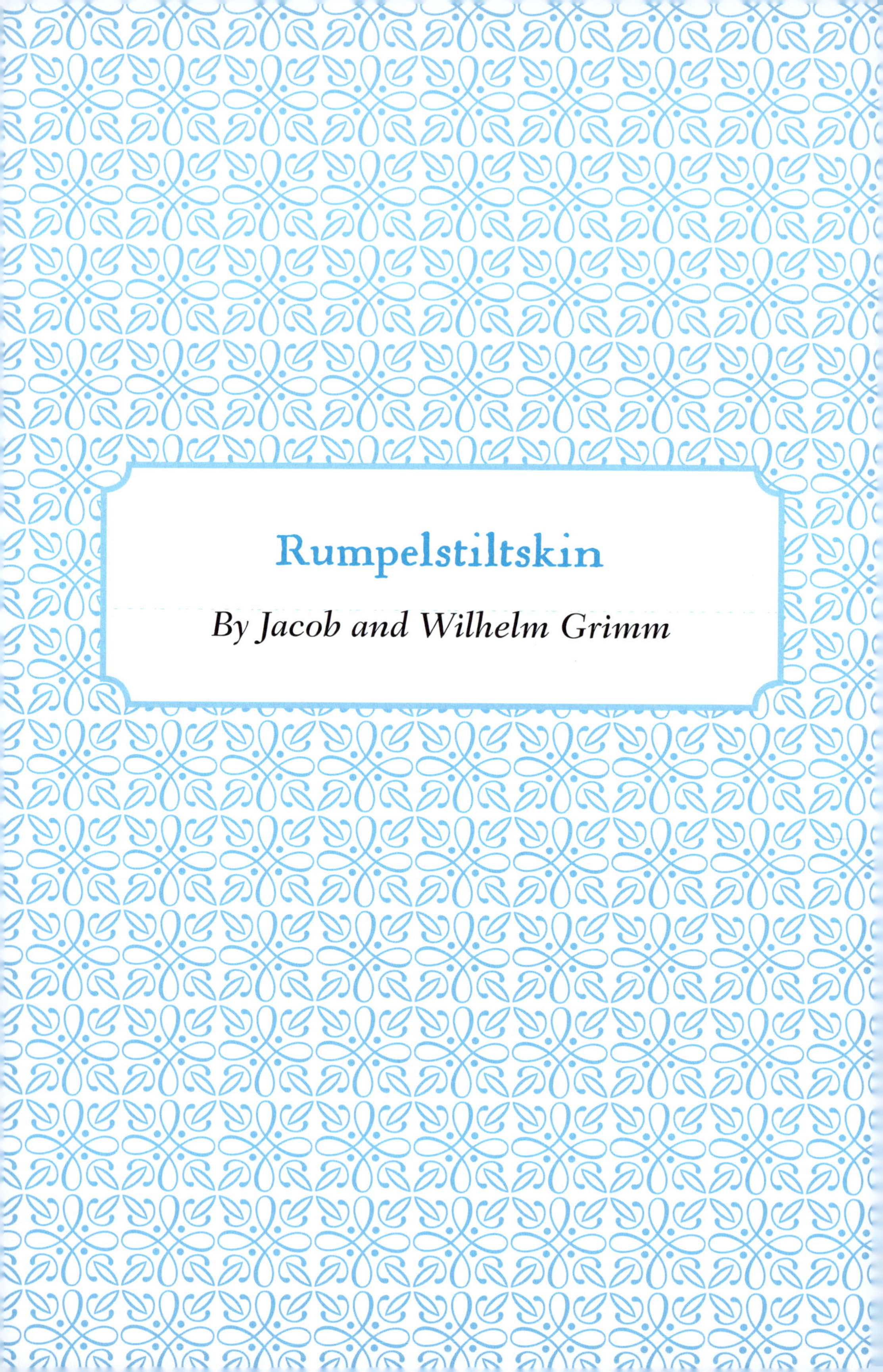

Rumpelstiltskin

By Jacob and Wilhelm Grimm

By the side of a wood, in a country a long way off, ran a fine stream of water; and upon the stream there stood a mill. The miller's house was close by, and the miller, you must know, had a very beautiful daughter. She was, moreover, very shrewd and clever; and the miller was so proud of her, that he one day told the king of the land, who used to come and hunt in the wood, that his daughter could spin gold out of straw. Now this king was very fond of money; and when he heard the miller's boast his greediness was raised, and he sent for the girl to be brought before him. Then he led her to a chamber in his palace where there was a great heap of straw, and gave her a spinning wheel, and said, "All this must be spun into gold before morning, as you love your life." It was in vain that the poor maiden said that it was only a silly boast of her father, for that she could do no such thing as spin straw into gold: the chamber door was locked, and she was left alone.

She sat down in one corner of the room, and began to bewail her hard fate; when on a sudden the door opened, and a droll-looking little man hobbled in, and said, "Good morrow to you, my good lass; what are you weeping for?"

"Alas!" said she, "I must spin this straw into gold, and I know not how."

"What will you give me," said the hobgoblin, "to do it for you?"

"My necklace," replied the maiden. He took her at her word, and sat himself down to the wheel, and whistled and sang:

"Round about, round about,
Lo and behold!
Reel away, reel away,
Straw into gold!"

And round about the wheel went merrily; the work was quickly done, and the straw was all spun into gold.

When the king came and saw this, he was greatly astonished and pleased; but his heart grew still more greedy of gain, and he shut up the poor miller's daughter again with a fresh task. Then she knew not what to do, and sat down once more to weep; but the dwarf soon opened the door, and said, "What will you give me to do your task?"

"The ring on my finger," said she. So her little friend took the ring, and began to work at the wheel again, and whistled and sang:

"Round about, round about,
Lo and behold!
Reel away, reel away,
Straw into gold!"

till, long before morning, all was done again.

The king was greatly delighted to see all this glittering treasure; but still he had not enough: so he took the miller's daughter to a yet larger heap, and said, "All this must be spun tonight; and if it is, you shall be my queen." As soon as she was alone that dwarf came in, and said, "What will you give me to spin gold for you this third time?"

"I have nothing left," said she.

"Then say you will give me," said the little man, "the first little child that you may have when you are queen."

"That may never be," thought the miller's daughter: and as she knew no other way to get her task done, she said she would do what he asked. Round went the wheel again to the old song, and the manikin once more spun the heap into gold. The king came in the morning, and, finding all he wanted, was forced to keep his word; so he married the miller's daughter, and she really became queen.

At the birth of her first little child she was very glad, and forgot the dwarf, and what she had said. But one day he came into her room, where she was sitting playing with her baby, and put her in mind of it. Then she grieved sorely at her misfortune, and said she would give him all the wealth of the kingdom if he would let her off, but in vain; till at last her tears softened him, and he said, "I will give you three days' grace, and if during that time you tell me my name, you shall keep your child."

Now the queen lay awake all night, thinking of all the odd names that she had ever heard; and she sent messengers all over the land to find out new ones. The next day the little man came, and she began with Timothy, Ichabod, Benjamin, Jeremiah, and all the names she could remember; but to all and each of them he said, "Madam, that is not my name."

The second day she began with all the comical names she could hear of, Bandy-Legs, Hatchback, Crookshanks, and so on; but the little gentleman still said to every one of them, "Madam, that is not my name."

The third day one of the messengers came back, and said, "I have travelled two days without hearing of any other names; but yesterday, as I was climbing a high hill, among the trees of the forest where the fox and the hare bid each other good night, I saw a little hut; and before the hut burnt a fire; and round about the fire a funny little dwarf was dancing upon one leg, and singing:

"Merrily the feast I'll make.
Today I'll brew, tomorrow bake;
Merrily I'll dance and sing,
For next day will a stranger bring.
Little does my lady dream
Rumpelstiltskin is my name!"

When the queen heard this she jumped for joy, and as soon as her little friend came she sat down upon her throne, and called all her court round to enjoy the fun; and the nurse stood by her side with the baby in her arms, as if it was quite ready to be given up. Then the little man began to chuckle at the thought of having the poor child, to take home with him to his hut in the woods; and he cried out, "Now, lady, what is my name?"

"Is it John?" asked she.

"No, madam!"

"Is it Tom?"

"No, madam!"

"Is it Jemmy?"

"It is not."

"Can your name be Rumpelstiltskin?" said the lady slyly.

"Some witch told you that! Some witch told you that!" cried the little man, and dashed his right foot in a rage so deep into the floor, that he was forced to lay hold of it with both hands to pull it out.

Then he made the best of his way off, while the nurse laughed and the baby crowed; and all the court jeered at him for having had so much trouble for nothing, and said, "We wish you a very good morning, and a merry feast, Mr. Rumpelstiltskin!"

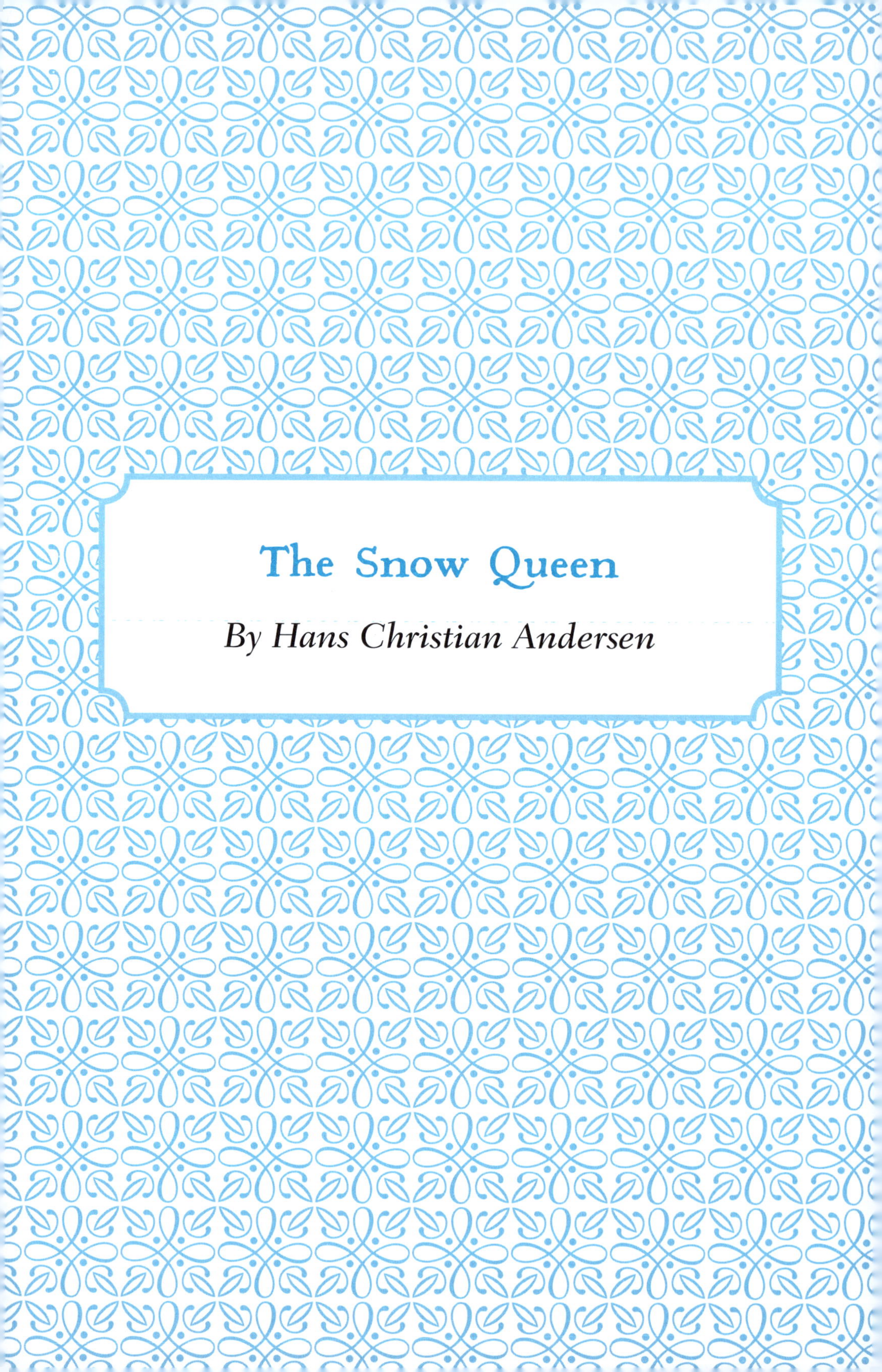

The Snow Queen

By Hans Christian Andersen

First Story: Which Describes a Looking Glass and Its Broken Fragments

You must attend to the beginning of this story, for when we get to the end we shall know more than we now do about a very wicked hobgoblin; he was one of the most mischievous of all sprites, for he was a real demon.

One day when he was in a merry mood he made a looking glass which had the power of making everything good or beautiful that was reflected in it shrink almost to nothing, while everything that was worthless and bad was magnified so as to look ten times worse than it really was.

The most lovely landscapes appeared like boiled spinach, and all the people became hideous and looked as if they stood on their heads and had no bodies. Their countenances were so distorted that no one could recognize them, and even one freckle on the face appeared to spread over the whole of the nose and mouth. The demon said this was very amusing. When a good or holy thought passed through the mind of anyone a wrinkle was seen in the mirror, and then how the demon laughed at his cunning invention.

All who went to the demon's school—for he kept a school—talked everywhere of the wonders they had seen, and declared that people could now, for the first time, see what the world and its inhabitants were really like. They carried the glass about everywhere, till at last there was not a land nor a people who had not been looked at through this distorted mirror.

They wanted even to fly with it up to heaven to see the angels, but the higher they flew the more slippery the glass became, and they could scarcely hold it. At last it slipped from their hands, fell to the earth, and was broken into millions of pieces.

But now the looking glass caused more unhappiness than ever, for some of the fragments were not so large as a grain of sand, and they flew about the world into every country. And when one of these tiny atoms flew into a person's eye it stuck there, unknown to himself, and from that moment he viewed everything the wrong way, and could see only the worst side of what he looked at, for even the smallest fragment retained the same power which had belonged to the whole mirror.

Some few persons even got a splinter of the looking glass in their hearts, and this was terrible, for their hearts became cold and hard like a lump of ice. A few of the pieces were so large that they could be used as windowpanes; it would have been a sad thing indeed to look at our friends through them. Other pieces were made into spectacles, and this was dreadful, for those who wore them could see nothing either rightly or justly. At all this the wicked demon laughed till his sides shook, to see the mischief he had done. There are still a number of these little fragments of glass floating about in the air, and now you shall hear what happened with one of them.

Second Story: A Little Boy and a Little Girl

In a large town full of houses and people there is not room for everybody to have even a little garden. Most people are obliged to content themselves with a few flowers in flowerpots.

In one of these large towns lived two poor children who had a garden somewhat larger and better than a few flowerpots. They were not brother and sister, but they loved each other almost as much as if they had been. Their parents lived opposite each other in two garrets where the roofs of neighboring houses nearly joined each other, and the water pipe ran between them. In each roof was a little window, so that anyone could step across the gutter from one window to the other.

The parents of each of these children had a large wooden box in which they cultivated kitchen vegetables for their own use, and in each box was a little rosebush which grew luxuriantly.

After a while the parents decided to place these two boxes across the water pipe, so that they reached from one window to the other and looked like two banks of flowers. Sweet peas drooped over the boxes, and the rosebushes shot forth long branches, which were trained about the windows and clustered together almost like a triumphal arch of leaves and flowers.

The boxes were very high, and the children knew they must not climb upon them without permission; but they often had leave to step out and sit upon their little stools under the rosebushes or play quietly together.

In winter all this pleasure came to an end, for the windows were sometimes quite frozen over. But they would warm copper pennies on the stove and hold the warm pennies against the frozen pane; then there would soon be a little round hole through which they could peep, and the soft, bright eyes of the little boy and girl would sparkle through the hole at each window as they looked at each other. Their names were Kay and Gerda. In summer they could be together with one jump from the window, but in winter they had to go up and down the long staircase and out through the snow before they could meet.

"See! there are the white bees swarming," said Kay's old grandmother one day when it was snowing.

"Have they a queen bee?" asked the little boy, for he knew that the real bees always had a queen.

"To be sure they have," said the grandmother. "She is flying there where the swarm is thickest. She is the largest of them all and never remains on the earth, but flies up to the dark clouds. Often at midnight she flies through the streets of the town and breathes with her frosty breath upon the windows; then the ice freezes on the panes into wonderful forms that look like flowers and castles."

"Yes, I have seen them," said both the children; and they knew it must be true.

"Can the Snow Queen come in here?" asked the little girl.

"Only let her come," said the boy. "I'll put her on the warm stove, and then she'll melt."

The grandmother smoothed his hair and told him more stories.

That same evening when little Kay was at home, half undressed, he climbed upon a chair by the window and peeped out through the little round hole. A few flakes of snow were falling, and one of them, rather larger than the rest, alighted on the edge of one of the flower boxes. Strange to say, this snowflake grew larger and larger till at last it took the form of a woman dressed in garments of white gauze, which looked like millions of starry snowflakes linked together. She was fair and beautiful, but made of ice—glittering, dazzling ice. Still, she was alive, and her eyes sparkled like bright stars, though there was neither peace nor rest in them. She nodded toward the window and waved her hand. The little boy was frightened and sprang from the chair, and at the same moment it seemed as if a large bird flew by the window.

On the following day there was a clear frost, and very soon came the spring. The sun shone; the young green leaves burst forth; the swallows built their nests; windows were opened, and the children sat once more in the garden on the roof, high above all the other rooms.

How beautifully the roses blossomed this summer! The little girl had learned a hymn in which roses were spoken of. She thought of their own roses, and she sang the hymn to the little boy, and he sang, too:

"Roses bloom and fade away;
The Christ child shall abide alway.
Blessed are we his face to see
And ever little children be."

Then the little ones held each other by the hand, and kissed the roses, and looked at the bright sunshine, and spoke to it as if the Christ child were really there. Those were glorious summer days. How beautiful and fresh it was out among the rosebushes, which seemed as if they would never leave off blooming.

One day Kay and Gerda sat looking at a book of pictures of animals and birds. Just then, as the clock in the church tower struck twelve, Kay said, "Oh, something has struck my heart!" and soon after, "There is certainly something in my eye."

The little girl put her arm round his neck and looked into his eye, but she could see nothing.

"I believe it is gone," he said. But it was not gone; it was one of those bits of the looking glass—that magic mirror of which we have spoken—the ugly glass which made everything great and good appear small and ugly, while all that was wicked and bad became more visible, and every little fault could be plainly seen. Poor little Kay had also received a small splinter in his heart, which very quickly turned to a lump of ice. He felt no more pain, but the glass was there still. "Why do you cry?" said he at last. "It makes you look ugly. There is nothing the matter with me now. Oh, fie!" he cried suddenly; "that rose is worm-eaten, and this one is quite crooked. After all, they are ugly roses, just like the box in which they stand." And then he kicked the boxes with his foot and pulled off the two roses.

"Why, Kay, what are you doing?" cried the little girl; and then when he saw how grieved she was he tore off another rose and jumped through his own window, away from sweet little Gerda.

When afterward she brought out the picture book he said, "It is only fit for babies in long clothes," and when grandmother told stories he would interrupt her with "but"; or sometimes when he could manage it he would get behind her chair, put on a pair of spectacles, and imitate her very cleverly to make the people laugh. By and by he began to mimic the speech and gait of persons in the street. All that was peculiar or disagreeable in a person he would imitate directly, and people said, "That boy will be very clever; he has a remarkable genius." But it was the piece of glass in his eye and the coldness in his heart that made him act like this. He would even tease little Gerda, who loved him with all her heart.

His games too were quite different; they were not so childlike. One winter's day, when it snowed, he brought out a burning glass, then, holding out the skirt of his blue coat, let the snowflakes fall upon it.

"Look in this glass, Gerda," said he, and she saw how every flake of snow was magnified and looked like a beautiful flower or a glittering star.

"Is it not clever," said Kay, "and much more interesting than looking at real flowers? There is not a single fault in it. The snowflakes are quite perfect till they begin to melt."

Soon after, Kay made his appearance in large, thick gloves and with his sledge at his back. He called upstairs to Gerda, "I've got leave to go into the great square, where the other boys play and ride." And away he went.

In the great square the boldest among the boys would often tie their sledges to the wagons of the country people and so get a ride. This was capital. But while they were all amusing themselves, and Kay with them, a great sledge came by; it was painted white, and in it sat someone wrapped in a rough white fur and wearing a white cap. The sledge drove twice round the square, and Kay fastened his own little sledge to it, so that when it went away he went with it. It went faster and faster right through the next street, and the person who drove turned round and nodded pleasantly to Kay as if they were well acquainted with each other; but whenever Kay wished to loosen his little sledge the driver turned and nodded as if to signify that he was to stay, so Kay sat still, and they drove out through the town gate.

Then the snow began to fall so heavily that the little boy could not see a hand's breadth before him, but still they drove on. He suddenly loosened the cord so that the large sledge might go on without him, but it was of no use; his little carriage held fast, and away they went like the wind. Then he called out loudly, but nobody heard him, while the snow beat upon him, and the sledge flew onward. Every now and then it gave a jump, as if they were going over hedges and ditches. The boy was frightened and tried to say a prayer, but he could remember nothing but the multiplication table.

The snowflakes became larger and larger, till they appeared like great white birds. All at once they sprang on one side, the great sledge stopped, and the person who had driven it rose up. The fur and the cap, which were made entirely of snow, fell off, and he saw a lady, tall and white; it was the Snow Queen.

"We have driven well," said she; "but why do you tremble so? Here, creep into my warm fur." Then she seated him beside her in the sledge, and as she wrapped the fur about him, he felt as if he were sinking into a snowdrift.

"Are you still cold?" she asked, as she kissed him on the forehead. The kiss was colder than ice; it went quite through to his heart, which was almost a lump of ice already. He felt as if he were going to die, but only for a moment—he soon seemed quite well and did not notice the cold all around him.

"My sledge! Don't forget my sledge," was his first thought, and then he looked and saw that it was bound fast to one of the white birds which flew behind him. The Snow Queen kissed little Kay again, and by this time he had forgotten little Gerda, his grandmother, and all at home.

"Now you must have no more kisses," she said, "or I should kiss you to death."

Kay looked at her. She was so beautiful, he could not imagine a more lovely face; she did not now seem to be made of ice as when he had seen her through his window and she had nodded to him.

In his eyes she was perfect, and he did not feel at all afraid. He told her he could do mental arithmetic as far as fractions, and that he knew the number of square miles and the number of inhabitants in the country. She smiled, and it occurred to him that she thought he did not yet know so very much.

He looked around the vast expanse as she flew higher and higher with him upon a black cloud, while the storm blew and howled as if it were singing songs of olden time. They flew over woods and lakes, over sea and land; below them roared the wild wind; wolves howled, and the snow crackled; over them flew the black, screaming crows, and above all shone the moon, clear and bright—and so Kay passed through the long, long winter's night, and by day he slept at the feet of the Snow Queen.

Third Story: The Enchanted Flower Garden

But how fared little Gerda in Kay's absence?

What had become of him no one knew, nor could anyone give the slightest information, excepting the boys, who said that he had tied his sledge to another very large one, which had driven through the street and out at the town gate. No one knew where it went. Many tears were shed for him, and little Gerda wept bitterly for a long time. She said she knew he must be dead, that he was drowned in the river which flowed close by the school. The long winter days were very dreary. But at last spring came with warm sunshine.

"Kay is dead and gone," said little Gerda.

"I don't believe it," said the sunshine.

"He is dead and gone," she said to the sparrows.

"We don't believe it," they replied, and at last little Gerda began to doubt it herself.

"I will put on my new red shoes," she said one morning, "those that Kay has never seen, and then I will go down to the river and ask for him."

It was quite early when she kissed her old grandmother, who was still asleep; then she put on her red shoes and went, quite alone, out of the town gate, toward the river.

"Is it true that you have taken my little playmate away from me?" she said to the river. "I will give you my red shoes if you will give him back to me."

And it seemed as if the waves nodded to her in a strange manner. Then she took off her red shoes, which she liked better than anything else, and threw them both into the river, but they fell near the bank, and the little waves carried them back to land, just as if the river would not take from her what she loved best, because it could not give her back little Kay.

But she thought the shoes had not been thrown out far enough. Then she crept into a boat that lay among the reeds, and threw the shoes again from the farther end of the boat into the water; but it was not fastened, and her movement sent it gliding away from the land. When she saw this she hastened to reach the end of the boat, but before she could do so it was more than a yard from the bank and drifting away faster than ever.

Little Gerda was very much frightened. She began to cry, but no one heard her except the sparrows, and they could not carry her to land, but they flew along by the shore and sang as if to comfort her: "Here we are! Here we are!"

The boat floated with the stream, and little Gerda sat quite still with only her stockings on her feet; the red shoes floated after her, but she could not reach them because the boat kept so much in advance.

The banks on either side of the river were very pretty. There were beautiful flowers, old trees, sloping fields in which cows and sheep were grazing, but not a human being to be seen.

"Perhaps the river will carry me to little Kay," thought Gerda, and then she became more cheerful, and raised her head and looked at the beautiful green banks; and so the boat sailed on for hours. At length she came to a large cherry orchard, in which stood a small house with strange red and blue windows. It had also a thatched roof, and outside were two wooden soldiers that presented arms to her as she sailed past. Gerda called out to them, for she thought they were alive; but of course they did not answer, and as the boat drifted nearer to the shore she saw what they really were.

Then Gerda called still louder, and there came a very old woman out of the house, leaning on a crutch. She wore a large hat to shade her from the sun, and on it were painted all sorts of pretty flowers.

"You poor little child," said the old woman, "how did you manage to come this long, long distance into the wide world on such a rapid, rolling stream?" And then the old woman walked into the water, seized the boat with her crutch, drew it to land, and lifted little Gerda out. And Gerda was glad to feel herself again on dry ground, although she was rather afraid of the strange old woman.

"Come and tell me who you are," said she, "and how you came here."

Then Gerda told her everything, while the old woman shook her head and said, "Hem-hem"; and when Gerda had finished she asked the old woman if she had not seen little Kay. She told her he had not passed that way, but he very likely would come. She told Gerda not to be sorrowful, but to taste the cherries and look at the flowers; they were better than any picture book, for each of them could tell a story. Then she took Gerda by the hand, and led her into the little house, and closed the door. The windows were very high, and as the panes were red, blue, and yellow, the daylight shone through them in all sorts of singular colors. On the table stood some beautiful cherries, and Gerda had permission to eat as many as she would. While she was eating them the old woman combed out her long flaxen ringlets with a golden comb, and the glossy curls hung down on each side of the little round, pleasant face, which looked fresh and blooming as a rose.

"I have long been wishing for a dear little maiden like you," said the old woman, "and now you must stay with me and see how happily we shall live together." And while she went on combing little Gerda's hair the child thought less and less about her adopted brother Kay, for the old woman was an enchantress, although she was not a wicked witch; she conjured only a little for her own amusement, and, now, because she wanted to keep Gerda. Therefore she went into the garden and stretched out her crutch toward all the rose trees, beautiful though they were, and they immediately sank into the dark earth, so that no one could tell where they had once stood. The old woman was afraid that if little Gerda saw roses, she would think of those at home and then remember little Kay and run away.

Then she took Gerda into the flower garden. How fragrant and beautiful it was! Every flower that could be thought of, for every season of the year, was here in full bloom; no picture book could have more beautiful colors. Gerda jumped for joy, and played till the sun went down behind the tall cherry trees; then she slept in an elegant bed, with red silk pillows embroidered with colored violets, and she dreamed as pleasantly as a queen on her wedding day.

The next day, and for many days after, Gerda played with the flowers in the warm sunshine. She knew every flower, and yet, although there were so many of them, it seemed as if one were missing, but what it was she could not tell. One day, however, as she sat looking at the old woman's hat with the painted flowers on it, she saw that the prettiest of them all was a rose. The old woman had forgotten to take it from her hat when she made all the roses sink into the earth. But it is difficult to keep the thoughts together in everything, and one little mistake upsets all our arrangements.

"What! are there no roses here?" cried Gerda, and she ran out into the garden and examined all the beds, and searched and searched. There was not one to be found. Then she sat down and wept, and her tears fell just on the place where one of the rose trees had sunk down. The warm tears moistened the earth, and the rose tree sprouted up at once, as blooming as when it had sunk; and Gerda embraced it, and kissed the roses, and thought of the beautiful roses at home, and, with them, of little Kay.

"Oh, how I have been detained!" said the little maiden. "I wanted to seek for little Kay. Do you know where he is?" she asked the roses; "do you think he is dead?"

And the roses answered: "No, he is not dead. We have been in the ground, where all the dead lie, but Kay is not there."

"Thank you," said little Gerda, and then she went to the other flowers and looked into their little cups and asked, "Do you know where little Kay is?" But each flower as it stood in the sunshine dreamed only of its own little fairy tale or history. Not one knew anything of Kay. Gerda heard many stories from the flowers, as she asked them one after another about him.

And then she ran to the other end of the garden. The door was fastened, but she pressed against the rusty latch, and it gave way. The door sprang open, and little Gerda ran out with bare feet into the wide world. She looked back three times, but no one seemed to be following her. At last she could run no longer, so she sat down to rest on a great stone, and when she looked around she saw that the summer was over and autumn very far advanced. She had known nothing of this in the beautiful garden where the sun shone and the flowers grew all the year round.

"Oh, how I have wasted my time!" said little Gerda. "It is autumn; I must not rest any longer," and she rose to go on. But her little feet were wounded and sore, and everything around her looked cold and bleak. The long willow leaves were quite yellow, the dewdrops fell like water, leaf after leaf dropped from the trees; the sloe thorn alone still bore fruit, but the sloes were sour and set the teeth on edge. Oh, how dark and weary the whole world appeared!

Fourth Story: The Prince and Princess

Gerda was obliged to rest again, and just opposite the place where she sat she saw a great crow come hopping toward her across the snow. He stood looking at her for some time, and then he wagged his head and said, "Caw, caw, good day, good day." He pronounced the words as plainly as he could, because he meant to be kind to the little girl, and then he asked her where she was going all alone in the wide world.

The word "alone" Gerda understood very well and felt how much it expressed. So she told the crow the whole story of her life and adventures and asked him if he had seen little Kay.

The crow nodded his head very gravely and said, "Perhaps I have—it may be."

"No! Do you really think you have?" cried little Gerda, and she kissed the crow and hugged him almost to death, with joy.

"Gently, gently," said the crow. "I believe I know. I think it may be little Kay; but he has certainly forgotten you by this time, for the princess."

"Does he live with a princess?" asked Gerda.

"Yes, listen," replied the crow; "but it is so difficult to speak your language. If you understand the crows' language, then I can explain it better. Do you?"

"No, I have never learned it," said Gerda, "but my grandmother understands it, and used to speak it to me. I wish I had learned it."

"It does not matter," answered the crow. "I will explain as well as I can, although it will be very badly done"; and he told her what he had heard.

"In this kingdom where we now are," said he, "there lives a princess who is so wonderfully clever that she has read all the newspapers in the world—and forgotten them too, although she is so clever.

"A short time ago, as she was sitting on her throne, which people say is not such an agreeable seat as is often supposed, she began to sing a song which commences with these words:

"Why should I not be married?

"Why not, indeed?' said she, and so she determined to marry if she could find a husband who knew what to say when he was spoken to, and not one who could only look grand, for that was so tiresome. She assembled all her court ladies at the beat of the drum, and when they heard of her intentions they were very much pleased.

"'We are so glad to hear of it,' said they. 'We were talking about it ourselves the other day.'

"You may believe that every word I tell you is true," said the crow, "for I have a tame sweetheart who hops freely about the palace, and she told me all this."

Of course his sweetheart was a crow, for "birds of a feather flock together," and one crow always chooses another crow.

"Newspapers were published immediately with a border of hearts and the initials of the princess among them. They gave notice that every young man who was handsome was free to visit the castle and speak with the princess, and those who could reply loud enough to be heard when spoken to were to make themselves quite at home at the palace, and the one who spoke best would be chosen as a husband for the princess.

"Yes, yes, you may believe me. It is all as true as I sit here," said the crow.

"The people came in crowds. There was a great deal of crushing and running about, but no one succeeded either on the first or the second day. They could all speak very well while they were outside in the streets, but when they entered the palace gates and saw the guards in silver uniforms and the footmen in their golden livery on the staircase and the great halls lighted up, they became quite confused. And when they stood before the throne on which the princess sat they could do nothing but repeat the last words she had said, and she had no particular wish to hear her own words over again. It was just as if they had all taken something to make them sleepy while they were in the palace, for they did not recover themselves nor speak till they got back again into the street. There was a long procession of them, reaching from the town gate to the palace.

"I went myself to see them," said the crow. "They were hungry and thirsty, for at the palace they did not even get a glass of water. Some of the wisest had taken a few slices of bread and butter with them, but they did not share it with their neighbors; they thought if the others went in to the princess looking hungry, there would be a better chance for themselves."

"But Kay! tell me about little Kay!" said Gerda. "Was he among the crowd?"

"Stop a bit; we are just coming to him. It was on the third day that there came marching cheerfully along to the palace a little personage without horses or carriage, his eyes sparkling like yours. He had beautiful long hair, but his clothes were very poor."

"That was Kay," said Gerda, joyfully. "Oh, then I have found him!" and she clapped her hands.

"He had a little knapsack on his back," added the crow.

"No, it must have been his sledge," said Gerda, "for he went away with it."

"It may have been so," said the crow; "I did not look at it very closely. But I know from my tame sweetheart that he passed through the palace gates, saw the guards in their silver uniform and the servants in their liveries of gold on the stairs, but was not in the least embarrassed.

"It must be very tiresome to stand on the stairs," he said. "I prefer to go in."

"The rooms were blazing with light; councilors and ambassadors walked about with bare feet, carrying golden vessels; it was enough to make any one feel serious. His boots creaked loudly as he walked, and yet he was not at all uneasy."

"It must be Kay," said Gerda; "I know he had new boots on. I heard them creak in grandmother's room."

"They really did creak," said the crow, "yet he went boldly up to the princess herself, who was sitting on a pearl as large as a spinning wheel. And all the ladies of the court were present with their maids and all the cavaliers with their servants, and each of the maids had another maid to wait upon her, and the cavaliers' servants had their own servants as well as each a page. They all stood in circles round the princess, and the nearer they stood to the door the prouder they looked. The servants' pages, who always wore slippers, could hardly be looked at, they held themselves up so proudly by the door."

"It must be quite awful," said little Gerda; "but did Kay win the princess?"

"If I had not been a crow," said he, "I would have married her myself, although I am engaged. He spoke as well as I do when I speak the crows' language. I heard this from my tame sweetheart. He was quite free and agreeable and said he had not come to woo the princess, but to hear her wisdom. And he was as pleased with her as she was with him."

"Oh, certainly that was Kay," said Gerda; "he was so clever; he could work mental arithmetic and fractions. Oh, will you take me to the palace?"

"It is very easy to ask that," replied the crow, "but how are we to manage it? However, I will speak about it to my tame sweetheart and ask her advice, for, I must tell you, it will be very difficult to gain permission for a little girl like you to enter the palace."

"Oh, yes, but I shall gain permission easily," said Gerda, "for when Kay hears that I am here he will come out and fetch me in immediately."

"Wait for me here by the palings," said the crow, wagging his head as he flew away.

It was late in the evening before the crow returned. "Caw, caw!" he said; "she sends you greeting, and here is a little roll which she took from the kitchen for you. There is plenty of bread there, and she thinks you must be hungry. It is not possible for you to enter the palace by the front entrance. The guards in silver uniform and the servants in gold livery would not allow it. But do not cry; we will manage to get you in. My sweetheart knows a little back staircase that leads to the sleeping apartments, and she knows where to find the key."

Then they went into the garden, through the great avenue, where the leaves were falling one after another, and they could see the lights in the palace being put out in the same manner. And the crow led little Gerda to a back door which stood ajar. Oh! how her heart beat with anxiety and longing; it was as if she were going to do something wrong, and yet she only wanted to know where little Kay was.

"It must be he," she thought, "with those clear eyes and that long hair."

She could fancy she saw him smiling at her as he used to at home when they sat among the roses. He would certainly be glad to see her, and to hear what a long distance she had come for his sake, and to know how sorry they had all been at home because he did not come back. Oh, what joy and yet what fear she felt!

They were now on the stairs, and in a small closet at the top a lamp was burning. In the middle of the floor stood the tame crow, turning her head from side to side and gazing at Gerda, who curtsied as her grandmother had taught her to do.

"My betrothed has spoken so very highly of you, my little lady," said the tame crow. "Your story is very touching. If you will take the lamp, I will walk before you. We will go straight along this way; then we shall meet no one."

"I feel as if somebody were behind us," said Gerda, as something rushed by her like a shadow on the wall; and then it seemed to her that horses with flying manes and thin legs, hunters, ladies and gentlemen on horseback, glided by her like shadows.

"They are only dreams," said the crow; "they are coming to carry the thoughts of the great people out hunting. All the better, for if their thoughts are out hunting, we shall be able to look at them in their beds more safely. I hope that when you rise to honor and favor you will show a grateful heart."

"You may be quite sure of that," said the crow from the forest.

They now came into the first hall, the walls of which were hung with rose-colored satin embroidered with artificial flowers. Here the dreams again flitted by them, but so quickly that Gerda could not distinguish the royal persons. Each hall appeared more splendid than the last. It was enough to bewilder one. At length they reached a bedroom. The ceiling was like a great palm tree, with glass leaves of the most costly crystal, and over the centre of the floor two beds, each resembling a lily, hung from a stem of gold. One, in which the princess lay, was white; the other was red. And in this Gerda had to seek for little Kay.

She pushed one of the red leaves aside and saw a little brown neck. Oh, that must be Kay! She called his name loudly and held the lamp over him. The dreams rushed back into the room on horseback. He woke and turned his head round—it was not little Kay! The prince was only like him; still he was young and pretty. Out of her white-lily bed peeped the princess, and asked what was the matter. Little Gerda wept and told her story, and all that the crows had done to help her.

"You poor child," said the prince and princess; then they praised the crows, and said they were not angry with them for what they had done, but that it must not happen again, and that this time they should be rewarded.

"Would you like to have your freedom?" asked the princess, "or would you prefer to be raised to the position of court crows, with all that is left in the kitchen for yourselves?"

Then both the crows bowed and begged to have a fixed appointment; for they thought of their old age, and it would be so comfortable, they said, to feel that they had made provision for it.

And then the prince got out of his bed and gave it up to Gerda—he could not do more—and she lay down. She folded her little hands and thought, "How good everybody is to me, both men and animals;" then she closed her eyes and fell into a sweet sleep. All the dreams came flying back again to her, looking like angels now, and one of them drew a little sledge, on which sat Kay, who nodded to her. But all this was only a dream. It vanished as soon as she awoke.

The following day she was dressed from head to foot in silk and velvet and invited to stay at the palace for a few days and enjoy herself; but she only begged for a pair of boots and a little carriage and a horse to draw it, so that she might go out into the wide world to seek for Kay.

And she obtained not only boots but a muff, and was neatly dressed; and when she was ready to go, there at the door she found a coach made of pure gold with the coat of arms of the prince and princess shining upon it like a star, and the coachman, footman, and outriders all wearing golden crowns upon their heads. The prince and princess themselves helped her into the coach and wished her success.

The forest crow, who was now married, accompanied her for the first three miles; he sat by Gerda's side, as he could not bear riding backwards. The tame crow stood in the doorway flapping her wings. She could not go with them, because she had been suffering from headache ever since the new appointment, no doubt from overeating. The coach was well stored with sweet cakes, and under the seat were fruit and gingerbread nuts.

"Farewell, farewell," cried the prince and princess, and little Gerda wept, and the crow wept; and then, after a few miles, the crow also said farewell, and this parting was even more sad. However, he flew to a tree and stood flapping his black wings as long as he could see the coach, which glittered like a sunbeam.

Fifth Story: The Little Robber Girl

The coach drove on through a thick forest, where it lighted up the way like a torch and dazzled the eyes of some robbers, who could not bear to let it pass them unmolested.

"It is gold! it is gold!" cried they, rushing forward and seizing the horses. Then they struck dead the little jockeys, the coachman, and the footman, and pulled little Gerda out of the carriage.

"She is plump and pretty. She has been fed with the kernels of nuts," said the old robber woman, who had a long beard, and eyebrows that hung over her eyes. "She is as good as a fatted lamb; how nice she will taste!" and as she said this she drew forth a shining knife, that glittered horribly. "Oh!" screamed the old woman at the same moment, for her own daughter, who held her back, had bitten her in the ear. "You naughty girl," said the mother, and now she had not time to kill Gerda.

"She shall play with me," said the little robber girl. "She shall give me her muff and her pretty dress, and sleep with me in my bed." And then she bit her mother again, and all the robbers laughed.

"I will have a ride in the coach," said the little robber girl, and she would have her own way, for she was self-willed and obstinate.

She and Gerda seated themselves in the coach and drove away over stumps and stones, into the depths of the forest. The little robber girl was about the same size as Gerda, but stronger; she had broader shoulders and a darker skin; her eyes were quite black, and she had a mournful look. She clasped little Gerda round the waist and said:

"They shall not kill you as long as you don't make me vexed with you. I suppose you are a princess."

"No," said Gerda; and then she told her all her history and how fond she was of little Kay.

The robber girl looked earnestly at her, nodded her head slightly, and said, "They shan't kill you even if I do get angry with you, for I will do it myself." And then she wiped Gerda's eyes and put her own hands into the beautiful muff, which was so soft and warm.

The coach stopped in the courtyard of a robber's castle, the walls of which were full of cracks from top to bottom. Ravens and crows flew in and out of the holes and crevices, while great bulldogs, each of which looked as if it could swallow a man, were jumping about; but they were not allowed to bark.

In the large old smoky hall a bright fire was burning on the stone floor. There was no chimney, so the smoke went up to the ceiling and found a way out for itself. Soup was boiling in a large cauldron, and hares and rabbits were roasting on the spit.

"You shall sleep with me and all my little animals tonight," said the robber girl after they had had something to eat and drink. So she took Gerda to a corner of the hall where some straw and carpets were laid down. Above them, on laths and perches, were more than a hundred pigeons that all seemed to be asleep, although they moved slightly when the two little girls came near them. "These all belong to me," said the robber girl, and she seized the nearest to her, held it by the feet, and shook it till it flapped its wings. "Kiss it," cried she, flapping it in Gerda's face.

"There sit the wood pigeons," continued she, pointing to a number of laths and a cage which had been fixed into the walls, near one of the openings. "Both rascals would fly away directly, if they were not closely locked up. And here is my old sweetheart 'Ba,'" and she dragged out a reindeer by the horn; he wore a bright copper ring round his neck and was tethered to the spot. "We are obliged to hold him tight too, else he would run away from us also. I tickle his neck every evening with my sharp knife, which frightens him very much." And the robber girl drew a long knife from a chink in the wall and let it slide gently over the reindeer's neck. The poor animal began to kick, and the little robber girl laughed and pulled down Gerda into bed with her.

"Will you have that knife with you while you are asleep?" asked Gerda, looking at it in great fright.

"I always sleep with the knife by me," said the robber girl. "No one knows what may happen. But now tell me again all about little Kay, and why you went out into the world."

Then Gerda repeated her story over again, while the wood pigeons in the cage over her cooed, and the other pigeons slept. The little robber girl put one arm across Gerda's neck, and held the knife in the other, and was soon fast asleep and snoring. But Gerda could not close her eyes at all; she knew not whether she was to live or to die. The robbers sat round the fire, singing and drinking. It was a terrible sight for a little girl to witness.

Then the wood pigeons said: "Coo, coo, we have seen little Kay. A white fowl carried his sledge, and he sat in the carriage of the Snow Queen, which drove through the wood while we were lying in our nest. She blew upon us, and all the young ones died, excepting us two. Coo, coo."

"What are you saying up there?" cried Gerda. "Where was the Snow Queen going? Do you know anything about it?"

"She was most likely traveling to Lapland, where there is always snow and ice. Ask the reindeer that is fastened up there with a rope."

"Yes, there is always snow and ice," said the reindeer, "and it is a glorious place; you can leap and run about freely on the sparkling icy plains. The Snow Queen has her summer tent there, but her strong castle is at the North Pole, on an island called Spitzbergen."

"O Kay, little Kay!" sighed Gerda.

"Lie still," said the robber girl, "or you shall feel my knife."

In the morning Gerda told her all that the wood pigeons had said, and the little robber girl looked quite serious, and nodded her head and said: "That is all talk, that is all talk. Do you know where Lapland is?" she asked the reindeer.

"Who should know better than I do?" said the animal, while his eyes sparkled. "I was born and brought up there and used to run about the snow-covered plains."

"Now listen," said the robber girl; "all our men are gone away; only mother is here, and here she will stay; but at noon she always drinks out of a great bottle, and afterwards sleeps for a little while; and then I'll do something for you." She jumped out of bed, clasped her mother round the neck, and pulled her by the beard, crying, "My own little nanny goat, good morning!" And her mother pinched her nose till it was quite red; yet she did it all for love.

When the mother had gone to sleep the little robber maiden went to the reindeer and said: "I should like very much to tickle your neck a few times more with my knife, for it makes you look so funny, but never mind—I will untie your cord and set you free, so that you may run away to Lapland; but you must make good use of your legs and carry this little maiden to the castle of the Snow Queen, where her playfellow is. You have heard what she told me, for she spoke loud enough, and you were listening."

The reindeer jumped for joy, and the little robber girl lifted Gerda on his back and had the forethought to tie her on and even to give her own little cushion to sit upon.

"Here are your fur boots for you," said she, "for it will be very cold; but I must keep the muff, it is so pretty. However, you shall not be frozen for the want of it; here are my mother's large warm mittens, they will reach up to your elbows. Let me put them on. There, now your hands look just like my mother's."

But Gerda wept for joy.

"I don't like to see you fret," said the little robber girl. "You ought to look quite happy now. And here are two loaves and a ham, so that you need not starve."

These were fastened upon the reindeer, and then the little robber maiden opened the door, coaxed in all the great dogs, cut the string with which the reindeer was fastened, with her sharp knife, and said, "Now run, but mind you take good care of the little girl." And Gerda stretched out her hand, with the great mitten on it, toward the little robber girl and said "Farewell," and away flew the reindeer over stumps and stones, through the great forest, over marshes and plains, as quickly as he could. The wolves howled and the ravens screamed, while up in the sky quivered red lights like flames of fire. "There are my old northern lights," said the reindeer; "see how they flash!" And he ran on day and night still faster and faster, but the loaves and the ham were all eaten by the time they reached Lapland.

Sixth Story: The Lapland Woman and the Finland Woman

They stopped at a little hut; it was very mean looking. The roof sloped nearly down to the ground, and the door was so low that the family had to creep in on their hands and knees when they went in and out. There was no one at home but an old Lapland woman who was dressing fish by the light of a train-oil lamp.

The reindeer told her all about Gerda's story after having first told his own, which seemed to him the most important. But Gerda was so pinched with the cold that she could not speak.

"Oh, you poor things," said the Lapland woman, "you have a long way to go yet. You must travel more than a hundred miles farther, to Finland. The Snow Queen lives there now, and she burns Bengal lights every evening. I will write a few words on a dried stockfish, for I have no paper, and you can take it from me to the Finland woman who lives there. She can give you better information than I can."

So when Gerda was warmed and had taken something to eat and drink, the woman wrote a few words on the dried fish and told Gerda to take great care of it. Then she tied her again on the back of the reindeer, and he sprang high into the air and set off at full speed. Flash, flash, went the beautiful blue northern lights the whole night long.

And at length they reached Finland and knocked at the chimney of the Finland woman's hut, for it had no door above the ground. They crept in, but it was so terribly hot inside that the woman wore scarcely any clothes. She was small and very dirty looking. She loosened little Gerda's dress and took off the fur boots and the mittens, or Gerda would have been unable to bear the heat; and then she placed a piece of ice on the reindeer's head and read what was written on the dried fish. After she had read it three times she knew it by heart, so she popped the fish into the soup saucepan, as she knew it was good to eat, and she never wasted anything.

The reindeer told his own story first and then little Gerda's, and the Finlander twinkled with her clever eyes, but said nothing.

"You are so clever," said the reindeer; "I know you can tie all the winds of the world with a piece of twine. If a sailor unties one knot, he has a fair wind; when he unties the second, it blows hard; but if the third and fourth are loosened, then comes a storm which will root up whole forests. Cannot you give this little maiden something which will make her as strong as twelve men, to overcome the Snow Queen?"

"The power of twelve men!" said the Finland woman. "That would be of very little use." But she went to a shelf and took down and unrolled a large skin on which were inscribed wonderful characters, and she read till the perspiration ran down from her forehead.

But the reindeer begged so hard for little Gerda, and Gerda looked at the Finland woman with such tender, tearful eyes, that her own eyes began to twinkle again. She drew the reindeer into a corner and whispered to him while she laid a fresh piece of ice on his head: "Little Kay is really with the Snow Queen, but he finds everything there so much to his taste and his liking that he believes it is the finest place in the world; and this is because he has a piece of broken glass in his heart and a little splinter of glass in his eye. These must be taken out, or he will never be a human being again, and the Snow Queen will retain her power over him."

"But can you not give little Gerda something to help her to conquer this power?"

"I can give her no greater power than she has already," said the woman; "don't you see how strong that is? how men and animals are obliged to serve her, and how well she has gotten through the world, barefooted as she is? She cannot receive any power from me greater than she now has, which consists in her own purity and innocence of heart. If she cannot herself obtain access to the Snow Queen and remove the glass fragments from little Kay, we can do nothing to help her. Two miles from here the Snow Queen's garden begins. You can carry the little girl so far, and set her down by the large bush which stands in the snow, covered with red berries. Do not stay gossiping, but come back here as quickly as you can." Then the Finland woman lifted little Gerda upon the reindeer, and he ran away with her as quickly as he could.

"Oh, I have forgotten my boots and my mittens," cried little Gerda, as soon as she felt the cutting cold; but the reindeer dared not stop, so he ran on till he reached the bush with the red berries. Here he set Gerda down, and he kissed her, and the great bright tears trickled over the animal's cheeks; then he left her and ran back as fast as he could.

There stood poor Gerda, without shoes, without gloves, in the midst of cold, dreary, icebound Finland. She ran forward as quickly as she could, when a whole regiment of snowflakes came round her. They did not, however, fall from the sky, which was quite clear and glittered with the northern lights. The snowflakes ran along the ground, and the nearer they came to her the larger they appeared. Gerda remembered how large and beautiful they looked through the burning glass. But these were really larger and much more terrible, for they were alive and were the guards of the Snow Queen and had the strangest shapes. Some were like great porcupines, others like twisted serpents with their heads stretching out, and some few were like little fat bears with their hair bristled; but all were dazzlingly white, and all were living snowflakes.

Little Gerda repeated the Lord's Prayer, and the cold was so great that she could see her own breath come out of her mouth like steam, as she uttered the words. The steam appeared to increase as she continued her prayer, till it took the shape of little angels, who grew larger the moment they touched the earth. They all wore helmets on their heads and carried spears and shields. Their number continued to increase more and more, and by the time Gerda had finished her prayers a whole legion stood round her. They thrust their spears into the terrible snowflakes so that they shivered into a hundred pieces, and little Gerda could go forward with courage and safety. The angels stroked her hands and feet, so that she felt the cold less as she hastened on to the Snow Queen's castle.

But now we must see what Kay is doing. In truth he thought not of little Gerda, and least of all that she could be standing at the front of the palace.

Seventh Story: The Palace of the Snow Queen and What Happened There at Last

The walls of the palace were formed of drifted snow, and the windows and doors of cutting winds. There were more than a hundred rooms in it, all as if they had been formed of snow blown together. The largest of them extended for several miles. They were all lighted up by the vivid light of the aurora, and were so large and empty, so icy cold and glittering!

There were no amusements here; not even a little bear's ball, when the storm might have been the music, and the bears could have danced on their hind legs and shown their good manners. There were no pleasant games of snapdragon, or touch, nor even a gossip over the tea table for the young-lady foxes. Empty, vast, and cold were the halls of the Snow Queen.

The flickering flames of the northern lights could be plainly seen, whether they rose high or low in the heavens, from every part of the castle. In the midst of this empty, endless hall of snow was a frozen lake, broken on its surface into a thousand forms; each piece resembled another, because each was in itself perfect as a work of art, and in the centre of this lake sat the Snow Queen when she was at home. She called the lake "The Mirror of Reason," and said that it was the best, and indeed the only one, in the world.

Little Kay was quite blue with cold—indeed, almost black—but he did not feel it; for the Snow Queen had kissed away the icy shiverings, and his heart was already a lump of ice. He dragged some sharp, flat pieces of ice to and fro and placed them together in all kinds of positions, as if he wished to make something out of them—just as we try to form various figures with little tablets of wood, which we call a "Chinese puzzle." Kay's figures were very artistic; it was the icy game of reason at which he played, and in his eyes the figures were very remarkable and of the highest importance; this opinion was owing to the splinter of glass still sticking in his eye. He composed many complete figures, forming different words, but there was one word he never could manage to form, although he wished it very much. It was the word "Eternity."

The Snow Queen had said to him, "When you can find out this, you shall be your own master, and I will give you the whole world and a new pair of skates." But he could not accomplish it.

"Now I must hasten away to warmer countries," said the Snow Queen. "I will go and look into the black craters of the tops of the burning mountains, Etna and Vesuvius, as they are called. I shall make them look white, which will be good for them and for the lemons and the grapes." And away flew the Snow Queen, leaving little Kay quite alone in the great hall which was so many miles in length. He sat and looked at his pieces of ice and was thinking so deeply and sat so still that anyone might have supposed he was frozen.

Just at this moment it happened that little Gerda came through the great door of the castle. Cutting winds were raging around her, but she offered up a prayer, and the winds sank down as if they were going to sleep. On she went till she came to the large, empty hall and caught sight of Kay. She knew him directly; she flew to him and threw her arms around his neck and held him fast while she exclaimed, "Kay, dear little Kay, I have found you at last!"

But he sat quite still, stiff and cold.

Then little Gerda wept hot tears, which fell on his breast, and penetrated into his heart, and thawed the lump of ice, and washed away the little piece of glass which had stuck there. Then he looked at her, and she sang:

"Roses bloom and fade away,
But we the Christ child see alway."

Then Kay burst into tears. He wept so that the splinter of glass swam out of his eye. Then he recognized Gerda and said joyfully, "Gerda, dear little Gerda, where have you been all this time, and where have I been?" And he looked all around him and said, "How cold it is, and how large and empty it all looks," and he clung to Gerda, and she laughed and wept for joy.

It was so pleasing to see them that even the pieces of ice danced, and when they were tired and went to lie down they formed themselves into the letters of the word which the Snow Queen had said he must find out before he could be his own master and have the whole world and a pair of new skates.

Gerda kissed his cheeks, and they became blooming; and she kissed his eyes till they shone like her own; she kissed his hands and feet, and he became quite healthy and cheerful. The Snow Queen might come home now when she pleased, for there stood his certainty of freedom, in the word she wanted, written in shining letters of ice.

Then they took each other by the hand and went forth from the great palace of ice. They spoke of the grandmother and of the roses on the roof, and as they went on the winds were at rest, and the sun burst forth. When they arrived at the bush with red berries, there stood the reindeer waiting for them, and he had brought another young reindeer with him, whose udders were full, and the children drank her warm milk and kissed her on the mouth.

They carried Kay and Gerda first to the Finland woman, where they warmed themselves thoroughly in the hot room and had directions about their journey home. Next they went to the Lapland woman, who had made some new clothes for them and put their sleighs in order. Both the reindeer ran by their side and followed them as far as the boundaries of the country, where the first green leaves were budding. And here they took leave of the two reindeer and the Lapland woman, and all said farewell.

Then birds began to twitter, and the forest too was full of green young leaves, and out of it came a beautiful horse, which Gerda remembered, for it was one which had drawn the golden coach. A young girl was riding upon it, with a shining red cap on her head and pistols in her belt. It was the little robber maiden, who had got tired of staying at home; she was going first to the north, and if that did not suit her, she meant to try some other part of the world. She knew Gerda directly, and Gerda remembered her; it was a joyful meeting.

"You are a fine fellow to go gadding about in this way," said she to little Kay. "I should like to know whether you deserve that anyone should go to the end of the world to find you."

But Gerda patted her cheeks and asked after the prince and princess.

"They are gone to foreign countries," said the robber girl.

"And the crow?" asked Gerda.

"Oh, the crow is dead," she replied. "His tame sweetheart is now a widow and wears a bit of black worsted round her leg. She mourns very pitifully, but it is all stuff. But now tell me how you managed to get him back."

Then Gerda and Kay told her all about it.

"Snip, snap, snurre! it's all right at last," said the robber girl.

She took both their hands and promised that if ever she should pass through the town, she would call and pay them a visit. And then she rode away into the wide world.

But Gerda and Kay went hand in hand toward home, and as they advanced, spring appeared more lovely with its green verdure and its beautiful flowers. Very soon they recognized the large town where they lived, and the tall steeples of the churches in which the sweet bells were ringing a merry peal, as they entered it and found their way to their grandmother's door.

They went upstairs into the little room, where all looked just as it used to do. The old clock was going "Tick, tick," and the hands pointed to the time of day, but as they passed through the door into the room they perceived that they were both grown up and become a man and woman.

The roses out on the roof were in full bloom and peeped in at the window, and there stood the little chairs on which they had sat when children, and Kay and Gerda seated themselves each on their own chair and held each other by the hand, while the cold, empty grandeur of the Snow Queen's palace vanished from their memories like a painful dream.

The grandmother sat in God's bright sunshine, and she read aloud from the Bible, "Except ye become as little children, ye shall in no wise enter into the kingdom of God." And Kay and Gerda looked into each other's eyes and all at once understood the words of the old song:

"Roses bloom and fade away,
But we the Christ child see alway."

And they both sat there, grown up, yet children at heart, and it was summer—warm, beautiful summer.

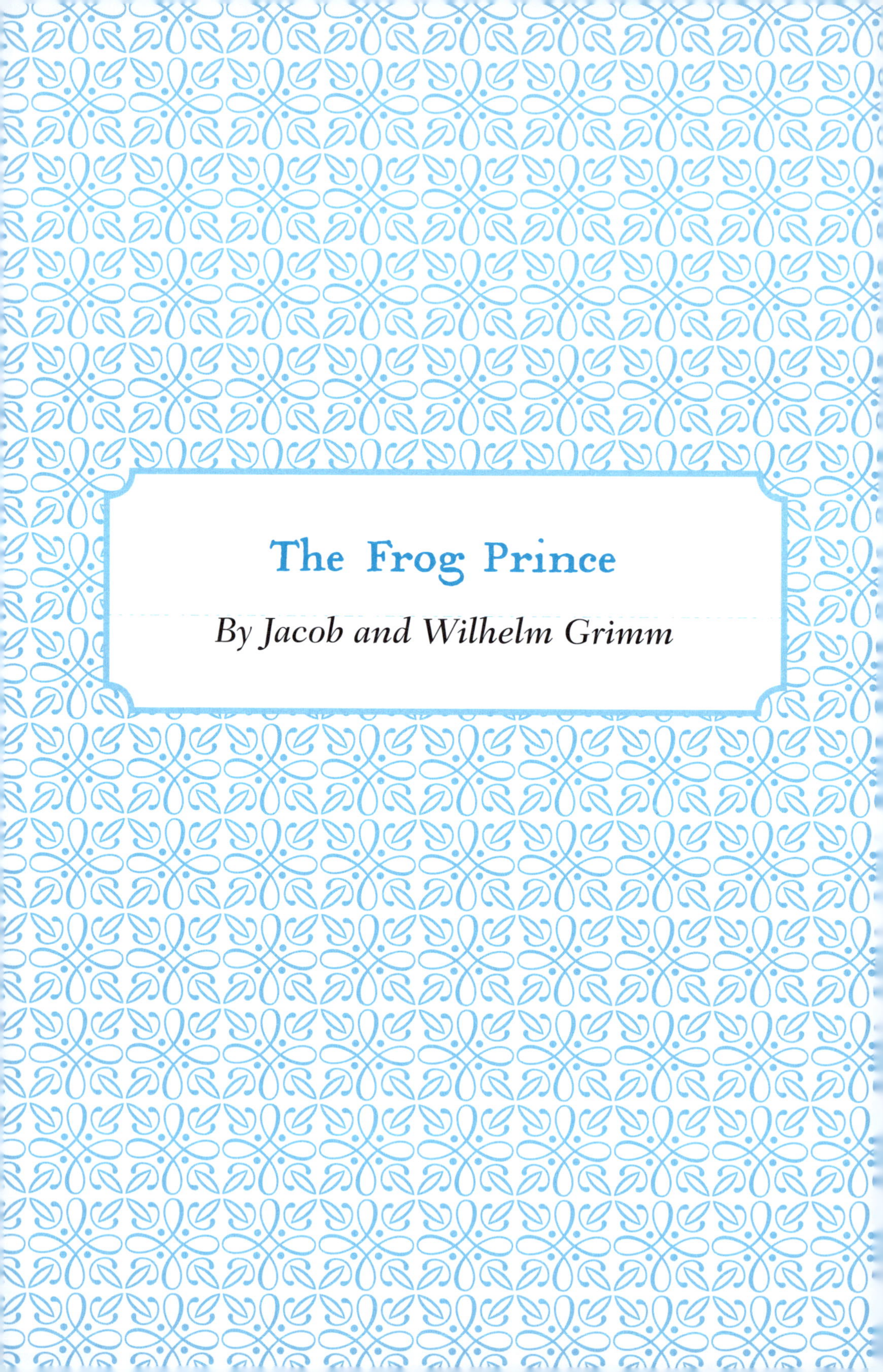

The Frog Prince

By Jacob and Wilhelm Grimm

One fine evening a young princess put on her bonnet and clogs, and went out to take a walk by herself in a wood; and when she came to a cool spring of water, that rose in the midst of it, she sat herself down to rest a while. Now she had a golden ball in her hand, which was her favourite plaything; and she was always tossing it up into the air, and catching it again as it fell. After a time she threw it up so high that she missed catching it as it fell; and the ball bounded away, and rolled along upon the ground, till at last it fell down into the spring. The princess looked into the spring after her ball, but it was very deep, so deep that she could not see the bottom of it. Then she began to bewail her loss, and said, "Alas! if I could only get my ball again, I would give all my fine clothes and jewels, and everything that I have in the world."

Whilst she was speaking, a frog put its head out of the water, and said, "Princess, why do you weep so bitterly?"

"Alas!" said she, "what can you do for me, you nasty frog? My golden ball has fallen into the spring."

The frog said, "I want not your pearls, and jewels, and fine clothes; but if you will love me, and let me live with you and eat from off your golden plate, and sleep upon your bed, I will bring you your ball again."

"What nonsense," thought the princess, "this silly frog is talking! He can never even get out of the spring to visit me, though he may be able to get my ball for me, and therefore I will tell him he shall have what he asks." So she said to the frog, "Well, if you will bring me my ball, I will do all you ask."

Then the frog put his head down, and dived deep under the water; and after a little while he came up again, with the ball in his mouth, and threw it on the edge of the spring. As soon as the young princess saw her ball, she ran to pick it up; and she was so overjoyed to have it in her hand again, that she never thought of the frog, but ran home with it as fast as she could. The frog called after her, "Stay, princess, and take me with you as you said." But she did not stop to hear a word.

The next day, just as the princess had sat down to dinner, she heard a strange noise—tap, tap, plash, plash—as if something was coming up the marble staircase: and soon afterwards there was a gentle knock at the door, and a little voice cried out and said:

"Open the door, my princess dear,
Open the door to thy true love here!
And mind the words that thou and I said
By the fountain cool, in the greenwood shade."

Then the princess ran to the door and opened it, and there she saw the frog, whom she had quite forgotten. At this sight she was sadly frightened, and shutting the door as fast as she could came back to her seat. The king, her father, seeing that something had frightened her, asked her what was the matter. "There is a nasty frog," said she, "at the door, that lifted my ball for me out of the spring this morning: I told him that he should live with me here, thinking that he could never get out of the spring; but there he is at the door, and he wants to come in."

While she was speaking the frog knocked again at the door, and said:

"Open the door, my princess dear,
Open the door to thy true love here!
And mind the words that thou and I said
By the fountain cool, in the greenwood shade."

Then the king said to the young princess, "As you have given your word you must keep it; so go and let him in." She did so, and the frog hopped into the room, and then straight on—tap, tap, plash, plash—from the bottom of the room to the top, till he came up close to the table where the princess sat.

"Pray lift me upon a chair," said he to the princess, "and let me sit next to you." As soon as she had done this, the frog said, "Put your plate nearer to me, that I may eat out of it." This she did, and when he had eaten as much as he could, he said, "Now I am tired; carry me upstairs, and put me into your bed." And the princess, though very unwilling, took him up in her hand, and put him upon the pillow of her own bed, where he slept all night long. As soon as it was light he jumped up, hopped downstairs, and went out of the house. "Now, then," thought the princess, "at last he is gone, and I shall be troubled with him no more."

But she was mistaken; for when night came again she heard the same tapping at the door; and the frog came once more, and said:

"Open the door, my princess dear,
Open the door to thy true love here!

And mind the words that thou and I said
By the fountain cool, in the greenwood shade."

And when the princess opened the door the frog came in, and slept upon her pillow as before, till the morning broke. And the third night he did the same. But when the princess awoke on the following morning she was astonished to see, instead of the frog, a handsome prince, gazing on her with the most beautiful eyes she had ever seen, and standing at the head of her bed.

He told her that he had been enchanted by a spiteful fairy, who had changed him into a frog; and that he had been fated so to abide till some princess should take him out of the spring, and let him eat from her plate, and sleep upon her bed for three nights. "You," said the prince, "have broken his cruel charm, and now I have nothing to wish for but that you should go with me into my father's kingdom, where I will marry you, and love you as long as you live."

The young princess, you may be sure, was not long in saying "Yes" to all this; and as they spoke a gay coach drove up, with eight beautiful horses, decked with plumes of feathers and a golden harness; and behind the coach rode the prince's servant, faithful Heinrich, who had bewailed the misfortunes of his dear master during his enchantment so long and so bitterly, that his heart had well-nigh burst.

They then took leave of the king, and got into the coach with eight horses, and all set out, full of joy and merriment, for the prince's kingdom, which they reached safely; and there they lived happily a great many years.

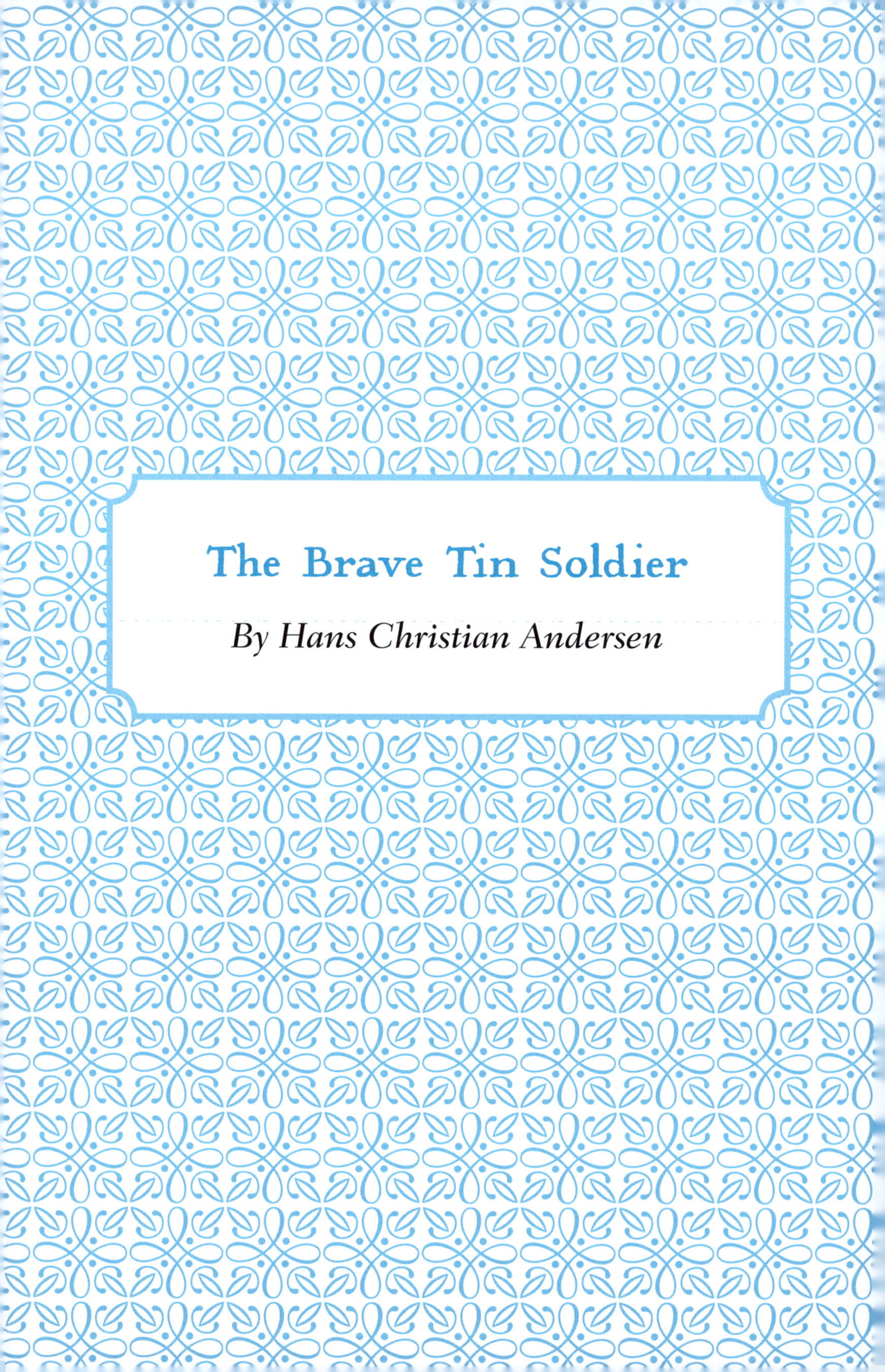

The Brave Tin Soldier

By Hans Christian Andersen

There were once five-and-twenty tin soldiers, who were all brothers, for they had been made out of the same old tin spoon. They shouldered arms and looked straight before them, and wore a splendid uniform, red and blue. The first thing in the world they ever heard were the words, "Tin soldiers!" uttered by a little boy, who clapped his hands with delight when the lid of the box, in which they lay, was taken off. They were given him for a birthday present, and he stood at the table to set them up. The soldiers were all exactly alike, excepting one, who had only one leg; he had been left to the last, and then there was not enough of the melted tin to finish him, so they made him to stand firmly on one leg, and this caused him to be very remarkable.

The table on which the tin soldiers stood, was covered with other playthings, but the most attractive to the eye was a pretty little paper castle. Through the small windows the rooms could be seen. In front of the castle a number of little trees surrounded a piece of looking glass, which was intended to represent a transparent lake. Swans, made of wax, swam on the lake, and were reflected in it. All this was very pretty, but the prettiest of all was a tiny little lady, who stood at the open door of the castle; she, also, was made of paper, and she wore a dress of clear muslin, with a narrow blue ribbon over her shoulders just like a scarf. In front of these was fixed a glittering tinsel rose, as large as her whole face. The little lady was a dancer, and she stretched out both her arms, and raised one of her legs so high, that the tin soldier could not see it at all, and he thought that she, like himself, had only one leg. "That is the wife for me," he thought; "but she is too grand, and lives in a castle, while I have only a box to live in, five-and-twenty of us altogether, that is no place for her. Still I must try and make her acquaintance." Then he laid himself at full length on the table behind a snuffbox that stood upon it, so that he could peep at the little delicate lady, who continued to stand on one leg without losing her balance. When evening came, the other tin soldiers were all placed in the box, and the people of the house went to bed. Then the playthings began to have their own games together, to pay visits, to have sham fights, and to give balls. The tin soldiers rattled in their box; they wanted to get out and join the amusements, but they could not open the lid. The nutcrackers played at leapfrog, and the pencil jumped about the table. There was such a noise that the canary woke up and began to talk, and in poetry too. Only the tin soldier and the dancer remained in their places. She stood on tiptoe, with her legs stretched out, as firmly as he did on his one leg. He never took his eyes from her for even a moment. The clock struck twelve, and, with a bounce, up sprang the lid of the snuffbox; but, instead of snuff, there jumped up a little black goblin; for the snuffbox was a toy puzzle.

"Tin soldier," said the goblin, "don't wish for what does not belong to you."

But the tin soldier pretended not to hear.

"Very well; wait till tomorrow, then," said the goblin.

When the children came in the next morning, they placed the tin soldier in the window. Now, whether it was the goblin who did it, or the draught, is not known, but the window flew open, and out fell the tin soldier, heels over head, from the third story, into the street beneath. It was a terrible fall; for he came head downwards, his helmet and his bayonet stuck in between the flagstones, and his one leg up in the air. The servant maid and the little boy went downstairs directly to look for him; but he was nowhere to be seen, although once they nearly trod upon him. If he had called out, "Here I am," it would have been all right, but he was too proud to cry out for help while he wore a uniform.

Presently it began to rain, and the drops fell faster and faster, till there was a heavy shower. When it was over, two boys happened to pass by, and one of them said, "Look, there is a tin soldier. He ought to have a boat to sail in."

So they made a boat out of a newspaper, and placed the tin soldier in it, and sent him sailing down the gutter, while the two boys ran by the side of it, and clapped their hands. Good gracious, what large waves arose in that gutter! and how fast the stream rolled on! for the rain had been very heavy. The paper boat rocked up and down, and turned itself round sometimes so quickly that the tin soldier trembled; yet he remained firm; his countenance did not change; he looked straight before him, and shouldered his musket. Suddenly the boat shot under a bridge which formed a part of a drain, and then it was as dark as the tin soldier's box.

"Where am I going now?" thought he. "This is the black goblin's fault, I am sure. Ah, well, if the little lady were only here with me in the boat, I should not care for any darkness."

Suddenly there appeared a great water rat, who lived in the drain.

"Have you a passport?" asked the rat, "give it to me at once." But the tin soldier remained silent and held his musket tighter than ever. The boat sailed on and the rat followed it. How he did gnash his teeth and cry out to the bits of wood and straw, "Stop him, stop him; he has not paid toll, and has not shown his pass." But the stream rushed on stronger and stronger. The tin soldier could already see daylight shining where the arch ended. Then he heard a roaring sound quite terrible enough to frighten the bravest man. At the end of the tunnel the drain fell into a large canal over a steep place, which made it as dangerous for him as a waterfall would be to us. He was too close to it to stop, so the boat rushed on, and the poor tin soldier could only hold himself as stiffly as possible, without moving an eyelid, to show that he was not afraid. The boat whirled round three or four times, and then filled with water to the very edge; nothing could save it from sinking. He now stood up to his neck in water, while deeper and deeper sank the boat, and the paper became soft and loose with the wet, till at last the water closed over the soldier's head. He thought of the elegant little dancer whom he should never see again, and the words of the song sounded in his ears—

"Farewell, warrior! ever brave,
Drifting onward to thy grave."

Then the paper boat fell to pieces, and the soldier sank into the water and immediately afterwards was swallowed up by a great fish. Oh how dark it was inside the fish! A great deal darker than in the tunnel, and narrower too, but the tin soldier continued firm, and lay at full length shouldering his musket. The fish swam to and fro, making the most wonderful movements, but at last he became quite still. After a while, a flash of lightning seemed to pass through him, and then the daylight approached, and a voice cried out, "I declare, here is the tin soldier." The fish had been caught, taken to the market and sold to the cook, who took him into the kitchen and cut him open with a large knife. She picked up the soldier and held him by the waist between her finger and thumb, and carried him into the room. They were all anxious to see this wonderful soldier who had travelled about inside a fish; but he was not at all proud. They placed him on the table, and—how many curious things do happen in the world—there he was in the very same room from the window of which he had fallen, there were the same children, the same playthings, standing on the table, and the pretty castle with the elegant little dancer at the door; she still balanced herself on one leg, and held up the other, so she was as firm as himself. It touched the tin soldier so much to see her that he almost wept tin tears, but he kept them back. He only looked at her and they both remained silent.

Presently one of the little boys took up the tin soldier, and threw him into the stove. He had no reason for doing so, therefore it must have been the fault of the black goblin who lived in the snuffbox. The flames lighted up the tin soldier, as he stood; the heat was very terrible, but whether it proceeded from the real fire or from the fire of love he could not tell. Then he could see that the bright colors were faded from his uniform, but whether they had been washed off during his journey or from the effects of his sorrow, no one could say. He looked at the little lady, and she looked at him. He felt himself melting away, but he still remained firm with his gun on his shoulder. Suddenly the door of the room flew open and the draught of air caught up the little dancer; she fluttered like a sylph right into the stove by the side of the tin soldier, and was instantly in flames and was gone. The tin soldier melted down into a lump, and the next morning, when the maid servant took the ashes out of the stove, she found him in the shape of a little tin heart. But of the little dancer nothing remained but the tinsel rose, which was burnt black as a cinder.

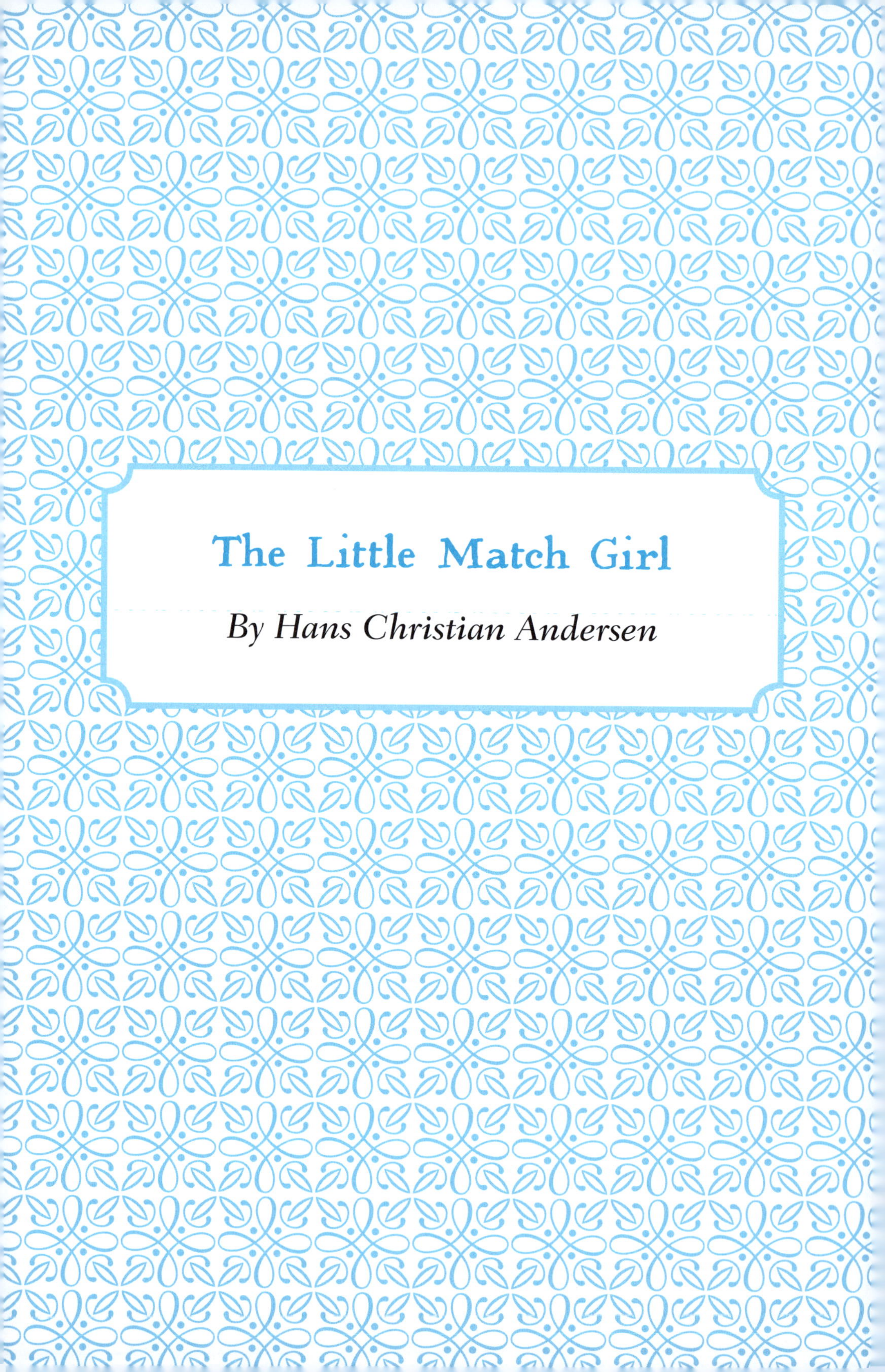

The Little Match Girl

By Hans Christian Andersen

It was dreadfully cold; it was snowing fast, and was almost dark, as evening came on—the last evening of the year. In the cold and the darkness, there went along the street a poor little girl, bareheaded and with naked feet. When she left home she had slippers on, it is true; but they were much too large for her feet—slippers that her mother had used till then, and the poor little girl lost them in running across the street when two carriages were passing terribly fast. When she looked for them, one was not to be found, and a boy seized the other and ran away with it, saying he would use it for a cradle someday, when he had children of his own.

So on the little girl went with her bare feet, that were red and blue with cold. In an old apron that she wore were bundles of matches, and she carried a bundle also in her hand. No one had bought so much as a bunch all the long day, and no one had given her even a penny.

Poor little girl! Shivering with cold and hunger she crept along, a perfect picture of misery.

The snowflakes fell on her long flaxen hair, which hung in pretty curls about her throat; but she thought not of her beauty nor of the cold. Lights gleamed in every window, and there came to her the savory smell of roast goose, for it was New Year's Eve. And it was this of which she thought.

In a corner formed by two houses, one of which projected beyond the other, she sat cowering down. She had drawn under her little feet, but still she grew colder and colder; yet she dared not go home, for she had sold no matches and could not bring a penny of money. Her father would certainly beat her; and, besides, it was cold enough at home, for they had only the house roof above them, and though the largest holes had been stopped with straw and rags, there were left many through which the cold wind could whistle.

And now her little hands were nearly frozen with cold. Alas! a single match might do her good if she might only draw it from the bundle, rub it against the wall, and warm her fingers by it. So at last she drew one out. Whisht! How it blazed and burned! It gave out a warm, bright flame like a little candle, as she held her hands over it. A wonderful little light it was. It really seemed to the little girl as if she sat before a great iron stove with polished brass feet and brass shovel and tongs. So blessedly it burned that the little maiden stretched out her feet to warm them also. How comfortable she was! But lo! the flame went out, the stove vanished, and nothing remained but the little burned match in her hand.

She rubbed another match against the wall. It burned brightly, and where the light fell upon the wall it became transparent like a veil, so that she could see through it into the room. A snow-white cloth was spread upon the table, on which was a beautiful china dinner service, while a roast goose, stuffed with apples and prunes, steamed famously and sent forth a most savory smell. And what was more delightful still, and wonderful, the goose jumped from the dish, with knife and fork still in its breast, and waddled along the floor straight to the little girl.

But the match went out then, and nothing was left to her but the thick, damp wall.

She lighted another match. And now she was under a most beautiful Christmas tree, larger and far more prettily trimmed than the one she had seen through the glass doors at the rich merchant's. Hundreds of wax tapers were burning on the green branches, and gay figures, such as she had seen in shop windows, looked down upon her. The child stretched out her hands to them; then the match went out.

Still the lights of the Christmas tree rose higher and higher. She saw them now as stars in heaven, and one of them fell, forming a long trail of fire.

"Now someone is dying," murmured the child softly; for her grandmother, the only person who had loved her, and who was now dead, had told her that whenever a star falls a soul mounts up to God.

She struck yet another match against the wall, and again it was light; and in the brightness there appeared before her the dear old grandmother, bright and radiant, yet sweet and mild, and happy as she had never looked on earth.

"Oh, grandmother," cried the child, "take me with you. I know you will go away when the match burns out. You, too, will vanish, like the warm stove, the splendid New Year's feast, the beautiful Christmas tree." And lest her grandmother should disappear, she rubbed the whole bundle of matches against the wall.

And the matches burned with such a brilliant light that it became brighter than noonday. Her grandmother had never looked so grand and beautiful. She took the little girl in her arms, and both flew together, joyously and gloriously, mounting higher and higher, far above the earth; and for them there was neither hunger, nor cold, nor care—they were with God.

But in the corner, at the dawn of day, sat the poor girl, leaning against the wall, with red cheeks and smiling mouth—frozen to death on the last evening of the old year. Stiff and cold she sat, with the matches, one bundle of which was burned.

"She wanted to warm herself, poor little thing," people said. No one imagined what sweet visions she had had, or how gloriously she had gone with her grandmother to enter upon the joys of a new year.

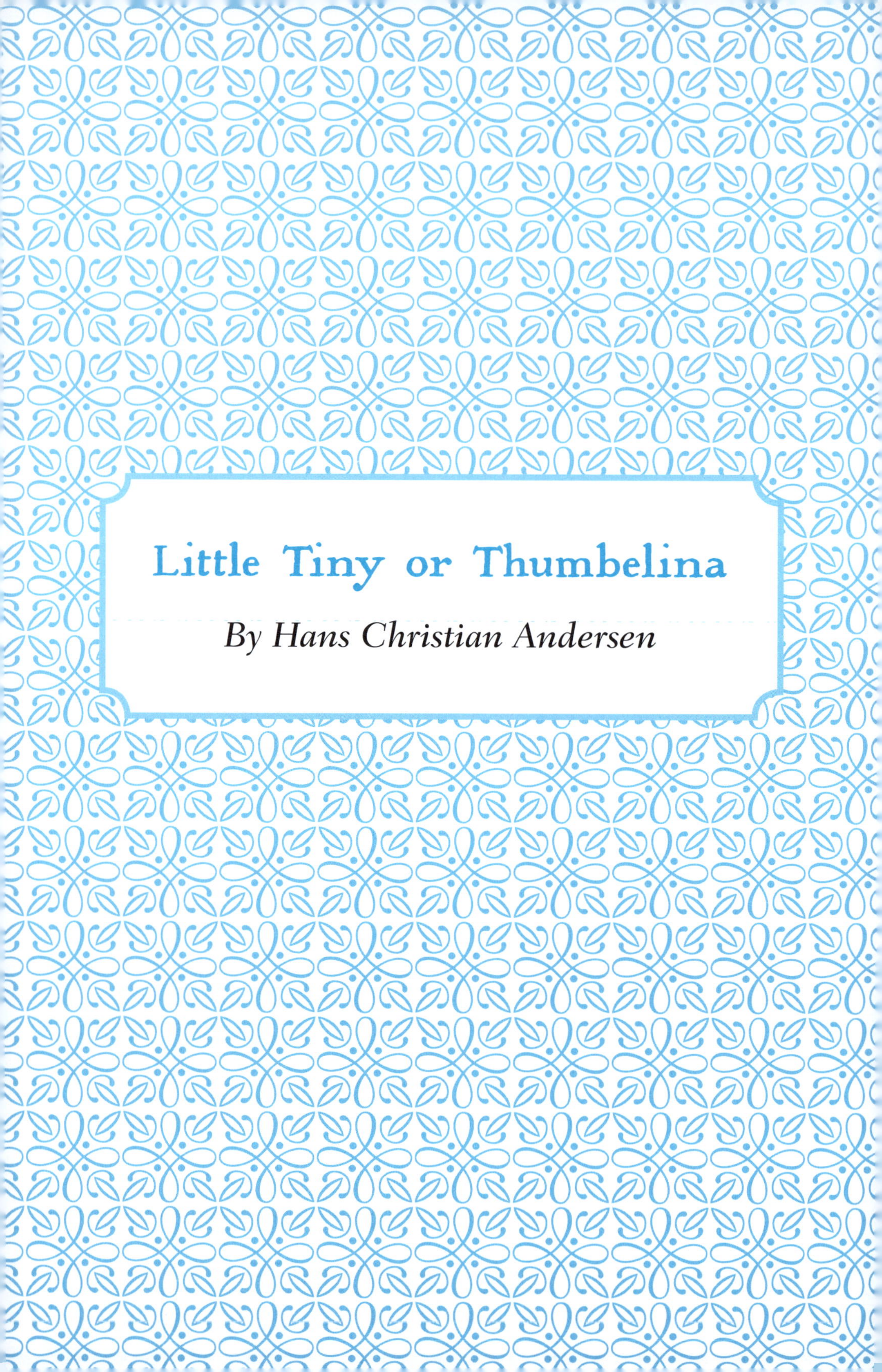

Little Tiny or Thumbelina

By Hans Christian Andersen

There was once a woman who wished very much to have a little child, but she could not obtain her wish. At last she went to a fairy, and said, "I should so very much like to have a little child; can you tell me where I can find one?"

"Oh, that can be easily managed," said the fairy. "Here is a barleycorn of a different kind to those which grow in the farmer's fields, and which the chickens eat; put it into a flowerpot, and see what will happen."

"Thank you," said the woman, and she gave the fairy twelve shillings, which was the price of the barleycorn. Then she went home and planted it, and immediately there grew up a large handsome flower, something like a tulip in appearance, but with its leaves tightly closed as if it were still a bud. "It is a beautiful flower," said the woman, and she kissed the red, and golden-colored leaves, and while she did so the flower opened, and she could see that it was a real tulip. Within the flower, upon the green velvet stamens, sat a very delicate and graceful little maiden. She was scarcely half as long as a thumb, and they gave her the name of "Thumbelina," or Tiny, because she was so small. A walnut shell, elegantly polished, served her for a cradle; her bed was formed of blue violet leaves, with a rose leaf for a counterpane. Here she slept at night, but during the day she amused herself on a table, where the woman had placed a plateful of water. Round this plate were wreaths of flowers with their stems in the water, and upon it floated a large tulip leaf, which served Tiny for a boat. Here the little maiden sat and rowed herself from side to side, with two oars made of white horsehair. It really was a very pretty sight. Tiny could, also, sing so softly and sweetly that nothing like her singing had ever before been heard. One night, while she lay in her pretty bed, a large, ugly, wet toad crept through a broken pane of glass in the window, and leaped right upon the table where Tiny lay sleeping under her rose leaf quilt.

"What a pretty little wife this would make for my son," said the toad, and she took up the walnut shell in which little Tiny lay asleep, and jumped through the window with it into the garden.

In the swampy margin of a broad stream in the garden lived the toad, with her son. He was uglier even than his mother, and when he saw the pretty little maiden in her elegant bed, he could only cry, "Croak, croak, croak."

"Don't speak so loud, or she will wake," said the toad, "and then she might run away, for she is as light as swan's down. We will place her on one of the waterlily leaves out in the stream; it will be like an island to her, she is so light and small, and then she cannot escape; and, while she is away, we will make haste and prepare the stateroom under the marsh, in which you are to live when you are married."

Far out in the stream grew a number of waterlilies, with broad green leaves, which seemed to float on the top of the water. The largest of these leaves appeared farther off than the rest, and the old toad swam out to it with the walnut shell, in which little Tiny lay still asleep. The tiny little creature woke very early in the morning, and began to cry bitterly when she found where she was, for she could see nothing but water on every side of the large green leaf, and no way of reaching the land. Meanwhile the old toad was very busy under the marsh, decking her room with rushes and wild yellow flowers, to make it look pretty for her new daughter-in-law. Then she swam out with her ugly son to the leaf on which she had placed poor little Tiny. She wanted to fetch the pretty bed, that she might put it in the bridal chamber to be ready for her. The old toad bowed low to her in the water, and said, "Here is my son, he will be your husband, and you will live happily in the marsh by the stream."

"Croak, croak, croak," was all her son could say for himself; so the toad took up the elegant little bed, and swam away with it, leaving Tiny all alone on the green leaf, where she sat and wept. She could not bear to think of living with the old toad, and having her ugly son for a husband. The little fishes, who swam about in the water beneath, had seen the toad, and heard what she said, so they lifted their heads above the water to look at the little maiden. As soon as they caught sight of her, they saw she was very pretty, and it made them very sorry to think that she must go and live with the ugly toads. "No, it must never be!" So they assembled together in the water, round the green stalk which held the leaf on which the little maiden stood, and gnawed it away at the root with their teeth. Then the leaf floated down the stream, carrying Tiny far away out of reach of land.

Tiny sailed past many towns, and the little birds in the bushes saw her, and sang, "What a lovely little creature"; so the leaf swam away with her farther and farther, till it brought her to other lands. A graceful little white butterfly constantly fluttered round her, and at last alighted on the leaf. Tiny pleased him, and she was glad of it, for now the toad could not possibly reach her, and the country through which she sailed was beautiful, and the sun shone upon the water, till it glittered like liquid gold. She took off her girdle and tied one end of it round the butterfly, and the other end of the ribbon she fastened to the leaf, which now glided on much faster than ever, taking little Tiny with it as she stood. Presently a large cockchafer flew by; the moment he caught sight of her, he seized her round her delicate waist with his claws, and flew with her into a tree. The green leaf floated away on the brook, and the butterfly flew with it, for he was fastened to it, and could not get away.

Oh, how frightened little Tiny felt when the cockchafer flew with her to the tree! But especially was she sorry for the beautiful white butterfly which she had fastened to the leaf, for if he could not free himself he would die of hunger. But the cockchafer did not trouble himself at all about the matter. He seated himself by her side on a large green leaf, gave her some honey from the flowers to eat, and told her she was very pretty, though not in the least like a cockchafer. After a time, all the cockchafers turned up their feelers, and said, "She has only two legs! how ugly that looks." "She has no feelers," said another. "Her waist is quite slim. Pooh! she is like a human being."

"Oh! she is ugly," said all the lady cockchafers, although Tiny was very pretty. Then the cockchafer who had run away with her, believed all the others when they said she was ugly, and would have nothing more to say to her, and told her she might go where she liked. Then he flew down with her from the tree, and placed her on a daisy, and she wept at the thought that she was so ugly that even the cockchafers would have nothing to say to her. And all the while she was really the loveliest creature that one could imagine, and as tender and delicate as a beautiful rose leaf. During the whole summer poor little Tiny lived quite alone in the wide forest. She wove herself a bed with blades of grass, and hung it up under a broad leaf, to protect herself from the rain. She sucked the honey from the flowers for food, and drank the dew from their leaves every morning. So passed away the summer and the autumn, and then came the winter—the long, cold winter. All the birds who had sung to her so sweetly were flown away, and the trees and the flowers had withered. The large clover leaf under the shelter of which she had lived, was now rolled together and shrivelled up, nothing remained but a yellow withered stalk. She felt dreadfully cold, for her clothes were torn, and she was herself so frail and delicate, that poor little Tiny was nearly frozen to death. It began to snow too; and the snowflakes, as they fell upon her, were like a whole shovelful falling upon one of us, for we are tall, but she was only an inch high. Then she wrapped herself up in a dry leaf, but it cracked in the middle and could not keep her warm, and she shivered with cold. Near the wood in which she had been living lay a cornfield, but the corn had been cut a long time; nothing remained but the bare dry stubble standing up out of the frozen ground. It was to her like struggling through a large wood. Oh! how she shivered with the cold. She came at last to the door of a fieldmouse, who had a little den under the corn stubble. There dwelt the fieldmouse in warmth and comfort, with a whole roomful of corn, a kitchen, and a beautiful dining room. Poor little Tiny stood before the door just like a little beggar girl, and begged for a small piece of barleycorn, for she had been without a morsel to eat for two days.

"You poor little creature," said the fieldmouse, who was really a good old fieldmouse, "come into my warm room and dine with me." She was very pleased with Tiny, so she said, "You are quite welcome to stay with me all the winter, if you like; but you must keep my rooms clean and neat, and tell me stories, for I shall like to hear them very much." And Tiny did all the fieldmouse asked her, and found herself very comfortable.

"We shall have a visitor soon," said the fieldmouse one day; "my neighbor pays me a visit once a week. He is better off than I am; he has large rooms, and wears a beautiful black velvet coat. If you could only have him for a husband, you would be well provided for indeed. But he is blind, so you must tell him some of your prettiest stories."

But Tiny did not feel at all interested about this neighbor, for he was a mole. However, he came and paid his visit dressed in his black velvet coat.

"He is very rich and learned, and his house is twenty times larger than mine," said the fieldmouse.

He was rich and learned, no doubt, but he always spoke slightingly of the sun and the pretty flowers, because he had never seen them. Tiny was obliged to sing to him, "Ladybird, ladybird, fly away home," and many other pretty songs. And the mole fell in love with her because she had such a sweet voice; but he said nothing yet, for he was very cautious. A short time before, the mole had dug a long passage under the earth, which led from the dwelling of the fieldmouse to his own, and here she had permission to walk with Tiny whenever she liked. But he warned them not to be alarmed at the sight of a dead bird which lay in the passage. It was a perfect bird, with a beak and feathers, and could not have been dead long, and was lying just where the mole had made his passage. The mole took a piece of phosphorescent wood in his mouth, and it glittered like fire in the dark; then he went before them to light them through the long, dark passage. When they came to the spot where lay the dead bird, the mole pushed his broad nose through the ceiling, the earth gave way, so that there was a large hole, and the daylight shone into the passage. In the middle of the floor lay a dead swallow, his beautiful wings pulled close to his sides, his feet and his head drawn up under his feathers; the poor bird had evidently died of the cold. It made little Tiny very sad to see it, she did so love the little birds; all the summer they had sung and twittered for her so beautifully. But the mole pushed it aside with his crooked legs, and said, "He will sing no more now. How miserable it must be to be born a little bird! I am thankful that none of my children will ever be birds, for they can do nothing but cry, 'Tweet, tweet,' and always die of hunger in the winter."

"Yes, you may well say that, as a clever man!" exclaimed the field-mouse, "What is the use of his twittering, for when winter comes he must either starve or be frozen to death. Still birds are very high bred."

Tiny said nothing; but when the two others had turned their backs on the bird, she stooped down and stroked aside the soft feathers which covered the head, and kissed the closed eyelids. "Perhaps this was the one who sang to me so sweetly in the summer," she said; "and how much pleasure it gave me, you dear, pretty bird."

The mole now stopped up the hole through which the daylight shone, and then accompanied the lady home. But during the night Tiny could not sleep; so she got out of bed and wove a large, beautiful carpet of hay; then she carried it to the dead bird, and spread it over him, with some down from the flowers which she had found in the fieldmouse's room. It was as soft as wool, and she spread some of it on each side of the bird, so that he might lie warmly in the cold earth. "Farewell, you pretty little bird," said she, "farewell; thank you for your delightful singing during the summer, when all the trees were green, and the warm sun shone upon us." Then she laid her head on the bird's breast, but she was alarmed immediately, for it seemed as if something inside the bird went "thump, thump." It was the bird's heart; he was not really dead, only benumbed with the cold, and the warmth had restored him to life. In autumn, all the swallows fly away into warm countries, but if one happens to linger, the cold seizes it, it becomes frozen, and falls down as if dead; it remains where it fell, and the cold snow covers it. Tiny trembled very much; she was quite frightened, for the bird was large, a great deal larger than herself—she was only an inch high. But she took courage, laid the wool more thickly over the poor swallow, and then took a leaf which she had used for her own counterpane, and laid it over the head of the poor bird. The next morning she again stole out to see him. He was alive but very weak; he could only open his eyes for a moment to look at Tiny, who stood by holding a piece of decayed wood in her hand, for she had no other lantern. "Thank you, pretty little maiden," said the sick swallow; "I have been so nicely warmed, that I shall soon regain my strength, and be able to fly about again in the warm sunshine."

"Oh," said she, "it is cold out of doors now; it snows and freezes. Stay in your warm bed; I will take care of you."

Then she brought the swallow some water in a flower leaf, and after he had drank, he told her that he had wounded one of his wings in a thornbush, and could not fly as fast as the others, who were soon far away on their journey to warm countries. Then at last he had fallen to the earth, and could remember no more, nor how he came to be where she had found him. The whole winter the swallow remained underground, and Tiny nursed him with care and love. Neither the mole nor the fieldmouse knew anything about it, for they did not like swallows. Very soon the springtime came, and the sun warmed the earth. Then the swallow bade farewell to Tiny, and she opened the hole in the ceiling which the mole had made. The sun shone in upon them so beautifully, that the swallow asked her if she would go with him; she could sit on his back, he said, and he would fly away with her into the green woods. But Tiny knew it would make the fieldmouse very grieved if she left her in that manner, so she said, "No, I cannot."

"Farewell, then, farewell, you good, pretty little maiden," said the swallow; and he flew out into the sunshine.

Tiny looked after him, and the tears rose in her eyes. She was very fond of the poor swallow.

"Tweet, tweet," sang the bird, as he flew out into the green woods, and Tiny felt very sad. She was not allowed to go out into the warm sunshine. The corn which had been sown in the field over the house of the fieldmouse had grown up high into the air, and formed a thick wood to Tiny, who was only an inch in height.

"You are going to be married, Tiny," said the fieldmouse. "My neighbor has asked for you. What good fortune for a poor child like you. Now we will prepare your wedding clothes. They must be both woollen and linen. Nothing must be wanting when you are the mole's wife."

Tiny had to turn the spindle, and the fieldmouse hired four spiders, who were to weave day and night. Every evening the mole visited her, and was continually speaking of the time when the summer would be over. Then he would keep his wedding day with Tiny; but now the heat of the sun was so great that it burned the earth, and made it quite hard, like a stone. As soon as the summer was over, the wedding should take place. But Tiny was not at all pleased; for she did not like the tiresome mole. Every morning when the sun rose, and every evening when it went down, she would creep out at the door, and as the wind blew aside the ears of corn, so that she could see the blue sky, she thought how beautiful and bright it seemed out there, and wished so much to see her dear swallow again. But he never returned; for by this time he had flown far away into the lovely green forest.

When autumn arrived, Tiny had her outfit quite ready; and the fieldmouse said to her, "In four weeks the wedding must take place."

Then Tiny wept, and said she would not marry the disagreeable mole.

"Nonsense," replied the fieldmouse. "Now don't be obstinate, or I shall bite you with my white teeth. He is a very handsome mole; the queen herself does not wear more beautiful velvets and furs. His kitchen and cellars are quite full. You ought to be very thankful for such good fortune."

So the wedding day was fixed, on which the mole was to fetch Tiny away to live with him, deep under the earth, and never again to see the warm sun, because he did not like it. The poor child was very unhappy at the thought of saying farewell to the beautiful sun, and as the fieldmouse had given her permission to stand at the door, she went to look at it once more.

"Farewell bright sun," she cried, stretching out her arm towards it; and then she walked a short distance from the house; for the corn had been cut, and only the dry stubble remained in the fields. "Farewell, farewell," she repeated, twining her arm round a little red flower that grew just by her side. "Greet the little swallow from me, if you should see him again."

"Tweet, tweet," sounded over her head suddenly. She looked up, and there was the swallow himself flying close by. As soon as he spied Tiny, he was delighted; and then she told him how unwilling she felt to marry the ugly mole, and to live always beneath the earth, and never to see the bright sun anymore. And as she told him she wept.

"Cold winter is coming," said the swallow, "and I am going to fly away into warmer countries. Will you go with me? You can sit on my back, and fasten yourself on with your sash. Then we can fly away from the ugly mole and his gloomy rooms—far away, over the mountains, into warmer countries, where the sun shines more brightly than here; where it is always summer, and the flowers bloom in greater beauty. Fly now with me, dear little Tiny; you saved my life when I lay frozen in that dark passage."

"Yes, I will go with you," said Tiny; and she seated herself on the bird's back, with her feet on his outstretched wings, and tied her girdle to one of his strongest feathers.

Then the swallow rose in the air, and flew over forest and over sea, high above the highest mountains, covered with eternal snow. Tiny would have been frozen in the cold air, but she crept under the bird's warm feathers, keeping her little head uncovered, so that she might admire the beautiful lands over which they passed. At length they reached the warm countries, where the sun shines brightly, and the sky seems so much higher above the earth. Here, on the hedges, and by the wayside, grew purple, green, and white grapes; lemons and oranges hung from trees in the woods; and the air was fragrant with myrtles and orange blossoms. Beautiful children ran along the country lanes, playing with large gay butterflies; and as the swallow flew farther and farther, every place appeared still more lovely.

At last they came to a blue lake, and by the side of it, shaded by trees of the deepest green, stood a palace of dazzling white marble, built in the olden times. Vines clustered round its lofty pillars, and at the top were many swallows' nests, and one of these was the home of the swallow who carried Tiny.

"This is my house," said the swallow; "but it would not do for you to live there—you would not be comfortable. You must choose for yourself one of those lovely flowers, and I will put you down upon it, and then you shall have everything that you can wish to make you happy."

"That will be delightful," she said, and clapped her little hands for joy.

A large marble pillar lay on the ground, which, in falling, had been broken into three pieces. Between these pieces grew the most beautiful large white flowers; so the swallow flew down with Tiny, and placed her on one of the broad leaves. But how surprised she was to see in the middle of the flower, a tiny little man, as white and transparent as if he had been made of crystal! He had a gold crown on his head, and delicate wings at his shoulders, and was not much larger than Tiny herself. He was the angel of the flower; for a tiny man and a tiny woman dwell in every flower; and this was the king of them all.

"Oh, how beautiful he is!" whispered Tiny to the swallow.

The little prince was at first quite frightened at the bird, who was like a giant, compared to such a delicate little creature as himself; but when he saw Tiny, he was delighted, and thought her the prettiest little maiden he had ever seen. He took the gold crown from his head, and placed it on hers, and asked her name, and if she would be his wife, and queen over all the flowers.

This certainly was a very different sort of husband to the son of a toad, or the mole, with his black velvet and fur; so she said, "Yes," to the handsome prince. Then all the flowers opened, and out of each came a little lady or a tiny lord, all so pretty it was quite a pleasure to look at them. Each of them brought Tiny a present; but the best gift was a pair of beautiful wings, which had belonged to a large white fly, and they fastened them to Tiny's shoulders, so that she might fly from flower to flower. Then there was much rejoicing, and the little swallow who sat above them, in his nest, was asked to sing a wedding song, which he did as well as he could; but in his heart he felt sad, for he was very fond of Tiny, and would have liked never to part from her again.

"You must not be called Tiny anymore," said the spirit of the flowers to her. "It is an ugly name, and you are so very pretty. We will call you Maia."

"Farewell, farewell," said the swallow, with a heavy heart as he left the warm countries to fly back into Denmark. There he had a nest over the window of a house in which dwelt the writer of fairy tales. The swallow sang, "Tweet, tweet," and from his song came the whole story.

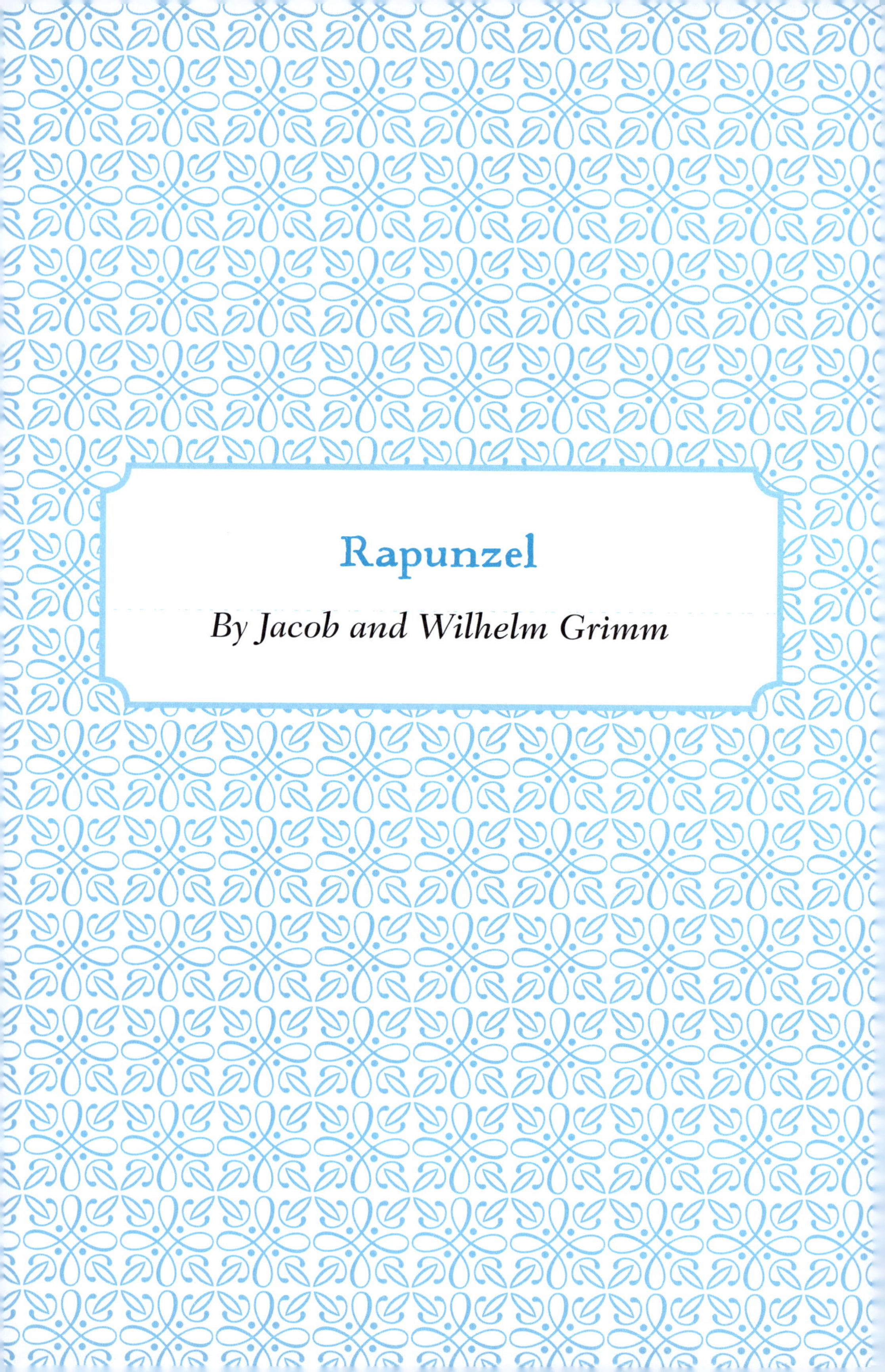

Rapunzel

By Jacob and Wilhelm Grimm

There were once a man and a woman who had long in vain wished for a child. At length the woman hoped that God was about to grant her desire. These people had a little window at the back of their house from which a splendid garden could be seen, which was full of the most beautiful flowers and herbs. It was, however, surrounded by a high wall, and no one dared to go into it because it belonged to an enchantress, who had great power and was dreaded by all the world. One day the woman was standing by this window and looking down into the garden, when she saw a bed which was planted with the most beautiful rampion (Rapunzel), and it looked so fresh and green that she longed for it, she quite pined away, and began to look pale and miserable. Then her husband was alarmed, and asked: "What ails you, dear wife?"

"Ah," she replied, "if I can't eat some of the rampion, which is in the garden behind our house, I shall die."

The man, who loved her, thought: "Sooner than let your wife die, bring her some of the rampion yourself, let it cost what it will."

At twilight, he clambered down over the wall into the garden of the enchantress, hastily clutched a handful of rampion, and took it to his wife. She at once made herself a salad of it, and ate it greedily. It tasted so good to her—so very good, that the next day she longed for it three times as much as before. If he was to have any rest, her husband must once more descend into the garden. In the gloom of evening therefore, he let himself down again; but when he had clambered down the wall he was terribly afraid, for he saw the enchantress standing before him.

"How can you dare," said she with angry look, "descend into my garden and steal my rampion like a thief? You shall suffer for it!"

"Ah," answered he, "let mercy take the place of justice, I only made up my mind to do it out of necessity. My wife saw your rampion from the window, and felt such a longing for it that she would have died if she had not got some to eat."

Then the enchantress allowed her anger to be softened, and said to him: "If the case be as you say, I will allow you to take away with you as much rampion as you will, only I make one condition, you must give me the child which your wife will bring into the world; it shall be well treated, and I will care for it like a mother."

The man in his terror consented to everything, and when the woman was brought to bed, the enchantress appeared at once, gave the child the name of Rapunzel, and took it away with her.

Rapunzel grew into the most beautiful child under the sun. When she was twelve years old, the enchantress shut her into a tower, which lay in a forest, and had neither stairs nor door, but quite at the top was a little window. When the enchantress wanted to go in, she placed herself beneath it and cried:

"Rapunzel, Rapunzel,
Let down your hair to me."

Rapunzel had magnificent long hair, fine as spun gold, and when she heard the voice of the enchantress she unfastened her braided tresses, wound them round one of the hooks of the window above, and then the hair fell twenty ells down, and the enchantress climbed up by it.

After a year or two, it came to pass that the king's son rode through the forest and passed by the tower. Then he heard a song, which was so charming that he stood still and listened. This was Rapunzel, who in her solitude passed her time in letting her sweet voice resound. The king's son wanted to climb up to her, and looked for the door of the tower, but none was to be found. He rode home, but the singing had so deeply touched his heart, that every day he went out into the forest and listened to it. Once when he was thus standing behind a tree, he saw that an enchantress came there, and he heard how she cried:

"Rapunzel, Rapunzel,
Let down your hair to me."

Then Rapunzel let down the braids of her hair, and the enchantress climbed up to her. "If that is the ladder by which one mounts, I too will try my fortune," said he, and the next day when it began to grow dark, he went to the tower and cried:

"Rapunzel, Rapunzel,
Let down your hair to me."

Immediately the hair fell down and the king's son climbed up.

At first Rapunzel was terribly frightened when a man, such as her eyes had never yet beheld, came to her; but the king's son began to talk to her quite like a friend, and told her that his heart had been so stirred that it had let him have no rest, and he had been forced to see her. Then Rapunzel lost her fear, and when he asked her if she would take him for her husband, and she saw that he was young and handsome, she thought: "He will love me more than old Dame Gothel does"; and she said yes, and laid her hand in his. She said: "I will willingly go away with you, but I do not know how to get down. Bring with you a skein of silk every time that you come, and I will weave a ladder with it, and when that is ready I will descend, and you will take me on your horse." They agreed that until that time he should come to her every evening, for the old woman came by day. The enchantress remarked nothing of this, until once Rapunzel said to her: "Tell me, Dame Gothel, how it happens that you are so much heavier for me to draw up than the young king's son—he is with me in a moment."

"Ah! you wicked child," cried the enchantress. "What do I hear you say! I thought I had separated you from all the world, and yet you have deceived me!" In her anger she clutched Rapunzel's beautiful tresses, wrapped them twice round her left hand, seized a pair of scissors with the right, and snip, snap, they were cut off, and the lovely braids lay on the ground. And she was so pitiless that she took poor Rapunzel into a desert where she had to live in great grief and misery.

On the same day that she cast out Rapunzel, however, the enchantress fastened the braids of hair, which she had cut off, to the hook of the window, and when the king's son came and cried:

"Rapunzel, Rapunzel,
Let down your hair to me."

She let the hair down. The king's son ascended, but instead of finding his dearest Rapunzel, he found the enchantress, who gazed at him with wicked and venomous looks. "Aha!" she cried mockingly, "you would fetch your dearest, but the beautiful bird sits no longer singing in the nest; the cat has got it, and will scratch out your eyes as well. Rapunzel is lost to you; you will never see her again."

The king's son was beside himself with pain, and in his despair he leapt down from the tower. He escaped with his life, but the thorns into which he fell pierced his eyes. Then he wandered quite blind about the forest, ate nothing but roots and berries, and did naught but lament and weep over the loss of his dearest wife. Thus he roamed about in misery for some years, and at length came to the desert where Rapunzel, with the twins to which she had given birth, a boy and a girl, lived in wretchedness. He heard a voice, and it seemed so familiar to him that he went towards it, and when he approached, Rapunzel knew him and fell on his neck and wept. Two of her tears wetted his eyes and they grew clear again, and he could see with them as before. He led her to his kingdom where he was joyfully received, and they lived for a long time afterwards, happy and contented.

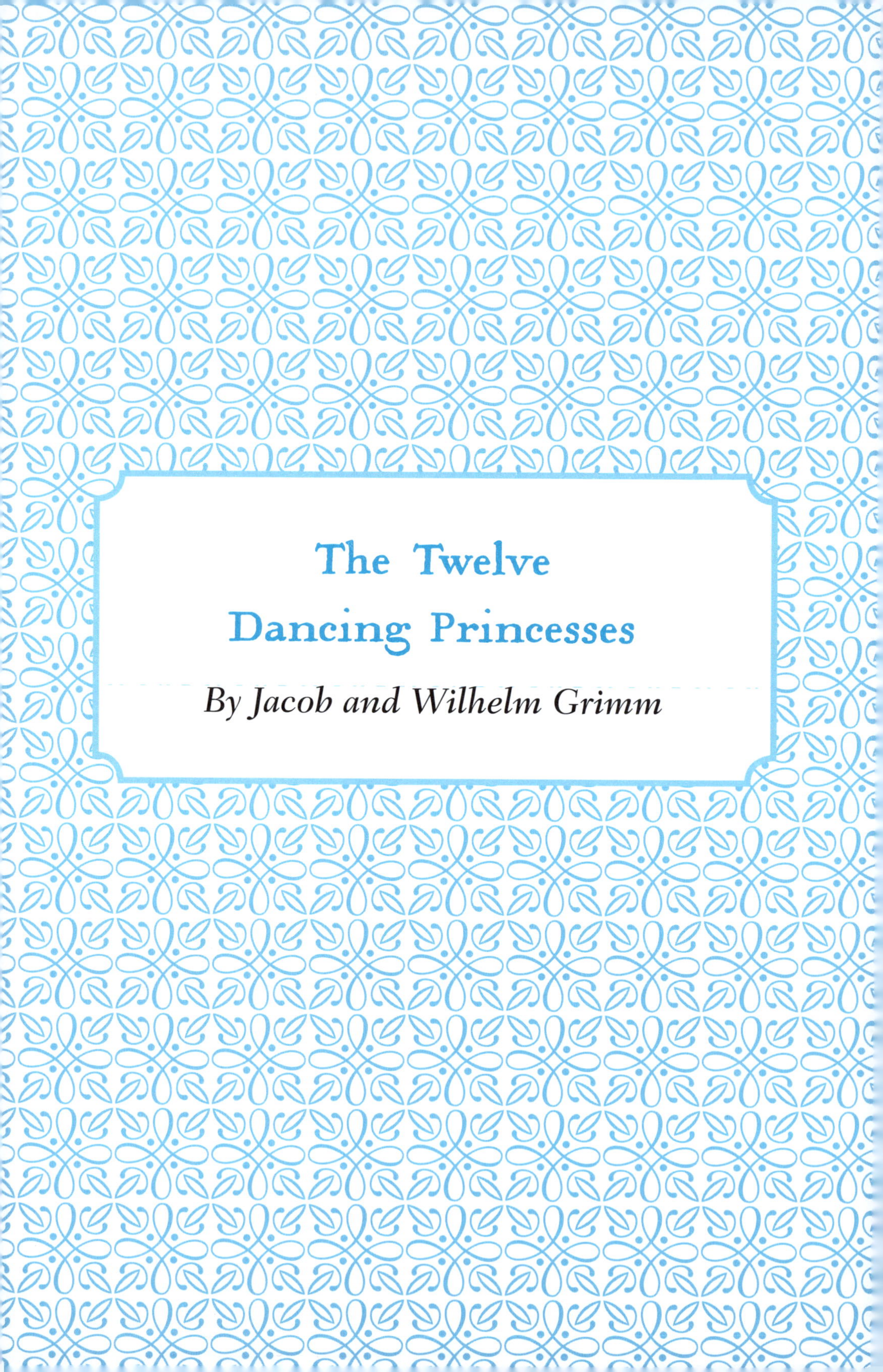
The Twelve
Dancing Princesses
By Jacob and Wilhelm Grimm

There was a king who had twelve beautiful daughters. They slept in twelve beds all in one room; and when they went to bed, the doors were shut and locked up; but every morning their shoes were found to be quite worn through as if they had been danced in all night; and yet nobody could find out how it happened, or where they had been.

Then the king made it known to all the land, that if any person could discover the secret, and find out where it was that the princesses danced in the night, he should have the one he liked best for his wife, and should be king after his death; but whoever tried and did not succeed, after three days and nights, should be put to death.

A king's son soon came. He was well entertained, and in the evening was taken to the chamber next to the one where the princesses lay in their twelve beds. There he was to sit and watch where they went to dance; and, in order that nothing might pass without his hearing it, the door of his chamber was left open. But the king's son soon fell asleep; and when he awoke in the morning he found that the princesses had all been dancing, for the soles of their shoes were full of holes. The same thing happened the second and third night: so the king ordered his head to be cut off. After him came several others; but they had all the same luck, and all lost their lives in the same manner.

Now it chanced that an old soldier, who had been wounded in battle and could fight no longer, passed through the country where this king reigned: and as he was travelling through a wood, he met an old woman, who asked him where he was going. "I hardly know where I am going, or what I had better do," said the soldier; "but I think I should like very well to find out where it is that the princesses dance, and then in time I might be a king."

"Well," said the old dame, "that is no very hard task: only take care not to drink any of the wine which one of the princesses will bring to you in the evening; and as soon as she leaves you pretend to be fast asleep."

Then she gave him a cloak, and said, "As soon as you put that on you will become invisible, and you will then be able to follow the princesses wherever they go." When the soldier heard all this good counsel, he determined to try his luck: so he went to the king, and said he was willing to undertake the task.

He was as well received as the others had been, and the king ordered fine royal robes to be given him; and when the evening came he was led to the outer chamber. Just as he was going to lie down, the eldest of the princesses brought him a cup of wine; but the soldier threw it all away secretly, taking care not to drink a drop. Then he laid himself down on his bed, and in a little while began to snore very loud as if he was fast asleep. When the twelve princesses heard this they laughed heartily; and the eldest said, "This fellow too might have done a wiser thing than lose his life in this way!" Then they rose up and opened their drawers and boxes, and took out all their fine clothes, and dressed themselves at the glass, and skipped about as if they were eager to begin dancing. But the youngest said, "I don't know how it is, while you are so happy I feel very uneasy; I am sure some mischance will befall us."

"You simpleton," said the eldest, "you are always afraid; have you forgotten how many kings' sons have already watched in vain? And as for this soldier, even if I had not given him his sleeping draught, he would have slept soundly enough."

When they were all ready, they went and looked at the soldier; but he snored on, and did not stir hand or foot: so they thought they were quite safe; and the eldest went up to her own bed and clapped her hands, and the bed sank into the floor and a trapdoor flew open. The soldier saw them going down through the trapdoor one after another, the eldest leading the way; and thinking he had no time to lose, he jumped up, put on the cloak which the old woman had given him, and followed them; but in the middle of the stairs he trod on the gown of the youngest princess, and she cried out to her sisters, "All is not right; someone took hold of my gown."

"You silly creature!" said the eldest, "it is nothing but a nail in the wall." Then down they all went, and at the bottom they found themselves in a most delightful grove of trees; and the leaves were all of silver, and glittered and sparkled beautifully. The soldier wished to take away some token of the place; so he broke off a little branch, and there came a loud noise from the tree. Then the youngest daughter said again, "I am sure all is not right—did not you hear that noise? That never happened before."

But the eldest said, "It is only our princes, who are shouting for joy at our approach."

Then they came to another grove of trees, where all the leaves were of gold; and afterwards to a third, where the leaves were all glittering diamonds. And the soldier broke a branch from each; and every time there was a loud noise, which made the youngest sister tremble with fear; but the eldest still said, it was only the princes, who were crying for joy. So they went on till they came to a great lake; and at the side of the lake there lay twelve little boats with twelve handsome princes in them, who seemed to be waiting there for the princesses.

One of the princesses went into each boat, and the soldier stepped into the same boat with the youngest. As they were rowing over the lake, the prince who was in the boat with the youngest princess and the soldier said, "I do not know why it is, but though I am rowing with all my might we do not get on so fast as usual, and I am quite tired: the boat seems very heavy today."

"It is only the heat of the weather," said the princess: "I feel it very warm too."

On the other side of the lake stood a fine illuminated castle, from which came the merry music of horns and trumpets. There they all landed, and went into the castle, and each prince danced with his princess; and the soldier, who was all the time invisible, danced with them too; and when any of the princesses had a cup of wine set by her, he drank it all up, so that when she put the cup to her mouth it was empty. At this, too, the youngest sister was terribly frightened, but the eldest always silenced her. They danced on till three o'clock in the morning, and then all their shoes were worn out, so that they were obliged to leave off. The princes rowed them back again over the lake (but this time the soldier placed himself in the boat with the eldest princess); and on the opposite shore they took leave of each other, the princesses promising to come again the next night.

When they came to the stairs, the soldier ran on before the princesses, and laid himself down; and as the twelve sisters slowly came up very much tired, they heard him snoring in his bed; so they said, "Now all is quite safe"; then they undressed themselves, put away their fine clothes, pulled off their shoes, and went to bed. In the morning the soldier said nothing about what had happened, but determined to see more of this strange adventure, and went again the second and third night; and everything happened just as before; the princesses danced each time till their shoes were worn to pieces, and then returned home. However, on the third night the soldier carried away one of the golden cups as a token of where he had been.

As soon as the time came when he was to declare the secret, he was taken before the king with the three branches and the golden cup; and the twelve princesses stood listening behind the door to hear what he would say. And when the king asked him, "Where do my twelve daughters dance at night?" he answered, "With twelve princes in a castle underground." And then he told the king all that had happened, and showed him the three branches and the golden cup which he had brought with him. Then the king called for the princesses, and asked them whether what the soldier said was true: and when they saw that they were discovered, and that it was of no use to deny what had happened, they confessed it all. And the king asked the soldier which of them he would choose for his wife; and he answered, "I am not very young, so I will have the eldest." And they were married that very day, and the soldier was chosen to be the king's heir.

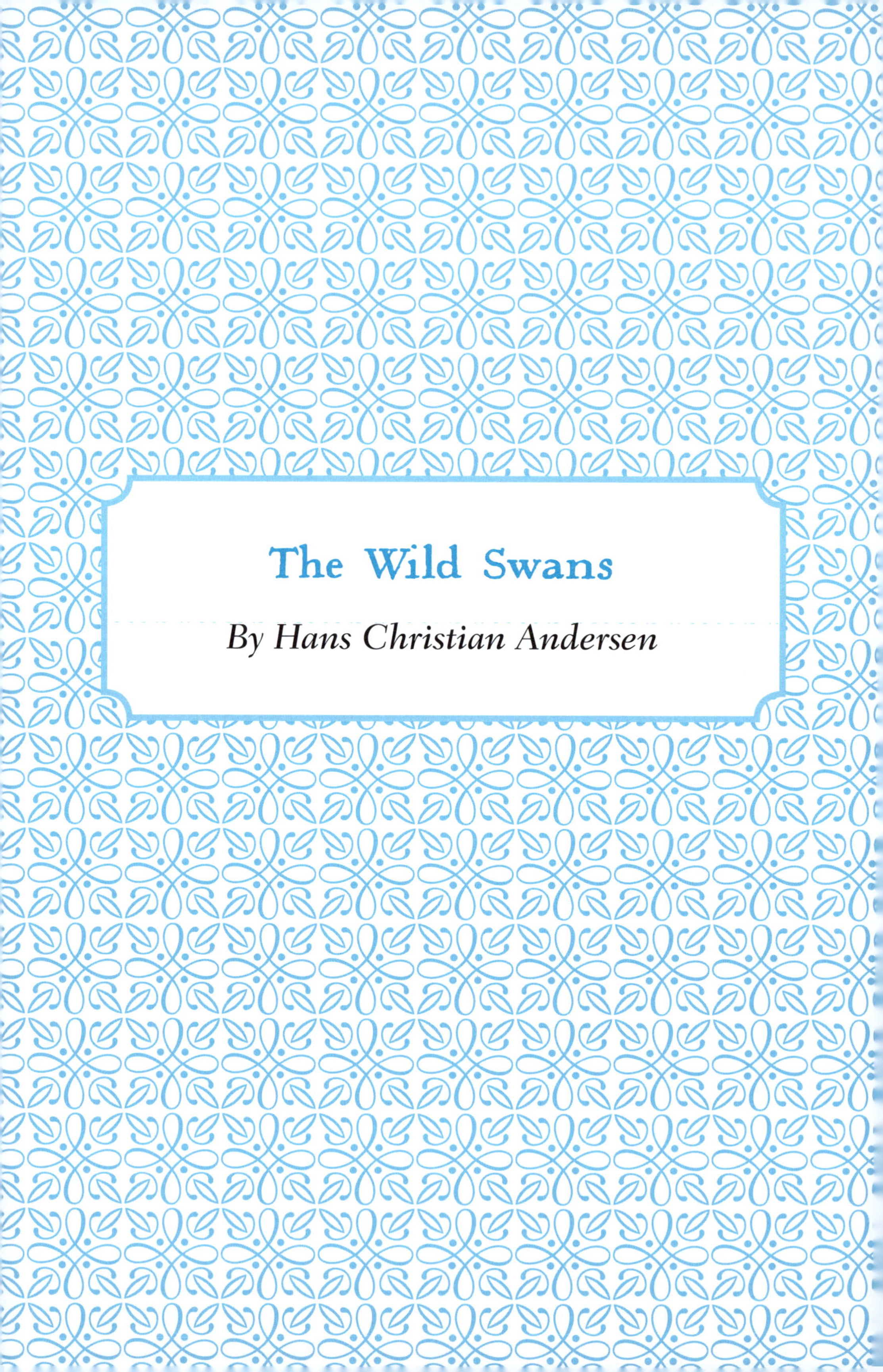

The Wild Swans

By Hans Christian Andersen

Far away in the land to which the swallows fly when it is winter, dwelt a king who had eleven sons, and one daughter, named Eliza. The eleven brothers were princes, and each went to school with a star on his breast, and a sword by his side. They wrote with diamond pencils on gold slates, and learnt their lessons so quickly and read so easily that everyone might know they were princes. Their sister Eliza sat on a little stool of plate glass, and had a book full of pictures, which had cost as much as half a kingdom. Oh, these children were indeed happy, but it was not to remain so always. Their father, who was king of the country, married a very wicked queen, who did not love the poor children at all. They knew this from the very first day after the wedding.

In the palace there were great festivities, and the children played at receiving company; but instead of having, as usual, all the cakes and apples that were left, she gave them some sand in a teacup, and told them to pretend it was cake. The week after, she sent little Eliza into the country to a peasant and his wife, and then she told the king so many untrue things about the young princes, that he gave himself no more trouble respecting them.

"Go out into the world and get your own living," said the queen. "Fly like great birds, who have no voice." But she could not make them ugly as she wished, for they were turned into eleven beautiful wild swans. Then, with a strange cry, they flew through the windows of the palace, over the park, to the forest beyond. It was early morning when they passed the peasant's cottage, where their sister Eliza lay asleep in her room. They hovered over the roof, twisted their long necks and flapped their wings, but no one heard them or saw them, so they were at last obliged to fly away, high up in the clouds; and over the wide world they flew till they came to a thick, dark wood, which stretched far away to the seashore. Poor little Eliza was alone in her room playing with a green leaf, for she had no other playthings, and she pierced a hole through the leaf, and looked through it at the sun, and it was as if she saw her brothers' clear eyes, and when the warm sun shone on her cheeks, she thought of all the kisses they had given her.

One day passed just like another; sometimes the winds rustled through the leaves of the rosebush, and would whisper to the roses,

"Who can be more beautiful than you!" But the roses would shake their heads, and say, "Eliza is." And when the old woman sat at the cottage door on Sunday, and read her hymnbook, the wind would flutter the leaves, and say to the book, "Who can be more pious than you?" and then the hymnbook would answer "Eliza." And the roses and the hymnbook told the real truth.

At fifteen she returned home, but when the queen saw how beautiful she was, she became full of spite and hatred towards her. Willingly would she have turned her into a swan, like her brothers, but she did not dare to do so yet, because the king wished to see his daughter. Early one morning the queen went into the bathroom; it was built of marble, and had soft cushions, trimmed with the most beautiful tapestry. She took three toads with her, and kissed them, and said to one, "When Eliza comes to the bath, seat yourself upon her head, that she may become as stupid as you are." Then she said to another, "Place yourself on her forehead, that she may become as ugly as you are, and that her father may not know her." "Rest on her heart," she whispered to the third, "then she will have evil inclinations, and suffer in consequence."

So she put the toads into the clear water, and they turned green immediately. She next called Eliza, and helped her to undress and get into the bath. As Eliza dipped her head under the water, one of the toads sat on her hair, a second on her forehead, and a third on her breast, but she did not seem to notice them, and when she rose out of the water, there were three red poppies floating upon it. Had not the creatures been venomous or been kissed by the witch, they would have been changed into red roses. At all events they became flowers, because they had rested on Eliza's head, and on her heart. She was too good and too innocent for witchcraft to have any power over her. When the wicked queen saw this, she rubbed mud on her face, so that she was quite brown; then she tangled her beautiful hair and smeared it with disgusting ointment, till it was quite impossible to recognize the beautiful Eliza.

When her father saw her, he was much shocked, and declared she was not his daughter. No one but the watchdog and the swallows knew her; and they were only poor animals, and could say nothing. Then poor Eliza wept, and thought of her eleven brothers, who were all away. Sorrowfully, she stole away from the palace, and walked, the whole day, over fields and moors, till she came to the great forest. She knew not in what direction to go; but she was so unhappy, and longed so for her brothers, who had been, like herself, driven out into the world, that she was determined to seek them. She had been but a short time in the wood when night came on, and she quite lost the path; so she laid herself down on the soft moss, offered up her evening prayer, and leaned her head against the stump of a tree. All nature was still, and the soft, mild air fanned her forehead. The light of hundreds of glowworms shone amidst the grass and the moss, like green fire; and if she touched a twig with her hand, ever so lightly, the brilliant insects fell down around her, like shooting stars.

All night long she dreamt of her brothers. She and they were children again, playing together. She saw them writing with their diamond pencils on golden slates, while she looked at the beautiful picture book which had cost half a kingdom. They were not writing lines and letters, as they used to do; but descriptions of the noble deeds they had performed, and of all they had discovered and seen. In the picture book, too, everything was living. The birds sang, and the people came out of the book, and spoke to Eliza and her brothers; but, as the leaves turned over, they darted back again to their places, that all might be in order.

When she awoke, the sun was high in the heavens; yet she could not see him, for the lofty trees spread their branches thickly over her head; but his beams were glancing through the leaves here and there, like a golden mist. There was a sweet fragrance from the fresh green verdure, and the birds almost perched upon her shoulders. She heard water rippling from a number of springs, all flowing in a lake with golden sands. Bushes grew thickly round the lake, and at one spot an opening had been made by a deer, through which Eliza went down to the water. The lake was so clear that, had not the wind rustled the branches of the trees and the bushes, so that they moved, they would have appeared as if painted in the depths of the lake; for every leaf was reflected in the water, whether it stood in the shade or the sunshine.

As soon as Eliza saw her own face, she was quite terrified at finding it caked with mud; but when she wetted her little hand, and rubbed her eyes and forehead, her skin gleamed forth once more; and, after she had undressed, and dipped herself in the fresh water, a more beautiful king's daughter could not be found in the wide world.

As soon as she had dressed herself again, and braided her long hair, she went to the bubbling spring, and drank some water out of the hollow of her hand. Then she wandered far into the forest, not knowing whither she went. She thought of her brothers, and felt sure that God would not forsake her. It is God who makes the wild apples grow in the wood, to satisfy the hungry, and He now led her to one of these trees, which was so loaded with fruit, that the boughs bent beneath the weight. Here she held her noonday repast, placed props under the boughs, and then went into the gloomiest depths of the forest. It was so still that she could hear the sound of her own footsteps, as well as the rustling of every withered leaf which she crushed under her feet. Not a bird was to be seen, not a sunbeam could penetrate through the large, dark boughs of the trees. Their lofty trunks stood so close together, that, when she looked before her, it seemed as if she were enclosed within trelliswork. Such solitude she had never known before. The night was very dark. Not a single glow worm glittered in the moss.

Sorrowfully she laid herself down to sleep; and, after a while, it seemed to her as if the branches of the trees parted over her head, and that the mild eyes of angels looked down upon her from heaven. When she awoke in the morning, she knew not whether she had dreamt this, or if it had really been so. Then she continued her wandering; but she had not gone many steps forward, when she met an old woman with berries in her basket, and she gave her a few to eat. Then Eliza asked her if she had not seen eleven princes riding through the forest.

"No," replied the old woman. "But I saw yesterday eleven swans, with gold crowns on their heads, swimming on the river close by." Then she led Eliza a little distance farther to a sloping bank, and at the foot of it wound a little river. The trees on its banks stretched their long leafy branches across the water towards each other, and where the growth prevented them from meeting naturally, the roots had torn themselves away from the ground, so that the branches might mingle their foliage as they hung over the water. Eliza bade the old woman farewell, and walked by the flowing river, till she reached the shore of the open sea. And there, before the young maiden's eyes, lay the glorious ocean, but not a sail appeared on its surface, not even a boat could be seen. How was she to go farther? She noticed how the countless pebbles on the seashore had been smoothed and rounded by the action of the water. Glass, iron, stones, everything that lay there mingled together, had taken its shape from the same power, and felt as smooth, or even smoother than her own delicate hand. "The water rolls on without weariness," she said, "till all that is hard becomes smooth; so will I be unwearied in my task. Thanks for your lessons, bright rolling waves; my heart tells me you will lead me to my dear brothers."

On the foam-covered seaweeds, lay eleven white swan feathers, which she gathered up and placed together. Drops of water lay upon them; whether they were dewdrops or tears no one could say. Lonely as it was on the seashore, she did not observe it, for the ever-moving sea showed more changes in a few hours than the most varying lake could produce during a whole year. If a black heavy cloud arose, it was as if the sea said, "I can look dark and angry too"; and then the wind blew, and the waves turned to white foam as they rolled. When the wind slept, and the clouds glowed with the red sunlight, then the sea looked like a rose leaf. But however quietly its white glassy surface rested, there was still a motion on the shore, as its waves rose and fell like the breast of a sleeping child.

When the sun was about to set, Eliza saw eleven white swans with golden crowns on their heads, flying towards the land, one behind the other, like a long white ribbon. Then Eliza went down the slope from the shore, and hid herself behind the bushes. The swans alighted quite close to her and flapped their great white wings. As soon as the sun had disappeared under the water, the feathers of the swans fell off, and eleven beautiful princes, Eliza's brothers, stood near her. She uttered a loud cry, for, although they were very much changed, she knew them immediately. She sprang into their arms, and called them each by name. Then, how happy the princes were at meeting their little sister again, for they recognized her, although she had grown so tall and beautiful. They laughed, and they wept, and very soon understood how wickedly their mother had acted to them all. "We brothers," said the eldest, "fly about as wild swans, so long as the sun is in the sky; but as soon as it sinks behind the hills, we recover our human shape. Therefore must we always be near a resting place for our feet before sunset; for if we should be flying towards the clouds at the time we recovered our natural shape as men, we should sink deep into the sea. We do not dwell here, but in a land just as fair, that lies beyond the ocean, which we have to cross for a long distance; there is no island in our passage upon which we could pass the night; nothing but a little rock rising out of the sea, upon which we can scarcely stand with safety, even closely crowded together. If the sea is rough, the foam dashes over us, yet we thank God even for this rock; we have passed whole nights upon it, or we should never have reached our beloved fatherland, for our flight across the sea occupies two of the longest days in the year. We have permission to visit out home once in every year, and to remain eleven days, during which we fly across the forest to look once more at the palace where our father dwells, and where we were born, and at the church, where our mother lies buried. Here it seems as if the very trees and bushes were related to us. The wild horses leap over the plains as we have seen them in our childhood. The charcoal burners sing the old songs, to which we have danced as children. This is our fatherland, to which we are drawn by loving ties; and here we have found you, our dear little sister. Two days longer we can remain here, and then must we fly away to a beautiful land which is not our home; and how can we take you with us? We have neither ship nor boat."

"How can I break this spell?" said their sister. And then she talked about it nearly the whole night, only slumbering for a few hours.

Eliza was awakened by the rustling of the swans' wings as they soared above. Her brothers were again changed to swans, and they flew in circles wider and wider, till they were far away; but one of them, the youngest swan, remained behind, and laid his head in his sister's lap, while she stroked his wings; and they remained together the whole day.

Towards evening, the rest came back, and as the sun went down they resumed their natural forms. "Tomorrow," said one, "we shall fly away, not to return again till a whole year has passed. But we cannot leave you here. Have you courage to go with us? My arm is strong enough to carry you through the wood; and will not all our wings be strong enough to fly with you over the sea?"

"Yes, take me with you," said Eliza. Then they spent the whole night in weaving a net with the pliant willow and rushes. It was very large and strong. Eliza laid herself down on the net, and when the sun rose, and her brothers again became wild swans, they took up the net with their beaks, and flew up to the clouds with their dear sister, who still slept. The sunbeams fell on her face, therefore one of the swans soared over her head, so that his broad wings might shade her. They were far from the land when Eliza woke. She thought she must still be dreaming, it seemed so strange to her to feel herself being carried so high in the air over the sea. By her side lay a branch full of beautiful ripe berries, and a bundle of sweet roots; the youngest of her brothers had gathered them for her, and placed them by her side. She smiled her thanks to him; she knew it was the same who had hovered over her to shade her with his wings.

They were now so high, that a large ship beneath them looked like a white seagull skimming the waves. A great cloud floating behind them appeared like a vast mountain, and upon it Eliza saw her own shadow and those of the eleven swans, looking gigantic in size. Altogether it formed a more beautiful picture than she had ever seen; but as the sun rose higher, and the clouds were left behind, the shadowy picture vanished away. Onward the whole day they flew through the air like a winged arrow, yet more slowly than usual, for they had their sister to carry. The weather seemed inclined to be stormy, and Eliza watched the sinking sun with great anxiety, for the little rock in the ocean was not yet in sight. It appeared to her as if the swans were making great efforts with their wings. Alas! she was the cause of their not advancing more quickly. When the sun set, they would change to men, fall into the sea and be drowned. Then she offered a prayer from her inmost heart, but still no appearance of the rock. Dark clouds came nearer, the gusts of wind told of a coming storm, while from a thick, heavy mass of clouds the lightning burst forth flash after flash. The sun had reached the edge of the sea, when the swans darted down so swiftly, that Eliza's head trembled; she believed they were falling, but they again soared onward. Presently she caught sight of the rock just below them, and by this time the sun was half hidden by the waves. The rock did not appear larger than a seal's head thrust out of the water. They sunk so rapidly, that at the moment their feet touched the rock, it shone only like a star, and at last disappeared like the last spark in a piece of burnt paper. Then she saw her brothers standing closely round her with their arms linked together. There was but just room enough for them, and not the smallest space to spare.

The sea dashed against the rock, and covered them with spray. The heavens were lighted up with continual flashes, and peal after peal of thunder rolled. But the sister and brothers sat holding each other's hands, and singing hymns, from which they gained hope and courage. In the early dawn the air became calm and still, and at sunrise the swans flew away from the rock with Eliza. The sea was still rough, and from their high position in the air, the white foam on the dark green waves looked like millions of swans swimming on the water. As the sun rose higher, Eliza saw before her, floating on the air, a range of mountains, with shining masses of ice on their summits. In the centre, rose a castle apparently a mile long, with rows of columns, rising one above another, while, around it, palm trees waved and flowers bloomed as large as mill wheels. She asked if this was the land to which they were hastening. The swans shook their heads, for what she beheld were the beautiful ever-changing cloud palaces of the "Fata Morgana," into which no mortal can enter. Eliza was still gazing at the scene, when mountains, forests, and castles melted away, and twenty stately churches rose in their stead, with high towers and pointed gothic windows. Eliza even fancied she could hear the tones of the organ, but it was the music of the murmuring sea which she heard. As they drew nearer to the churches, they also changed into a fleet of ships, which seemed to be sailing beneath her; but as she looked again, she found it was only a sea mist gliding over the ocean. So there continued to pass before her eyes a constant change of scene, till at last she saw the real land to which they were bound, with its blue mountains, its cedar forests, and its cities and palaces. Long before the sun went down, she sat on a rock, in front of a large cave, on the floor of which the overgrown yet delicate green creeping plants looked like an embroidered carpet. "Now we shall expect to hear what you dream of tonight," said the youngest brother, as he showed his sister her bedroom.

"Heaven grant that I may dream how to save you," she replied. And this thought took such hold upon her mind that she prayed earnestly to God for help, and even in her sleep she continued to pray. Then it appeared to her as if she were flying high in the air, towards the cloudy palace of the "Fata Morgana," and a fairy came out to meet her, radiant and beautiful in appearance, and yet very much like the old woman who had given her berries in the wood, and who had told her of the swans with golden crowns on their heads. "Your brothers can be released," said she, "if you have only courage and perseverance. True, water is softer than your own delicate hands, and yet it polishes stones into shapes; it feels no pain as your fingers would feel, it has no soul, and cannot suffer such agony and torment as you will have to endure. Do you see the stinging nettle which I hold in my hand? Quantities of the same sort grow round the cave in which you sleep, but none will be of any use to you unless they grow upon the graves in a churchyard. These you must gather even while they burn blisters on your hands. Break them to pieces with your hands and feet, and they will become flax, from which you must spin and weave eleven coats with long sleeves; if these are then thrown over the eleven swans, the spell will be broken. But remember, that from the moment you commence your task until it is finished, even should it occupy years of your life, you must not speak. The first word you utter will pierce through the hearts of your brothers like a deadly dagger. Their lives hang upon your tongue. Remember all I have told you." And as she finished speaking, she touched her hand lightly with the nettle, and a pain, as of burning fire, awoke Eliza.

It was broad daylight, and close by where she had been sleeping lay a nettle like the one she had seen in her dream. She fell on her knees and offered her thanks to God. Then she went forth from the cave to begin her work with her delicate hands. She groped in amongst the ugly nettles, which burnt great blisters on her hands and arms, but she determined to bear it gladly if she could only release her dear brothers. So she bruised the nettles with her bare feet and spun the flax. At sunset her brothers returned and were very much frightened when they found her dumb. They believed it to be some new sorcery of their wicked stepmother. But when they saw her hands they understood what she was doing on their behalf, and the youngest brother wept, and where his tears fell the pain ceased, and the burning blisters vanished. She kept to her work all night, for she could not rest till she had released her dear brothers. During the whole of the following day, while her brothers were absent, she sat in solitude, but never before had the time flown so quickly. One coat was already finished and she had begun the second, when she heard the huntsman's horn, and was struck with fear. The sound came nearer and nearer, she heard the dogs barking, and fled with terror into the cave. She hastily bound together the nettles she had gathered into a bundle and sat upon them. Immediately a great dog came bounding towards her out of the ravine, and then another and another; they barked loudly, ran back, and then came again. In a very few minutes all the huntsmen stood before the cave, and the handsomest of them was the king of the country. He advanced towards her, for he had never seen a more beautiful maiden.

"How did you come here, my sweet child?" he asked.

Eliza shook her head. She dared not speak, at the cost of her brothers' lives. And she hid her hands under her apron, so that the king might not see how she must be suffering.

"Come with me," he said; "here you cannot remain. If you are as good as you are beautiful, I will dress you in silk and velvet, I will place a golden crown upon your head, and you shall dwell, and rule, and make your home in my richest castle." And then he lifted her on his horse. She wept and wrung her hands, but the king said, "I wish only for your happiness. A time will come when you will thank me for this." And then he galloped away over the mountains, holding her before him on this horse, and the hunters followed behind them.

As the sun went down, they approached a fair royal city, with churches, and cupolas. On arriving at the castle the king led her into marble halls, where large fountains played, and where the walls and the ceilings were covered with rich paintings. But she had no eyes for all these glorious sights, she could only mourn and weep. Patiently she allowed the women to array her in royal robes, to weave pearls in her hair, and draw soft gloves over her blistered fingers. As she stood before them in all her rich dress, she looked so dazzlingly beautiful that the court bowed low in her presence. Then the king declared his intention of making her his bride, but the archbishop shook his head, and whispered that the fair young maiden was only a witch who had blinded the king's eyes and bewitched his heart. But the king would not listen to this; he ordered the music to sound, the daintiest dishes to be served, and the loveliest maidens to dance. Afterwards he led her through fragrant gardens and lofty halls, but not a smile appeared on her lips or sparkled in her eyes. She looked the very picture of grief. Then the king opened the door of a little chamber in which she was to sleep; it was adorned with rich green tapestry, and resembled the cave in which he had found her. On the floor lay the bundle of flax which she had spun from the nettles, and under the ceiling hung the coat she had made. These things had been brought away from the cave as curiosities by one of the huntsmen.

"Here you can dream yourself back again in the old home in the cave," said the king; "here is the work with which you employed yourself. It will amuse you now in the midst of all this splendor to think of that time."

When Eliza saw all these things which lay so near her heart, a smile played around her mouth, and the crimson blood rushed to her cheeks. She thought of her brothers, and their release made her so joyful that she kissed the king's hand. Then he pressed her to his heart. Very soon the joyous church bells announced the marriage feast, and that the beautiful dumb girl out of the wood was to be made the queen of the country. Then the archbishop whispered wicked words in the king's ear, but they did not sink into his heart. The marriage was still to take place, and the archbishop himself had to place the crown on the bride's head; in his wicked spite, he pressed the narrow circlet so tightly on her forehead that it caused her pain. But a heavier weight encircled her heart—sorrow for her brothers. She felt not bodily pain. Her mouth was closed; a single word would cost the lives of her brothers. But she loved the kind, handsome king, who did everything to make her happy more and more each day; she loved him with all her heart, and her eyes beamed with the love she dared not speak. Oh! if she had only been able to confide in him and tell him of her grief. But dumb she must remain till her task was finished. Therefore at night she crept away into her little chamber, which had been decked out to look like the cave, and quickly wove one coat after another.

But when she began the seventh she found she had no more flax. She knew that the nettles she wanted to use grew in the churchyard, and that she must pluck them herself. How should she get out there? "Oh, what is the pain in my fingers to the torment which my heart endures?" said she. "I must venture, I shall not be denied help from heaven." Then with a trembling heart, as if she were about to perform a wicked deed, she crept into the garden in the broad moonlight, and passed through the narrow walks and the deserted streets, till she reached the churchyard. Then she saw on one of the broad tombstones a group of ghouls. These hideous creatures took off their rags, as if they intended to bathe, and then clawing open the fresh graves with their long, skinny fingers, pulled out the dead bodies and ate the flesh! Eliza had to pass close by them, and they fixed their wicked glances upon her, but she prayed silently, gathered the burning nettles, and carried them home with her to the castle. One person only had seen her, and that was the archbishop—he was awake while everybody was asleep. Now he thought his opinion was evidently correct. All was not right with the queen. She was a witch, and had bewitched the king and all the people. Secretly he told the king what he had seen and what he feared, and as the hard words came from his tongue, the carved images of the saints shook their heads as if they would say, "It is not so. Eliza is innocent."

But the archbishop interpreted it in another way; he believed that they witnessed against her, and were shaking their heads at her wickedness. Two large tears rolled down the king's cheeks, and he went home with doubt in his heart, and at night he pretended to sleep, but there came no real sleep to his eyes, for he saw Eliza get up every night and disappear in her own chamber. From day to day his brow became darker, and Eliza saw it and did not understand the reason, but it alarmed her and made her heart tremble for her brothers. Her hot tears glittered like pearls on the regal velvet and diamonds, while all who saw her were wishing they could be queens. In the meantime she had almost finished her task; only one coat of mail was wanting, but she had no flax left, and not a single nettle. Once more only, and for the last time, must she venture to the churchyard and pluck a few handfuls. She thought with terror of the solitary walk, and of the horrible ghouls, but her will was firm, as well as her trust in Providence. Eliza went, and the king and the archbishop followed her. They saw her vanish through the wicket gate into the churchyard, and when they came nearer they saw the ghouls sitting on the tombstone, as Eliza had seen them, and the king turned away his head, for he thought she was with them—she whose head had rested on his breast that very evening.

"The people must condemn her," said he, and she was very quickly condemned by everyone to suffer death by fire. Away from the gorgeous regal halls was she led to a dark, dreary cell, where the wind whistled through the iron bars. Instead of the velvet and silk dresses, they gave her the coats of mail which she had woven to cover her, and the bundle of nettles for a pillow; but nothing they could give her would have pleased her more. She continued her task with joy, and prayed for help, while the street-boys sang jeering songs about her, and not a soul comforted her with a kind word. Towards evening, she heard at the grating the flutter of a swan's wing, it was her youngest brother—he had found his sister, and she sobbed for joy, although she knew that very likely this would be the last night she would have to live. But still she could hope, for her task was almost finished, and her brothers were come. Then the archbishop arrived, to be with her during her last hours, as he had promised the king. But she shook her head, and begged him, by looks and gestures, not to stay; for in this night she knew she must finish her task, otherwise all her pain and tears and sleepless nights would have been suffered in vain. The archbishop withdrew, uttering bitter words against her; but poor Eliza knew that she was innocent, and diligently continued her work.

The little mice ran about the floor, they dragged the nettles to her feet, to help as well as they could; and the thrush sat outside the grating of the window, and sang to her the whole night long, as sweetly as possible, to keep up her spirits.

It was still twilight, and at least an hour before sunrise, when the eleven brothers stood at the castle gate, and demanded to be brought before the king. They were told it could not be, it was yet almost night, and as the king slept they dared not disturb him. They threatened, they entreated. Then the guard appeared, and even the king himself, inquiring what all the noise meant. At this moment the sun rose. The eleven brothers were seen no more, but eleven wild swans flew away over the castle.

And now all the people came streaming forth from the gates of the city, to see the witch burnt. An old horse drew the cart on which she sat. They had dressed her in a garment of coarse sackcloth. Her lovely hair hung loose on her shoulders, her cheeks were deadly pale, her lips moved silently, while her fingers still worked at the green flax. Even on the way to death, she would not give up her task. The ten coats of mail lay at her feet, she was working hard at the eleventh, while the mob jeered her and said, "See the witch, how she mutters! She has no hymnbook in her hand. She sits there with her ugly sorcery. Let us tear it in a thousand pieces."

And then they pressed towards her, and would have destroyed the coats of mail, but at the same moment eleven wild swans flew over her, and alighted on the cart. Then they flapped their large wings, and the crowd drew on one side in alarm.

"It is a sign from heaven that she is innocent," whispered many of them; but they ventured not to say it aloud.

As the executioner seized her by the hand, to lift her out of the cart, she hastily threw the eleven coats of mail over the swans, and they immediately became eleven handsome princes; but the youngest had a swan's wing, instead of an arm; for she had not been able to finish the last sleeve of the coat.

"Now I may speak," she exclaimed. "I am innocent."

Then the people, who saw what happened, bowed to her, as before a saint; but she sank lifeless in her brothers' arms, overcome with suspense, anguish, and pain.

"Yes, she is innocent," said the eldest brother; and then he related all that had taken place; and while he spoke there rose in the air a fragrance as from millions of roses. Every piece of faggot in the pile had taken root, and threw out branches, and appeared a thick hedge, large and high, covered with roses; while above all bloomed a white and shining flower, that glittered like a star. This flower the king plucked, and placed in Eliza's bosom, when she awoke from her swoon, with peace and happiness in her heart. And all the church bells rang of themselves, and the birds came in great troops. And a marriage procession returned to the castle, such as no king had ever before seen.

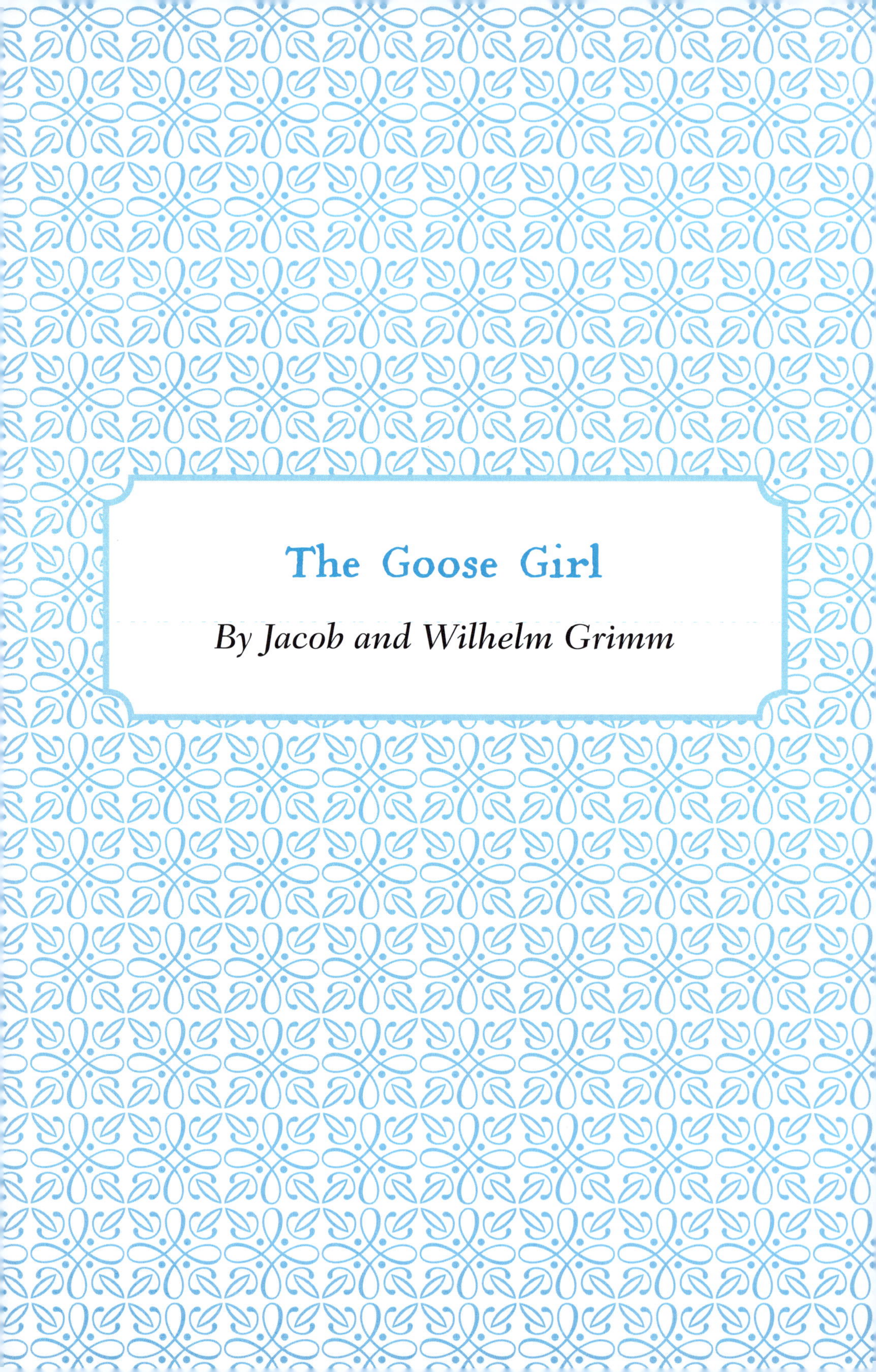
The Goose Girl
By Jacob and Wilhelm Grimm

The king of a great land died, and left his queen to take care of their only child. This child was a daughter, who was very beautiful; and her mother loved her dearly, and was very kind to her. And there was a good fairy too, who was fond of the princess, and helped her mother to watch over her. When she grew up, she was betrothed to a prince who lived a great way off; and as the time drew near for her to be married, she got ready to set off on her journey to his country. Then the queen, her mother, packed up a great many costly things; jewels, and gold, and silver; trinkets, fine dresses, and in short everything that became a royal bride. And she gave her a waiting maid to ride with her, and give her into the bridegroom's hands; and each had a horse for the journey. Now the princess's horse was the fairy's gift, and it was called Falada, and could speak.

When the time came for them to set out, the fairy went into her bedchamber, and took a little knife, and cut off a lock of her hair, and gave it to the princess, and said, "Take care of it, dear child; for it is a charm that may be of use to you on the road." Then they all took a sorrowful leave of the princess; and she put the lock of hair into her bosom, got upon her horse, and set off on her journey to her bridegroom's kingdom.

One day, as they were riding along by a brook, the princess began to feel very thirsty: and she said to her maid, "Pray get down, and fetch me some water in my golden cup out of yonder brook, for I want to drink."

"Nay," said the maid, "if you are thirsty, get off yourself, and stoop down by the water and drink; I shall not be your waiting maid any longer."

Then she was so thirsty that she got down, and knelt over the little brook, and drank; for she was frightened, and dared not bring out her golden cup; and she wept and said, "Alas! what will become of me?" And the lock answered her, and said:

"Alas! alas! if thy mother knew it,
Sadly, sadly, would she rue it."

But the princess was very gentle and meek, so she said nothing to her maid's ill behaviour, but got upon her horse again.

Then all rode farther on their journey, till the day grew so warm, and the sun so scorching, that the bride began to feel very thirsty again; and at last, when they came to a river, she forgot her maid's rude speech, and said, "Pray get down, and fetch me some water to drink in my golden cup."

But the maid answered her, and even spoke more haughtily than before: "Drink if you will, but I shall not be your waiting maid."

Then the princess was so thirsty that she got off her horse, and lay down, and held her head over the running stream, and cried and said, "What will become of me?" And the lock of hair answered her again:

"Alas! alas! if thy mother knew it,
Sadly, sadly, would she rue it."

And as she leaned down to drink, the lock of hair fell from her bosom, and floated away with the water. Now she was so frightened that she did not see it; but her maid saw it, and was very glad, for she knew the charm; and she saw that the poor bride would be in her power, now that she had lost the hair. So when the bride had done drinking, and would have got upon Falada again, the maid said, "I shall ride upon Falada, and you may have my horse instead"; so she was forced to give up her horse, and soon afterwards to take off her royal clothes and put on her maid's shabby ones.

At last, as they drew near the end of their journey, this treacherous servant threatened to kill her mistress if she ever told anyone what had happened. But Falada saw it all, and marked it well.

Then the waiting maid got upon Falada, and the real bride rode upon the other horse, and they went on in this way till at last they came to the royal court. There was great joy at their coming, and the prince flew to meet them, and lifted the maid from her horse, thinking she was the one who was to be his wife; and she was led upstairs to the royal chamber; but the true princess was told to stay in the court below.

Now the old king happened just then to have nothing else to do; so he amused himself by sitting at his kitchen window, looking at what was going on; and he saw her in the courtyard. As she looked very pretty, and too delicate for a waiting maid, he went up into the royal chamber to ask the bride who it was she had brought with her, that was thus left standing in the court below. "I brought her with me for the sake of her company on the road," said she; "pray give the girl some work to do, that she may not be idle."

The old king could not for some time think of any work for her to do;

but at last he said, "I have a lad who takes care of my geese; she may go and help him." Now the name of this lad, that the real bride was to help in watching the king's geese, was Curdken.

But the false bride said to the prince, "Dear husband, pray do me one piece of kindness."

"That I will," said the prince. "Then tell one of your slaughterers to cut off the head of the horse I rode upon, for it was very unruly, and plagued me sadly on the road"; but the truth was, she was very much afraid lest Falada should some day or other speak, and tell all she had done to the princess. She carried her point, and the faithful Falada was killed; but when the true princess heard of it, she wept, and begged the man to nail up Falada's head against a large dark gate of the city, through which she had to pass every morning and evening, that there she might still see him sometimes. Then the slaughterer said he would do as she wished; and cut off the head, and nailed it up under the dark gate.

Early the next morning, as she and Curdken went out through the gate, she said sorrowfully:

"Falada, Falada, there thou hangest!"

and the head answered:

"Bride, bride, there thou gangest!
Alas! alas! if thy mother knew it,
Sadly, sadly, would she rue it."

Then they went out of the city, and drove the geese on. And when she came to the meadow, she sat down upon a bank there, and let down her waving locks of hair, which were all of pure silver; and when Curdken saw it glitter in the sun, he ran up, and would have pulled some of the locks out, but she cried:

"Blow, breezes, blow!
Let Curdken's hat go!
Blow, breezes, blow!
Let him after it go!
O'er hills, dales, and rocks,
Away be it whirl'd

Till the silvery locks
Are all comb'd and curl'd!"

Then there came a wind, so strong that it blew off Curdken's hat; and away it flew over the hills: and he was forced to turn and run after it; till, by the time he came back, she had done combing and curling her hair, and had put it up again safe. Then he was very angry and sulky, and would not speak to her at all; but they watched the geese until it grew dark in the evening, and then drove them homewards.

The next morning, as they were going through the dark gate, the poor girl looked up at Falada's head, and cried:

"Falada, Falada, there thou hangest!"

and the head answered:

"Bride, bride, there thou gangest!
Alas! alas! if thy mother knew it,
Sadly, sadly, would she rue it."

Then she drove on the geese, and sat down again in the meadow, and began to comb out her hair as before; and Curdken ran up to her, and wanted to take hold of it; but she cried out quickly:

"Blow, breezes, blow!
Let Curdken's hat go!
Blow, breezes, blow!
Let him after it go!
O'er hills, dales, and rocks,
Away be it whirl'd
Till the silvery locks
Are all comb'd and curl'd!"

Then the wind came and blew away his hat; and off it flew a great way, over the hills and far away, so that he had to run after it; and when he came back she had bound up her hair again, and all was safe. So they watched the geese till it grew dark.

In the evening, after they came home, Curdken went to the old king, and said, "I cannot have that strange girl to help me to keep the geese any longer."

"Why?" said the king.

"Because, instead of doing any good, she does nothing but tease me all day long." Then the king made him tell him what had happened.

And Curdken said, "When we go in the morning through the dark gate with our flock of geese, she cries and talks with the head of a horse that hangs upon the wall, and says:

"Falada, Falada, there thou hangest!"

and the head answers:

"Bride, bride, there thou gangest!
Alas! alas! if thy mother knew it,
Sadly, sadly, would she rue it."

And Curdken went on telling the king what had happened upon the meadow where the geese fed; how his hat was blown away; and how he was forced to run after it, and to leave his flock of geese to themselves. But the old king told the boy to go out again the next day: and when morning came, he placed himself behind the dark gate, and heard how she spoke to Falada, and how Falada answered. Then he went into the field, and hid himself in a bush by the meadow's side; and he soon saw with his own eyes how they drove the flock of geese; and how, after a little time, she let down her hair that glittered in the sun. And then he heard her say:

"Blow, breezes, blow!
Let Curdken's hat go!
Blow, breezes, blow!
Let him after it go!
O'er hills, dales, and rocks,
Away be it whirl'd
Till the silvery locks
Are all comb'd and curl'd!"

And soon came a gale of wind, and carried away Curdken's hat, and away went Curdken after it, while the girl went on combing and curling her hair. All this the old king saw: so he went home without being seen; and when the little goose girl came back in the evening he called her aside, and asked her why she did so: but she burst into tears, and said, "That I must not tell you or any man, or I shall lose my life."

But the old king begged so hard, that she had no peace till she had told him all the tale, from beginning to end, word for word. And it was very lucky for her that she did so, for when she had done the king ordered royal clothes to be put upon her, and gazed on her with wonder, she was so beautiful. Then he called his son and told him that he had only a false bride; for that she was merely a waiting maid, while the true bride stood by. And the young king rejoiced when he saw her beauty, and heard how meek and patient she had been; and without saying anything to the false bride, the king ordered a great feast to be got ready for all his court. The bridegroom sat at the top, with the false princess on one side, and the true one on the other; but nobody knew her again, for her beauty was quite dazzling to their eyes; and she did not seem at all like the little goose girl, now that she had her brilliant dress on.

When they had eaten and drank, and were very merry, the old king said he would tell them a tale. So he began, and told all the story of the princess, as if it was one that he had once heard; and he asked the true waiting maid what she thought ought to be done to anyone who would behave thus. "Nothing better," said this false bride, "than that she should be thrown into a cask stuck round with sharp nails, and that two white horses should be put to it, and should drag it from street to street till she was dead."

"Thou art she!" said the old king; "and as thou has judged thyself, so shall it be done to thee." And the young king was then married to his true wife, and they reigned over the kingdom in peace and happiness all their lives; and the good fairy came to see them, and restored the faithful Falada to life again.

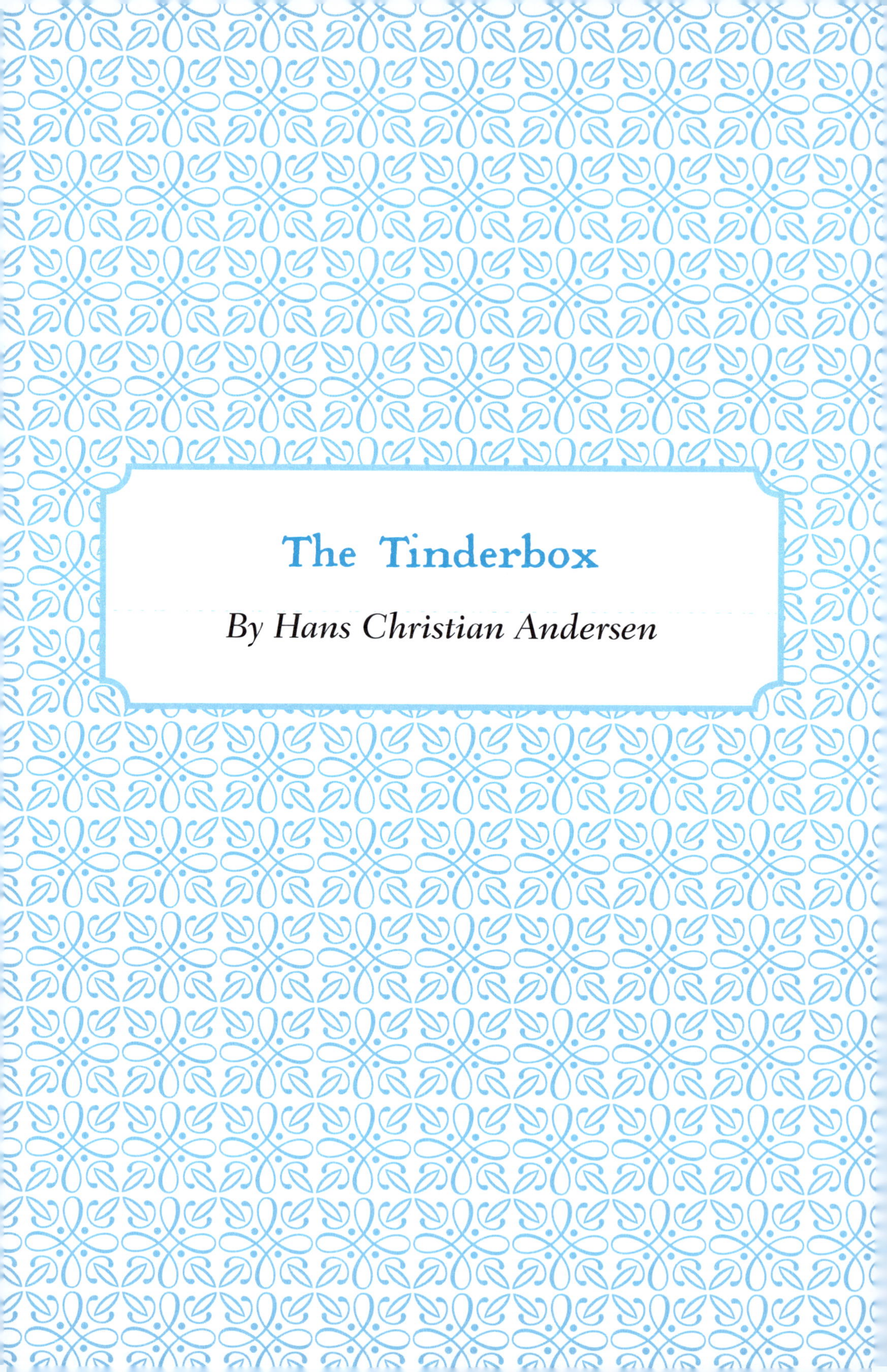

The Tinderbox

By Hans Christian Andersen

A soldier came marching along the high road: "Left, right—left, right." He had his knapsack on his back, and a sword at his side; he had been to the wars, and was now returning home.

As he walked on, he met a very frightful-looking old witch in the road. Her underlip hung quite down on her breast, and she stopped and said, "Good evening, soldier; you have a very fine sword, and a large knapsack, and you are a real soldier; so you shall have as much money as ever you like."

"Thank you, old witch," said the soldier.

"Do you see that large tree," said the witch, pointing to a tree which stood beside them. "Well, it is quite hollow inside, and you must climb to the top, when you will see a hole, through which you can let yourself down into the tree to a great depth. I will tie a rope round your body, so that I can pull you up again when you call out to me."

"But what am I to do, down there in the tree?" asked the soldier.

"Get money," she replied, "for you must know that when you reach the ground under the tree, you will find yourself in a large hall, lighted up by three hundred lamps; you will then see three doors, which can be easily opened, for the keys are in all the locks. On entering the first of the chambers, to which these doors lead, you will see a large chest, standing in the middle of the floor, and upon it a dog seated, with a pair of eyes as large as teacups. But you need not be at all afraid of him; I will give you my blue checked apron, which you must spread upon the floor, and then boldly seize hold of the dog, and place him upon it. You can then open the chest, and take from it as many pence as you please, they are only copper pence; but if you would rather have silver money, you must go into the second chamber. Here you will find another dog, with eyes as big as millwheels; but do not let that trouble you. Place him upon my apron, and then take what money you please. If, however, you like gold best, enter the third chamber, where there is another chest full of it. The dog who sits on this chest is very dreadful; his eyes are as big as a tower, but do not mind him. If he also is placed upon my apron, he cannot hurt you, and you may take from the chest what gold you will."

"This is not a bad story," said the soldier; "but what am I to give you, you old witch? for, of course, you do not mean to tell me all this for nothing."

"No," said the witch; "but I do not ask for a single penny. Only promise to bring me an old tinderbox, which my grandmother left behind the last time she went down there."

"Very well; I promise. Now tie the rope round my body."

"Here it is," replied the witch; "and here is my blue checked apron."

As soon as the rope was tied, the soldier climbed up the tree, and let himself down through the hollow to the ground beneath; and here he found, as the witch had told him, a large hall, in which many hundred lamps were all burning. Then he opened the first door. "Ah!" there sat the dog, with the eyes as large as teacups, staring at him.

"You're a pretty fellow," said the soldier, seizing him, and placing him on the witch's apron, while he filled his pockets from the chest with as many pieces as they would hold. Then he closed the lid, seated the dog upon it again, and walked into another chamber, And, sure enough, there sat the dog with eyes as big as millwheels.

"You had better not look at me in that way," said the soldier; "you will make your eyes water"; and then he seated him also upon the apron, and opened the chest. But when he saw what a quantity of silver money it contained, he very quickly threw away all the coppers he had taken, and filled his pockets and his knapsack with nothing but silver.

Then he went into the third room, and there the dog was really hideous; his eyes were, truly, as big as towers, and they turned round and round in his head like wheels.

"Good morning," said the soldier, touching his cap, for he had never seen such a dog in his life. But after looking at him more closely, he thought he had been civil enough, so he placed him on the floor, and opened the chest. Good gracious, what a quantity of gold there was! enough to buy all the sugar-sticks of the sweet-stuff women; all the tin soldiers, whips, and rocking horses in the world, or even the whole town itself. There was, indeed, an immense quantity. So the soldier now threw away all the silver money he had taken, and filled his pockets and his knapsack with gold instead; and not only his pockets and his knapsack, but even his cap and boots, so that he could scarcely walk.

He was really rich now; so he replaced the dog on the chest, closed the door, and called up through the tree, "Now pull me out, you old witch."

"Have you got the tinderbox?" asked the witch.

"No; I declare I quite forgot it." So he went back and fetched the tinderbox, and then the witch drew him up out of the tree, and he stood again in the high road, with his pockets, his knapsack, his cap, and his boots full of gold.

"What are you going to do with the tinderbox?" asked the soldier.

"That is nothing to you," replied the witch; "you have the money, now give me the tinderbox."

"I tell you what," said the soldier, "if you don't tell me what you are going to do with it, I will draw my sword and cut off your head."

"No," said the witch.

The soldier immediately cut off her head, and there she lay on the ground. Then he tied up all his money in her apron, and slung it on his back like a bundle, put the tinderbox in his pocket, and walked off to the nearest town. It was a very nice town, and he put up at the best inn, and ordered a dinner of all his favorite dishes, for now he was rich and had plenty of money.

The servant, who cleaned his boots, thought they certainly were a shabby pair to be worn by such a rich gentleman, for he had not yet bought any new ones. The next day, however, he procured some good clothes and proper boots, so that our soldier soon became known as a fine gentleman, and the people visited him, and told him all the wonders that were to be seen in the town, and of the king's beautiful daughter, the princess.

"Where can I see her?" asked the soldier.

"She is not to be seen at all," they said; "she lives in a large copper castle, surrounded by walls and towers. No one but the king himself can pass in or out, for there has been a prophecy that she will marry a common soldier, and the king cannot bear to think of such a marriage."

"I should like very much to see her," thought the soldier; but he could not obtain permission to do so. However, he passed a very pleasant time; went to the theatre, drove in the king's garden, and gave a great deal of money to the poor, which was very good of him; he remembered what it had been in olden times to be without a shilling. Now he was rich, had fine clothes, and many friends, who all declared he was a fine fellow and a real gentleman, and all this gratified him exceedingly. But his money would not last forever; and as he spent and gave away a great deal daily, and received none, he found himself at last with only two shillings left.

So he was obliged to leave his elegant rooms, and live in a little garret under the roof, where he had to clean his own boots, and even mend them with a large needle. None of his friends came to see him, there were too many stairs to mount up. One dark evening, he had not even a penny to buy a candle; then all at once he remembered that there was a piece of candle stuck in the tinderbox, which he had brought from the old tree, into which the witch had helped him.

He found the tinderbox, but no sooner had he struck a few sparks from the flint and steel, than the door flew open and the dog with eyes as big as teacups, whom he had seen while down in the tree, stood before him, and said, "What orders, master?"

"Hallo," said the soldier; "well this is a pleasant tinderbox, if it brings me all I wish for."

"Bring me some money," said he to the dog.

He was gone in a moment, and presently returned, carrying a large bag of coppers in his month. The soldier very soon discovered after this the value of the tinderbox. If he struck the flint once, the dog who sat on the chest of copper money made his appearance; if twice, the dog came from the chest of silver; and if three times, the dog with eyes like towers, who watched over the gold. The soldier had now plenty of money; he returned to his elegant rooms, and reappeared in his fine clothes, so that his friends knew him again directly, and made as much of him as before.

After a while he began to think it was very strange that no one could get a look at the princess. "Everyone says she is very beautiful," thought he to himself; "but what is the use of that if she is to be shut up in a copper castle surrounded by so many towers. Can I by any means get to see her? Stop! Where is my tinderbox?" Then he struck a light, and in a moment the dog, with eyes as big as teacups, stood before him.

"It is midnight," said the soldier, "yet I should very much like to see the princess, if only for a moment."

The dog disappeared instantly, and before the soldier could even look round, he returned with the princess. She was lying on the dog's back asleep, and looked so lovely, that everyone who saw her would know she was a real princess. The soldier could not help kissing her, true soldier as he was. Then the dog ran back with the princess; but in the morning, while at breakfast with the king and queen, she told them what a singular dream she had had during the night, of a dog and a soldier, that she had ridden on the dog's back, and been kissed by the soldier.

"That is a very pretty story, indeed," said the queen. So the next night one of the old ladies of the court was set to watch by the princess's bed, to discover whether it really was a dream, or what else it might be.

The soldier longed very much to see the princess once more, so he sent for the dog again in the night to fetch her, and to run with her as fast as ever he could. But the old lady put on water boots, and ran after him as quickly as he did, and found that he carried the princess into a large house. She thought it would help her to remember the place if she made a large cross on the door with a piece of chalk. Then she went home to bed, and the dog presently returned with the princess. But when he saw that a cross had been made on the door of the house, where the soldier lived, he took another piece of chalk and made crosses on all the doors in the town, so that the lady-in-waiting might not be able to find out the right door.

Early the next morning the king and queen accompanied the lady and all the officers of the household, to see where the princess had been.

"Here it is," said the king, when they came to the first door with a cross on it.

"No, my dear husband, it must be that one," said the queen, pointing to a second door having a cross also.

"And here is one, and there is another!" they all exclaimed; for there were crosses on all the doors in every direction.

So they felt it would be useless to search any farther. But the queen was a very clever woman; she could do a great deal more than merely ride in a carriage. She took her large gold scissors, cut a piece of silk into squares, and made a neat little bag. This bag she filled with buckwheat flour, and tied it round the princess's neck; and then she cut a small hole in the bag, so that the flour might be scattered on the ground as the princess went along. During the night, the dog came again and carried the princess on his back, and ran with her to the soldier, who loved her very much, and wished that he had been a prince, so that he might have her for a wife. The dog did not observe how the flour ran out of the bag all the way from the castle wall to the soldier's house, and even up to the window, where he had climbed with the princess. Therefore in the morning the king and queen found out where their daughter had been, and the soldier was taken up and put in prison.

Oh, how dark and disagreeable it was as he sat there, and the people said to him, "Tomorrow you will be hanged." It was not very pleasant news, and besides, he had left the tinderbox at the inn. In the morning he could see through the iron grating of the little window how the people were hastening out of the town to see him hanged; he heard the drums beating, and saw the soldiers marching. Everyone ran out to look at them, and a shoemaker's boy, with a leather apron and slippers on, galloped by so fast, that one of his slippers flew off and struck against the wall where the soldier sat looking through the iron grating. "Hallo, you shoemaker's boy, you need not be in such a hurry," cried the soldier to him. "There will be nothing to see till I come; but if you will run to the house where I have been living, and bring me my tinderbox, you shall have four shillings, but you must put your best foot foremost."

The shoemaker's boy liked the idea of getting the four shillings, so he ran very fast and fetched the tinderbox, and gave it to the soldier. And now we shall see what happened. Outside the town a large gibbet had been erected, round which stood the soldiers and several thousands of people. The king and the queen sat on splendid thrones opposite to the judges and the whole council. The soldier already stood on the ladder; but as they were about to place the rope around his neck, he said that an innocent request was often granted to a poor criminal before he suffered death. He wished very much to smoke a pipe, as it would be the last pipe he should ever smoke in the world. The king could not refuse this request, so the soldier took his tinderbox, and struck fire, once, twice, thrice, and there in a moment stood all the dogs—the one with eyes as big as teacups, the one with eyes as large as millwheels, and the third, whose eyes were like towers. "Help me now, that I may not be hanged," cried the soldier.

And the dogs fell upon the judges and all the councillors; seized one by the legs, and another by the nose, and tossed them many feet high in the air, so that they fell down and were dashed to pieces.

"I will not be touched," said the king. But the largest dog seized him, as well as the queen, and threw them after the others. Then the soldiers and all the people were afraid, and cried, "Good soldier, you shall be our king, and you shall marry the beautiful princess."

So they placed the soldier in the king's carriage, and the three dogs ran on in front and cried "Hurrah!" and the little boys whistled through their fingers, and the soldiers presented arms. The princess came out of the copper castle, and became queen, which was very pleasing to her. The wedding festivities lasted a whole week, and the dogs sat at the table, and stared with all their eyes.

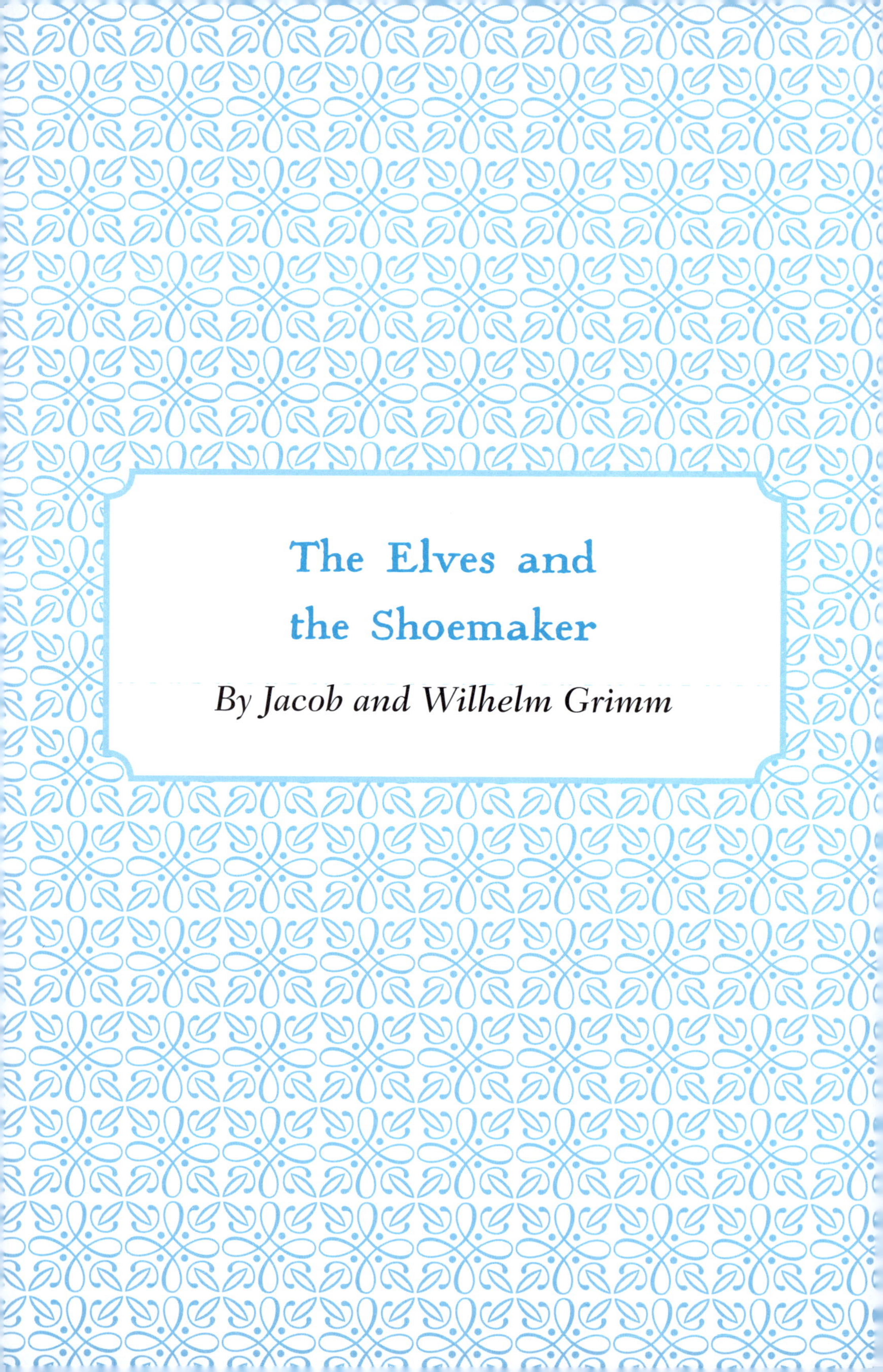

The Elves and the Shoemaker

By Jacob and Wilhelm Grimm

There was once a shoemaker, who worked very hard and was very honest: but still he could not earn enough to live upon; and at last all he had in the world was gone, save just leather enough to make one pair of shoes.

Then he cut his leather out, all ready to make up the next day, meaning to rise early in the morning to his work. His conscience was clear and his heart light amidst all his troubles; so he went peaceably to bed, left all his cares to heaven, and soon fell asleep. In the morning after he had said his prayers, he sat himself down to his work; when, to his great wonder, there stood the shoes all ready made, upon the table. The good man knew not what to say or think at such an odd thing happening. He looked at the workmanship; there was not one false stitch in the whole job; all was so neat and true, that it was quite a masterpiece.

The same day a customer came in, and the shoes suited him so well that he willingly paid a price higher than usual for them; and the poor shoemaker, with the money, bought leather enough to make two pairs more. In the evening he cut out the work, and went to bed early, that he might get up and begin betimes next day; but he was saved all the trouble, for when he got up in the morning the work was done ready to his hand. Soon in came buyers, who paid him handsomely for his goods, so that he bought leather enough for four pair more. He cut out the work again overnight and found it done in the morning, as before; and so it went on for some time: what was got ready in the evening was always done by daybreak, and the good man soon became thriving and well-off again.

One evening, about Christmastime, as he and his wife were sitting over the fire chatting together, he said to her, "I should like to sit up and watch tonight, that we may see who it is that comes and does my work for me." The wife liked the thought; so they left a light burning, and hid themselves in a corner of the room, behind a curtain that was hung up there, and watched what would happen.

As soon as it was midnight, there came in two little naked dwarfs; and they sat themselves upon the shoemaker's bench, took up all the work that was cut out, and began to ply with their little fingers, stitching and rapping and tapping away at such a rate, that the shoemaker was all wonder, and could not take his eyes off them. And on they went, till the job was quite done, and the shoes stood ready for use upon the table. This was long before daybreak; and then they bustled away as quick as lightning.

The next day the wife said to the shoemaker. "These little wights have made us rich, and we ought to be thankful to them, and do them a good turn if we can. I am quite sorry to see them run about as they do; and indeed it is not very decent, for they have nothing upon their backs to keep off the cold. I'll tell you what, I will make each of them a shirt, and a coat and waistcoat, and a pair of pantaloons into the bargain; and do you make each of them a little pair of shoes."

The thought pleased the good cobbler very much; and one evening, when all the things were ready, they laid them on the table, instead of the work that they used to cut out, and then went and hid themselves, to watch what the little elves would do.

About midnight in they came, dancing and skipping, hopped round the room, and then went to sit down to their work as usual; but when they saw the clothes lying for them, they laughed and chuckled, and seemed mightily delighted.

Then they dressed themselves in the twinkling of an eye, and danced and capered and sprang about, as merry as could be; till at last they danced out at the door, and away over the green.

The good couple saw them no more; but everything went well with them from that time forward, as long as they lived.

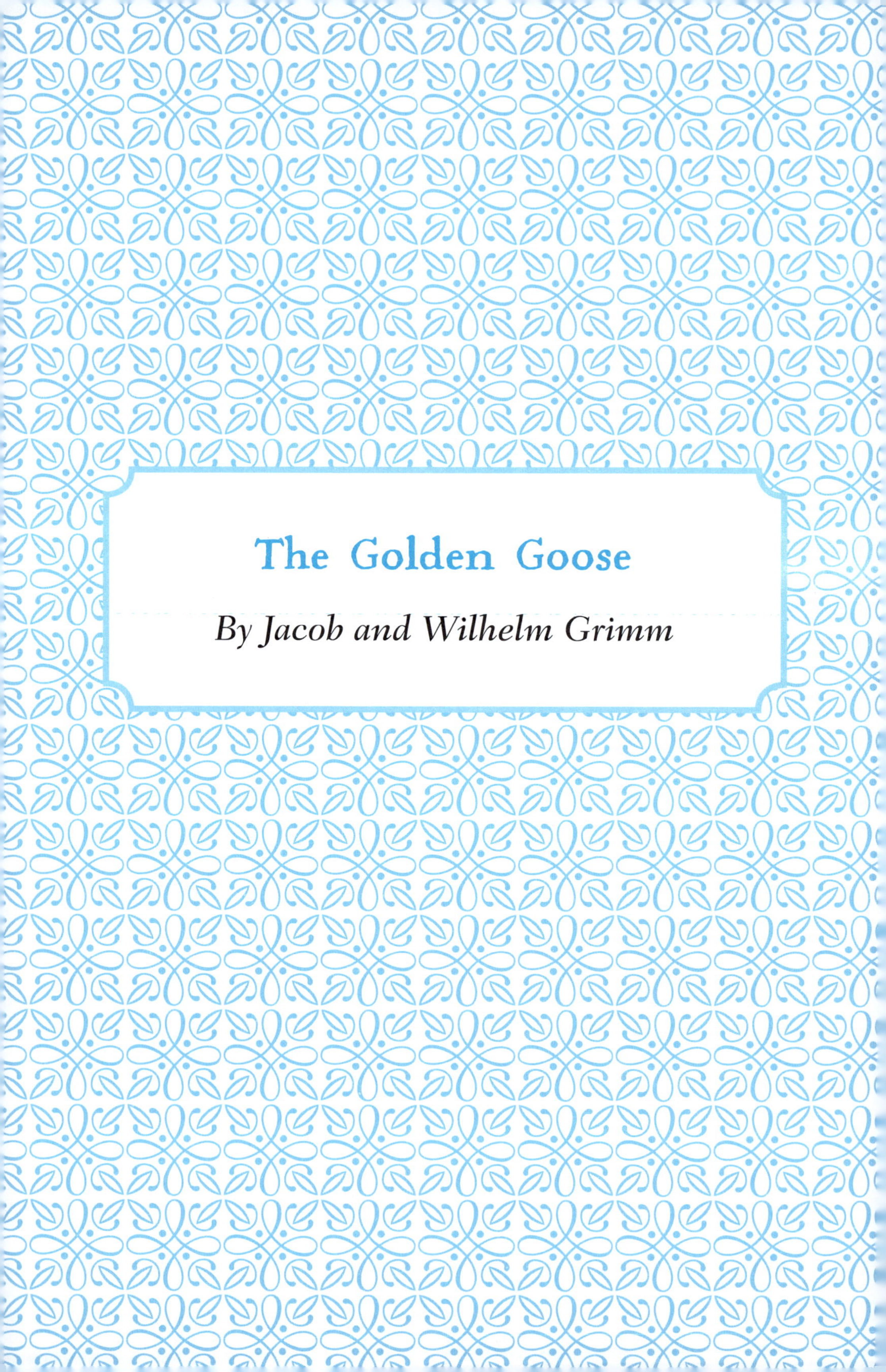

The Golden Goose

By Jacob and Wilhelm Grimm

There was a man who had three sons, the youngest of whom was called Dummling, and was despised, mocked, and sneered at on every occasion.

It happened that the eldest wanted to go into the forest to hew wood, and before he went his mother gave him a beautiful sweet cake and a bottle of wine in order that he might not suffer from hunger or thirst.

When he entered the forest he met a little grey-haired old man who bade him good day, and said: "Do give me a piece of cake out of your pocket, and let me have a draught of your wine; I am so hungry and thirsty."

But the clever son answered: "If I give you my cake and wine, I shall have none for myself; be off with you," and he left the little man standing and went on.

But when he began to hew down a tree, it was not long before he made a false stroke, and the axe cut him in the arm, so that he had to go home and have it bound up. And this was the little grey man's doing.

After this the second son went into the forest, and his mother gave him, like the eldest, a cake and a bottle of wine. The little old grey man met him likewise, and asked him for a piece of cake and a drink of wine. But the second son, too, said sensibly enough: "What I give you will be taken away from myself; be off!" and he left the little man standing and went on. His punishment, however, was not delayed; when he had made a few blows at the tree he struck himself in the leg, so that he had to be carried home.

Then Dummling said: "Father, do let me go and cut wood."

The father answered: "Your brothers have hurt themselves with it, leave it alone, you do not understand anything about it."

But Dummling begged so long that at last he said: "Just go then, you will get wiser by hurting yourself." His mother gave him a cake made with water and baked in the cinders, and with it a bottle of sour beer.

When he came to the forest the little old grey man met him likewise, and greeting him, said: "Give me a piece of your cake and a drink out of your bottle; I am so hungry and thirsty."

Dummling answered: "I have only cinder cake and sour beer; if that pleases you, we will sit down and eat." So they sat down, and when

Dummling pulled out his cinder cake, it was a fine sweet cake, and the sour beer had become good wine. So they ate and drank, and after that the little man said: "Since you have a good heart, and are willing to divide what you have, I will give you good luck. There stands an old tree; cut it down, and you will find something at the roots." Then the little man took leave of him.

Dummling went and cut down the tree, and when it fell there was a goose sitting in the roots with feathers of pure gold. He lifted her up, and taking her with him, went to an inn where he thought he would stay the night. Now the host had three daughters, who saw the goose and were curious to know what such a wonderful bird might be, and would have liked to have one of its golden feathers.

The eldest thought: "I shall soon find an opportunity of pulling out a feather," and as soon as Dummling had gone out she seized the goose by the wing, but her finger and hand remained sticking fast to it.

The second came soon afterwards, thinking only of how she might get a feather for herself, but she had scarcely touched her sister than she was held fast.

At last the third also came with the like intent, and the others screamed out: "Keep away; for goodness' sake keep away!" But she did not understand why she was to keep away. "The others are there," she thought, "I may as well be there too," and ran to them; but as soon as she had touched her sister, she remained sticking fast to her. So they had to spend the night with the goose.

The next morning Dummling took the goose under his arm and set out, without troubling himself about the three girls who were hanging on to it. They were obliged to run after him continually, now left, now right, wherever his legs took him.

In the middle of the fields the parson met them, and when he saw the procession he said: "For shame, you good-for-nothing girls, why are you running across the fields after this young man? Is that seemly?" At the same time he seized the youngest by the hand in order to pull her away, but as soon as he touched her he likewise stuck fast, and was himself obliged to run behind.

Before long the sexton came by and saw his master, the parson, running behind three girls. He was astonished at this and called out: "Hi! your reverence, whither away so quickly? Do not forget that we have a christening today!" and running after him he took him by the sleeve, but was also held fast to it.

Whilst the five were trotting thus one behind the other, two labourers came with their hoes from the fields; the parson called out to them and begged that they would set him and the sexton free. But they had scarcely touched the sexton when they were held fast, and now there were seven of them running behind Dummling and the goose.

Soon afterwards he came to a city, where a king ruled who had a daughter who was so serious that no one could make her laugh. So he had put forth a decree that whosoever should be able to make her laugh should marry her. When Dummling heard this, he went with his goose and all her train before the king's daughter, and as soon as she saw the seven people running on and on, one behind the other, she began to laugh quite loudly, and as if she would never stop. Thereupon Dummling asked to have her for his wife; but the king did not like the son-in-law, and made all manner of excuses and said he must first produce a man who could drink a cellarful of wine. Dummling thought of the little grey man, who could certainly help him; so he went into the forest, and in the same place where he had felled the tree, he saw a man sitting, who had a very sorrowful face. Dummling asked him what he was taking to heart so sorely, and he answered: "I have such a great thirst and cannot quench it; cold water I cannot stand, a barrel of wine I have just emptied, but that to me is like a drop on a hot stone!"

"There, I can help you," said Dummling, "just come with me and you shall be satisfied."

He led him into the king's cellar, and the man bent over the huge barrels, and drank and drank till his loins hurt, and before the day was out he had emptied all the barrels. Then Dummling asked once more for his bride, but the king was vexed that such an ugly fellow, whom everyone called Dummling, should take away his daughter, and he made a new condition; he must first find a man who could eat a whole mountain of bread. Dummling did not think long, but went straight into the forest, where in the same place there sat a man who was tying up his body with a strap, and making an awful face, and saying: "I have eaten a whole overfull of rolls, but what good is that when one has such a hunger as I? My stomach remains empty, and I must tie myself up if I am not to die of hunger."

At this Dummling was glad, and said: "Get up and come with me; you shall eat yourself full." He led him to the king's palace where all the flour in the whole kingdom was collected, and from it he caused a huge mountain of bread to be baked. The man from the forest stood before it, began to eat, and by the end of one day the whole mountain had vanished. Then Dummling for the third time asked for his bride; but the king again sought a way out, and ordered a ship which could sail on land and on water. "As soon as you come sailing back in it," said he, "you shall have my daughter for wife."

Dummling went straight into the forest, and there sat the little grey man to whom he had given his cake. When he heard what Dummling wanted, he said: "Since you have given me to eat and to drink, I will give you the ship; and I do all this because you once were kind to me." Then he gave him the ship which could sail on land and water, and when the king saw that, he could no longer prevent him from having his daughter. The wedding was celebrated, and after the king's death, Dummling inherited his kingdom and lived for a long time contentedly with his wife.

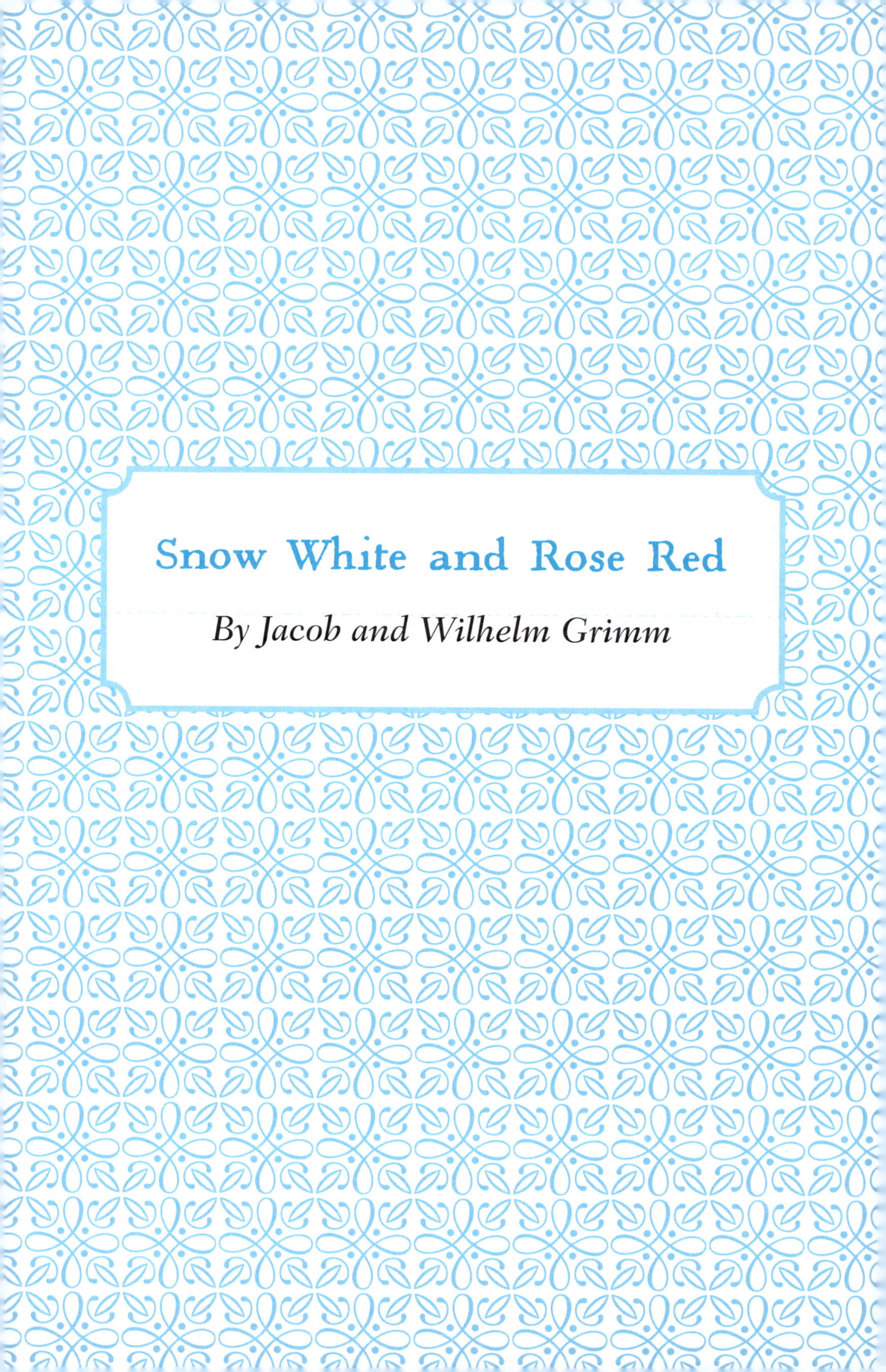

Snow White and Rose Red

By Jacob and Wilhelm Grimm

There was once a poor widow who lived in a lonely cottage. In front of the cottage was a garden wherein stood two rose trees, one of which bore white and the other red roses. She had two children who were like the two rose trees, and one was called Snow White, and the other Rose Red. They were as good and happy, as busy and cheerful as ever two children in the world were, only Snow White was more quiet and gentle than Rose Red. Rose Red liked better to run about in the meadows and fields seeking flowers and catching butterflies; but Snow White sat at home with her mother, and helped her with her housework, or read to her when there was nothing to do.

The two children were so fond of one another that they always held each other by the hand when they went out together, and when Snow White said: "We will not leave each other," Rose Red answered: "Never so long as we live," and their mother would add: "What one has she must share with the other."

They often ran about the forest alone and gathered red berries, and no beasts did them any harm, but came close to them trustfully. The little hare would eat a cabbage leaf out of their hands, the roe grazed by their side, the stag leapt merrily by them, and the birds sat still upon the boughs, and sang whatever they knew.

No mishap overtook them; if they had stayed too late in the forest, and night came on, they laid themselves down near one another upon the moss, and slept until morning came, and their mother knew this and did not worry on their account.

Once when they had spent the night in the wood and the dawn had roused them, they saw a beautiful child in a shining white dress sitting near their bed. He got up and looked quite kindly at them, but said nothing and went into the forest. And when they looked round they found that they had been sleeping quite close to a precipice, and would certainly have fallen into it in the darkness if they had gone only a few paces further. And their mother told them that it must have been the angel who watches over good children.

Snow White and Rose Red kept their mother's little cottage so neat that it was a pleasure to look inside it. In the summer Rose Red took care of the house, and every morning laid a wreath of flowers by her mother's bed before she awoke, in which was a rose from each tree. In the winter Snow White lit the fire and hung the kettle on the hob. The kettle was of brass and shone like gold, so brightly was it polished. In the evening, when the snowflakes fell, the mother said: "Go, Snow White, and bolt the door," and then they sat round the hearth, and the mother took her spectacles and read aloud out of a large book, and the two girls listened as they sat and spun. And close by them lay a lamb upon the floor, and behind them upon a perch sat a white dove with its head hidden beneath its wings.

One evening, as they were thus sitting comfortably together, someone knocked at the door as if he wished to be let in. The mother said: "Quick, Rose Red, open the door, it must be a traveller who is seeking shelter." Rose Red went and pushed back the bolt, thinking that it was a poor man, but it was not; it was a bear that stretched his broad, black head within the door.

Rose Red screamed and sprang back, the lamb bleated, the dove fluttered, and Snow White hid herself behind her mother's bed. But the bear began to speak and said: "Do not be afraid, I will do you no harm! I am half-frozen, and only want to warm myself a little beside you."

"Poor bear," said the mother, "lie down by the fire, only take care that you do not burn your coat." Then she cried: "Snow White, Rose Red, come out, the bear will do you no harm, he means well." So they both came out, and by and by the lamb and dove came nearer, and were not afraid of him. The bear said: "Here, children, knock the snow out of my coat a little"; so they brought the broom and swept the bear's hide clean; and he stretched himself by the fire and growled contentedly and comfortably. It was not long before they grew quite at home, and played tricks with their clumsy guest. They tugged his hair with their hands, put their feet upon his back and rolled him about, or they took a hazel switch and beat him, and when he growled they laughed. But the bear took it all in good part, only when they were too rough he called out:

"Leave me alive, children,
Snow White, Rose Red,
Will you beat your wooer dead?"

When it was bedtime, and the others went to bed, the mother said to the bear: "You can lie there by the hearth, and then you will be safe from the cold and the bad weather." As soon as day dawned the two children let him out, and he trotted across the snow into the forest.

Henceforth the bear came every evening at the same time, laid himself down by the hearth, and let the children amuse themselves with him as much as they liked; and they got so used to him that the doors were never fastened until their black friend had arrived.

When spring had come and all outside was green, the bear said one morning to Snow White: "Now I must go away, and cannot come back for the whole summer."

"Where are you going, then, dear bear?" asked Snow White.

"I must go into the forest and guard my treasures from the wicked dwarfs. In the winter, when the earth is frozen hard, they are obliged to stay below and cannot work their way through; but now, when the sun has thawed and warmed the earth, they break through it, and come out to pry and steal; and what once gets into their hands, and in their caves, does not easily see daylight again."

Snow White was quite sorry at his departure, and as she unbolted the door for him, and the bear was hurrying out, he caught against the bolt and a piece of his hairy coat was torn off, and it seemed to Snow White as if she had seen gold shining through it, but she was not sure about it. The bear ran away quickly, and was soon out of sight behind the trees.

A short time afterwards the mother sent her children into the forest to get firewood. There they found a big tree which lay felled on the ground, and close by the trunk something was jumping backwards and forwards in the grass, but they could not make out what it was. When they came nearer they saw a dwarf with an old, withered face and a snow white beard a yard long. The end of the beard was caught in a crevice of the tree, and the little fellow was jumping about like a dog tied to a rope, and did not know what to do.

He glared at the girls with his fiery red eyes and cried: "Why do you stand there? Can you not come here and help me?"

"What are you up to, little man?" asked Rose Red.

"You stupid, prying goose!" answered the dwarf: "I was going to split the tree to get a little wood for cooking. The little bit of food that we people get is immediately burnt up with heavy logs; we do not swallow so much as you coarse, greedy folk. I had just driven the wedge safely in, and everything was going as I wished; but the cursed wedge was too smooth and suddenly sprang out, and the tree closed so quickly that

I could not pull out my beautiful white beard; so now it is tight and I cannot get away, and the silly, sleek, milk-faced things laugh! Ugh! how odious you are!"

The children tried very hard, but they could not pull the beard out, it was caught too fast. "I will run and fetch someone," said Rose Red.

"You senseless goose!" snarled the dwarf; "why should you fetch someone? You are already two too many for me; can you not think of something better?"

"Don't be impatient," said Snow White, "I will help you," and she pulled her scissors out of her pocket, and cut off the end of the beard.

As soon as the dwarf felt himself free he laid hold of a bag which lay amongst the roots of the tree, and which was full of gold, and lifted it up, grumbling to himself: "Uncouth people, to cut off a piece of my fine beard. Bad luck to you!" and then he swung the bag upon his back, and went off without even once looking at the children.

Some time afterwards Snow White and Rose Red went to catch a dish of fish. As they came near the brook they saw something like a large grasshopper jumping towards the water, as if it were going to leap in. They ran to it and found it was the dwarf. "Where are you going?" said Rose Red; "you surely don't want to go into the water?"

"I am not such a fool!" cried the dwarf; "don't you see that the accursed fish wants to pull me in?" The little man had been sitting there fishing, and unluckily the wind had tangled up his beard with the fishing-line; a moment later a big fish made a bite and the feeble creature had not strength to pull it out; the fish kept the upper hand and pulled the dwarf towards him. He held on to all the reeds and rushes, but it was of little good, for he was forced to follow the movements of the fish, and was in urgent danger of being dragged into the water.

The girls came just in time; they held him fast and tried to free his beard from the line, but all in vain, beard and line were entangled fast together. There was nothing to do but to bring out the scissors and cut the beard, whereby a small part of it was lost. When the dwarf saw that he screamed out: "Is that civil, you toadstool, to disfigure a man's face? Was it not enough to clip off the end of my beard? Now you have cut off the best part of it. I cannot let myself be seen by my people. I wish you had been made to run the soles off your shoes!" Then he took out a sack of pearls which lay in the rushes, and without another word he dragged it away and disappeared behind a stone.

It happened that soon afterwards the mother sent the two children to the town to buy needles and thread, and laces and ribbons. The road led them across a heath upon which huge pieces of rock lay strewn about. There they noticed a large bird hovering in the air, flying slowly round and round above them; it sank lower and lower, and at last settled near a rock not far away. Immediately they heard a loud, piteous cry. They ran up and saw with horror that the eagle had seized their old acquaintance the dwarf, and was going to carry him off.

The children, full of pity, at once took tight hold of the little man, and pulled against the eagle so long that at last he let his booty go. As soon as the dwarf had recovered from his first fright he cried with his shrill voice: "Could you not have done it more carefully! You dragged at my brown coat so that it is all torn and full of holes, you clumsy creatures!" Then he took up a sack full of precious stones, and slipped away again under the rock into his hole. The girls, who by this time were used to his ingratitude, went on their way and did their business in town.

As they crossed the heath again on their way home they surprised the dwarf, who had emptied out his bag of precious stones in a clean spot, and had not thought that anyone would come there so late. The evening sun shone upon the brilliant stones; they glittered and sparkled with all colours so beautifully that the children stood still and stared at them. "Why do you stand gaping there?" cried the dwarf, and his ashen-grey face became copper red with rage. He was still cursing when a loud growling was heard, and a black bear came trotting towards them out of the forest. The dwarf sprang up in a fright, but he could not reach his cave, for the bear was already close. Then in the dread of his heart he cried: "Dear Mr. Bear, spare me, I will give you all my treasures; look, the beautiful jewels lying there! Grant me my life; what do you want with such a slender little fellow as I? you would not feel me between your teeth. Come, take these two wicked girls, they are tender morsels for you, fat as young quails; for mercy's sake eat them!" The bear took no heed of his words, but gave the wicked creature a single blow with his paw, and he did not move again.

The girls had run away, but the bear called to them: "Snow White and Rose Red, do not be afraid; wait, I will come with you." Then they recognized his voice and waited, and when he came up to them suddenly his bearskin fell off, and he stood there a handsome man, clothed all in gold. "I am a king's son," he said, "and I was bewitched by that wicked dwarf, who had stolen my treasures; I have had to run about the forest as a savage bear until I was freed by his death. Now he has got his well-deserved punishment.

Snow White was married to him, and Rose Red to his brother, and they divided between them the great treasure which the dwarf had gathered together in his cave. The old mother lived peacefully and happily with her children for many years. She took the two rose trees with her, and they stood before her window, and every year bore the most beautiful roses, white and red.

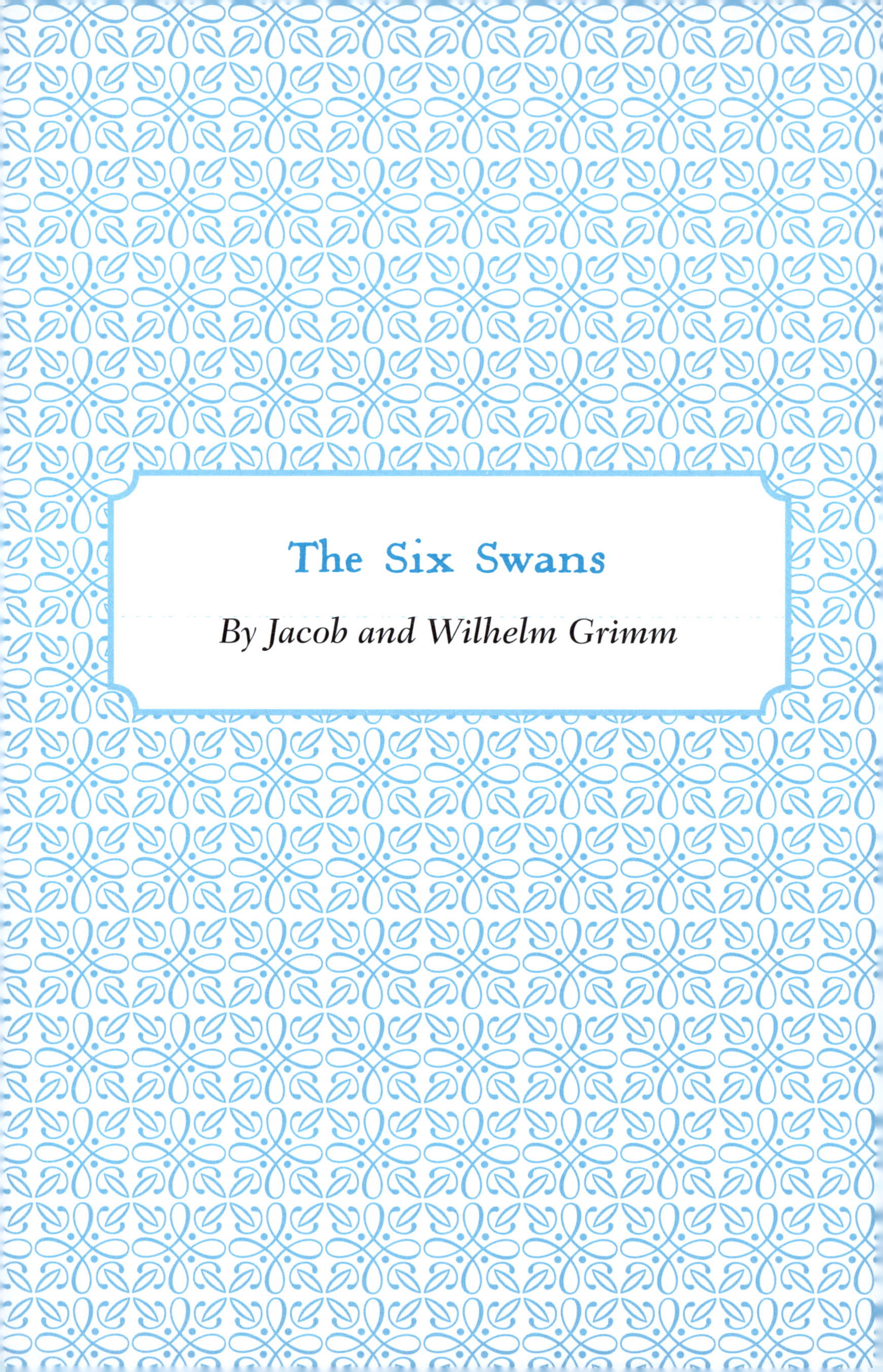
The Six Swans
By Jacob and Wilhelm Grimm

A King was once hunting in a large wood, and pursued his game so hotly that none of his courtiers could follow him. But when evening approached he stopped, and looking around him perceived that he had lost himself. He sought a path out of the forest but could not find one, and presently he saw an old woman, with a nodding head, who came up to him. "My good woman," said he to her, "can you not show me the way out of the forest?"

"Oh, yes, my lord King," she replied; "I can do that very well, but upon one condition, which if you do not fulfil, you will never again get out of the wood, but will die of hunger."

"What, then, is this condition?" asked the King.

"I have a daughter," said the old woman, "who is as beautiful as any one you can find in the whole world, and well deserves to be your bride. Now, if you will make her your Queen, I will show you your way out of the wood." In the anxiety of his heart, the King consented, and the old woman led him to her cottage, where the daughter was sitting by the fire. She received the King as if she had expected him, and he saw at once that she was very beautiful, but yet she did not quite please him, for he could not look at her without a secret shuddering. However, he took the maiden upon his horse, and the old woman showed him the way, and the King arrived safely at his palace, where the wedding was to be celebrated.

The King had been married once before, and had seven children by his first wife, six boys and a girl, whom he loved above everything else in the world. He became afraid, soon, that the stepmother might not treat his children very well, and might even do them some great injury, so he took them away to a lonely castle which stood in the midst of a forest. The castle was so entirely hidden, and the way to it was so difficult to discover, that he himself could not have found it if a wise woman had not given him a ball of cotton which had the wonderful property, when he threw it before him, of unrolling itself and showing him the right path. The King went, however, so often to see his dear children, that the Queen, noticing his absence, became inquisitive, and wished to know what he went to fetch out of the forest. So she gave his servants a great quantity of money, and they disclosed to her the secret, and also told her of the ball of cotton which alone could show her the way. She had now no peace until she discovered where this ball was concealed, and then she made some fine silken shirts, and, as she had learnt of her mother, she sewed within each a charm. One day soon after, when the King was gone out hunting, she took the little shirts and went into the forest, and the cotton showed her the path. The children, seeing someone coming in the distance, thought it was their dear father, and ran out full of joy. Then she threw over each of them a shirt, that, as it touched their bodies, changed them into Swans, which flew away over the forest. The Queen then went home quite contented, and thought she was free of her stepchildren; but the little girl had not met her with the brothers, and the Queen did not know of her.

The following day the King went to visit his children, but he found only the Maiden. "Where are your brothers?" asked he.

"Ah, dear father," she replied, "they are gone away and have left me alone"; and she told him how she had looked out of the window and seen them changed into Swans, which had flown over the forest; and then she showed him the feathers which they had dropped in the courtyard, and which she had collected together. The King was much grieved, but he did not think that his wife could have done this wicked deed, and, as he feared the girl might also be stolen away, he took her with him. She was, however, so much afraid of the stepmother, that she begged him not to stop more than one night in the castle.

The poor Maiden thought to herself, "This is no longer my place; I will go and seek my brothers"; and when night came she escaped and went quite deep into the wood. She walked all night long, and a great part of the next day, until she could go no further from weariness. Just then she saw a rough-looking hut, and going in, she found a room with six little beds, but she dared not get into one, so crept under, and laying herself upon the hard earth, prepared to pass the night there. Just as the sun was setting, she heard a rustling, and saw six white Swans come flying in at the window. They settled on the ground and began blowing one another until they had blown all their feathers off, and their swan's down slipped from them like a shirt. Then the Maiden knew them at once for her brothers, and gladly crept out from under the bed, and the brothers were not less glad to see their sister, but their joy was of short duration. "Here you must not stay," said they to her; "this is a robbers' hiding place; if they should return and find you here, they would murder you."

"Can you not protect me, then?" inquired the sister.

"No," they replied; "for we can only lay aside our swan's feathers for a quarter of an hour each evening, and for that time we regain our human form, but afterwards we resume our changed appearance."

Their sister then asked them, with tears, "Can you not be restored again?"

"Oh, no," replied they; "the conditions are too difficult. For six long years you must neither speak nor laugh, and during that time you must sew together for us six little shirts of starflowers, and should there fall a single word from your lips, then all your labour will be in vain." Just as the brothers finished speaking, the quarter of an hour elapsed, and they all flew out of the window again like Swans.

The little sister, however, made a solemn resolution to rescue her brothers, or die in the attempt; and she left the cottage, and, penetrating deep into the forest, passed the night amid the branches of a tree. The next morning she went out and collected the starflowers to sew together. She had no one to converse with and for laughing she had no spirits, so there up in the tree she sat, intent upon her work.

After she had passed some time there, it happened that the King of that country was hunting in the forest, and his huntsmen came beneath the tree on which the Maiden sat. They called to her and asked, "Who art thou?" But she gave no answer. "Come down to us," continued they; "we will do thee no harm." She simply shook her head, and when they pressed her further with questions, she threw down to them her gold necklace, hoping therewith to satisfy them. They did not, however, leave her, and she threw down her girdle, but in vain! and even her rich dress did not make them desist. At last the huntsman himself climbed the tree and brought down the Maiden, and took her before the King.

The King asked her, "Who art thou? What dost thou upon that tree?" But she did not answer; and then he questioned her in all the languages that he knew, but she remained dumb to all, as a fish. Since, however, she was so beautiful, the King's heart was touched, and he conceived for her a strong affection. Then he put around her his cloak, and, placing her before him on his horse, took her to his castle. There he ordered rich clothing to be made for her, and, although her beauty shone as the sunbeams, not a word escaped her. The King placed her by his side at table, and there her dignified mien and manners so won upon him, that he said, "This Maiden will I marry, and no other in the world"; and after some days he wedded her.

Now, the King had a wicked stepmother, who was discontented with his marriage, and spoke evil of the young Queen. "Who knows whence the wench comes?" said she. "She who cannot speak is not worthy of a King." A year after, when the Queen brought her firstborn into the world, the old woman took him away. Then she went to the King and complained that the Queen was a murderess. The King, however, would not believe it, and suffered no one to do any injury to his wife, who sat composedly sewing at her shirts and paying attention to nothing else. When a second child was born, the false stepmother used the same deceit, but the King again would not listen to her words, saying, "She is too pious and good to act so; could she but speak and defend herself, her innocence would come to light." But when again, the old woman stole away the third child, and then accused the Queen, who answered not a word to the accusation, the King was obliged to give her up to be tried, and she was condemned to suffer death by fire.

When the time had elapsed, and the sentence was to be carried out, it happened that the very day had come round when her dear brothers should be set free; the six shirts were also ready, all but the last, which yet wanted the left sleeve. As she was led to the scaffold, she placed the shirts upon her arm, and just as she had mounted it, and the fire was about to be kindled, she looked around, and saw six Swans come flying through the air. Her heart leapt for joy as she perceived her deliverers approaching, and soon the Swans, flying towards her, alighted so near that she was enabled to throw over them the shirts, and as soon as she had done so, their feathers fell off and the brothers stood up alive and well; but the youngest was without his left arm, instead of which he had a swan's wing. They embraced and kissed each other, and the Queen, going to the King, who was thunderstruck, began to say, "Now may I speak, my dear husband, and prove to you that I am innocent and falsely accused"; and then she told him how the wicked woman had stolen away and hidden her three children. When she had concluded, the King was overcome with joy, and the wicked stepmother was led to the scaffold and bound to the stake and burnt to ashes. The King and Queen for ever after lived in peace and prosperity with their six brothers.

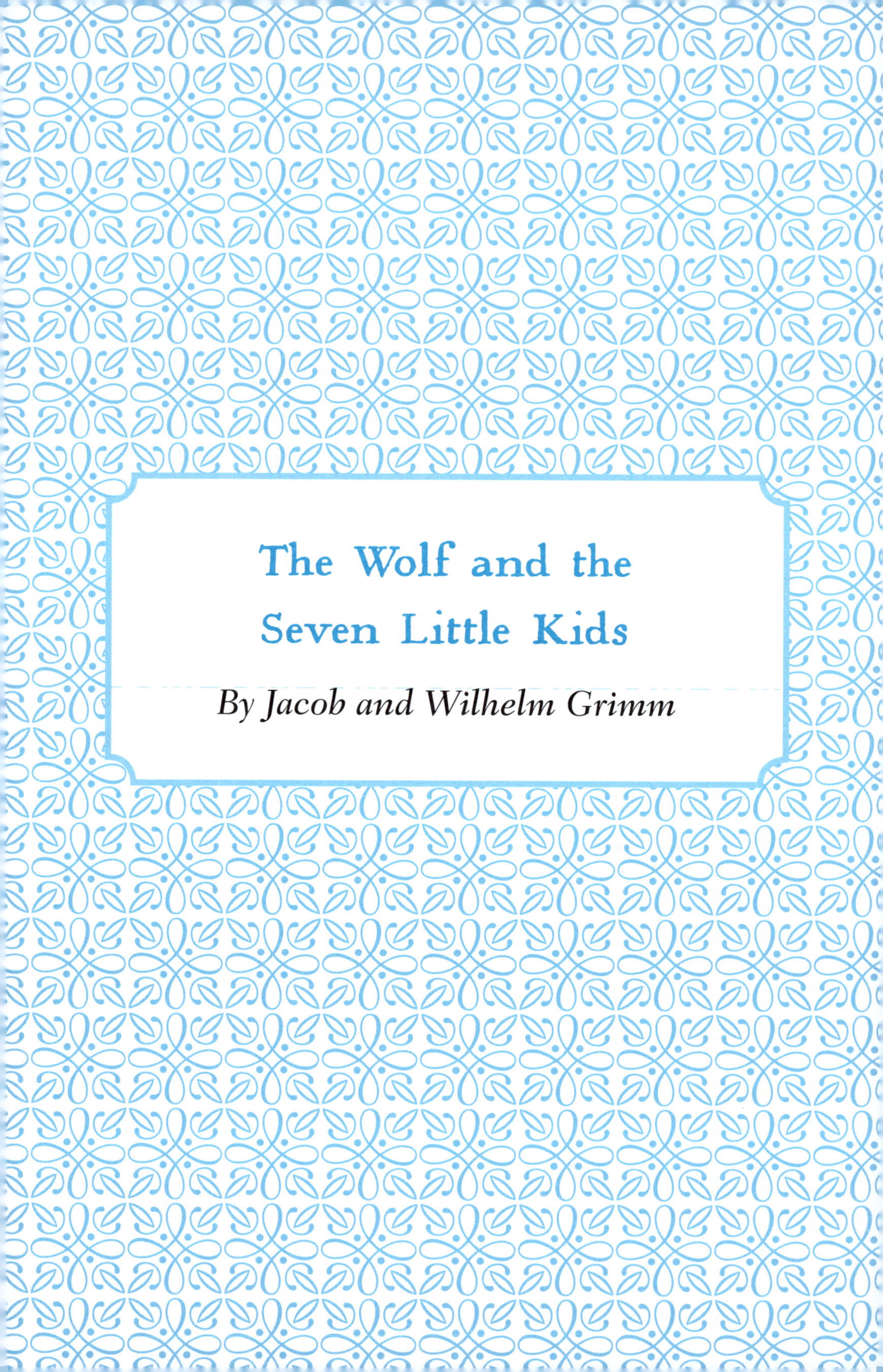

The Wolf and the Seven Little Kids

By Jacob and Wilhelm Grimm

There was once upon a time an old goat who had seven little kids, and loved them with all the love of a mother for her children. One day she wanted to go into the forest and fetch some food. So she called all seven to her and said: "Dear children, I have to go into the forest, be on your guard against the wolf; if he comes in, he will devour you all—skin, hair, and everything. The wretch often disguises himself, but you will know him at once by his rough voice and his black feet."

The kids said: "Dear mother, we will take good care of ourselves; you may go away without any anxiety." Then the old one bleated, and went on her way with an easy mind.

It was not long before someone knocked at the house door and called: "Open the door, dear children; your mother is here, and has brought something back with her for each of you."

But the little kids knew that it was the wolf, by the rough voice. "We will not open the door," cried they, "you are not our mother. She has a soft, pleasant voice, but your voice is rough; you are the wolf!" Then the wolf went away to a shopkeeper and bought himself a great lump of chalk, ate this and made his voice soft with it. Then he came back, knocked at the door of the house, and called: "Open the door, dear children, your mother is here and has brought something back with her for each of you." But the wolf had laid his black paws against the window, and the children saw them and cried: "We will not open the door, our mother has not black feet like you: you are the wolf!"

Then the wolf ran to a baker and said: "I have hurt my feet, rub some dough over them for me." And when the baker had rubbed his feet over, he ran to the miller and said: "Strew some white meal over my feet for me." The miller thought to himself: "The wolf wants to deceive someone," and refused; but the wolf said: "If you will not do it, I will devour you." Then the miller was afraid, and made his paws white for him. Truly, this is the way of mankind.

So now the wretch went for the third time to the house door, knocked at it and said: "Open the door for me, children, your dear little mother has come home, and has brought every one of you something back from the forest with her." The little kids cried: "First show us your paws that we may know if you are our dear little mother." Then he put his paws in through the window and when the kids saw that they were white, they believed that all he said was true, and opened the door. But who should come in but the wolf! They were terrified and wanted to hide themselves. One sprang under the table, the second into the bed, the third into the stove, the fourth into the kitchen, the fifth into the cupboard, the sixth under the washing bowl, and the seventh into the clock case. But the wolf found them all, and used no great ceremony; one after the other he swallowed them down his throat. The youngest, who was in the clock case, was the only one he did not find. When the wolf had satisfied his appetite he took himself off, laid himself down under a tree in the green meadow outside, and began to sleep. Soon afterwards the old goat came home again from the forest. Ah! what a sight she saw there! The house door stood wide open. The table, chairs, and benches were thrown down, the washing bowl lay broken to pieces, and the quilts and pillows were pulled off the bed. She sought her children, but they were nowhere to be found. She called them one after another by name, but no one answered. At last, when she came to the youngest, a soft voice cried: "Dear mother, I am in the clock case." She took the kid out, and it told her that the wolf had come and had eaten all the others. Then you may imagine how she wept over her poor children.

At length in her grief she went out, and the youngest kid ran with her. When they came to the meadow, there lay the wolf by the tree and snored so loud that the branches shook. She looked at him on every side and saw that something was moving and struggling in his gorged belly. "Ah, heavens," she said, "is it possible that my poor children whom he has swallowed down for his supper, can be still alive?" Then the kid had to run home and fetch scissors, and a needle and thread, and the goat cut open the monster's stomach, and hardly had she made one cut, than one little kid thrust its head out, and when she had cut farther, all six sprang out one after another, and were all still alive, and had suffered no injury whatever, for in his greediness the monster had swallowed them down whole. What rejoicing there was! They embraced their dear mother, and jumped like a tailor at his wedding. The mother, however, said: "Now go and look for some big stones, and we will fill the wicked beast's stomach with them while he is still asleep." Then the seven kids dragged the stones thither with all speed, and put as many of them into this stomach as they could get in; and the mother sewed him up again in the greatest haste, so that he was not aware of anything and never once stirred.

When the wolf at length had had his fill of sleep, he got on his legs, and as the stones in his stomach made him very thirsty, he wanted to go to a well to drink. But when he began to walk and to move about, the stones in his stomach knocked against each other and rattled. Then cried he:

"What rumbles and tumbles
Against my poor bones?
I thought 'twas six kids,
But it feels like big stones."

And when he got to the well and stooped over the water to drink, the heavy stones made him fall in, and he drowned miserably. When the seven kids saw that, they came running to the spot and cried aloud: "The wolf is dead! The wolf is dead!" and danced for joy round about the well with their mother.

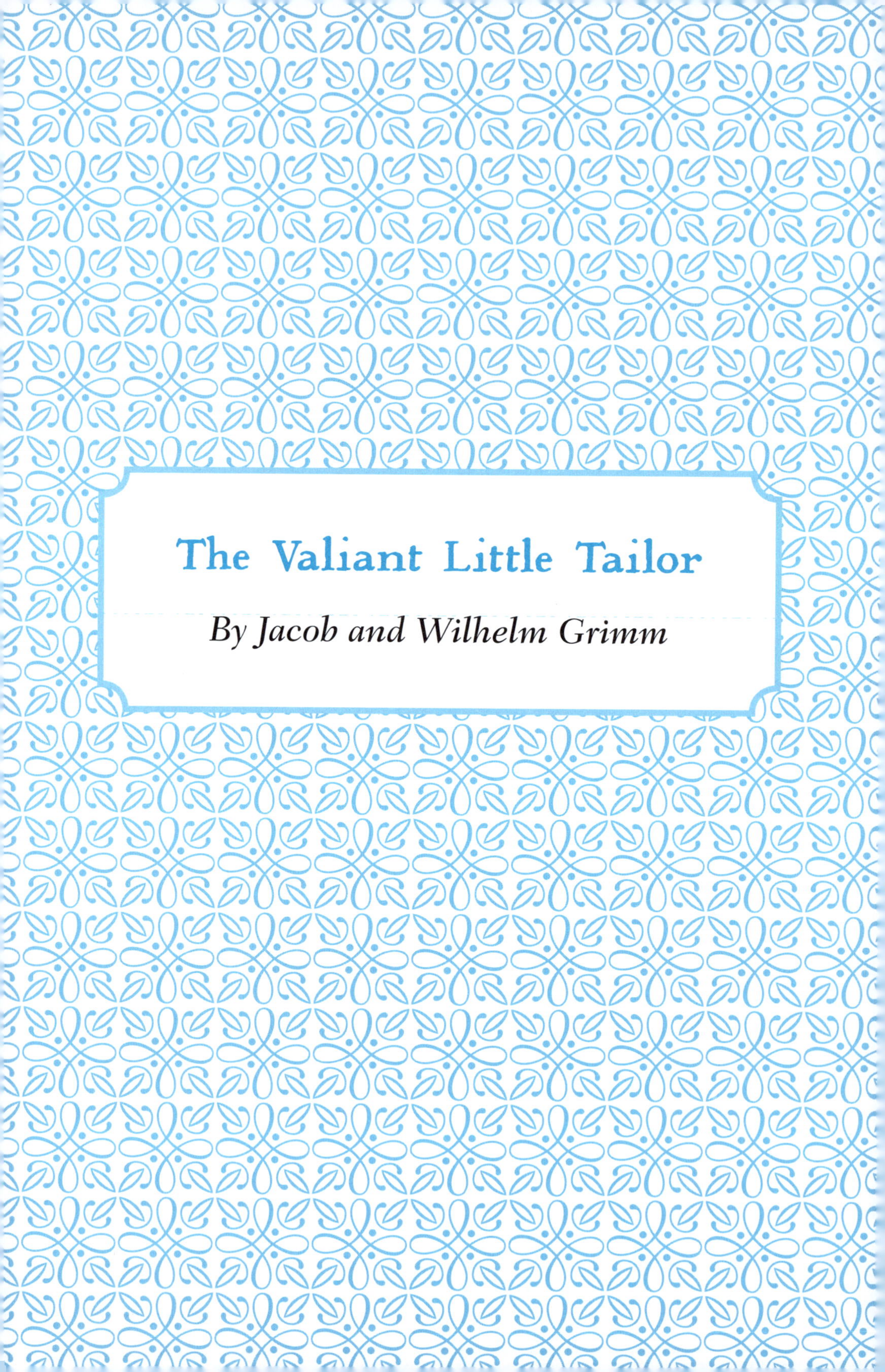

The Valiant Little Tailor

By Jacob and Wilhelm Grimm

One summer's morning a little tailor was sitting on his table by the window; he was in good spirits, and sewed with all his might. Then came a peasant woman down the street crying: "Good jams, cheap! Good jams, cheap!"

This rang pleasantly in the tailor's ears; he stretched his delicate head out of the window, and called: "Come up here, dear woman; here you will get rid of your goods." The woman came up the three steps to the tailor with her heavy basket, and he made her unpack all the pots for him. He inspected each one, lifted it up, put his nose to it, and at length said: "The jam seems to me to be good, so weigh me out four ounces, dear woman, and if it is a quarter of a pound that is of no consequence."

The woman who had hoped to find a good sale, gave him what he desired, but went away quite angry and grumbling. "Now, this jam shall be blessed by God," cried the little tailor, "and give me health and strength"; so he brought the bread out of the cupboard, cut himself a piece right across the loaf and spread the jam over it. "This won't taste bitter," said he, "but I will just finish the jacket before I take a bite." He laid the bread near him, sewed on, and in his joy, made bigger and bigger stitches. In the meantime the smell of the sweet jam rose to where the flies were sitting in great numbers, and they were attracted and descended on it in hosts. "Hi! who invited you?" said the little tailor, and drove the unbidden guests away. The flies, however, who understood no German, would not be turned away, but came back again in ever-increasing companies. The little tailor at last lost all patience, and drew a piece of cloth from the hole under his worktable, and saying: "Wait, and I will give it to you," struck it mercilessly on them. When he drew it away and counted, there lay before him no fewer than seven, dead and with legs stretched out. "Are you a fellow of that sort?" said he, and could not help admiring his own bravery. "The whole town shall know of this!" And the little tailor hastened to cut himself a girdle, stitched it, and embroidered on it in large letters: "Seven at one stroke!" "What, the town!" he continued, "the whole world shall hear of it!" and his heart wagged with joy like a lamb's tail.

The tailor put on the girdle, and resolved to go forth into the world, because he thought his workshop was too small for his valour. Before he went away, he sought about in the house to see if there was anything which he could take with him; however, he found nothing but an old cheese, and that he put in his pocket. In front of the door he observed a bird which had caught itself in the thicket. It had to go into his pocket with the cheese. Now he took to the road boldly, and as he was light and nimble, he felt no fatigue. The road led him up a mountain, and when he had reached the highest point of it, there sat a powerful giant looking peacefully about him. The little tailor went bravely up, spoke to him, and said: "Good day, comrade, so you are sitting there overlooking the widespread world! I am just on my way thither, and want to try my luck. Have you any inclination to go with me?"

The giant looked contemptuously at the tailor, and said: "You ragamuffin! You miserable creature!"

"Oh, indeed?" answered the little tailor, and unbuttoned his coat, and showed the giant the girdle, "there may you read what kind of a man I am!"

The giant read: "Seven at one stroke," and thought that they had been men whom the tailor had killed, and began to feel a little respect for the tiny fellow. Nevertheless, he wished to try him first, and took a stone in his hand and squeezed it together so that water dropped out of it. "Do that likewise," said the giant, "if you have strength."

"Is that all?" said the tailor, "that is child's play with us!" and put his hand into his pocket, brought out the soft cheese, and pressed it until the liquid ran out of it. "Faith," said he, "that was a little better, wasn't it?"

The giant did not know what to say, and could not believe it of the little man. Then the giant picked up a stone and threw it so high that the eye could scarcely follow it. "Now, little mite of a man, do that likewise."

"Well thrown," said the tailor, "but after all the stone came down to earth again; I will throw you one which shall never come back at all," and he put his hand into his pocket, took out the bird, and threw it into the air. The bird, delighted with its liberty, rose, flew away and did not come back. "How does that shot please you, comrade?" asked the tailor.

"You can certainly throw," said the giant, "but now we will see if you are able to carry anything properly." He took the little tailor to a mighty oak tree which lay there felled on the ground, and said: "If you are strong enough, help me to carry the tree out of the forest."

"Readily," answered the little man; "take you the trunk on your shoulders, and I will raise up the branches and twigs; after all, they are the heaviest." The giant took the trunk on his shoulder, but the tailor seated himself on a branch, and the giant, who could not look round, had to carry away the whole tree, and the little tailor into the bargain: he behind, was quite merry and happy, and whistled the song: "Three tailors rode forth from the gate," as if carrying the tree were child's play. The giant, after he had dragged the heavy burden part of the way, could go no further, and cried: "Hark you, I shall have to let the tree fall!" The tailor sprang nimbly down, seized the tree with both arms as if he had been carrying it, and said to the giant: "You are such a great fellow, and yet cannot even carry the tree!"

They went on together, and as they passed a cherry tree, the giant laid hold of the top of the tree where the ripest fruit was hanging, bent it down, gave it into the tailor's hand, and bade him eat. But the little tailor was much too weak to hold the tree, and when the giant let it go, it sprang back again, and the tailor was tossed into the air with it. When he had fallen down again without injury, the giant said: "What is this? Have you not strength enough to hold the weak twig?"

"There is no lack of strength," answered the little tailor. "Do you think that could be anything to a man who has struck down seven at one blow? I leapt over the tree because the huntsmen are shooting down there in the thicket. Jump as I did, if you can do it." The giant made the attempt but he could not get over the tree, and remained hanging in the branches, so that in this also the tailor kept the upper hand.

The giant said: "If you are such a valiant fellow, come with me into our cavern and spend the night with us." The little tailor was willing, and followed him. When they went into the cave, other giants were sitting there by the fire, and each of them had a roasted sheep in his hand and was eating it. The little tailor looked round and thought: "It is much more spacious here than in my workshop." The giant showed him a bed, and said he was to lie down in it and sleep. The bed, however, was too big for the little tailor; he did not lie down in it, but crept into a corner. When it was midnight, and the giant thought that the little tailor was lying in a sound sleep, he got up, took a great iron bar, cut through the bed with one blow, and thought he had finished off the grasshopper for good. With the earliest dawn the giants went into the forest, and had quite forgotten the little tailor, when all at once he walked up to them quite merrily and boldly. The giants were terrified, they were afraid that he would strike them all dead, and ran away in a great hurry.

The little tailor went onwards, always following his own pointed nose.

After he had walked for a long time, he came to the courtyard of a royal palace, and as he felt weary, he lay down on the grass and fell asleep. Whilst he lay there, the people came and inspected him on all sides, and read on his girdle: "Seven at one stroke."

"Ah!" said they, "what does the great warrior want here in the midst of peace? He must be a mighty lord." They went and announced him to the king, and gave it as their opinion that if war should break out, this would be a weighty and useful man who ought on no account to be allowed to depart. The counsel pleased the king, and he sent one of his courtiers to the little tailor to offer him military service when he awoke. The ambassador remained standing by the sleeper, waited until he stretched his limbs and opened his eyes, and then conveyed to him this proposal. "For this very reason have I come here," the tailor replied, "I am ready to enter the king's service." He was therefore honourably received, and a special dwelling was assigned him.

The soldiers, however, were set against the little tailor, and wished him a thousand miles away. "What is to be the end of this?" they said among themselves. "If we quarrel with him, and he strikes about him, seven of us will fall at every blow; not one of us can stand against him." They came therefore to a decision, betook themselves in a body to the king, and begged for their dismissal. "We are not prepared," said they, "to stay with a man who kills seven at one stroke." The king was sorry that for the sake of one he should lose all his faithful servants, wished that he had never set eyes on the tailor, and would willingly have been rid of him again. But he did not venture to give him his dismissal, for he dreaded lest he should strike him and all his people dead, and place himself on the royal throne. He thought about it for a long time, and at last found good counsel. He sent to the little tailor and caused him to be informed that as he was a great warrior, he had one request to make to him. In a forest of his country lived two giants, who caused great mischief with their robbing, murdering, ravaging, and burning, and no one could approach them without putting himself in danger of death. If the tailor conquered and killed these two giants, he would give him his only daughter to wife, and half of his kingdom as a dowry, likewise one hundred horsemen should go with him to assist him. "That would indeed be a fine thing for a man like me!" thought the little tailor. "One is not offered a beautiful princess and half a kingdom every day of one's life!" "Oh, yes," he replied, "I will soon subdue the giants, and do not require the help of the hundred horsemen to do it; he who can hit seven with one blow has no need to be afraid of two."

The little tailor went forth, and the hundred horsemen followed him. When he came to the outskirts of the forest, he said to his followers: "Just stay waiting here, I alone will soon finish off the giants." Then he bounded into the forest and looked about right and left. After a while he perceived both giants. They lay sleeping under a tree, and snored so that the branches waved up and down. The little tailor, not idle, gathered two pocketsful of stones, and with these climbed up the tree. When he was halfway up, he slipped down by a branch, until he sat just above the sleepers, and then let one stone after another fall on the breast of one of the giants. For a long time the giant felt nothing, but at last he awoke, pushed his comrade, and said: "Why are you knocking me?"

"You must be dreaming," said the other, "I am not knocking you."

They laid themselves down to sleep again, and then the tailor threw a stone down on the second.

"What is the meaning of this?" cried the other. "Why are you pelting me?"

"I am not pelting you," answered the first, growling. They disputed about it for a time, but as they were weary they let the matter rest, and their eyes closed once more. The little tailor began his game again, picked out the biggest stone, and threw it with all his might on the breast of the first giant.

"That is too bad!" cried he, and sprang up like a madman, and pushed his companion against the tree until it shook. The other paid him back in the same coin, and they got into such a rage that they tore up trees and belaboured each other so long, that at last they both fell down dead on the ground at the same time. Then the little tailor leapt down. "It is a lucky thing," said he, "that they did not tear up the tree on which I was sitting, or I should have had to sprint on to another like a squirrel; but we tailors are nimble." He drew out his sword and gave each of them a couple of thrusts in the breast, and then went out to the horsemen and said: "The work is done; I have finished both of them off, but it was hard work! They tore up trees in their sore need, and defended themselves with them, but all that is to no purpose when a man like myself comes, who can kill seven at one blow."

"But are you not wounded?" asked the horsemen.

"You need not concern yourself about that," answered the tailor, "they have not bent one hair of mine." The horsemen would not believe him, and rode into the forest; there they found the giants swimming in their blood, and all round about lay the torn up trees.

The little tailor demanded of the king the promised reward; he, however, repented of his promise, and again bethought himself how he could get rid of the hero.

"Before you receive my daughter, and the half of my kingdom," said he to him, "you must perform one more heroic deed. In the forest roams a unicorn which does great harm, and you must catch it first."

"I fear one unicorn still less than two giants. Seven at one blow is my kind of affair." He took a rope and an axe with him, went forth into the forest, and again bade those who were sent with him to wait outside. He had not long to seek. The unicorn soon came towards him, and rushed directly on the tailor, as if it would gore him with its horn without more ado. "Softly, softly; it can't be done as quickly as that," said he, and stood still and waited until the animal was quite close, and then sprang nimbly behind the tree. The unicorn ran against the tree with all its strength, and stuck its horn so fast in the trunk that it had not the strength enough to draw it out again, and thus it was caught. "Now, I have got the bird," said the tailor, and came out from behind the tree and put the rope round its neck, and then with his axe he hewed the horn out of the tree, and when all was ready he led the beast away and took it to the king.

The king still would not give him the promised reward, and made a third demand. Before the wedding the tailor was to catch him a wild boar that made great havoc in the forest, and the huntsmen should give him their help.

"Willingly," said the tailor, "that is child's play!" He did not take the huntsmen with him into the forest, and they were well pleased that he did not, for the wild boar had several times received them in such a manner that they had no inclination to lie in wait for him. When the boar perceived the tailor, it ran on him with foaming mouth and whetted tusks, and was about to throw him to the ground, but the hero fled and sprang into a chapel which was near and up to the window at once, and in one bound out again. The boar ran after him, but the tailor ran round outside and shut the door behind it, and then the raging beast, which was much too heavy and awkward to leap out of the window, was caught. The little tailor called the huntsmen thither that they might see the prisoner with their own eyes. The hero, however, went to the king, who was now, whether he liked it or not, obliged to keep his promise, and gave his daughter and the half of his kingdom. Had he known that it was no warlike hero, but a little tailor who was standing before him, it would have gone to his heart still more than it did. The wedding was held with great magnificence and small joy, and out of a tailor a king was made.

After some time the young queen heard her husband say in his dreams at night: "Boy, make me the doublet, and patch the pantaloons, or else I will rap the yard measure over your ears." Then she discovered in what state of life the young lord had been born, and next morning complained of her wrongs to her father, and begged him to help her to get rid of her husband, who was nothing else but a tailor. The king comforted her and said: "Leave your bedroom door open this night, and my servants shall stand outside, and when he has fallen asleep shall go in, bind him, and take him on board a ship which shall carry him into the wide world." The woman was satisfied with this, but the king's armour-bearer, who had heard all, was friendly with the young lord, and informed him of the whole plot. "I'll put a screw into that business," said the little tailor. At night he went to bed with his wife at the usual time, and when she thought that he had fallen asleep, she got up, opened the door, and then lay down again. The little tailor, who was only pretending to be asleep, began to cry out in a clear voice: "Boy, make me the doublet and patch me the pantaloons, or I will rap the yard measure over your ears. I smote seven at one blow. I killed two giants, I brought away one unicorn, and caught a wild boar, and am I to fear those who are standing outside the room?" When these men heard the tailor speaking thus, they were overcome by a great dread, and ran as if the wild huntsman were behind them, and none of them would venture anything further against him. So the little tailor was and remained a king to the end of his life.

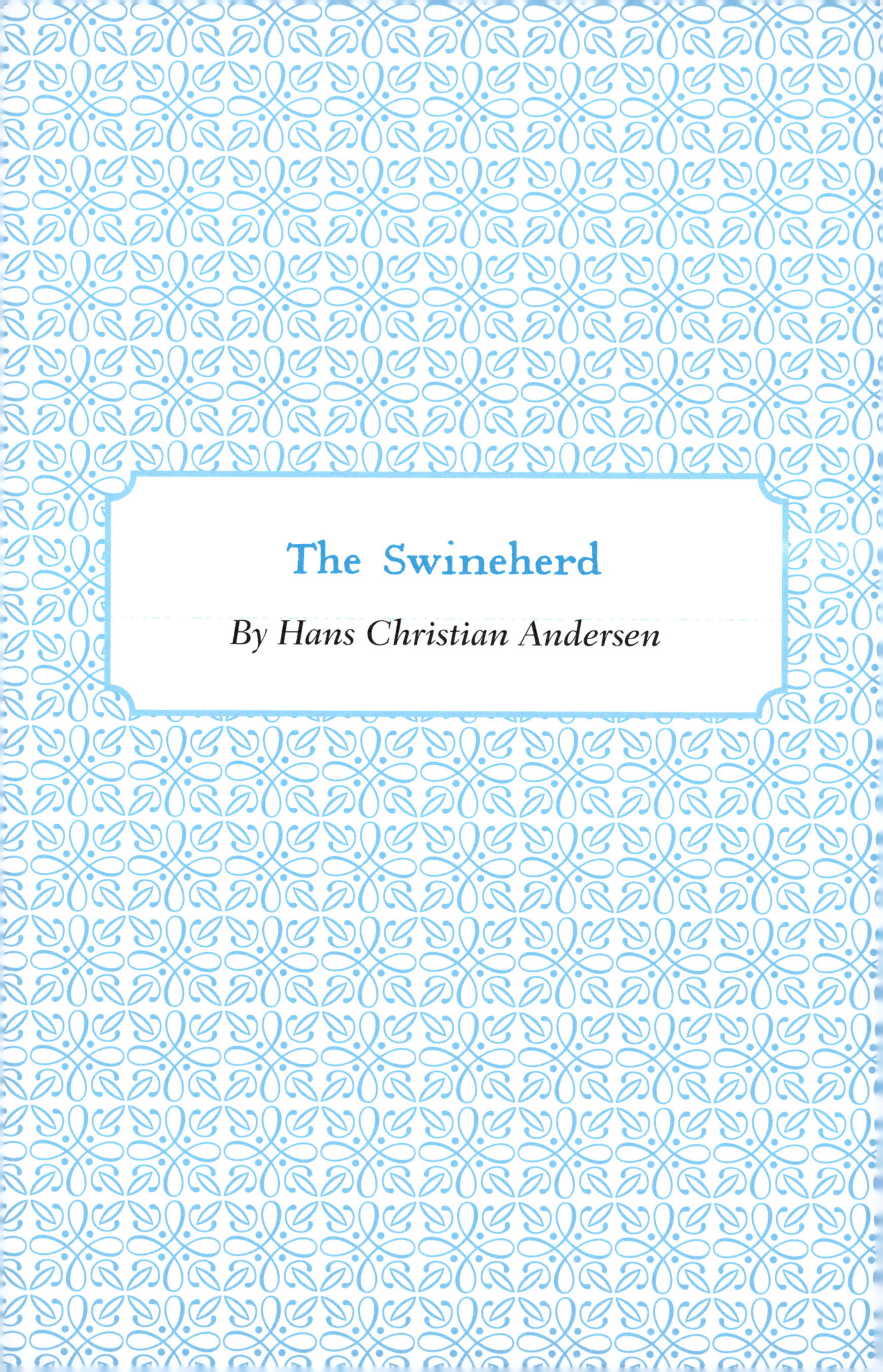

The Swineherd

By Hans Christian Andersen

Once upon a time lived a poor prince; his kingdom was very small, but it was large enough to enable him to marry, and marry he would. It was rather bold of him that he went and asked the emperor's daughter: "Will you marry me?" but he ventured to do so, for his name was known far and wide, and there were hundreds of princesses who would have gladly accepted him, but would she do so? Now we shall see.

On the grave of the prince's father grew a rose tree, the most beautiful of its kind. It bloomed only once in five years, and then it had only one single rose upon it, but what a rose! It had such a sweet scent that one instantly forgot all sorrow and grief when one smelt it. He had also a nightingale, which could sing as if every sweet melody was in its throat. This rose and the nightingale he wished to give to the princess; and therefore both were put into big silver cases and sent to her.

The emperor ordered them to be carried into the great hall where the princess was just playing "Visitors are coming" with her ladies-in-waiting; when she saw the large cases with the presents therein, she clapped her hands for joy.

"I wish it were a little pussy cat," she said. But then the rose tree with the beautiful rose was unpacked.

"Oh, how nicely it is made," exclaimed the ladies.

"It is more than nice," said the emperor, "it is charming."

The princess touched it and nearly began to cry.

"For shame, pa," she said, "it is not artificial, it is natural!"

"For shame, it is natural," repeated all her ladies.

"Let us first see what the other case contains before we are angry," said the emperor; then the nightingale was taken out, and it sang so beautifully that no one could possibly say anything unkind about it.

"Superbe, charmant," said the ladies of the court, for they all prattled French, one worse than the other.

"How much the bird reminds me of the musical box of the late lamented empress," said an old courtier, "it has exactly the same tone, the same execution."

"You are right," said the emperor, and began to cry like a little child.

"I hope it is not natural," said the princess.

"Yes, certainly it is natural," replied those who had brought the presents.

"Then let it fly," said the princess, and refused to see the prince.

But the prince was not discouraged. He painted his face, put on common clothes, pulled his cap over his forehead, and came back.

"Good day, emperor," he said, "could you not give me some employment at the court?"

"There are so many," replied the emperor, "who apply for places, that for the present I have no vacancy, but I will remember you. But wait a moment; it just comes into my mind, I require somebody to look after my pigs, for I have a great many."

Thus the prince was appointed imperial swineherd, and as such he lived in a wretchedly small room near the pigsty; there he worked all day long, and when it was night he had made a pretty little pot. There were little bells round the rim, and when the water began to boil in it, the bells began to play the old tune:

"A jolly old sow once lived in a sty,
Three little piggies had she."

But what was more wonderful was that, when one put a finger into the steam rising from the pot, one could at once smell what meals they were preparing on every fire in the whole town. That was indeed much more remarkable than the rose. When the princess with her ladies passed by and heard the tune, she stopped and looked quite pleased, for she also could play it—in fact, it was the only tune she could play, and she played it with one finger.

"That is the tune I know," she exclaimed. "He must be a well-educated swineherd. Go and ask him how much the instrument is."

One of the ladies had to go and ask; but she put on pattens.

"What will you take for your pot?" asked the lady.

"I will have ten kisses from the princess," said the swineherd.

"God forbid," said the lady.

"Well, I cannot sell it for less," replied the swineherd.

"What did he say?" said the princess.

"I really cannot tell you," replied the lady.

"You can whisper it into my ear."

"It is very naughty," said the princess, and walked off.

But when she had gone a little distance, the bells rang again so sweetly:

"A jolly old sow once lived in a sty,
Three little piggies had she."

"Ask him," said the princess, "if he will be satisfied with ten kisses from one of my ladies."

"No, thank you," said the swineherd: "ten kisses from the princess, or I keep my pot."

"That is tiresome," said the princess. "But you must stand before me, so that nobody can see it."

The ladies placed themselves in front of her and spread out their dresses, and she gave the swineherd ten kisses and received the pot.

That was a pleasure! Day and night the water in the pot was boiling; there was not a single fire in the whole town of which they did not know what was preparing on it, the chamberlain's as well as the shoemaker's. The ladies danced and clapped their hands for joy.

"We know who will eat soup and pancakes; we know who will eat porridge and cutlets; oh, how interesting!"

"Very interesting, indeed," said the mistress of the household. "But you must not betray me, for I am the emperor's daughter."

"Of course not," they all said.

The swineherd— hat is to say, the prince, but they did not know otherwise than that he was a real swineherd—did not waste a single day without doing something; he made a rattle, which, when turned quickly round, played all the waltzes, galops, and polkas known since the creation of the world.

"But that is superbe," said the princess passing by. "I have never heard a more beautiful composition. Go down and ask him what the instrument costs; but I shall not kiss him again."

"He will have a hundred kisses from the princess," said the lady, who had gone down to ask him.

"I believe he is mad," said the princess, and walked off, but soon she stopped. "One must encourage art," she said. "I am the emperor's daughter! Tell him I will give him ten kisses, as I did the other day; the remainder one of my ladies can give him.

"But we do not like to kiss him," said the ladies.

"That is nonsense," said the princess; "if I can kiss him, you can also do it. Remember that I give you food and employment." And the lady had to go down once more.

"A hundred kisses from the princess," said the swineherd, "or everybody keeps his own."

"Place yourselves before me," said the princess then. They did as they were bidden, and the princess kissed him.

"I wonder what that crowd near the pigsty means!" said the emperor, who had just come out on his balcony. He rubbed his eyes and put his spectacles on.

"The ladies of the court are up to some mischief, I think. I shall have to go down and see." He pulled up his shoes, for they were down at the heels, and he was very quick about it. When he had come down into the courtyard he walked quite softly, and the ladies were so busily engaged in counting the kisses, that all should be fair, that they did not notice the emperor. He raised himself on tiptoe.

"What does this mean?" he said, when he saw that his daughter was kissing the swineherd, and then hit their heads with his shoe just as the swineherd received the sixty-eighth kiss.

"Go out of my sight," said the emperor, for he was very angry; and both the princess and the swineherd were banished from the empire. There she stood and cried, the swineherd scolded her, and the rain came down in torrents.

"Alas, unfortunate creature that I am!" said the princess, "I wish I had accepted the prince. Oh, how wretched I am!"

The swineherd went behind a tree, wiped his face, threw off his poor attire and stepped forth in his princely garments; he looked so beautiful that the princess could not help bowing to him.

"I have now learnt to despise you," he said. "You refused an honest prince; you did not appreciate the rose and the nightingale; but you did not mind kissing a swineherd for his toys; you have no one but yourself to blame!"

And then he returned into his kingdom and left her behind. She could now sing at her leisure:

"A jolly old sow once lived in a sty,
Three little piggies has she."

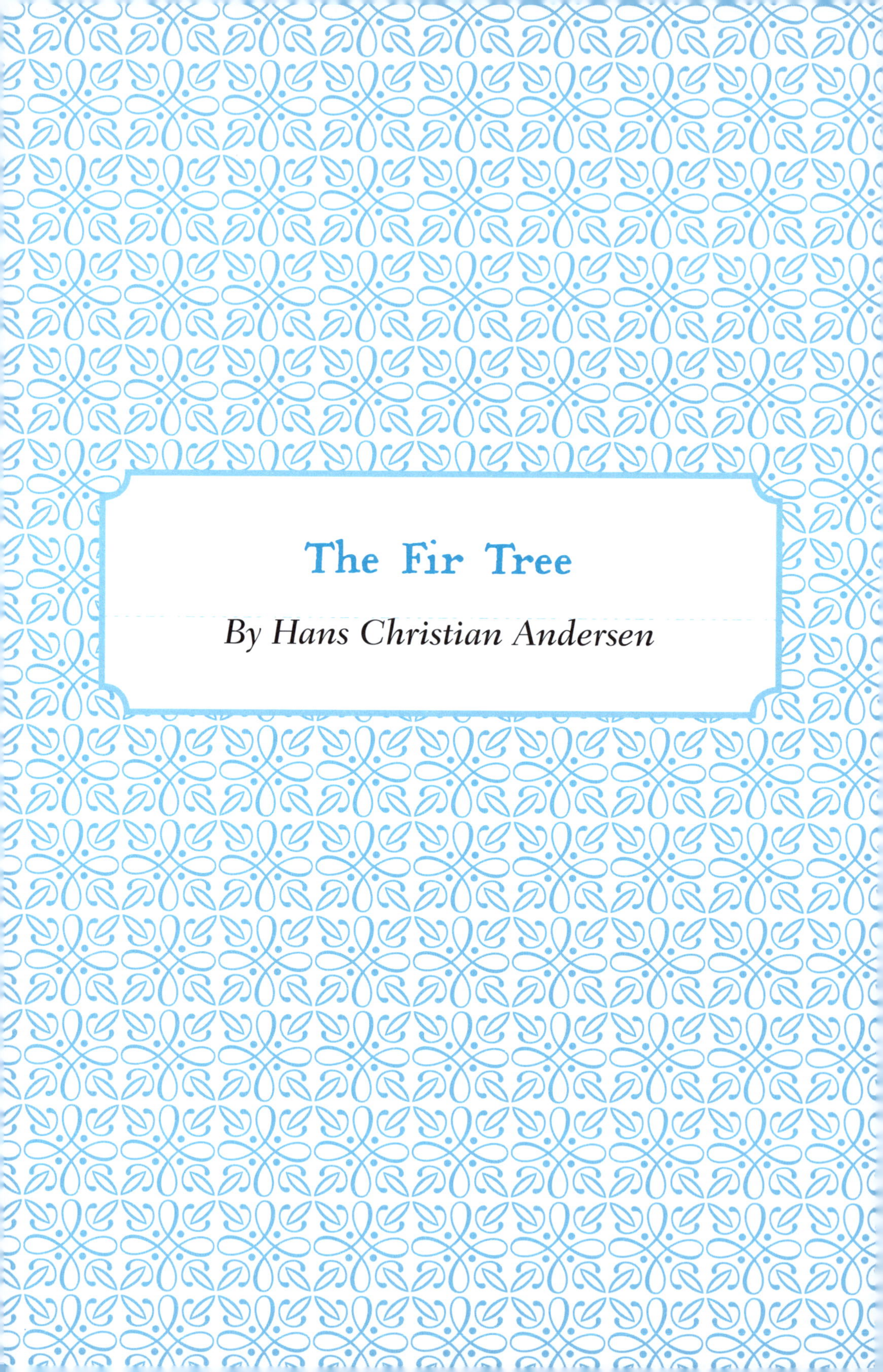

The Fir Tree

By Hans Christian Andersen

Far down in the forest, where the warm sun and the fresh air made a sweet resting place, grew a pretty little fir tree; and yet it was not happy, it wished so much to be tall like its companions—the pines and firs which grew around it. The sun shone, and the soft air fluttered its leaves, and the little peasant children passed by, prattling merrily, but the fir tree heeded them not. Sometimes the children would bring a large basket of raspberries or strawberries, wreathed on a straw, and seat themselves near the fir tree, and say, "Is it not a pretty little tree?" which made it feel more unhappy than before. And yet all this while the tree grew a notch or joint taller every year; for by the number of joints in the stem of a fir tree we can discover its age. Still, as it grew, it complained, "Oh! how I wish I were as tall as the other trees, then I would spread out my branches on every side, and my top would overlook the wide world. I should have the birds building their nests on my boughs, and when the wind blew, I should bow with stately dignity like my tall companions."

The tree was so discontented, that it took no pleasure in the warm sunshine, the birds, or the rosy clouds that floated over it morning and evening. Sometimes, in winter, when the snow lay white and glittering on the ground, a hare would come springing along, and jump right over the little tree; and then how mortified it would feel! Two winters passed, and when the third arrived, the tree had grown so tall that the hare was obliged to run round it. Yet it remained unsatisfied, and would exclaim, "Oh, if I could but keep on growing tall and old! There is nothing else worth caring for in the world!" In the autumn, as usual, the woodcutters came and cut down several of the tallest trees, and the young fir tree, which was now grown to its full height, shuddered as the noble trees fell to the earth with a crash. After the branches were lopped off, the trunks looked so slender and bare, that they could scarcely be recognized. Then they were placed upon wagons, and drawn by horses out of the forest. "Where were they going? What would become of them?" The young fir tree wished very much to know; so in the spring, when the swallows and the storks came, it asked, "Do you know where those trees were taken? Did you meet them?"

The swallows knew nothing, but the stork, after a little reflection, nodded his head, and said, "Yes, I think I do. I met several new ships when I flew from Egypt, and they had fine masts that smelt like fir. I think these must have been the trees; I assure you they were stately, very stately."

"Oh, how I wish I were tall enough to go on the sea," said the fir tree. "What is the sea, and what does it look like?"

"It would take too much time to explain," said the stork, flying quickly away.

"Rejoice in thy youth," said the sunbeam; "rejoice in thy fresh growth, and the young life that is in thee."

And the wind kissed the tree, and the dew watered it with tears; but the fir tree regarded them not.

Christmastime drew near, and many young trees were cut down, some even smaller and younger than the fir tree who enjoyed neither rest nor peace with longing to leave its forest home. These young trees, which were chosen for their beauty, kept their branches, and were also laid on wagons and drawn by horses out of the forest.

"Where are they going?" asked the fir tree. "They are not taller than I am: indeed, one is much less; and why are the branches not cut off? Where are they going?"

"We know, we know," sang the sparrows; "we have looked in at the windows of the houses in the town, and we know what is done with them. They are dressed up in the most splendid manner. We have seen them standing in the middle of a warm room, and adorned with all sorts of beautiful things—honey cakes, gilded apples, playthings, and many hundreds of wax tapers."

"And then," asked the fir tree, trembling through all its branches, "and then what happens?"

"We did not see any more," said the sparrows; "but this was enough for us."

"I wonder whether anything so brilliant will ever happen to me," thought the fir tree. "It would be much better than crossing the sea. I long for it almost with pain. Oh! when will Christmas be here? I am now as tall and well grown as those which were taken away last year. Oh! that I were now laid on the wagon, or standing in the warm room, with all that brightness and splendor around me! Something better and more beautiful is to come after, or the trees would not be so decked out. Yes, what follows will be grander and more splendid. What can it be? I am weary with longing. I scarcely know how I feel."

"Rejoice with us," said the air and the sunlight. "Enjoy thine own bright life in the fresh air."

But the tree would not rejoice, though it grew taller every day; and, winter and summer, its dark-green foliage might be seen in the forest, while passersby would say, "What a beautiful tree!"

A short time before Christmas, the discontented fir tree was the first to fall. As the axe cut through the stem, and divided the pith, the tree fell with a groan to the earth, conscious of pain and faintness, and forgetting all its anticipations of happiness, in sorrow at leaving its home in the forest. It knew that it should never again see its dear old companions, the trees, nor the little bushes and many-colored flowers that had grown by its side; perhaps not even the birds. Neither was the journey at all pleasant. The tree first recovered itself while being unpacked in the courtyard of a house, with several other trees; and it heard a man say, "We only want one, and this is the prettiest."

Then came two servants in grand livery, and carried the fir tree into a large and beautiful apartment. On the walls hung pictures, and near the great stove stood great china vases, with lions on the lids. There were rocking chairs, silken sofas, large tables, covered with pictures, books, and playthings, worth a great deal of money—at least, the children said so. Then the fir tree was placed in a large tub, full of sand; but green baize hung all around it, so that no one could see it was a tub, and it stood on a very handsome carpet. How the fir tree trembled! "What was going to happen to him now?" Some young ladies came, and the servants helped them to adorn the tree. On one branch they hung little bags cut out of colored paper, and each bag was filled with sweetmeats; from other branches hung gilded apples and walnuts, as if they had grown there; and above, and all round, were hundreds of red, blue, and white tapers, which were fastened on the branches. Dolls, exactly like real babies, were placed under the green leaves—the tree had never seen such things before—and at the very top was fastened a glittering star, made of tinsel. Oh, it was very beautiful!

"This evening," they all exclaimed, "how bright it will be!" "Oh, that the evening were come," thought the tree, "and the tapers lighted! then I shall know what else is going to happen. Will the trees of the forest come to see me? I wonder if the sparrows will peep in at the windows as they fly? shall I grow faster here, and keep on all these ornaments summer and winter?" But guessing was of very little use; it made his bark ache, and this pain is as bad for a slender fir tree, as headache is for us. At last the tapers were lighted, and then what a glistening blaze of light the tree presented! It trembled so with joy in all its branches, that one of the candles fell among the green leaves and burnt some of them. "Help! help!" exclaimed the young ladies, but there was no danger, for they quickly extinguished the fire. After this, the tree tried not to tremble at all, though the fire frightened him; he was so anxious not to hurt any of the beautiful ornaments, even while their brilliancy dazzled him. And now the folding doors were thrown open, and a troop of children rushed in as if they intended to upset the tree; they were followed more silently by their elders. For a moment the little ones stood silent with astonishment, and then they shouted for joy, till the room rang, and they danced merrily round the tree, while one present after another was taken from it.

"What are they doing? What will happen next?" thought the fir. At last the candles burnt down to the branches and were put out. Then the children received permission to plunder the tree.

Oh, how they rushed upon it, till the branches cracked, and had it not been fastened with the glistening star to the ceiling, it must have been thrown down. The children then danced about with their pretty toys, and no one noticed the tree, except the children's maid who came and peeped among the branches to see if an apple or a fig had been forgotten.

"A story, a story," cried the children, pulling a little fat man towards the tree.

"Now we shall be in the green shade," said the man, as he seated himself under it, "and the tree will have the pleasure of hearing also, but I shall only relate one story; what shall it be? Ivede-Avede, or Humpty Dumpty, who fell downstairs, but soon got up again, and at last married a princess."

"Ivede-Avede," cried some. "Humpty Dumpty," cried others, and there was a fine shouting and crying out. But the fir tree remained quite still, and thought to himself, "Shall I have anything to do with all this?" but he had already amused them as much as they wished. Then the old man told them the story of Humpty Dumpty, how he fell downstairs, and was raised up again, and married a princess. And the children clapped their hands and cried, "Tell another, tell another," for they wanted to hear the story of "Ivede-Avede"; but they only had "Humpty Dumpty." After this the fir tree became quite silent and thoughtful; never had the birds in the forest told such tales as "Humpty Dumpty," who fell downstairs, and yet married a princess.

"Ah! yes, so it happens in the world," thought the fir tree; he believed it all, because it was related by such a nice man. "Ah! well," he thought, "who knows? perhaps I may fall down too, and marry a princess"; and he looked forward joyfully to the next evening, expecting to be again decked out with lights and playthings, gold and fruit. "Tomorrow I will not tremble," thought he; "I will enjoy all my splendor, and I shall hear the story of Humpty Dumpty again, and perhaps Ivede-Avede." And the tree remained quiet and thoughtful all night.

In the morning the servants and the housemaid came in. "Now," thought the fir, "all my splendor is going to begin again." But they dragged him out of the room and upstairs to the garret, and threw him on the floor, in a dark corner, where no daylight shone, and there they left him. "What does this mean?" thought the tree, "what am I to do here? I can hear nothing in a place like this," and he had time enough to think, for days and nights passed and no one came near him, and when at last somebody did come, it was only to put away large boxes in a corner. So the tree was completely hidden from sight as if it had never existed. "It is winter now," thought the tree, "the ground is hard and covered with snow, so that people cannot plant me. I shall be sheltered here, I dare say, until spring comes. How thoughtful and kind everybody is to me! Still I wish this place were not so dark, as well as lonely, with not even a little hare to look at. How pleasant it was out in the forest while the snow lay on the ground, when the hare would run by, yes, and jump over me too, although I did not like it then. Oh, it is terribly lonely here."

"Squeak, squeak," said a little mouse, creeping cautiously towards the tree; then came another; and they both sniffed at the fir tree and crept between the branches.

"Oh, it is very cold," said the little mouse, "or else we should be so comfortable here, shouldn't we, you old fir tree?"

"I am not old," said the fir tree, "there are many who are older than I am."

"Where do you come from? and what do you know?" asked the mice, who were full of curiosity. "Have you seen the most beautiful places in the world, and can you tell us all about them? and have you been in the store-room, where cheeses lie on the shelf, and hams hang from the ceiling? One can run about on tallow candles there, and go in thin and come out fat."

"I know nothing of that place," said the fir tree, "but I know the wood where the sun shines and the birds sing." And then the tree told the little mice all about its youth. They had never heard such an account in their lives; and after they had listened to it attentively, they said, "What a number of things you have seen! You must have been very happy."

"Happy!" exclaimed the fir tree, and then as he reflected upon what he had been telling them, he said, "Ah, yes! after all those were happy days." But when he went on and related all about Christmas Eve, and how he had been dressed up with cakes and lights, the mice said, "How happy you must have been, you old fir tree."

"I am not old at all," replied the tree, "I only came from the forest this winter, I am now checked in my growth."

"What splendid stories you can relate," said the little mice. And the next night four other mice came with them to hear what the tree had to tell. The more he talked the more he remembered, and then he thought to himself, "Those were happy days, but they may come again. Humpty Dumpty fell downstairs, and yet he married the princess; perhaps I may marry a princess too." And the fir tree thought of the pretty little birch tree that grew in the forest, which was to him a real beautiful princess.

"Who is Humpty Dumpty?" asked the little mice. And then the tree related the whole story; he could remember every single word, and the little mice were so delighted with it, that they were ready to jump to the top of the tree. The next night a great many more mice made their appearance, and on Sunday two rats came with them; but they said, it was not a pretty story at all, and the little mice were very sorry, for it made them also think less of it.

"Do you know only one story?" asked the rats.

"Only one," replied the fir tree; "I heard it on the happiest evening of my life; but I did not know I was so happy at the time."

"We think it is a very miserable story," said the rats. "Don't you know any story about bacon, or tallow in the storeroom?"

"No," replied the tree.

"Many thanks to you then," replied the rats, and they marched off.

The little mice also kept away after this, and the tree sighed, and said, "It was very pleasant when the merry little mice sat round me and listened while I talked. Now that is all passed too. However, I shall consider myself happy when someone comes to take me out of this place." But would this ever happen? Yes; one morning people came to clear out the garret, the boxes were packed away, and the tree was pulled out of the corner, and thrown roughly on the garret floor; then the servant dragged it out upon the staircase where the daylight shone. "Now life is beginning again," said the tree, rejoicing in the sunshine and fresh air. Then it was carried downstairs and taken into the courtyard so quickly, that it forgot to think of itself, and could only look about, there was so much to be seen. The court was close to a garden, where everything looked blooming. Fresh and fragrant roses hung over the little palings. The linden trees were in blossom; while the swallows flew here and there, crying, "Twit, twit, twit, my mate is coming"—but it was not the fir tree they meant. "Now I shall live," cried the tree, joyfully spreading out its branches; but alas! they were all withered and yellow, and it lay in a corner amongst weeds and nettles. The star of gold paper still stuck in the top of the tree and glittered in the sunshine. In the same courtyard two of the merry children were playing who had danced round the tree at Christmas, and had been so happy.

The youngest saw the gilded star, and ran and pulled it off the tree. "Look what is sticking to the ugly old fir tree," said the child, treading on the branches till they crackled under his boots. And the tree saw all the fresh bright flowers in the garden, and then looked at itself, and wished it had remained in the dark corner of the garret. It thought of its fresh youth in the forest, of the merry Christmas evening, and of the little mice who had listened to the story of "Humpty Dumpty."

"Past! past!" said the old tree; "Oh, had I but enjoyed myself while I could have done so! but now it is too late." Then a lad came and chopped the tree into small pieces, till a large bundle lay in a heap on the ground. The pieces were placed in a fire under the copper, and they quickly blazed up brightly, while the tree sighed so deeply that each sigh was like a pistol shot.

Then the children, who were at play, came and seated themselves in front of the fire, and looked at it and cried, "Pop, pop." But at each "pop," which was a deep sigh, the tree was thinking of a summer day in the forest; and of Christmas evening, and of "Humpty Dumpty," the only story it had ever heard or knew how to relate, till at last it was consumed. The boys still played in the garden, and the youngest wore the golden star on his breast, with which the tree had been adorned during the happiest evening of its existence. Now all was past; the tree's life was past, and the story also—for all stories must come to an end at last.

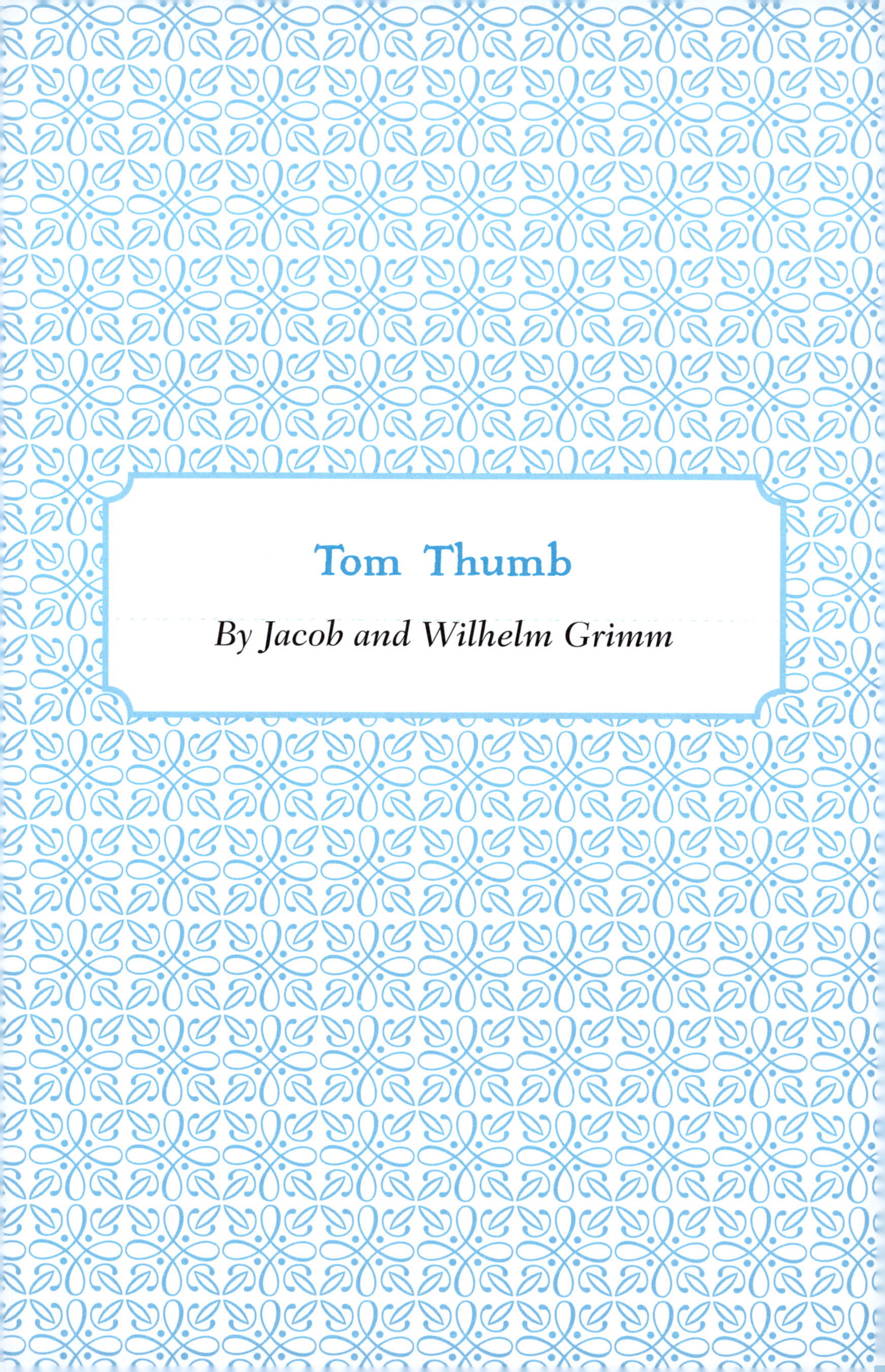
Tom Thumb
By Jacob and Wilhelm Grimm

A poor woodman sat in his cottage one night, smoking his pipe by the fireside, while his wife sat by his side spinning. "How lonely it is, wife," said he, as he puffed out a long curl of smoke, "for you and me to sit here by ourselves, without any children to play about and amuse us while other people seem so happy and merry with their children!"

"What you say is very true," said the wife, sighing, and turning round her wheel; "how happy should I be if I had but one child! If it were ever so small—nay, if it were no bigger than my thumb—I should be very happy, and love it dearly." Now—odd as you may think it—it came to pass that this good woman's wish was fulfilled, just in the very way she had wished it; for, not long afterwards, she had a little boy, who was quite healthy and strong, but was not much bigger than her thumb. So they said, "Well, we cannot say we have not got what we wished for, and, little as he is, we will love him dearly." And they called him Thomas Thumb.

They gave him plenty of food, yet for all they could do he never grew bigger, but kept just the same size as he had been when he was born. Still, his eyes were sharp and sparkling, and he soon showed himself to be a clever little fellow, who always knew well what he was about.

One day, as the woodman was getting ready to go into the wood to cut fuel, he said, "I wish I had someone to bring the cart after me, for I want to make haste."

"Oh, father," cried Tom, "I will take care of that; the cart shall be in the wood by the time you want it."

Then the woodman laughed, and said, "How can that be? you cannot reach up to the horse's bridle."

"Never mind that, father," said Tom; "if my mother will only harness the horse, I will get into his ear and tell him which way to go."

"Well," said the father, "we will try for once."

When the time came the mother harnessed the horse to the cart, and put Tom into his ear; and as he sat there the little man told the beast how to go, crying out, "Go on!" and "Stop!" as he wanted: and thus the horse went on just as well as if the woodman had driven it himself into the wood. It happened that as the horse was going a little too fast, and Tom was calling out, "Gently! gently!" two strangers came up.

"What an odd thing that is!" said one: "there is a cart going along, and I hear a carter talking to the horse, but yet I can see no one."

"That is queer, indeed," said the other; "let us follow the cart, and see where it goes." So they went on into the wood, till at last they came to the place where the woodman was.

Then Tom Thumb, seeing his father, cried out, "See, father, here I am with the cart, all right and safe! now take me down!" So his father took hold of the horse with one hand, and with the other took his son out of the horse's ear, and put him down upon a straw, where he sat as merry as you please.

The two strangers were all this time looking on, and did not know what to say for wonder. At last one took the other aside, and said, "That little urchin will make our fortune, if we can get him, and carry him about from town to town as a show; we must buy him." So they went up to the woodman, and asked him what he would take for the little man.

"He will be better off," said they, "with us than with you." "I won't sell him at all," said the father; "my own flesh and blood is dearer to me than all the silver and gold in the world." But Tom, hearing of the bargain they wanted to make, crept up his father's coat to his shoulder and whispered in his ear, "Take the money, father, and let them have me; I'll soon come back to you."

So the woodman at last said he would sell Tom to the strangers for a large piece of gold, and they paid the price. "Where would you like to sit?" said one of them.

"Oh, put me on the rim of your hat; that will be a nice gallery for me; I can walk about there and see the country as we go along." So they did as he wished; and when Tom had taken leave of his father they took him away with them.

They journeyed on till it began to be dusky, and then the little man said, "Let me get down, I'm tired." So the man took off his hat, and put him down on a clod of earth, in a ploughed field by the side of the road. But Tom ran about amongst the furrows, and at last slipped into an old mouse hole. "Good night, my masters!" said he, "I'm off! mind and look sharp after me the next time." Then they ran at once to the place, and poked the ends of their sticks into the mouse hole, but all in vain; Tom only crawled farther and farther in; and at last it became quite dark, so that they were forced to go their way without their prize, as sulky as could be.

When Tom found they were gone, he came out of his hiding place. "What dangerous walking it is," said he, "in this ploughed field! If I were to fall from one of these great clods, I should undoubtedly break my neck." At last, by good luck, he found a large empty snail shell. "This is lucky," said he, "I can sleep here very well"; and in he crept.

Just as he was falling asleep, he heard two men passing by, chatting together; and one said to the other, "How can we rob that rich parson's house of his silver and gold?"

"I'll tell you!" cried Tom.

"What noise was that?" said the thief, frightened; "I'm sure I heard someone speak."

They stood still listening, and Tom said, "Take me with you, and I'll soon show you how to get the parson's money."

"But where are you?" said they.

"Look about on the ground," answered he, "and listen where the sound comes from."

At last the thieves found him out, and lifted him up in their hands. "You little urchin!" they said, "what can you do for us?"

"Why, I can get between the iron window bars of the parson's house, and throw you out whatever you want."

"That's a good thought," said the thieves; "come along, we shall see what you can do."

When they came to the parson's house, Tom slipped through the window bars into the room, and then called out as loud as he could bawl, "Will you have all that is here?"

At this the thieves were frightened, and said, "Softly, softly! Speak low, that you may not awaken anybody."

But Tom seemed as if he did not understand them, and bawled out again, "How much will you have? Shall I throw it all out?"

Now the cook lay in the next room; and hearing a noise she raised herself up in her bed and listened. Meantime the thieves were frightened, and ran off a little way; but at last they plucked up their hearts, and said, "The little urchin is only trying to make fools of us." So they came back and whispered softly to him, saying, "Now let us have no more of your roguish jokes; but throw us out some of the money."

Then Tom called out as loud as he could, "Very well! hold your hands! here it comes."

The cook heard this quite plain, so she sprang out of bed, and ran to open the door. The thieves ran off as if a wolf was at their tails: and the maid, having groped about and found nothing, went away for a light. By the time she came back, Tom had slipped off into the barn; and when she had looked about and searched every hole and corner, and found nobody, she went to bed, thinking she must have been dreaming with her eyes open.

The little man crawled about in the hay loft, and at last found a snug place to finish his night's rest in; so he laid himself down, meaning to sleep till daylight, and then find his way home to his father and mother. But alas! how woefully he was undone! what crosses and sorrows happen to us all in this world! The cook got up early, before daybreak, to feed the cows; and going straight to the hay loft, carried away a large bundle of hay, with the little man in the middle of it, fast asleep. He still, however, slept on, and did not awake till he found himself in the mouth of the cow; for the cook had put the hay into the cow's rick, and the cow had taken Tom up in a mouthful of it.

"Good lack-a-day!" said he, "how came I to tumble into the mill?" But he soon found out where he really was, and was forced to have all his wits about him, that he might not get between the cow's teeth, and so be crushed to death. At last down he went into her stomach. "It is rather dark," said he; "they forgot to build windows in this room to let the sun in; a candle would be no bad thing."

Though he made the best of his bad luck, he did not like his quarters at all; and the worst of it was, that more and more hay was always coming down, and the space left for him became smaller and smaller. At last he cried out as loud as he could, "Don't bring me any more hay! Don't bring me any more hay!"

The maid happened to be just then milking the cow; and hearing someone speak, but seeing nobody, and yet being quite sure it was the same voice that she had heard in the night, she was so frightened that she fell off her stool, and overset the milk pail. As soon as she could pick herself up out of the dirt, she ran off as fast as she could to her master the parson, and said, "Sir, sir, the cow is talking!" But the parson said, "Woman, thou art surely mad!" However, he went with her into the cow house, to try and see what was the matter.

Scarcely had they set foot on the threshold, when Tom called out, "Don't bring me any more hay!" Then the parson himself was frightened; and thinking the cow was surely bewitched, told his man to kill her on the spot. So the cow was killed, and cut up; and the stomach, in which Tom lay, was thrown out upon a dunghill.

Tom soon set himself to work to get out, which was not a very easy task; but at last, just as he had made room to get his head out, fresh ill-luck befell him. A hungry wolf sprang out, and swallowed up the whole stomach, with Tom in it, at one gulp, and ran away.

Tom, however, was still not disheartened; and thinking the wolf would not dislike having some chat with him as he was going along, he called out, "My good friend, I can show you a famous treat."

"Where's that?" said the wolf.

"In such and such a house," said Tom, describing his own father's house. "You can crawl through the drain into the kitchen and then into the pantry, and there you will find cakes, ham, beef, cold chicken, roast pig, apple-dumplings, and everything that your heart can wish."

The wolf did not want to be asked twice; so that very night he went to the house and crawled through the drain into the kitchen, and then into the pantry, and ate and drank there to his heart's content. As soon as he had had enough he wanted to get away; but he had eaten so much that he could not go out by the same way he came in.

This was just what Tom had reckoned upon; and now he began to set up a great shout, making all the noise he could. "Will you be easy?" said the wolf; "you'll awaken everybody in the house if you make such a clatter."

"What's that to me?" said the little man; "you have had your frolic, now I've a mind to be merry myself"; and he began, singing and shouting as loud as he could.

The woodman and his wife, being awakened by the noise, peeped through a crack in the door; but when they saw a wolf was there, you may well suppose that they were sadly frightened; and the woodman ran for his axe, and gave his wife a scythe. "Do you stay behind," said the woodman, "and when I have knocked him on the head you must rip him up with the scythe."

Tom heard all this, and cried out, "Father, father! I am here, the wolf has swallowed me."

And his father said, "Heaven be praised! we have found our dear child again"; and he told his wife not to use the scythe for fear she should hurt him. Then he aimed a great blow, and struck the wolf on the head, and killed him on the spot! And when he was dead they cut open his body, and set Tommy free.

"Ah!" said the father, "what fears we have had for you!"

"Yes, father," answered he; "I have travelled all over the world, I think, in one way or other, since we parted; and now I am very glad to come home and get fresh air again."

"Why, where have you been?" said his father. "I have been in a mouse hole, and in a snail shell, and down a cow's throat, and in the wolf's belly; and yet here I am again, safe and sound."

"Well," said they, "you are come back, and we will not sell you again for all the riches in the world."

Then they hugged and kissed their dear little son, and gave him plenty to eat and drink, for he was very hungry; and then they fetched new clothes for him, for his old ones had been quite spoiled on his journey. So Master Thumb stayed at home with his father and mother, in peace; for though he had been so great a traveller, and had done and seen so many fine things, and was fond enough of telling the whole story, he always agreed that, after all, there's no place like home!

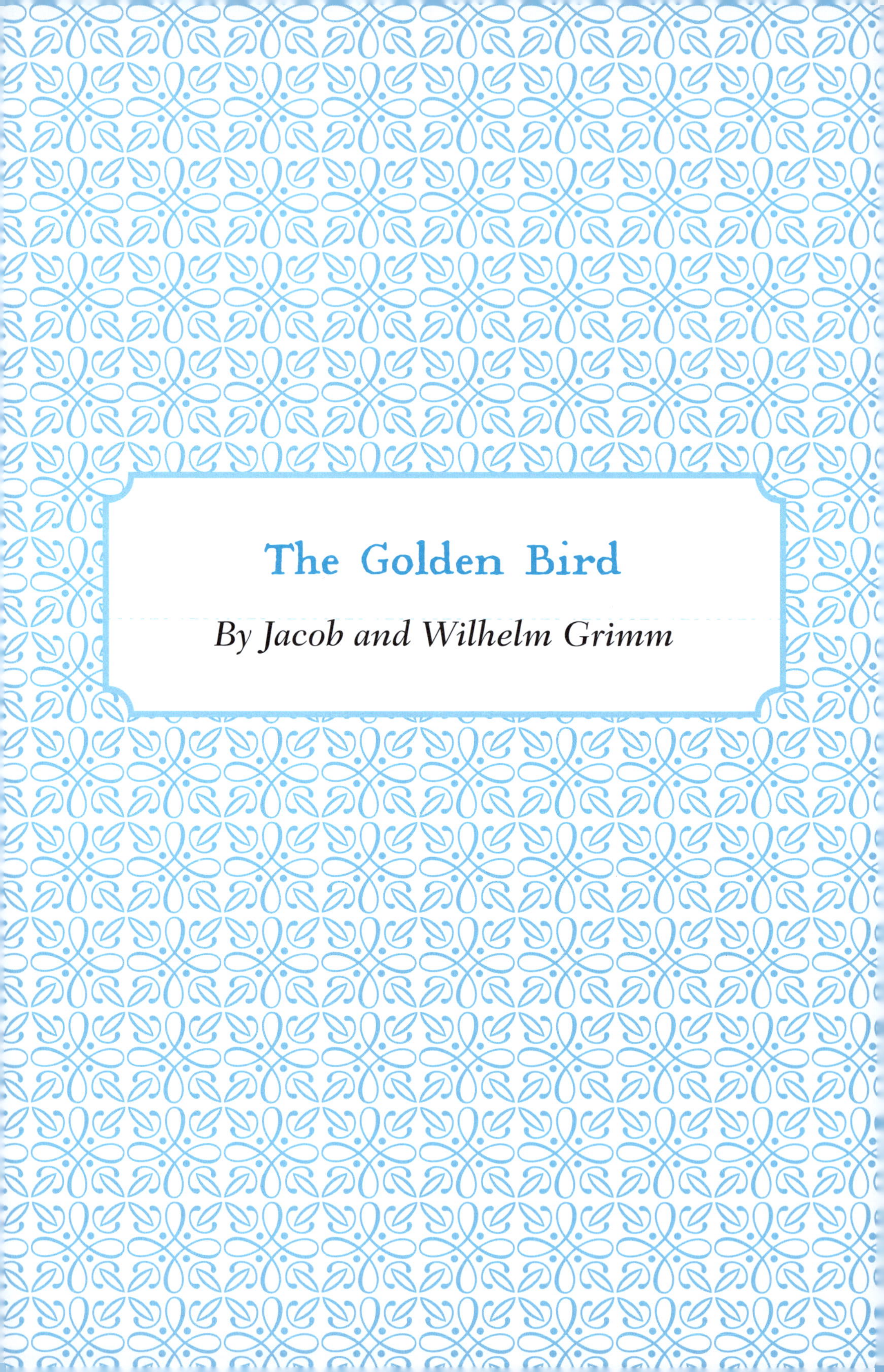

The Golden Bird

By Jacob and Wilhelm Grimm

A certain king had a beautiful garden, and in the garden stood a tree which bore golden apples. These apples were always counted, and about the time when they began to grow ripe it was found that every night one of them was gone. The king became very angry at this, and ordered the gardener to keep watch all night under the tree. The gardener set his eldest son to watch; but about twelve o'clock he fell asleep, and in the morning another of the apples was missing. Then the second son was ordered to watch; and at midnight he too fell asleep, and in the morning another apple was gone. Then the third son offered to keep watch; but the gardener at first would not let him, for fear some harm should come to him: however, at last he consented, and the young man laid himself under the tree to watch. As the clock struck twelve he heard a rustling noise in the air, and a bird came flying that was of pure gold; and as it was snapping at one of the apples with its beak, the gardener's son jumped up and shot an arrow at it. But the arrow did the bird no harm; only it dropped a golden feather from its tail, and then flew away. The golden feather was brought to the king in the morning, and all the council was called together. Everyone agreed that it was worth more than all the wealth of the kingdom: but the king said, "One feather is of no use to me, I must have the whole bird."

Then the gardener's eldest son set out and thought to find the golden bird very easily; and when he had gone but a little way, he came to a wood, and by the side of the wood he saw a fox sitting; so he took his bow and made ready to shoot at it. Then the fox said, "Do not shoot me, for I will give you good counsel; I know what your business is, and that you want to find the golden bird. You will reach a village in the evening; and when you get there, you will see two inns opposite to each other, one of which is very pleasant and beautiful to look at: go not in there, but rest for the night in the other, though it may appear to you to be very poor and mean."

But the son thought to himself, "What can such a beast as this know about the matter?" So he shot his arrow at the fox; but he missed it, and it set up its tail above its back and ran into the wood. Then he went his way, and in the evening came to the village where the two inns were; and in one of these were people singing, and dancing, and feasting; but the other looked very dirty, and poor. "I should be very silly," said he, "if I went to that shabby house, and left this charming place"; so he went into the smart house, and ate and drank at his ease, and forgot the bird, and his country too.

Time passed on; and as the eldest son did not come back, and no tidings were heard of him, the second son set out, and the same thing happened to him. He met the fox, who gave him the good advice: but when he came to the two inns, his eldest brother was standing at the window where the merrymaking was, and called to him to come in; and he could not withstand the temptation, but went in, and forgot the golden bird and his country in the same manner.

Time passed on again, and the youngest son too wished to set out into the wide world to seek for the golden bird; but his father would not listen to it for a long while, for he was very fond of his son, and was afraid that some ill luck might happen to him also, and prevent his coming back. However, at last it was agreed he should go, for he would not rest at home; and as he came to the wood, he met the fox, and heard the same good counsel. But he was thankful to the fox, and did not attempt his life as his brothers had done; so the fox said, "Sit upon my tail, and you will travel faster." So he sat down, and the fox began to run, and away they went over stock and stone so quick that their hair whistled in the wind.

When they came to the village, the son followed the fox's counsel, and without looking about him went to the shabby inn and rested there all night at his ease. In the morning came the fox again and met him as he was beginning his journey, and said, "Go straight forward, till you come to a castle, before which lie a whole troop of soldiers fast asleep and snoring: take no notice of them, but go into the castle and pass on and on till you come to a room, where the golden bird sits in a wooden cage; close by it stands a beautiful golden cage; but do not try to take the bird out of the shabby cage and put it into the handsome one, otherwise you will repent it." Then the fox stretched out his tail again, and the young man sat himself down, and away they went over stock and stone till their hair whistled in the wind.

Before the castle gate all was as the fox had said: so the son went in and found the chamber where the golden bird hung in a wooden cage, and below stood the golden cage, and the three golden apples that had been lost were lying close by it. Then thought he to himself, "It will be a very droll thing to bring away such a fine bird in this shabby cage"; so he opened the door and took hold of it and put it into the golden cage. But the bird set up such a loud scream that all the soldiers awoke, and they took him prisoner and carried him before the king. The next morning the court sat to judge him; and when all was heard, it sentenced him to die, unless he should bring the king the golden horse which could run as swiftly as the wind; and if he did this, he was to have the golden bird given him for his own.

So he set out once more on his journey, sighing, and in great despair, when on a sudden his friend the fox met him, and said, "You see now what has happened on account of your not listening to my counsel. I will still, however, tell you how to find the golden horse, if you will do as I bid you. You must go straight on till you come to the castle where the horse stands in his stall: by his side will lie the groom fast asleep and snoring: take away the horse quietly, but be sure to put the old leathern saddle upon him, and not the golden one that is close by it." Then the son sat down on the fox's tail, and away they went over stock and stone till their hair whistled in the wind.

All went right, and the groom lay snoring with his hand upon the golden saddle. But when the son looked at the horse, he thought it a great pity to put the leathern saddle upon it. "I will give him the good one," said he; "I am sure he deserves it." As he took up the golden saddle the groom awoke and cried out so loud, that all the guards ran in and took him prisoner, and in the morning he was again brought before the court to be judged, and was sentenced to die. But it was agreed, that, if he could bring thither the beautiful princess, he should live, and have the bird and the horse given him for his own.

Then he went his way very sorrowful; but the old fox came and said, "Why did not you listen to me? If you had, you would have carried away both the bird and the horse; yet will I once more give you counsel. Go straight on, and in the evening you will arrive at a castle. At twelve o'clock at night the princess goes to the bathing house: go up to her and give her a kiss, and she will let you lead her away; but take care you do not suffer her to go and take leave of her father and mother." Then the fox stretched out his tail, and so away they went over stock and stone till their hair whistled again.

As they came to the castle, all was as the fox had said, and at twelve o'clock the young man met the princess going to the bath and gave her the kiss, and she agreed to run away with him, but begged with many tears that he would let her take leave of her father. At first he refused, but she wept still more and more, and fell at his feet, till at last he consented; but the moment she came to her father's house the guards awoke and he was taken prisoner again.

Then he was brought before the king, and the king said, "You shall never have my daughter unless in eight days you dig away the hill that stops the view from my window." Now this hill was so big that the whole world could not take it away: and when he had worked for seven days, and had done very little, the fox came and said, "Lie down and go to sleep; I will work for you." And in the morning he awoke and the hill was gone; so he went merrily to the king, and told him that now that it was removed he must give him the princess.

Then the king was obliged to keep his word, and away went the young man and the princess; and the fox came and said to him, "We will have all three, the princess, the horse, and the bird."

"Ah!" said the young man, "that would be a great thing, but how can you contrive it?"

"If you will only listen," said the fox, "it can be done. When you come to the king, and he asks for the beautiful princess, you must say, 'Here she is!' Then he will be very joyful; and you will mount the golden horse that they are to give you, and put out your hand to take leave of them; but shake hands with the princess last. Then lift her quickly on to the horse behind you; clap your spurs to his side, and gallop away as fast as you can."

All went right: then the fox said, "When you come to the castle where the bird is, I will stay with the princess at the door, and you will ride in and speak to the king; and when he sees that it is the right horse, he will bring out the bird; but you must sit still, and say that you want to look at it, to see whether it is the true golden bird; and when you get it into your hand, ride away."

This, too, happened as the fox said; they carried off the bird, the princess mounted again, and they rode on to a great wood. Then the fox came, and said, "Pray kill me, and cut off my head and my feet." But the young man refused to do it: so the fox said, "I will at any rate give you good counsel: beware of two things; ransom no one from the gallows, and sit down by the side of no river." Then away he went. "Well," thought the young man, "it is no hard matter to keep that advice."

He rode on with the princess, till at last he came to the village where he had left his two brothers. And there he heard a great noise and uproar;

and when he asked what was the matter, the people said, "Two men are going to be hanged." As he came nearer, he saw that the two men were his brothers, who had turned robbers; so he said, "Cannot they in any way be saved?" But the people said "No," unless he would bestow all his money upon the rascals and buy their liberty. Then he did not stay to think about the matter, but paid what was asked, and his brothers were given up, and went on with him towards their home.

And as they came to the wood where the fox first met them, it was so cool and pleasant that the two brothers said, "Let us sit down by the side of the river, and rest a while, to eat and drink." So he said, "Yes," and forgot the fox's counsel, and sat down on the side of the river; and while he suspected nothing, they came behind, and threw him down the bank, and took the princess, the horse, and the bird, and went home to the king their master, and said, "All this have we won by our labour." Then there was great rejoicing made; but the horse would not eat, the bird would not sing, and the princess wept.

The youngest son fell to the bottom of the river's bed: luckily it was nearly dry, but his bones were almost broken, and the bank was so steep that he could find no way to get out. Then the old fox came once more, and scolded him for not following his advice; otherwise no evil would have befallen him: "Yet," said he, "I cannot leave you here, so lay hold of my tail and hold fast." Then he pulled him out of the river, and said to him, as he got upon the bank, "Your brothers have set watch to kill you, if they find you in the kingdom." So he dressed himself as a poor man, and came secretly to the king's court, and was scarcely within the doors when the horse began to eat, and the bird to sing, and the princess left off weeping. Then he went to the king, and told him all his brothers' roguery; and they were seized and punished, and he had the princess given to him again; and after the king's death he was heir to his kingdom.

A long while after, he went to walk one day in the wood, and the old fox met him, and besought him with tears in his eyes to kill him, and cut off his head and feet. And at last he did so, and in a moment the fox was changed into a man, and turned out to be the brother of the princess, who had been lost a great many, many years.

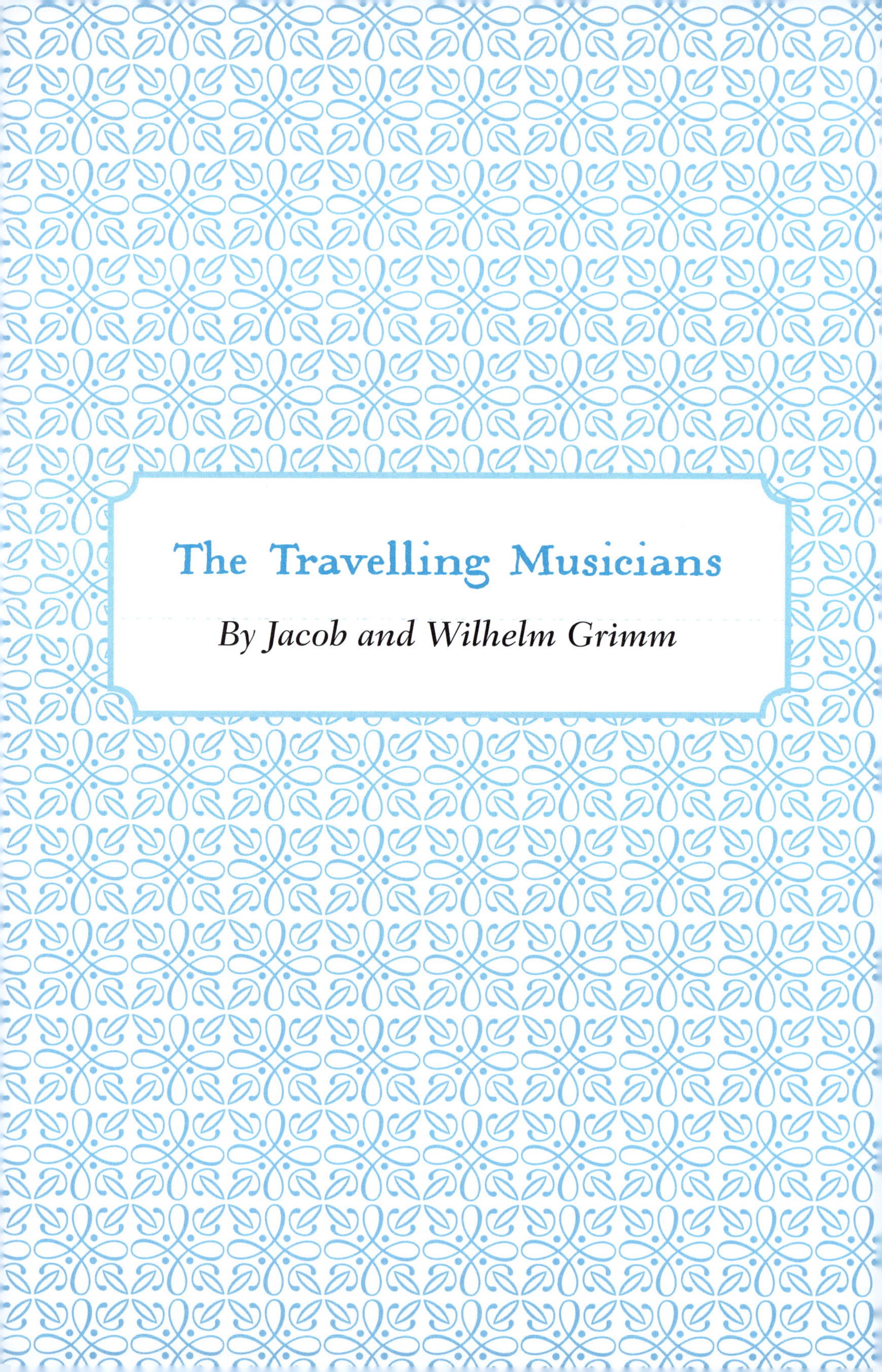

The Travelling Musicians

By Jacob and Wilhelm Grimm

An honest farmer had once a donkey that had been a faithful servant to him a great many years, but was now growing old and every day more and more unfit for work. His master therefore was tired of keeping him and began to think of putting an end to him; but the donkey, who saw that some mischief was in the wind, took himself slyly off, and began his journey towards the great city, "For there," thought he, "I may turn musician."

After he had travelled a little way, he spied a dog lying by the roadside and panting as if he were tired. "What makes you pant so, my friend?" said the donkey.

"Alas!" said the dog, "my master was going to knock me on the head, because I am old and weak, and can no longer make myself useful to him in hunting; so I ran away; but what can I do to earn my livelihood?"

"Hark ye!" said the donkey, "I am going to the great city to turn musician: suppose you go with me, and try what you can do in the same way?" The dog said he was willing, and they jogged on together.

They had not gone far before they saw a cat sitting in the middle of the road and making a most rueful face. "Pray, my good lady," said the donkey, "what's the matter with you? You look quite out of spirits!"

"Ah, me!" said the cat, "how can one be in good spirits when one's life is in danger? Because I am beginning to grow old, and had rather lie at my ease by the fire than run about the house after the mice, my mistress laid hold of me, and was going to drown me; and though I have been lucky enough to get away from her, I do not know what I am to live upon."

"Oh," said the donkey, "by all means go with us to the great city; you are a good night singer, and may make your fortune as a musician." The cat was pleased with the thought, and joined the party.

Soon afterwards, as they were passing by a farmyard, they saw a cock perched upon a gate, and screaming out with all his might and main. "Bravo!" said the donkey; "upon my word, you make a famous noise; pray what is all this about?"

"Why," said the cock, "I was just now saying that we should have fine weather for our washing day, and yet my mistress and the cook don't thank me for my pains, but threaten to cut off my head tomorrow, and make broth of me for the guests that are coming on Sunday!"

"Heaven forbid!" said the donkey, "come with us Master Chanticleer; it will be better, at any rate, than staying here to have your head cut off! Besides, who knows? If we care to sing in tune, we may get up some kind of a concert; so come along with us."

"With all my heart," said the cock: so they all four went on jollily together.

They could not, however, reach the great city the first day; so when night came on, they went into a wood to sleep. The donkey and the dog laid themselves down under a great tree, and the cat climbed up into the branches; while the cock, thinking that the higher he sat the safer he should be, flew up to the very top of the tree, and then, according to his custom, before he went to sleep, looked out on all sides of him to see that everything was well. In doing this, he saw afar off something bright and shining and calling to his companions said, "There must be a house no great way off, for I see a light."

"If that be the case," said the donkey, "we had better change our quarters, for our lodging is not the best in the world!"

"Besides," added the dog, "I should not be the worse for a bone or two, or a bit of meat." So they walked off together towards the spot where Chanticleer had seen the light, and as they drew near it became larger and brighter, till they at last came close to a house in which a gang of robbers lived.

The donkey, being the tallest of the company, marched up to the window and peeped in. "Well, Donkey," said Chanticleer, "what do you see?"

"What do I see?" replied the donkey. "Why, I see a table spread with all kinds of good things, and robbers sitting round it making merry."

"That would be a noble lodging for us," said the cock.

"Yes," said the donkey, "if we could only get in"; so they consulted together how they should contrive to get the robbers out; and at last they hit upon a plan. The donkey placed himself upright on his hind legs, with his forefeet resting against the window; the dog got upon his back; the cat scrambled up to the dog's shoulders, and the cock flew up and sat upon the cat's head. When all was ready a signal was given, and they began their music. The donkey brayed, the dog barked, the cat mewed, and the cock screamed; and then they all broke through the window at once, and came tumbling into the room, amongst the broken glass, with a most hideous clatter! The robbers, who had been not a little frightened by the opening concert, had now no doubt that some frightful hobgoblin had broken in upon them, and scampered away as fast as they could.

The coast once clear, our travellers soon sat down and dispatched what the robbers had left, with as much eagerness as if they had not expected to eat again for a month. As soon as they had satisfied themselves, they put out the lights, and each once more sought out a resting place to his own liking. The donkey laid himself down upon a heap of straw in the yard, the dog stretched himself upon a mat behind the door, the cat rolled herself up on the hearth before the warm ashes, and the cock perched upon a beam on the top of the house; and, as they were all rather tired with their journey, they soon fell asleep.

But about midnight, when the robbers saw from afar that the lights were out and that all seemed quiet, they began to think that they had been in too great a hurry to run away; and one of them, who was bolder than the rest, went to see what was going on. Finding everything still, he marched into the kitchen, and groped about till he found a match in order to light a candle; and then, espying the glittering fiery eyes of the cat, he mistook them for live coals, and held the match to them to light it. But the cat, not understanding this joke, sprang at his face, and spat, and scratched at him. This frightened him dreadfully, and away he ran to the back door; but there the dog jumped up and bit him in the leg; and as he was crossing over the yard the donkey kicked him; and the cock, who had been awakened by the noise, crowed with all his might. At this the robber ran back as fast as he could to his comrades, and told the captain how a horrid witch had got into the house, and had spat at him and scratched his face with her long bony fingers; how a man with a knife in his hand had hidden himself behind the door, and stabbed him in the leg; how a black monster stood in the yard and struck him with a club; and how the devil had sat upon the top of the house and cried out, "Throw the rascal up here!" After this the robbers never dared to go back to the house; but the musicians were so pleased with their quarters that they took up their abode there; and there they are, I dare say, at this very day.

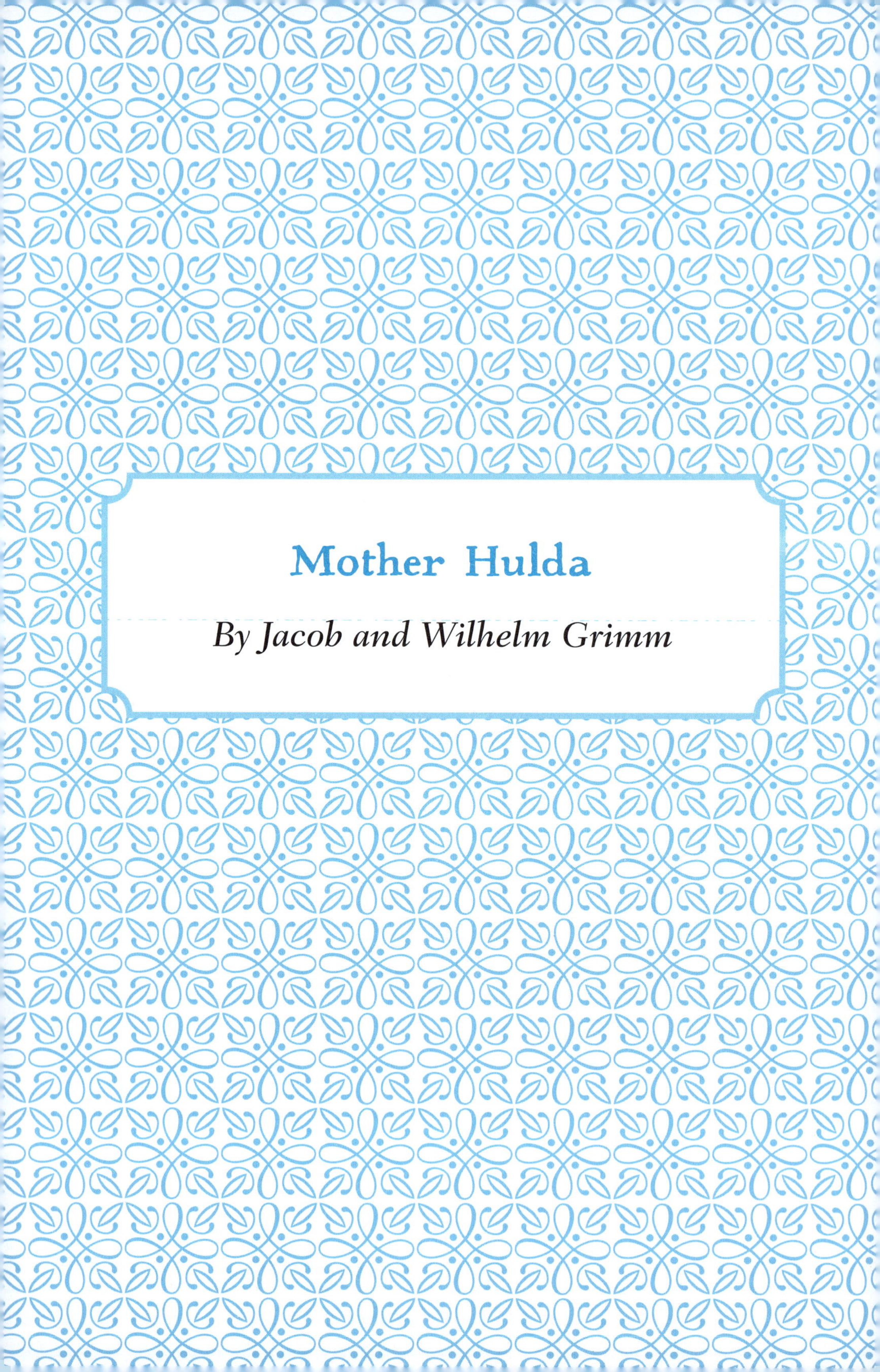

Mother Hulda

By Jacob and Wilhelm Grimm

Once upon a time there was a widow who had two daughters; one of them was beautiful and industrious, the other ugly and lazy. The mother, however, loved the ugly and lazy one best, because she was her own daughter, and so the other, who was only her stepdaughter, was made to do all the work of the house, and was quite the Cinderella of the family. Her stepmother sent her out every day to sit by the well in the high road, there to spin until she made her fingers bleed. Now it chanced one day that some blood fell on to the spindle, and as the girl stopped over the well to wash it off, the spindle suddenly sprang out of her hand and fell into the well. She ran home crying to tell of her misfortune, but her stepmother spoke harshly to her, and after giving her a violent scolding, said unkindly, "As you have let the spindle fall into the well you may go yourself and fetch it out."

The girl went back to the well not knowing what to do, and at last in her distress she jumped into the water after the spindle.

She remembered nothing more until she awoke and found herself in a beautiful meadow, full of sunshine, and with countless flowers blooming in every direction.

She walked over the meadow, and presently she came upon a baker's oven full of bread, and the loaves cried out to her, "Take us out, take us out, or alas! we shall be burnt to a cinder; we were baked through long ago." So she took the bread shovel and drew them all out.

She went on a little farther, till she came to a tree full of apples. "Shake me, shake me, I pray," cried the tree; "my apples, one and all, are ripe." So she shook the tree, and the apples came falling down upon her like rain; but she continued shaking until there was not a single apple left upon it. Then she carefully gathered the apples together in a heap and walked on again.

The next thing she came to was a little house, and there she saw an old woman looking out, with such large teeth, that she was terrified, and turned to run away. But the old woman called after her, "What are you afraid of, dear child? Stay with me; if you will do the work of my house properly for me, I will make you very happy. You must be very careful, however, to make my bed in the right way, for I wish you always to shake it thoroughly, so that the feathers fly about; then they say, down there in the world, that it is snowing; for I am Mother Hulda." The old woman spoke so kindly, that the girl summoned up courage and agreed to enter into her service.

She took care to do everything according to the old woman's bidding and every time she made the bed she shook it with all her might, so that the feathers flew about like so many snowflakes. The old woman was as good as her word: she never spoke angrily to her, and gave her roast and boiled meats every day.

So she stayed on with Mother Hulda for some time, and then she began to grow unhappy. She could not at first tell why she felt sad, but she became conscious at last of great longing to go home; then she knew she was homesick, although she was a thousand times better off with Mother Hulda than with her mother and sister. After waiting awhile, she went to Mother Hulda and said, "I am so homesick, that I cannot stay with you any longer, for although I am so happy here, I must return to my own people."

Then Mother Hulda said, "I am pleased that you should want to go back to your own people, and as you have served me so well and faithfully, I will take you home myself."

Thereupon she led the girl by the hand up to a broad gateway. The gate was opened, and as the girl passed through, a shower of gold fell upon her, and the gold clung to her, so that she was covered with it from head to foot.

"That is a reward for your industry," said Mother Hulda, and as she spoke she handed her the spindle which she had dropped into the well.

The gate was then closed, and the girl found herself back in the old world close to her mother's house. As she entered the courtyard, the cock, who was perched on the well, called out:

"Cock-a-doodle-doo!
Your golden daughter's come back to you."

Then she went in to her mother and sister, and as she was so richly covered with gold, they gave her a warm welcome. She related to them all that had happened, and when the mother heard how she had come by her great riches, she thought she should like her ugly, lazy daughter to go and try her fortune. So she made the sister go and sit by the well and spin, and the girl pricked her finger and thrust her hand into a thornbush, so that she might drop some blood on to the spindle; then she threw it into the well, and jumped in herself.

Like her sister she awoke in the beautiful meadow, and walked over it till she came to the oven. "Take us out, take us out, or alas! we shall be burnt to a cinder; we were baked through long ago," cried the loaves as before. But the lazy girl answered, "Do you think I am going to dirty my hands for you?" and walked on.

Presently she came to the apple tree. "Shake me, shake me, I pray; my apples, one and all, are ripe," it cried. But she only answered, "A nice thing to ask me to do, one of the apples might fall on my head," and passed on.

At last she came to Mother Hulda's house, and as she had heard all about the large teeth from her sister, she was not afraid of them, and engaged herself without delay to the old woman.

The first day she was very obedient and industrious, and exerted herself to please Mother Hulda, for she thought of the gold she should get in return. The next day, however, she began to dawdle over her work, and the third day she was more idle still; then she began to lie in bed in the mornings and refused to get up. Worse still, she neglected to make the old woman's bed properly, and forgot to shake it so that the feathers might fly about. So Mother Hulda very soon got tired of her, and told her she might go. The lazy girl was delighted at this, and thought to herself, "The gold will soon be mine." Mother Hulda led her, as she had led her sister, to the broad gateway; but as she was passing through, instead of the shower of gold, a great bucketful of pitch came pouring over her.

"That is in return for your services," said the old woman, and she shut the gate.

So the lazy girl had to go home covered with pitch, and the cock on the well called out as he saw her:

"Cock-a-doodle-doo!
Your dirty daughter's come back to you."

But, try what she would, she could not get the pitch off and it stuck to her as long as she lived.

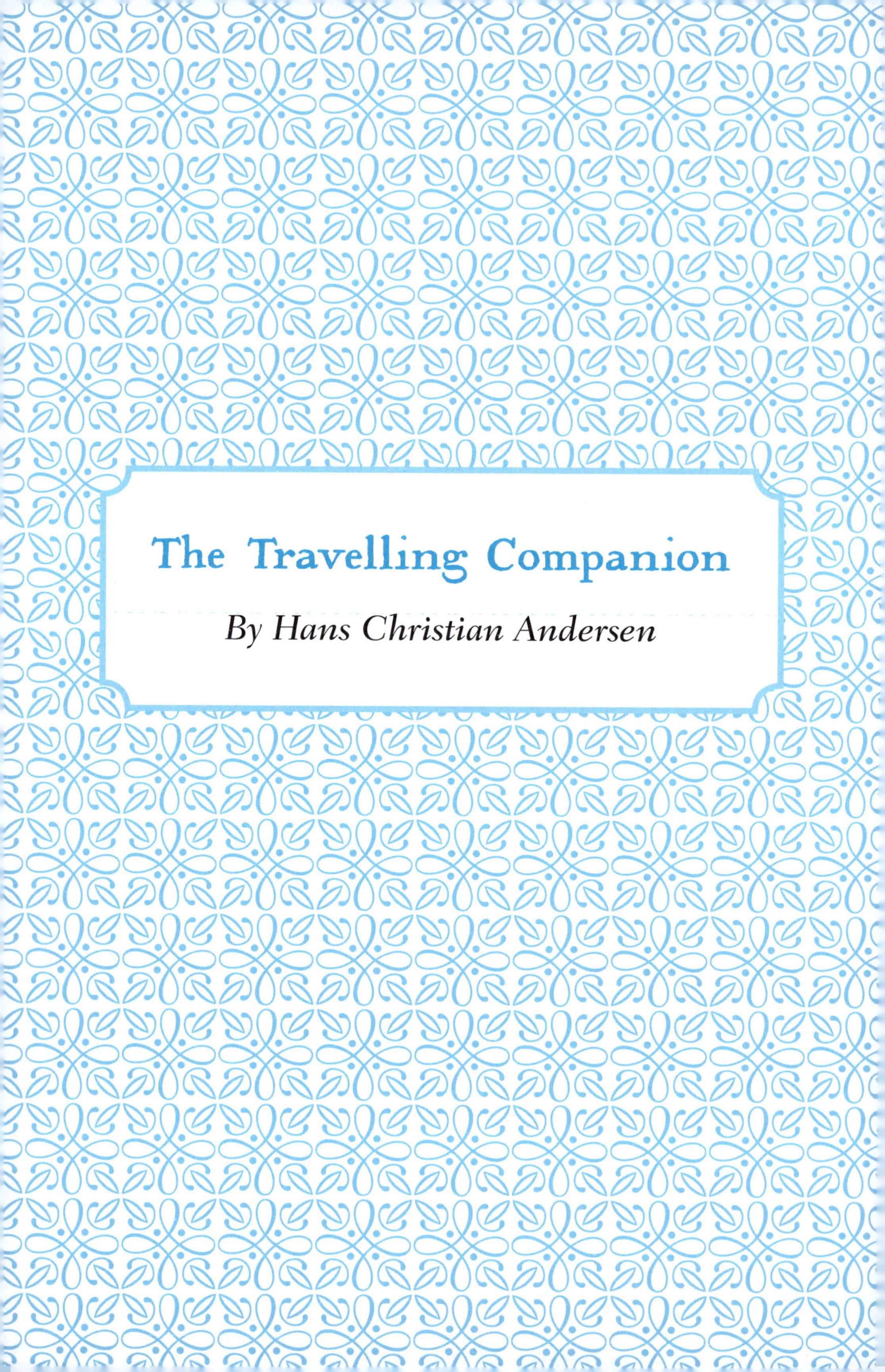
The Travelling Companion
By Hans Christian Andersen

Poor John was very sad; for his father was so ill, he had no hope of his recovery. John sat alone with the sick man in the little room, and the lamp had nearly burnt out; for it was late in the night.

"You have been a good son, John," said the sick father, "and God will help you on in the world." He looked at him, as he spoke, with mild, earnest eyes, drew a deep sigh, and died; yet it appeared as if he still slept.

John wept bitterly. He had no one in the wide world now; neither father, mother, brother, nor sister. Poor John! he knelt down by the bed, kissed his dead father's hand, and wept many, many bitter tears. But at last his eyes closed, and he fell asleep with his head resting against the hard bedpost. Then he dreamed a strange dream; he thought he saw the sun shining upon him, and his father alive and well, and even heard him laughing as he used to do when he was very happy. A beautiful girl, with a golden crown on her head, and long, shining hair, gave him her hand; and his father said, "See what a bride you have won. She is the loveliest maiden on the whole earth." Then he awoke, and all the beautiful things vanished before his eyes, his father lay dead on the bed, and he was all alone. Poor John!

During the following week the dead man was buried. The son walked behind the coffin which contained his father, whom he so dearly loved, and would never again behold. He heard the earth fall on the coffin-lid, and watched it till only a corner remained in sight, and at last that also disappeared. He felt as if his heart would break with its weight of sorrow, till those who stood round the grave sang a psalm, and the sweet, holy tones brought tears into his eyes, which relieved him. The sun shone brightly down on the green trees, as if it would say, "You must not be so sorrowful, John. Do you see the beautiful blue sky above you? Your father is up there, and he prays to the loving Father of all, that you may do well in the future."

"I will always be good," said John, "and then I shall go to be with my father in heaven. What joy it will be when we see each other again! How much I shall have to relate to him, and how many things he will be able to explain to me of the delights of heaven, and teach me as he once did on earth. Oh, what joy it will be!"

He pictured it all so plainly to himself, that he smiled even while the tears ran down his cheeks.

The little birds in the chestnut trees twittered, "Tweet, tweet"; they were so happy, although they had seen the funeral; but they seemed as if they knew that the dead man was now in heaven, and that he had wings much larger and more beautiful than their own; and he was happy now, because he had been good here on earth, and they were glad of it. John saw them fly away out of the green trees into the wide world, and he longed to fly with them; but first he cut out a large wooden cross, to place on his father's grave; and when he brought it there in the evening, he found the grave decked out with gravel and flowers. Strangers had done this; they who had known the good old father who was now dead, and who had loved him very much.

Early the next morning, John packed up his little bundle of clothes, and placed all his money, which consisted of fifty dollars and a few shillings, in his girdle; with this he determined to try his fortune in the world. But first he went into the churchyard; and, by his father's grave, he offered up a prayer, and said, "Farewell."

As he passed through the fields, all the flowers looked fresh and beautiful in the warm sunshine, and nodded in the wind, as if they wished to say, "Welcome to the green wood, where all is fresh and bright."

Then John turned to have one more look at the old church, in which he had been christened in his infancy, and where his father had taken him every Sunday to hear the service and join in singing the psalms. As he looked at the old tower, he espied the ringer standing at one of the narrow openings, with his little pointed red cap on his head, and shading his eyes from the sun with his bent arm. John nodded farewell to him, and the little ringer waved his red cap, laid his hand on his heart, and kissed his hand to him a great many times, to show that he felt kindly towards him, and wished him a prosperous journey.

John continued his journey, and thought of all the wonderful things he should see in the large, beautiful world, till he found himself farther away from home than ever he had been before. He did not even know the names of the places he passed through, and could scarcely understand the language of the people he met, for he was far away, in a strange land. The first night he slept on a haystack, out in the fields, for there was no other bed for him; but it seemed to him so nice and comfortable that even a king need not wish for a better. The field, the brook, the haystack, with the blue sky above, formed a beautiful sleeping room. The green grass, with the little red and white flowers, was the carpet; the elder bushes and the hedges of wild roses looked like garlands on the walls; and for a bath he could have the clear, fresh water of the brook; while the rushes bowed their heads to him, to wish him good morning and good evening. The moon, like a large lamp, hung high up in the blue ceiling, and he had no fear of its setting fire to his curtains. John slept here quite safely all night; and when he awoke, the sun was up, and all the little birds were singing round him, "Good morning, good morning. Are you not up yet?"

It was Sunday, and the bells were ringing for church. As the people went in, John followed them; he heard God's word, joined in singing the psalms, and listened to the preacher. It seemed to him just as if he were in his own church, where he had been christened, and had sung the psalms with his father. Out in the churchyard were several graves, and on some of them the grass had grown very high. John thought of his father's grave, which he knew at last would look like these, as he was not there to weed and attend to it. Then he set to work, pulled up the high grass, raised the wooden crosses which had fallen down, and replaced the wreaths which had been blown away from their places by the wind, thinking all the time, "Perhaps someone is doing the same for my father's grave, as I am not there to do it."

Outside the church door stood an old beggar, leaning on his crutch. John gave him his silver shillings, and then he continued his journey, feeling lighter and happier than ever. Towards evening, the weather became very stormy, and he hastened on as quickly as he could, to get shelter; but it was quite dark by the time he reached a little lonely church which stood on a hill. "I will go in here," he said, "and sit down in a corner; for I am quite tired, and want rest."

So he went in, and seated himself; then he folded his hands, and offered up his evening prayer, and was soon fast asleep and dreaming, while the thunder rolled and the lightning flashed without. When he awoke, it was still night; but the storm had ceased, and the moon shone in upon him through the windows. Then he saw an open coffin standing in the centre of the church, which contained a dead man, waiting for burial. John was not at all timid; he had a good conscience, and he knew also that the dead can never injure anyone. It is living wicked men who do harm to others. Two such wicked persons stood now by the dead man, who had been brought to the church to be buried. Their evil intentions were to throw the poor dead body outside the church door, and not leave him to rest in his coffin.

"Why do you do this?" asked John, when he saw what they were going to do; "it is very wicked. Leave him to rest in peace, in Christ's name."

"Nonsense," replied the two dreadful men. "He has cheated us; he owed us money which he could not pay, and now he is dead we shall not get a penny; so we mean to have our revenge, and let him lie like a dog outside the church door."

"I have only fifty dollars," said John, "it is all I possess in the world, but I will give it to you if you will promise me faithfully to leave the dead man in peace. I shall be able to get on without the money; I have strong and healthy limbs, and God will always help me."

"Why, of course," said the horrid men, "if you will pay his debt we will both promise not to touch him. You may depend upon that"; and then they took the money he offered them, laughed at him for his good nature, and went their way.

Then he laid the dead body back in the coffin, folded the hands, and took leave of it; and went away contentedly through the great forest. All around him he could see the prettiest little elves dancing in the moonlight, which shone through the trees. They were not disturbed by his appearance, for they knew he was good and harmless among men. They are wicked people only who can never obtain a glimpse of fairies. Some of them were not taller than the breadth of a finger, and they wore golden combs in their long, yellow hair. They were rocking themselves two together on the large dewdrops with which the leaves and the high grass were sprinkled. Sometimes the dewdrops would roll away, and then they fell down between the stems of the long grass, and caused a great deal of laughing and noise among the other little people. It was quite charming to watch them at play. Then they sang songs, and John remembered that he had learnt those pretty songs when he was a little boy. Large speckled spiders, with silver crowns on their heads, were employed to spin suspension bridges and palaces from one hedge to another, and when the tiny drops fell upon them, they glittered in the moonlight like shining glass. This continued till sunrise. Then the little elves crept into the flower buds, and the wind seized the bridges and palaces, and fluttered them in the air like cobwebs.

As John left the wood, a strong man's voice called after him, "Hallo, comrade, where are you travelling?"

"Into the wide world," he replied, "I am only a poor lad, I have neither father nor mother, but God will help me."

"I am going into the wide world also," replied the stranger; "shall we keep each other company?"

"With all my heart," he said, and so they went on together. Soon they began to like each other very much, for they were both good; but John found out that the stranger was much more clever than himself. He had travelled all over the world, and could describe almost everything. The sun was high in the heavens when they seated themselves under a large tree to eat their breakfast, and at the same moment an old woman came towards them. She was very old and almost bent double. She leaned upon a stick and carried on her back a bundle of firewood, which she had collected in the forest; her apron was tied round it, and John saw three great stems of fern and some willow twigs peeping out. Just as she came close up to them, her foot slipped and she fell to the ground screaming loudly; poor old woman, she had broken her leg! John proposed directly that they should carry the old woman home to her cottage; but the stranger opened his knapsack and took out a box, in which he said he had a salve that would quickly make her leg well and strong again, so that she would be able to walk home herself, as if her leg had never been broken. And all that he would ask in return was the three fern stems which she carried in her apron.

"That is rather too high a price," said the old woman, nodding her head quite strangely. She did not seem at all inclined to part with the fern stems. However, it was not very agreeable to lie there with a broken leg, so she gave them to him; and such was the power of the ointment, that no sooner had he rubbed her leg with it than the old mother rose up and walked even better than she had done before. But then this wonderful ointment could not be bought at a chemist's.

"What can you want with those three fern rods?" asked John of his fellow traveller.

"Oh, they will make capital brooms," said he; "and I like them because I have strange whims sometimes." Then they walked on together for a long distance.

"How dark the sky is becoming," said John; "and look at those thick, heavy clouds."

"Those are not clouds," replied his fellow traveller; "they are mountains—large lofty mountains—on the tops of which we should be above the clouds, in the pure, free air. Believe me, it is delightful to ascend so high, tomorrow we shall be there." But the mountains were not so near as they appeared; they had to travel a whole day before they reached them, and pass through black forests and piles of rock as large as a town. The journey had been so fatiguing that John and his fellow traveller stopped to rest at a roadside inn, so that they might gain strength for their journey on the morrow. In the large public room of the inn a great many persons were assembled to see a comedy performed by dolls. The showman had just erected his little theatre, and the people were sitting round the room to witness the performance. Right in front, in the very best place, sat a stout butcher, with a great bulldog by his side who seemed very much inclined to bite. He sat staring with all his eyes, and so indeed did everyone else in the room. And then the play began. It was a pretty piece, with a king and a queen in it, who sat on a beautiful throne, and had gold crowns on their heads. The trains to their dresses were very long, according to the fashion; while the prettiest of wooden dolls, with glass eyes and large mustaches, stood at the doors, and opened and shut them, that the fresh air might come into the room. It was a very pleasant play, not at all mournful; but just as the queen stood up and walked across the stage, the great bulldog, who should have been held back by his master, made a spring forward, and caught the queen in the teeth by the slender wrist, so that it snapped in two. This was a very dreadful disaster. The poor man, who was exhibiting the dolls, was much annoyed, and quite sad about his queen; she was the prettiest doll he had, and the bulldog had broken her head and shoulders off. But after all the people were gone away, the stranger, who came with John, said that he could soon set her to rights. And then he brought out his box and rubbed the doll with some of the salve with which he had cured the old woman when she broke her leg. As soon as this was done the doll's back became quite right again; her head and shoulders were fixed on, and she could even move her limbs herself: there was now no occasion to pull the wires, for the doll acted just like a living creature, excepting that she could not speak. The man to whom the show belonged was quite delighted at having a doll who could dance of herself without being pulled by the wires; none of the other dolls could do this.

During the night, when all the people at the inn were gone to bed, someone was heard to sigh so deeply and painfully, and the sighing continued for so long a time, that everyone got up to see what could be the matter. The showman went at once to his little theatre and found that it proceeded from the dolls, who all lay on the floor sighing piteously, and staring with their glass eyes; they all wanted to be rubbed with the ointment, so that, like the queen, they might be able to move of themselves. The queen threw herself on her knees, took off her beautiful crown, and, holding it in her hand, cried, "Take this from me, but do rub my husband and his courtiers."

The poor man who owned the theatre could scarcely refrain from weeping; he was so sorry that he could not help them. Then he immediately spoke to John's comrade, and promised him all the money he might receive at the next evening's performance, if he would only rub the ointment on four or five of his dolls. But the fellow traveller said he did not require anything in return, excepting the sword which the showman wore by his side. As soon as he received the sword he anointed six of the dolls with the ointment, and they were able immediately to dance so gracefully that all the living girls in the room could not help joining in the dance. The coachman danced with the cook, and the waiters with the chambermaids, and all the strangers joined; even the tongs and the fire shovel made an attempt, but they fell down after the first jump. So after all it was a very merry night. The next morning John and his companion left the inn to continue their journey through the great pine forests and over the high mountains. They arrived at last at such a great height that towns and villages lay beneath them, and the church steeples looked like little specks between the green trees. They could see for miles round, far away to places they had never visited, and John saw more of the beautiful world than he had ever known before. The sun shone brightly in the blue firmament above, and through the clear mountain air came the sound of the huntsman's horn, and the soft, sweet notes brought tears into his eyes, and he could not help exclaiming, "How good and loving God is to give us all this beauty and loveliness in the world to make us happy!"

His fellow traveller stood by with folded hands, gazing on the dark wood and the towns bathed in the warm sunshine. At this moment there sounded over their heads sweet music. They looked up, and discovered a large white swan hovering in the air, and singing as never bird sang before. But the song soon became weaker and weaker, the bird's head drooped, and he sunk slowly down, and lay dead at their feet.

"It is a beautiful bird," said the traveller, "and these large white wings are worth a great deal of money. I will take them with me. You see now that a sword will be very useful."

So he cut off the wings of the dead swan with one blow, and carried them away with him.

They now continued their journey over the mountains for many miles, till they at length reached a large city, containing hundreds of towers, that shone in the sunshine like silver. In the midst of the city stood a splendid marble palace, roofed with pure red gold, in which dwelt the king. John and his companion would not go into the town immediately; so they stopped at an inn outside the town, to change their clothes; for they wished to appear respectable as they walked through the streets. The landlord told them that the king was a very good man, who never injured anyone: but as to his daughter, "Heaven defend us!"

She was indeed a wicked princess. She possessed beauty enough—nobody could be more elegant or prettier than she was; but what of that? for she was a wicked witch; and in consequence of her conduct many noble young princes had lost their lives. Any one was at liberty to make her an offer; were he a prince or a beggar, it mattered not to her. She would ask him to guess three things which she had just thought of, and if he succeed, he was to marry her, and be king over all the land when her father died; but if he could not guess these three things, then she ordered him to be hanged or to have his head cut off. The old king, her father, was very much grieved at her conduct, but he could not prevent her from being so wicked, because he once said he would have nothing more to do with her lovers; she might do as she pleased. Each prince who came and tried the three guesses, so that he might marry the princess, had been unable to find them out, and had been hanged or beheaded. They had all been warned in time, and might have left her alone, if they would. The old king became at last so distressed at all these dreadful circumstances, that for a whole day every year he and his soldiers knelt and prayed that the princess might become good; but she continued as wicked as ever. The old women who drank brandy would color it quite black before they drank it, to show how they mourned; and what more could they do?

"What a horrible princess!" said John; "she ought to be well flogged. If I were the old king, I would have her punished in some way."

Just then they heard the people outside shouting, "Hurrah!" and, looking out, they saw the princess passing by; and she was really so beautiful that everybody forgot her wickedness, and shouted "Hurrah!" Twelve lovely maidens in white silk dresses, holding golden tulips in their hands, rode by her side on coal-black horses. The princess herself had a snow-white steed, decked with diamonds and rubies. Her dress was of cloth of gold, and the whip she held in her hand looked like a sunbeam. The golden crown on her head glittered like the stars of heaven, and her mantle was formed of thousands of butterflies' wings sewn together. Yet she herself was more beautiful than all.

When John saw her, his face became as red as a drop of blood, and he could scarcely utter a word. The princess looked exactly like the beautiful lady with the golden crown, of whom he had dreamed on the night his father died. She appeared to him so lovely that he could not help loving her.

"It could not be true," he thought, "that she was really a wicked witch, who ordered people to be hanged or beheaded, if they could not guess her thoughts. Everyone has permission to go and ask her hand, even the poorest beggar. I shall pay a visit to the palace," he said; "I must go, for I cannot help myself."

Then they all advised him not to attempt it; for he would be sure to share the same fate as the rest. His fellowtraveller also tried to persuade him against it; but John seemed quite sure of success. He brushed his shoes and his coat, washed his face and his hands, combed his soft flaxen hair, and then went out alone into the town, and walked to the palace.

"Come in," said the king, as John knocked at the door. John opened it, and the old king, in a dressing gown and embroidered slippers, came towards him. He had the crown on his head, carried his sceptre in one hand, and the orb in the other. "Wait a bit," said he, and he placed the orb under his arm, so that he could offer the other hand to John; but when he found that John was another suitor, he began to weep so violently, that both the sceptre and the orb fell to the floor, and he was obliged to wipe his eyes with his dressing gown. Poor old king! "Let her alone," he said; "you will fare as badly as all the others. Come, I will show you." Then he led him out into the princess's pleasure gardens, and there he saw a frightful sight. On every tree hung three or four king's sons who had wooed the princess, but had not been able to guess the riddles she gave them. Their skeletons rattled in every breeze, so that the terrified birds never dared to venture into the garden. All the flowers were supported by human bones instead of sticks, and human skulls in the flowerpots grinned horribly. It was really a doleful garden for a princess. "Do you see all this?" said the old king; "your fate will be the same as those who are here, therefore do not attempt it. You really make me very unhappy—I take these things to heart so very much."

John kissed the good old king's hand, and said he was sure it would be all right, for he was quite enchanted with the beautiful princess. Then the princess herself came riding into the palace yard with all her ladies, and he wished her "Good morning." She looked wonderfully fair and lovely when she offered her hand to John, and he loved her more than ever. How could she be a wicked witch, as all the people asserted? He accompanied her into the hall, and the little pages offered them gingerbread nuts and sweetmeats, but the old king was so unhappy he could eat nothing, and besides, gingerbread nuts were too hard for him. It was decided that John should come to the palace the next day, when the judges and the whole of the counsellors would be present, to try if he could guess the first riddle. If he succeeded, he would have to come a second time; but if not, he would lose his life—and no one had ever been able to guess even one. However, John was not at all anxious about the result of his trial; on the contrary, he was very merry. He thought only of the beautiful princess, and believed that in some way he should have help, but how he knew not, and did not like to think about it; so he danced along the high road as he went back to the inn, where he had left his fellow traveller waiting for him. John could not refrain from telling him how gracious the princess had been, and how beautiful she looked. He longed for the next day so much, that he might go to the palace and try his luck at guessing the riddles. But his comrade shook his head, and looked very mournful. "I do so wish you to do well," said he; "we might have continued together much longer, and now I am likely to lose you; you poor, dear John! I could shed tears, but I will not make you unhappy on the last night we may be together. We will be merry, really merry this evening; tomorrow, after you are gone, I shall be able to weep undisturbed."

It was very quickly known among the inhabitants of the town that another suitor had arrived for the princess, and there was great sorrow in consequence. The theatre remained closed, the women who sold sweetmeats tied crape round the sugar sticks, and the king and the priests were on their knees in the church. There was a great lamentation, for no one expected John to succeed better than those who had been suitors before.

In the evening John's comrade prepared a large bowl of punch, and said, "Now let us be merry, and drink to the health of the princess." But after drinking two glasses, John became so sleepy, that he could not keep his eyes open, and fell fast asleep. Then his fellow traveller lifted him gently out of his chair, and laid him on the bed; and as soon as it was quite dark, he took the two large wings which he had cut from the dead swan, and tied them firmly to his own shoulders. Then he put into his pocket the largest of the three rods which he had obtained from the old woman who had fallen and broken her leg. After this he opened the window, and flew away over the town, straight towards the palace, and seated himself in a corner, under the window which looked into the bedroom of the princess.

The town was perfectly still when the clocks struck a quarter to twelve. Presently the window opened, and the princess, who had large black wings to her shoulders, and a long white mantle, flew away over the city towards a high mountain. The fellow traveller, who had made himself invisible, so that she could not possibly see him, flew after her through the air, and whipped the princess with his rod, so that the blood came whenever he struck her. Ah, it was a strange flight through the air! The wind caught her mantle, so that it spread out on all sides, like the large sail of a ship, and the moon shone through it. "How it hails, to be sure!" said the princess, at each blow she received from the rod; and it served her right to be whipped.

At last she reached the side of the mountain, and knocked. The mountain opened with a noise like the roll of thunder, and the princess went in. The traveller followed her; no one could see him, as he had made himself invisible. They went through a long, wide passage. A thousand gleaming spiders ran here and there on the walls, causing them to glitter as if they were illuminated with fire. They next entered a large hall built of silver and gold. Large red and blue flowers shone on the walls, looking like sunflowers in size, but no one could dare to pluck them, for the stems were hideous poisonous snakes, and the flowers were flames of fire, darting out of their jaws. Shining glowworms covered the ceiling, and sky-blue bats flapped their transparent wings. Altogether the place had a frightful appearance. In the middle of the floor stood a throne supported by four skeleton horses, whose harness had been made by fiery red spiders. The throne itself was made of milk-white glass, and the cushions were little black mice, each biting the other's tail. Over it hung a canopy of rose-colored spider's webs, spotted with the prettiest little green flies, which sparkled like precious stones. On the throne sat an old magician with a crown on his ugly head, and a sceptre in his hand. He kissed the princess on the forehead, seated her by his side on the splendid throne, and then the music commenced. Great black grasshoppers played the mouth organ, and the owl struck herself on the body instead of a drum. It was altogether a ridiculous concert. Little black goblins with false lights in their caps danced about the hall; but no one could see the traveller, and he had placed himself just behind the throne where he could see and hear everything. The courtiers who came in afterwards looked noble and grand; but anyone with common sense could see what they really were, only broomsticks, with cabbages for heads. The magician had given them life, and dressed them in embroidered robes. It answered very well, as they were only wanted for show. After there had been a little dancing, the princess told the magician that she had a new suitor, and asked him what she could think of for the suitor to guess when he came to the castle the next morning.

"Listen to what I say," said the magician, "you must choose something very easy, he is less likely to guess it then. Think of one of your shoes, he will never imagine it is that. Then cut his head off; and mind you do not forget to bring his eyes with you tomorrow night, that I may eat them."

The princess curtsied low, and said she would not forget the eyes.

The magician then opened the mountain and she flew home again, but the traveller followed and flogged her so much with the rod, that she sighed quite deeply about the heavy hailstorm, and made as much haste as she could to get back to her bedroom through the window. The traveller then returned to the inn where John still slept, took off his wings and laid down on the bed, for he was very tired. Early in the morning John awoke, and when his fellow traveller got up, he said that he had a very wonderful dream about the princess and her shoe; he therefore advised John to ask her if she had not thought of her shoe. Of course the traveller knew this from what the magician in the mountain had said.

"I may as well say that as anything," said John. "Perhaps your dream may come true; still I will say farewell, for if I guess wrong I shall never see you again."

Then they embraced each other, and John went into the town and walked to the palace. The great hall was full of people, and the judges sat in armchairs, with eiderdown cushions to rest their heads upon, because they had so much to think of. The old king stood near, wiping his eyes with his white pocket handkerchief. When the princess entered, she looked even more beautiful than she had appeared the day before, and greeted everyone present most gracefully; but to John she gave her hand, and said, "Good morning to you."

Now came the time for John to guess what she was thinking of; and oh, how kindly she looked at him as she spoke. But when he uttered the single word shoe, she turned as pale as a ghost; all her wisdom could not help her, for he had guessed rightly. Oh, how pleased the old king was! It was quite amusing to see how he capered about. All the people clapped their hands, both on his account and John's, who had guessed rightly the first time. His fellow traveller was glad also, when he heard how successful John had been. But John folded his hands, and thanked God, who, he felt quite sure, would help him again; and he knew he had to guess twice more. The evening passed pleasantly like the one preceding. While John slept, his companion flew behind the princess to the mountain, and flogged her even harder than before; this time he had taken two rods with him. No one saw him go in with her, and he heard all that was said. The princess this time was to think of a glove, and he told John as if he had again heard it in a dream. The next day, therefore, he was able to guess correctly the second time, and it caused great rejoicing at the palace. The whole court jumped about as they had seen the king do the day before, but the princess lay on the sofa, and would not say a single word. All now depended upon John. If he only guessed rightly the third time, he would marry the princess, and reign over the kingdom after the death of the old king: but if he failed, he would lose his life, and the magician would have his beautiful blue eyes. That evening John said his prayers and went to bed very early, and soon fell asleep calmly. But his companion tied on his wings to his shoulders, took three rods, and, with his sword at his side, flew to the palace. It was a very dark night, and so stormy that the tiles flew from the roofs of the houses, and the trees in the garden upon which the skeletons hung bent themselves like reeds before the wind. The lightning flashed, and the thunder rolled in one long-continued peal all night. The window of the castle opened, and the princess flew out. She was pale as death, but she laughed at the storm as if it were not bad enough. Her white mantle fluttered in the wind like a large sail, and the traveller flogged her with the three rods till the blood trickled down, and at last she could scarcely fly; she contrived, however, to reach the mountain. "What a hailstorm!" she said, as she entered; "I have never been out in such weather as this."

"Yes, there may be too much of a good thing sometimes," said the magician.

Then the princess told him that John had guessed rightly the second time, and if he succeeded the next morning, he would win, and she could never come to the mountain again, or practice magic as she had done, and therefore she was quite unhappy. "I will find out something for you to think of which he will never guess, unless he is a greater conjuror than myself. But now let us be merry."

Then he took the princess by both hands, and they danced with all the little goblins and Jack-o'-lanterns in the room. The red spiders sprang here and there on the walls quite as merrily, and the flowers of fire appeared as if they were throwing out sparks. The owl beat the drum, the crickets whistled and the grasshoppers played the mouth organ. It was a very ridiculous ball. After they had danced enough, the princess was obliged to go home, for fear she should be missed at the palace. The magician offered to go with her, that they might be company to each other on the way. Then they flew away through the bad weather, and the traveller followed them, and broke his three rods across their shoulders. The magician had never been out in such a hailstorm as this. Just by the palace the magician stopped to wish the princess farewell, and to whisper in her ear, "Tomorrow think of my head."

But the traveller heard it, and just as the princess slipped through the window into her bedroom, and the magician turned round to fly back to the mountain, he seized him by the long black beard, and with his sabre cut off the wicked conjuror's head just behind the shoulders, so that he could not even see who it was. He threw the body into the sea to the fishes, and after dipping the head into the water, he tied it up in a silk handkerchief, took it with him to the inn, and then went to bed. The next morning he gave John the handkerchief, and told him not to untie it till the princess asked him what she was thinking of. There were so many people in the great hall of the palace that they stood as thick as radishes tied together in a bundle. The council sat in their armchairs with the white cushions. The old king wore new robes, and the golden crown and sceptre had been polished up so that he looked quite smart. But the princess was very pale, and wore a black dress as if she were going to a funeral.

"What have I thought of?" asked the princess, of John. He immediately untied the handkerchief, and was himself quite frightened when he saw the head of the ugly magician. Everyone shuddered, for it was terrible to look at; but the princess sat like a statue, and could not utter a single word. At length she rose and gave John her hand, for he had guessed rightly.

She looked at no one, but sighed deeply, and said, "You are my master now; this evening our marriage must take place."

"I am very pleased to hear it," said the old king. "It is just what I wish."

Then all the people shouted "Hurrah." The band played music in the streets, the bells rang, and the cake women took the black crape off the sugar sticks. There was universal joy. Three oxen, stuffed with ducks and chickens, were roasted whole in the marketplace, where everyone might help himself to a slice. The fountains spouted forth the most delicious wine, and whoever bought a penny loaf at the baker's received six large buns, full of raisins, as a present. In the evening the whole town was illuminated. The soldiers fired off cannons, and the boys let off crackers. There was eating and drinking, dancing and jumping everywhere. In the palace, the high-born gentlemen and beautiful ladies danced with each other, and they could be heard at a great distance singing the following song:

"Here are maidens, young and fair,
Dancing in the summer air;
Like two spinning-wheels at play,
Pretty maidens dance away—
Dance the spring and summer through
Till the sole falls from your shoe."

But the princess was still a witch, and she could not love John. His fellow traveller had thought of that, so he gave John three feathers out of the swan's wings, and a little bottle with a few drops in it. He told him to place a large bath full of water by the princess's bed, and put the feathers and the drops into it. Then, at the moment she was about to get into bed, he must give her a little push, so that she might fall into the water, and then dip her three times. This would destroy the power of the magician, and she would love him very much. John did all that his companion told him to do. The princess shrieked aloud when he dipped her under the water the first time, and struggled under his hands in the form of a great black swan with fiery eyes. As she rose the second time from the water, the swan had become white, with a black ring round its neck. John allowed the water to close once more over the bird, and at the same time it changed into a most beautiful princess. She was more lovely even than before, and thanked him, while her eyes sparkled with tears, for having broken the spell of the magician. The next day, the king came with the whole court to offer their congratulations, and stayed till quite late. Last of all came the travelling companion; he had his staff in his hand and his knapsack on his back. John kissed him many times and told him he must not go, he must remain with him, for he was the cause of all his good fortune. But the traveller shook his head, and said gently and kindly, "No: my time is up now; I have only paid my debt to you. Do you remember the dead man whom the bad people wished to throw out of his coffin? You gave all you possessed that he might rest in his grave; I am that man." As he said this, he vanished.

The wedding festivities lasted a whole month. John and his princess loved each other dearly, and the old king lived to see many a happy day, when he took their little children on his knees and let them play with his sceptre. And John became king over the whole country.

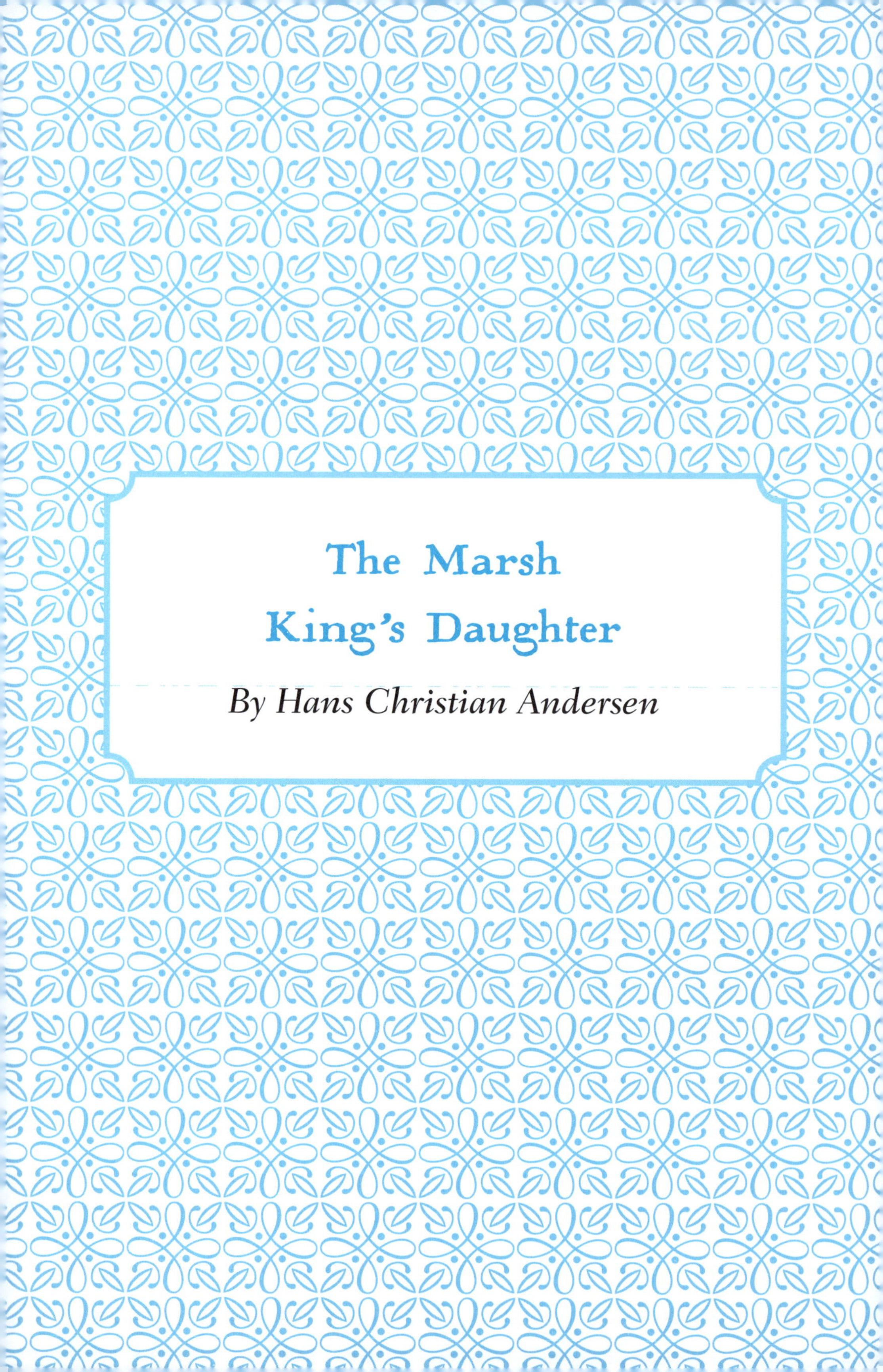

The Marsh King's Daughter

By Hans Christian Andersen

The storks relate to their little ones a great many stories, and they are all about moors and reed banks, and suited to their age and capacity. The youngest of them are quite satisfied with "kribble, krabble," or such nonsense, and think it very grand; but the elder ones want something with a deeper meaning, or at least something about their own family.

We are only acquainted with one of the two longest and oldest stories which the storks relate—it is about Moses, who was exposed by his mother on the banks of the Nile, and was found by the king's daughter, who gave him a good education, and he afterwards became a great man; but where he was buried is still unknown.

Everyone knows this story, but not the second; very likely because it is quite an inland story. It has been repeated from mouth to mouth, from one stork-mamma to another, for thousands of years; and each has told it better than the last; and now we mean to tell it better than all.

The first stork pair who related it lived at the time it happened, and had their summer residence on the rafters of the Viking's house, which stood near the wild moorlands of Wendsyssell; that is, to speak more correctly, the great moorheath, high up in the north of Jutland, by the Skjagen peak. This wilderness is still an immense wild heath of marshy ground, about which we can read in the "Official Directory." It is said that in olden times the place was a lake, the ground of which had heaved up from beneath, and now the moorland extends for miles in every direction, and is surrounded by damp meadows, trembling, undulating swamps, and marshy ground covered with turf, on which grow bilberry bushes and stunted trees. Mists are almost always hovering over this region, which, seventy years ago, was overrun with wolves. It may well be called the Wild Moor; and one can easily imagine, with such a wild expanse of marsh and lake, how lonely and dreary it must have been a thousand years ago. Many things may be noticed now that existed then. The reeds grow to the same height, and bear the same kind of long, purple-brown leaves, with their feathery tips. There still stands the birch, with its white bark and its delicate, loosely hanging leaves; and with regard to the living beings who frequented this spot, the fly still wears a gauzy dress of the same cut, and the favorite colors of the stork are white, with black and red for stockings. The people, certainly, in those days, wore very different dresses to those they now wear, but if any of them, be he huntsman or squire, master or servant, ventured on the wavering, undulating, marshy ground of the moor, they met with the same fate a thousand years ago as they would now. The wanderer sank, and went down to the Marsh King, as he is named, who rules in the great moorland empire beneath. They also called him "Gunkel King," but we like the name of "Marsh King" better, and we will give him that name as the storks do. Very little is known of the Marsh King's rule, but that, perhaps, is a good thing.

In the neighborhood of the moorlands, and not far from the great arm of the North Sea and the Cattegat which is called the Lumfjorden, lay the castle of the Viking, with its watertight stone cellars, its tower, and its three projecting storeys. On the ridge of the roof the stork had built his nest, and there the stork-mamma sat on her eggs and felt sure her hatching would come to something.

One evening, stork-papa stayed out rather late, and when he came home he seemed quite busy, bustling, and important. "I have something very dreadful to tell you," said he to the stork-mamma.

"Keep it to yourself then," she replied. "Remember that I am hatching eggs; it may agitate me, and will affect them."

"You must know it at once," said he. "The daughter of our host in Egypt has arrived here. She has ventured to take this journey, and now she is lost."

"She who sprung from the race of the fairies, is it?" cried the mother stork. "Oh, tell me all about it; you know I cannot bear to be kept waiting at a time when I am hatching eggs."

"Well, you see, mother," he replied, "she believed what the doctors said, and what I have heard you state also, that the moor flowers which grow about here would heal her sick father; and she has flown to the north in swan's plumage, in company with some other swan princesses, who come to these parts every year to renew their youth. She came, and where is she now!"

"You enter into particulars too much," said the mamma stork, "and the eggs may take cold; I cannot bear such suspense as this."

"Well," said he, "I have kept watch; and this evening I went among the rushes where I thought the marshy ground would bear me, and while I was there three swans came. Something in their manner of flying seemed to say to me, 'Look carefully now; there is one not all swan, only swan's feathers.' You know, mother, you have the same intuitive feeling that I have; you know whether a thing is right or not immediately."

"Yes, of course," said she; "but tell me about the princess; I am tired of hearing about the swan's feathers."

"Well, you know that in the middle of the moor there is something like a lake," said the stork-papa. "You can see the edge of it if you raise yourself a little. Just there, by the reeds and the green banks, lay the trunk of an elder tree; upon this the three swans stood flapping their wings, and looking about them; one of them threw off her plumage, and I immediately recognized her as one of the princesses of our home in Egypt. There she sat, without any covering but her long, black hair. I heard her tell the two others to take great care of the swan's plumage, while she dipped down into the water to pluck the flowers which she fancied she saw there. The others nodded, and picked up the feather dress, and took possession of it. I wonder what will become of it, thought I, and she most likely asked herself the same question. If so, she received an answer, a very practical one; for the two swans rose up and flew away with her swan's plumage. 'Dive down now!' they cried; 'thou shalt never more fly in the swan's plumage, thou shalt never again see Egypt; here, on the moor, thou wilt remain.' So saying, they tore the swan's plumage into a thousand pieces, the feathers drifted about like a snow shower, and then the two deceitful princesses flew away."

"Why, that is terrible," said the stork-mamma; "I feel as if I could hardly bear to hear any more, but you must tell me what happened next."

"The princess wept and lamented aloud; her tears moistened the elder stump, which was really not an elder stump but the Marsh King himself, he who in marshy ground lives and rules. I saw myself how the stump of the tree turned round, and was a tree no more, while long, clammy branches, like arms, were extended from it. Then the poor child was terribly frightened, and started up to run away. She hastened to cross the green, slimy ground; but it will not bear any weight, much less hers. She quickly sank, and the elder stump dived immediately after her; in fact, it was he who drew her down. Great black bubbles rose up out of the moor slime, and with these every trace of the two vanished. And now the princess is buried in the wild marsh, she will never now carry flowers to Egypt to cure her father. It would have broken your heart, mother, had you seen it."

"You ought not to have told me," said she, "at such a time as this; the eggs might suffer. But I think the princess will soon find help; someone will rise up to help her. Ah! if it had been you or I, or one of our people, it would have been all over with us."

"I mean to go every day," said he, "to see if anything comes to pass"; and so he did.

A long time went by, but at last he saw a green stalk shooting up out of the deep, marshy ground. As it reached the surface of the marsh, a leaf spread out, and unfolded itself broader and broader, and close to it came forth a bud.

One morning, when the stork-papa was flying over the stem, he saw that the power of the sun's rays had caused the bud to open, and in the cup of the flower lay a charming child—a little maiden, looking as if she had just come out of a bath. The little one was so like the Egyptian princess, that the stork, at the first moment, thought it must be the princess herself, but after a little reflection he decided that it was much more likely to be the daughter of the princess and the Marsh King; and this explained also her being placed in the cup of a waterlily. "But she cannot be left to lie here," thought the stork, "and in my nest there are already so many. But stay, I have thought of something: the wife of the Viking has no children, and how often she has wished for a little one. People always say the stork brings the little ones; I will do so in earnest this time. I shall fly with the child to the Viking's wife; what rejoicing there will be!"

And then the stork lifted the little girl out of the flower cup, flew to the castle, picked a hole with his beak in the bladder-covered window, and laid the beautiful child in the bosom of the Viking's wife. Then he flew back quickly to the stork-mamma and told her what he had seen and done; and the little storks listened to it all, for they were then quite old enough to do so. "So you see," he continued, "that the princess is not dead, for she must have sent her little one up here; and now I have found a home for her."

"Ah, I said it would be so from the first," replied the stork-mamma; "but now think a little of your own family. Our travelling time draws near, and I sometimes feel a little irritation already under the wings. The cuckoos and the nightingale are already gone, and I heard the quails say they should go too as soon as the wind was favorable. Our youngsters will go through all the manoeuvres at the review very well, or I am much mistaken in them."

The Viking's wife was above measure delighted when she awoke the next morning and found the beautiful little child lying in her bosom. She kissed it and caressed it; but it cried terribly, and struck out with its arms and legs, and did not seem to be pleased at all. At last it cried itself to sleep; and as it lay there so still and quiet, it was a most beautiful sight to see. The Viking's wife was so delighted, that body and soul were full of joy. Her heart felt so light within her, that it seemed as if her husband and his soldiers, who were absent, must come home as suddenly and unexpectedly as the little child had done. She and her whole household therefore busied themselves in preparing everything for the reception of her lord. The long, colored tapestry, on which she and her maidens had worked pictures of their idols, Odin, Thor, and Friga, was hung up. The slaves polished the old shields that served as ornaments; cushions were placed on the seats, and dry wood laid on the fireplaces in the centre of the hall, so that the flames might be fanned up at a moment's notice. The Viking's wife herself assisted in the work, so that at night she felt very tired, and quickly fell into a sound sleep. When she awoke, just before morning, she was terribly alarmed to find that the infant had vanished. She sprang from her couch, lighted a pine chip, and searched all round the room, when, at last, in that part of the bed where her feet had been, lay, not the child, but a great, ugly frog. She was quite disgusted at this sight, and seized a heavy stick to kill the frog; but the creature looked at her with such strange, mournful eyes, that she was unable to strike the blow. Once more she searched round the room; then she started at hearing the frog utter a low, painful croak. She sprang from the couch and opened the window hastily; at the same moment the sun rose, and threw its beams through the window, till it rested on the couch where the great frog lay. Suddenly it appeared as if the frog's broad mouth contracted, and became small and red. The limbs moved and stretched out and extended themselves till they took a beautiful shape; and behold there was the pretty child lying before her, and the ugly frog was gone. "How is this?" she cried, "have I had a wicked dream? Is it not my own lovely cherub that lies there?" Then she kissed it and fondled it; but the child struggled and fought, and bit as if she had been a little wild cat.

The Viking did not return on that day, nor the next; he was, however, on the way home; but the wind, so favorable to the storks, was against him; for it blew towards the south. A wind in favor of one is often against another.

After two or three days had passed, it became clear to the Viking's wife how matters stood with the child; it was under the influence of a powerful sorcerer. By day it was charming in appearance as an angel of light, but with a temper wicked and wild; while at night, in the form of an ugly frog, it was quiet and mournful, with eyes full of sorrow. Here were two natures, changing inwardly and outwardly with the absence and return of sunlight. And so it happened that by day the child, with the actual form of its mother, possessed the fierce disposition of its father; at night, on the contrary, its outward appearance plainly showed its descent on the father's side, while inwardly it had the heart and mind of its mother. Who would be able to loosen this wicked charm which the sorcerer had worked upon it? The wife of the Viking lived in constant pain and sorrow about it. Her heart clung to the little creature, but she could not explain to her husband the circumstances in which it was placed. He was expected to return shortly; and were she to tell him, he would very likely, as was the custom at that time, expose the poor child in the public highway, and let anyone take it away who would. The good wife of the Viking could not let that happen, and she therefore resolved that the Viking should never see the child excepting by daylight.

One morning there sounded a rushing of storks' wings over the roof. More than a hundred pair of storks had rested there during the night, to recover themselves after their excursion; and now they soared aloft, and prepared for the journey southward.

"All the husbands are here, and ready!" they cried; "wives and children also!"

"How light we are!" screamed the young storks in chorus. "Something pleasant seems creeping over us, even down to our toes, as if we were full of live frogs. Ah, how delightful it is to travel into foreign lands!"

"Hold yourselves properly in the line with us," cried papa and mamma. "Do not use your beaks so much; it tries the lungs." And then the storks flew away.

About the same time sounded the clang of the warriors' trumpets across the heath. The Viking had landed with his men. They were returning home, richly laden with spoil from the Gallic coast, where the people, as did also the inhabitants of Britain, often cried in alarm, "Deliver us from the wild northmen."

Life and noisy pleasure came with them into the castle of the Viking on the moorland. A great cask of mead was drawn into the hall, piles of wood blazed, cattle were slain and served up, that they might feast in reality. The priest who offered the sacrifice sprinkled the devoted parishioners with the warm blood; the fire crackled, and the smoke rolled along beneath the roof; the soot fell upon them from the beams; but they were used to all these things. Guests were invited, and received handsome presents. All wrongs and unfaithfulness were forgotten. They drank deeply, and threw in each other's faces the bones that were left, which was looked upon as a sign of good feeling amongst them. A bard, who was a kind of musician as well as warrior, and who had been with the Viking in his expedition, and knew what to sing about, gave them one of his best songs, in which they heard all their warlike deeds praised, and every wonderful action brought forward with honor. Every verse ended with this refrain—

"Gold and possessions will flee away,
Friends and foes must die one day;
Every man on earth must die,
But a famous name will never die."

And with that they beat upon their shields, and hammered upon the table with knives and bones, in a most outrageous manner.

The Viking's wife sat upon a raised cross seat in the open hall. She wore a silk dress, golden bracelets, and large amber beads. She was in costly attire, and the bard named her in his song, and spoke of the rich treasure of gold which she had brought to her husband. Her husband had already seen the wonderfully beautiful child in the daytime, and was delighted with her beauty; even her wild ways pleased him. He said the little maiden would grow up to be a heroine, with the strong will and determination of a man. She would never wink her eyes, even if, in joke, an expert hand should attempt to cut off her eyebrows with a sharp sword.

The full cask of mead soon became empty, and a fresh one was brought in; for these were people who liked plenty to eat and drink. The old proverb, which everyone knows, says that "the cattle know when to leave their pasture, but a foolish man knows not the measure of his own appetite." Yes, they all knew this; but men may know what is right, and yet often do wrong. They also knew "that even the welcome guest becomes wearisome when he sits too long in the house." But there they remained; for pork and mead are good things. And so at the Viking's house they stayed, and enjoyed themselves; and at night the bondmen slept in the ashes, and dipped their fingers in the fat, and licked them. Oh, it was a delightful time!

Once more in the same year the Viking went forth, though the storms of autumn had already commenced to roar. He went with his warriors to the coast of Britain; he said that it was but an excursion of pleasure across the water, so his wife remained at home with the little girl. After a while, it is quite certain the foster mother began to love the poor frog, with its gentle eyes and its deep sighs, even better than the little beauty who bit and fought with all around her.

The heavy, damp mists of autumn, which destroy the leaves of the wood, had already fallen upon forest and heath. Feathers of plucked birds, as they call the snow, flew about in thick showers, and winter was coming. The sparrows took possession of the stork's nest, and conversed about the absent owners in their own fashion; and they, the stork pair and all their young ones, where were they staying now? The storks might have been found in the land of Egypt, where the sun's rays shone forth bright and warm, as it does here at midsummer. Tamarinds and acacias were in full bloom all over the country, the crescent of Mahomet glittered brightly from the cupolas of the mosques, and on the slender pinnacles sat many of the storks, resting after their long journey. Swarms of them took divided possession of the nests—nests which lay close to each other between the venerable columns, and crowded the arches of temples in forgotten cities. The date and the palm lifted themselves as a screen or as a sunshade over them. The gray pyramids looked like broken shadows in the clear air and the far-off desert, where the ostrich wheels his rapid flight, and the lion, with his subtle eyes, gazes at the marble sphinx which lies half buried in sand. The waters of the Nile had retreated, and the whole bed of the river was covered with frogs, which was a most acceptable prospect for the stork families. The young storks thought their eyes deceived them, everything around appeared so beautiful.

"It is always like this here, and this is how we live in our warm country," said the stork-mamma; and the thought made the young ones almost beside themselves with pleasure.

"Is there anything more to see?" they asked; "are we going farther into the country?"

"There is nothing further for us to see," answered the stork-mamma. "Beyond this delightful region there are immense forests, where the branches of the trees entwine round each other, while prickly, creeping plants cover the paths, and only an elephant could force a passage for himself with his great feet. The snakes are too large, and the lizards too lively for us to catch. Then there is the desert; if you went there, your eyes would soon be full of sand with the lightest breeze, and if it should blow great guns, you would most likely find yourself in a sand drift. Here is the best place for you, where there are frogs and locusts; here I shall remain, and so must you." And so they stayed.

The parents sat in the nest on the slender minaret, and rested, yet still were busily employed in cleaning and smoothing their feathers, and in sharpening their beaks against their red stockings; then they would stretch out their necks, salute each other, and gravely raise their heads with the high-polished forehead, and soft, smooth feathers, while their brown eyes shone with intelligence. The female young ones strutted about amid the moist rushes, glancing at the other young storks and making acquaintances, and swallowing a frog at every third step, or tossing a little snake about with their beaks, in a way they considered very becoming, and besides it tasted very good. The young male storks soon began to quarrel; they struck at each other with their wings, and pecked with their beaks till the blood came. And in this manner many of the young ladies and gentlemen were betrothed to each other: it was, of course, what they wanted, and indeed what they lived for. Then they returned to a nest, and there the quarrelling began afresh; for in hot countries people are almost all violent and passionate. But for all that it was pleasant, especially for the old people, who watched them with great joy: all that their young ones did suited them. Every day here there was sunshine, plenty to eat, and nothing to think of but pleasure. But in the rich castle of their Egyptian host, as they called him, pleasure was not to be found. The rich and mighty lord of the castle lay on his couch, in the midst of the great hall, with its many colored walls looking like the centre of a great tulip; but he was stiff and powerless in all his limbs, and lay stretched out like a mummy. His family and servants stood round him; he was not dead, although he could scarcely be said to live. The healing moor flower from the north, which was to have been found and brought to him by her who loved him so well, had not arrived. His young and beautiful daughter who, in swan's plumage, had flown over land and seas to the distant north, had never returned. She is dead, so the two swan maidens had said when they came home; and they made up quite a story about her, and this is what they told—

"We three flew away together through the air," said they: "a hunter caught sight of us, and shot at us with an arrow. The arrow struck our young friend and sister, and slowly singing her farewell song she sank down, a dying swan, into the forest lake. On the shores of the lake, under a spreading birch tree, we laid her in the cold earth. We had our revenge; we bound fire under the wings of a swallow, who had a nest on the thatched roof of the huntsman. The house took fire, and burst into flames; the hunter was burnt with the house, and the light was reflected over the sea as far as the spreading birch, beneath which we laid her sleeping dust. She will never return to the land of Egypt." And then they both wept. And stork-papa, who heard the story, snapped with his beak so that it might be heard a long way off.

"Deceit and lies!" cried he; "I should like to run my beak deep into their chests."

"And perhaps break it off," said the mamma stork, "then what a sight you would be. Think first of yourself, and then of your family; all others are nothing to us."

"Yes, I know," said the stork-papa; "but tomorrow I can easily place myself on the edge of the open cupola, when the learned and wise men assemble to consult on the state of the sick man; perhaps they may come a little nearer to the truth." And the learned and wise men assembled together, and talked a great deal on every point; but the stork could make no sense out of anything they said; neither were there any good results from their consultations, either for the sick man, or for his daughter in the marshy heath. When we listen to what people say in this world, we shall hear a great deal; but it is an advantage to know what has been said and done before, when we listen to a conversation. The stork did, and we know at least as much as he, the stork.

"Love is a life-giver. The highest love produces the highest life. Only through love can the sick man be cured." This had been said by many, and even the learned men acknowledged that it was a wise saying.

"What a beautiful thought!" exclaimed the papa stork immediately.

"I don't quite understand it," said the mamma stork, when her husband repeated it; "however, it is not my fault, but the fault of the thought; whatever it may be, I have something else to think of."

Now the learned men had spoken also of love between this one and that one; of the difference of the love which we have for our neighbor, to the love that exists between parents and children; of the love of the plant for the light, and how the germ springs forth when the sunbeam kisses the ground. All these things were so elaborately and learnedly explained, that it was impossible for stork-papa to follow it, much less to talk about it. His thoughts on the subject quite weighed him down; he stood the whole of the following day on one leg, with half-shut eyes, thinking deeply. So much learning was quite a heavy weight for him to carry. One thing, however, the papa stork could understand. Everyone, high and low, had from their inmost hearts expressed their opinion that it was a great misfortune for so many thousands of people—the whole country indeed—to have this man so sick, with no hopes of his recovery. And what joy and blessing it would spread around if he could by any means be cured! But where bloomed the flower that could bring him health? They had searched for it everywhere; in learned writings, in the shining stars, in the weather and wind. Inquiries had been made in every byway that could be thought of, until at last the wise and learned men had asserted, as we have been already told, that "love, the life-giver, could alone give new life to a father"; and in saying this, they had overdone it, and said more than they understood themselves. They repeated it, and wrote it down as a recipe, "Love is a life-giver." But how could such a recipe be prepared—that was a difficulty they could not overcome. At last it was decided that help could only come from the princess herself, whose whole soul was wrapped up in her father, especially as a plan had been adopted by her to enable her to obtain a remedy.

More than a year had passed since the princess had set out at night, when the light of the young moon was soon lost beneath the horizon. She had gone to the marble sphinx in the desert, shaking the sand from her sandals, and then passed through the long passage, which leads to the centre of one of the great pyramids, where the mighty kings of antiquity, surrounded with pomp and splendor, lie veiled in the form of mummies. She had been told by the wise men, that if she laid her head on the breast of one of them, from the head she would learn where to find life and recovery for her father. She had performed all this, and in a dream had learnt that she must bring home to her father the lotus flower, which grows in the deep sea, near the moors and heath in the Danish land. The very place and situation had been pointed out to her, and she was told that the flower would restore her father to health and strength. And, therefore, she had gone forth from the land of Egypt, flying over to the open marsh and the wild moor in the plumage of a swan.

The papa and mamma storks knew all this, and we also know it now. We know, too, that the Marsh King has drawn her down to himself, and that to the loved ones at home she is forever dead. One of the wisest of them said, as the stork-mamma also said, "That in some way she would, after all, manage to succeed"; and so at last they comforted themselves with this hope, and would wait patiently; in fact, they could do nothing better.

"I should like to get away the swan's feathers from those two treacherous princesses," said the papa stork; "then, at least, they would not be able to fly over again to the wild moor, and do more wickedness. I can hide the two suits of feathers over yonder, till we find some use for them."

"But where will you put them?" asked the mamma stork.

"In our nest on the moor. I and the young ones will carry them by turns during our flight across; and as we return, should they prove too heavy for us, we shall be sure to find plenty of places on the way in which we can conceal them till our next journey. Certainly one suit of swan's feathers would be enough for the princess, but two are always better. In those northern countries no one can have too many travelling wrappers."

"No one will thank you for it," said stork-mamma; "but you are master; and, excepting at breeding time, I have nothing to say."

In the Viking's castle on the wild moor, to which the storks directed their flight in the following spring, the little maiden still remained. They had named her Helga, which was rather too soft a name for a child with a temper like hers, although her form was still beautiful. Every month this temper showed itself in sharper outlines; and in the course of years, while the storks still made the same journeys in autumn to the hill, and in spring to the moors, the child grew to be almost a woman, and before anyone seemed aware of it, she was a wonderfully beautiful maiden of sixteen. The casket was splendid, but the contents were worthless. She was, indeed, wild and savage even in those hard, uncultivated times. It was a pleasure to her to splash about with her white hands in the warm blood of the horse which had been slain for sacrifice. In one of her wild moods she bit off the head of the black cock, which the priest was about to slay for the sacrifice. To her foster father she said one day, "If thine enemy were to pull down thine house about thy ears, and thou shouldest be sleeping in unconscious security, I would not wake thee; even if I had the power I would never do it, for my ears still tingle with the blow that thou gavest me years ago. I have never forgotten it." But the Viking treated her words as a joke; he was, like everyone else, bewitched with her beauty, and knew nothing of the change in the form and temper of Helga at night. Without a saddle, she would sit on a horse as if she were a part of it, while it rushed along at full speed; nor would she spring from its back, even when it quarrelled with other horses and bit them. She would often leap from the high shore into the sea with all her clothes on, and swim to meet the Viking, when his boat was steering home towards the shore. She once cut off a long lock of her beautiful hair, and twisted it into a string for her bow. "If a thing is to be done well," said she, "I must do it myself."

The Viking's wife was, for the time in which she lived, a woman of strong character and will; but, compared to her daughter, she was a gentle, timid woman, and she knew that a wicked sorcerer had the terrible child in his power. It was sometimes as if Helga acted from sheer wickedness, for often when her mother stood on the threshold of the door, or stepped into the yard, she would seat herself on the brink of the well, wave her arms and legs in the air, and suddenly fall right in. Here she was able, from her frog nature, to dip and dive about in the water of the deep well, until at last she would climb forth like a cat, and come back into the hall dripping with water, so that the green leaves that were strewed on the floor were whirled round, and carried away by the streams that flowed from her.

But there was one time of the day which placed a check upon Helga. It was the evening twilight; when this hour arrived she became quiet and thoughtful, and allowed herself to be advised and led; then also a secret feeling seemed to draw her towards her mother. And as usual, when the sun set, and the transformation took place, both in body and mind, inwards and outwards, she would remain quiet and mournful, with her form shrunk together in the shape of a frog. Her body was much larger than those animals ever are, and on this account it was much more hideous in appearance; for she looked like a wretched dwarf, with a frog's head, and webbed fingers. Her eyes had a most piteous expression; she was without a voice, excepting a hollow, croaking sound, like the smothered sobs of a dreaming child.

Then the Viking's wife took her on her lap, and forgot the ugly form, as she looked into the mournful eyes, and often said, "I could wish that thou wouldst always remain my dumb frog child, for thou art too terrible when thou art clothed in a form of beauty." And the Viking woman wrote

Runic characters against sorcery and spells of sickness, and threw them over the wretched child; but they did no good.

"One can scarcely believe that she was ever small enough to lie in the cup of the waterlily," said the papa stork; "and now she is grown up, and the image of her Egyptian mother, especially about the eyes. Ah, we shall never see her again; perhaps she has not discovered how to help herself, as you and the wise men said she would. Year after year have I flown across and across the moor, but there was no sign of her being still alive. Yes, and I may as well tell you that each year, when I arrived a few days before you to repair the nest, and put everything in its place, I have spent a whole night flying here and there over the marshy lake, as if I had been an owl or a bat, but all to no purpose. The two suit of swan's plumage, which I and the young ones dragged over here from the land of the Nile, are of no use; trouble enough it was to us to bring them here in three journeys, and now they are lying at the bottom of the nest; and if a fire should happen to break out, and the wooden house be burnt down, they would be destroyed."

"And our good nest would be destroyed, too," said the mamma stork; "but you think less of that than of your plumage stuff and your moor princess. Go and stay with her in the marsh if you like. You are a bad father to your own children, as I have told you already, when I hatched my first brood. I only hope neither we nor our children may have an arrow sent through our wings, owing to that wild girl. Helga does not know in the least what she is about. We have lived in this house longer than she has, she should think of that, and we have never forgotten our duty. We have paid every year our toll of a feather, an egg, and a young one, as it is only right we should do. You don't suppose I can wander about the courtyard, or go everywhere as I used to do in old times. I can do it in Egypt, where I can be a companion of the people, without forgetting myself. But here I cannot go and peep into the pots and kettles as I do there. No, I can only sit up here and feel angry with that girl, the little wretch; and I am angry with you, too; you should have left her lying in the waterlily, then no one would have known anything about her."

"You are far better than your conversation," said the papa stork; "I know you better than you know yourself." And with that he gave a hop, and flapped his wings twice, proudly; then he stretched his neck and flew, or rather soared away, without moving his outspread wings. He went on for some distance, and then he gave a great flap with his wings and flew on his course at a rapid rate, his head and neck bending proudly before him, while the sun's rays fell on his glossy plumage.

"He is the handsomest of them all," said the mamma stork, as she watched him; "but I won't tell him so."

Early in the autumn, the Viking again returned home laden with spoil, and bringing prisoners with him. Among them was a young Christian priest, one of those who condemned the gods of the north. Often lately there had been, both in hall and chamber, a talk of the new faith which was spreading far and wide in the south, and which, through the means of the holy Ansgarius, had already reached as far as Hedeby on the Schlei. Even Helga had heard of this belief in the teachings of One who was named Christ, and who for the love of mankind, and for their redemption, had given up His life. But to her all this had, as it were, gone in one ear and out the other. It seemed that she only understood the meaning of the word "love," when in the form of a miserable frog she crouched together in the corner of the sleeping chamber; but the Viking's wife had listened to the wonderful story, and had felt herself strangely moved by it.

On their return, after this voyage, the men spoke of the beautiful temples built of polished stone, which had been raised for the public worship of this holy love. Some vessels, curiously formed of massive gold, had been brought home among the booty. There was a peculiar fragrance about them all, for they were incense vessels, which had been swung before the altars in the temples by the Christian priests. In the deep stony cellars of the castle, the young Christian priest was immured, and his hands and feet tied together with strips of bark. The Viking's wife considered him as beautiful as Baldur, and his distress raised her pity; but Helga said he ought to have ropes fastened to his heels, and be tied to the tails of wild animals.

"I would let the dogs loose after him" she said, "over the moor and across the heath. Hurrah! that would be a spectacle for the gods, and better still to follow in its course."

But the Viking would not allow him to die such a death as that, especially as he was the disowned and despiser of the high gods. In a few days, he had decided to have him offered as a sacrifice on the bloodstone in the grove. For the first time, a man was to be sacrificed here. Helga begged to be allowed to sprinkle the assembled people with the blood of the priest. She sharpened her glittering knife; and when one of the great, savage dogs, who were running about the Viking's castle in great numbers, sprang towards her, she thrust the knife into his side, merely, as she said, to prove its sharpness.

The Viking's wife looked at the wild, badly disposed girl, with great sorrow; and when night came on, and her daughter's beautiful form and disposition were changed, she spoke in eloquent words to Helga of the sorrow and deep grief that was in her heart. The ugly frog, in its monstrous shape, stood before her, and raised its brown mournful eyes to her face, listening to her words, and seeming to understand them with the intelligence of a human being.

"Never once to my lord and husband has a word passed my lips of what I have to suffer through you; my heart is full of grief about you," said the Viking's wife. "The love of a mother is greater and more powerful than I ever imagined. But love never entered thy heart; it is cold and clammy, like the plants on the moor."

Then the miserable form trembled; it was as if these words had touched an invisible bond between body and soul, for great tears stood in the eyes.

"A bitter time will come for thee at last," continued the Viking's wife; "and it will be terrible for me too. It had been better for thee if thou hadst been left on the high road, with the cold night wind to lull thee to sleep." And the Viking's wife shed bitter tears, and went away in anger and sorrow, passing under the partition of furs, which hung loose over the beam and divided the hall.

The shrivelled frog still sat in the corner alone. Deep silence reigned around. At intervals, a half-stifled sigh was heard from its inmost soul; it was the soul of Helga. It seemed in pain, as if a new life were arising in her heart. Then she took a step forward and listened; then stepped again forward, and seized with her clumsy hands the heavy bar which was laid across the door. Gently, and with much trouble, she pushed back the bar, as silently lifted the latch, and then took up the glimmering lamp which stood in the antechamber of the hall. It seemed as if a stronger will than her own gave her strength. She removed the iron bolt from the closed cellar door, and slipped in to the prisoner. He was slumbering. She touched him with her cold, moist hand, and as he awoke and caught sight of the hideous form, he shuddered as if he beheld a wicked apparition. She drew her knife, cut through the bonds which confined his hands and feet, and beckoned to him to follow her. He uttered some holy names and made the sign of the cross, while the form remained motionless by his side.

"Who art thou?" he asked, "whose outward appearance is that of an animal, while thou willingly performest acts of mercy?"

The frog figure beckoned to him to follow her, and led him through a long gallery concealed by hanging drapery to the stables, and then pointed to a horse. He mounted upon it, and she sprang up also before him, and held tightly by the animal's mane. The prisoner understood her, and they rode on at a rapid trot, by a road which he would never have found by himself, across the open heath. He forgot her ugly form, and only thought how the mercy and loving-kindness of the Almighty was acting through this hideous apparition. As he offered pious prayers and sang holy songs of praise, she trembled. Was it the effect of prayer and praise that caused this? or, was she shuddering in the cold morning air at the thought of approaching twilight? What were her feelings? She raised herself up, and wanted to stop the horse and spring off, but the Christian priest held her back with all his might, and then sang a pious song, as if this could loosen the wicked charm that had changed her into the semblance of a frog.

And the horse galloped on more wildly than before. The sky painted itself red, the first sunbeam pierced through the clouds, and in the clear flood of sunlight the frog became changed. It was Helga again, young and beautiful, but with a wicked demoniac spirit. He held now a beautiful young woman in his arms, and he was horrified at the sight. He stopped the horse, and sprang from its back. He imagined that some new sorcery was at work. But Helga also leaped from the horse and stood on the ground. The child's short garment reached only to her knee. She snatched the sharp knife from her girdle, and rushed like lightning at the astonished priest. "Let me get at thee!" she cried; "let me get at thee, that I may plunge this knife into thy body. Thou art pale as ashes, thou beardless slave." She pressed in upon him. They struggled with each other in heavy combat, but it was as if an invisible power had been given to the Christian in the struggle. He held her fast, and the old oak under which they stood seemed to help him, for the loosened roots on the ground became entangled in the maiden's feet, and held them fast. Close by rose a bubbling spring, and he sprinkled Helga's face and neck with the water, commanded the unclean spirit to come forth, and pronounced upon her a Christian blessing. But the water of faith has no power unless the wellspring of faith flows within. And yet even here its power was shown; something more than the mere strength of a man opposed itself, through his means, against the evil which struggled within her. His holy action seemed to overpower her. She dropped her arms, glanced at him with pale cheeks and looks of amazement. He appeared to her a mighty magician skilled in secret arts; his language was the darkest magic to her, and the movements of his hands in the air were as the secret signs of a magician's wand. She would not have blinked had he waved over her head a sharp knife or a glittering axe; but she shrunk from him as he signed her with the sign of the cross on her forehead and breast, and sat before him like a tame bird, with her head bowed down. Then he spoke to her, in gentle words, of the deed of love she had performed for him during the night, when she had come to him in the form of an ugly frog, to loosen his bonds, and to lead him forth to life and light; and he told her that she was bound in closer fetters than he had been, and that she could recover also life and light by his means. He would take her to Hedeby to St. Ansgarius, and there, in that Christian town, the spell of the sorcerer would be removed. But he would not let her sit before him on the horse, though of her own free will she wished to do so. "Thou must sit behind me, not before me," said he. "Thy magic beauty has a magic power which comes from an evil origin, and I fear it; still I am sure to overcome through my faith in Christ." Then he knelt down, and prayed with pious fervor. It was as if the quiet woodland were a holy church consecrated by his worship. The birds sang as if they were also of this new congregation; and the fragrance of the wildflowers was as the ambrosial perfume of incense; while, above all, sounded the words of Scripture, "A light to them that sit in darkness and in the shadow of death, to guide their feet into the way of peace." And he spoke these words with the deep longing of his whole nature.

Meanwhile, the horse that had carried them in wild career stood quietly by, plucking at the tall bramble bushes, till the ripe young berries fell down upon Helga's hands, as if inviting her to eat. Patiently she allowed herself to be lifted on the horse, and sat there like a somnambulist—as one who walked in his sleep. The Christian bound two branches together with bark, in the form of a cross, and held it on high as they rode through the forest. The way gradually grew thicker of brushwood, as they rode along, till at last it became a trackless wilderness. Bushes of the wild sloe here and there blocked up the path, so that they had to ride over them. The bubbling spring formed not a stream, but a marsh, round which also they were obliged to guide the horse; still there were strength and refreshment in the cool forest breeze, and no trifling power in the gentle words spoken in faith and Christian love by the young priest, whose inmost heart yearned to lead this poor lost one into the way of light and life. It is said that raindrops can make a hollow in the hardest stone, and the waves of the sea can smooth and round the rough edges of the rocks; so did the dew of mercy fall upon Helga, softening what was hard, and smoothing what was rough in her character. These effects did not yet appear; she was not herself aware of them; neither does the seed in the lap of earth know, when the refreshing dew and the warm sunbeams fall upon it, that it contains within itself power by which it will flourish and bloom. The song of the mother sinks into the heart of the child, and the little one prattles the words after her, without understanding their meaning; but after a time the thoughts expand, and what has been heard in childhood seems to the mind clear and bright. So now the "Word," which is all-powerful to create, was working in the heart of Helga.

They rode forth from the thick forest, crossed the heath, and again entered a pathless wood. Here, towards evening, they met with robbers.

"Where hast thou stolen that beauteous maiden?" cried the robbers, seizing the horse by the bridle, and dragging the two riders from its back.

The priest had nothing to defend himself with, but the knife he had taken from Helga, and with this he struck out right and left. One of the robbers raised his axe against him; but the young priest sprang on one side, and avoided the blow, which fell with great force on the horse's neck, so that the blood gushed forth, and the animal sunk to the ground. Then Helga seemed suddenly to awake from her long, deep reverie; she threw herself hastily upon the dying animal. The priest placed himself before her, to defend and shelter her; but one of the robbers swung his iron axe against the Christian's head with such force that it was dashed to pieces, the blood and brains were scattered about, and he fell dead upon the ground. Then the robbers seized beautiful Helga by her white arms and slender waist; but at that moment the sun went down, and as its last ray disappeared, she was changed into the form of a frog. A greenish white mouth spread half over her face; her arms became thin and slimy; while broad hands, with webbed fingers, spread themselves out like fans. Then the robbers, in terror, let her go, and she stood among them, a hideous monster; and as is the nature of frogs to do, she hopped up as high as her own size, and disappeared in the thicket. Then the robbers knew that this must be the work of an evil spirit or some secret sorcery, and, in a terrible fright, they ran hastily from the spot.

The full moon had already risen, and was shining in all her radiant splendor over the earth, when from the thicket, in the form of a frog, crept poor Helga. She stood still by the corpse of the Christian priest, and the carcase of the dead horse. She looked at them with eyes that seemed to weep, and from the frog's head came forth a croaking sound, as when a child bursts into tears. She threw herself first upon one, and then upon the other; brought water in her hand, which, from being webbed, was large and hollow, and poured it over them; but they were dead, and dead they would remain. She understood that at last. Soon wild animals would come and tear their dead bodies; but no, that must not happen. Then she dug up the earth, as deep as she was able, that she might prepare a grave for them. She had nothing but a branch of a tree and her two hands, between the fingers of which the webbed skin stretched, and they were torn by the work, while the blood ran down her hands. She saw at last that her work would be useless, more than she could accomplish; so she fetched more water, and washed the face of the dead, and then covered it with fresh green leaves; she also brought large boughs and spread over him, and scattered dried leaves between the branches. Then she brought the heaviest stones that she could carry, and laid them over the dead body, filling up the crevices with moss, till she thought she had fenced in his resting place strongly enough. The difficult task had employed her the whole night; and as the sun broke forth, there stood the beautiful Helga in all her loveliness, with her bleeding hands, and, for the first time, with tears on her maiden cheeks. It was, in this transformation, as if two natures were striving together within her; her whole frame trembled, and she looked around her as if she had just awoke from a painful dream. She leaned for support against the trunk of a slender tree, and at last climbed to the topmost branches, like a cat, and seated herself firmly upon them. She remained there the whole day, sitting alone, like a frightened squirrel, in the silent solitude of the wood, where the rest and stillness is as the calm of death.

Butterflies fluttered around her, and close by were several anthills, each with its hundreds of busy little creatures moving quickly to and fro. In the air, danced myriads of gnats, swarm upon swarm, troops of buzzing flies, ladybirds, dragonflies with golden wings, and other little winged creatures. The worm crawled forth from the moist ground, and the moles crept out; but, excepting these, all around had the stillness of death: but when people say this, they do not quite understand themselves what they mean. None noticed Helga but a flock of magpies, which flew chattering round the top of the tree on which she sat. These birds hopped close to her on the branches with bold curiosity. A glance from her eyes was a signal to frighten them away, and they were not clever enough to find out who she was; indeed she hardly knew herself.

When the sun was near setting, and the evening's twilight about to commence, the approaching transformation aroused her to fresh exertion. She let herself down gently from the tree, and, as the last sunbeam vanished, she stood again in the wrinkled form of a frog, with the torn, webbed skin on her hands, but her eyes now gleamed with more radiant beauty than they had ever possessed in her most beautiful form of loveliness; they were now pure, mild maidenly eyes that shone forth in the face of a frog. They showed the existence of deep feeling and a human heart, and the beauteous eyes overflowed with tears, weeping precious drops that lightened the heart.

On the raised mound which she had made as a grave for the dead priest, she found the cross made of the branches of a tree, the last work of him who now lay dead and cold beneath it. A sudden thought came to Helga, and she lifted up the cross and planted it upon the grave, between the stones that covered him and the dead horse. The sad recollection brought the tears to her eyes, and in this gentle spirit she traced the same sign in the sand round the grave; and as she formed, with both her hands, the sign of the cross, the web skin fell from them like a torn glove. She washed her hands in the water of the spring, and gazed with astonishment at their delicate whiteness. Again she made the holy sign in the air, between herself and the dead man; her lips trembled, her tongue moved, and the name which she in her ride through the forest had so often heard spoken, rose to her lips, and she uttered the words, "Jesus Christ." Then the frog skin fell from her; she was once more a lovely maiden. Her head bent wearily, her tired limbs required rest, and then she slept.

Her sleep, however, was short. Towards midnight, she awoke; before her stood the dead horse, prancing and full of life, which shone forth from his eyes and from his wounded neck. Close by his side appeared the murdered Christian priest, more beautiful than Baldur, as the Viking's wife had said; but now he came as if in a flame of fire. Such gravity, such stern justice, such a piercing glance shone from his large, gentle eyes, that it seemed to penetrate into every corner of her heart. Beautiful Helga trembled at the look, and her memory returned with a power as if it had been the day of judgment. Every good deed that had been done for her, every loving word that had been said, were vividly before her mind. She understood now that love had kept her here during the day of her trial; while the creature formed of dust and clay, soul and spirit, had wrestled and struggled with evil. She acknowledged that she had only followed the impulses of an evil disposition, that she had done nothing to cure herself; everything had been given her, and all had happened as it were by the ordination of Providence. She bowed herself humbly, confessed her great imperfections in the sight of Him who can read every fault of the heart, and then the priest spoke. "Daughter of the moorland, thou hast come from the swamp and the marshy earth, but from this thou shalt arise. The sunlight shining into thy inmost soul proves the origin from which thou hast really sprung, and has restored the body to its natural form. I am come to thee from the land of the dead, and thou also must pass through the valley to reach the holy mountains where mercy and perfection dwell. I cannot lead thee to Hedeby that thou mayst receive Christian baptism, for first thou must remove the thick veil with which the waters of the moorland are shrouded, and bring forth from its depths the living author of thy being and thy life. Till this is done, thou canst not receive consecration."

Then he lifted her on the horse and gave her a golden censer, similar to those she had already seen at the Viking's house. A sweet perfume arose from it, while the open wound in the forehead of the slain priest, shone with the rays of a diamond. He took the cross from the grave, and held it aloft, and now they rode through the air over the rustling trees, over the hills where warriors lay buried each by his dead war horse; and the brazen monumental figures rose up and galloped forth, and stationed themselves on the summits of the hills. The golden crescent on their foreheads, fastened with golden knots, glittered in the moonlight, and their mantles floated in the wind. The dragon, that guards buried treasure, lifted his head and gazed after them. The goblins and the satyrs peeped out from beneath the hills, and flitted to and fro in the fields, waving blue, red, and green torches, like the glowing sparks in burning paper. Over woodland and heath, flood and fen, they flew on, till they reached the wild moor, over which they hovered in broad circles. The Christian priest held the cross aloft, and it glittered like gold, while from his lips sounded pious prayers. Beautiful Helga's voice joined with his in the hymns he sung, as a child joins in her mother's song. She swung the censer, and a wonderful fragrance of incense arose from it; so powerful, that the reeds and rushes of the moor burst forth into blossom. Each germ came forth from the deep ground: all that had life raised itself. Blooming waterlilies spread themselves forth like a carpet of wrought flowers, and upon them lay a slumbering woman, young and beautiful. Helga fancied that it was her own image she saw reflected in the still water. But it was her mother she beheld, the wife of the Marsh King, the princess from the land of the Nile.

The dead Christian priest desired that the sleeping woman should be lifted on the horse, but the horse sank beneath the load, as if he had been a funeral pall fluttering in the wind. But the sign of the cross made the airy phantom strong, and then the three rode away from the marsh to firm ground.

At the same moment the cock crew in the Viking's castle, and the dream figures dissolved and floated away in the air, but mother and daughter stood opposite to each other.

"Am I looking at my own image in the deep water?" said the mother.

"Is it myself that I see represented on a white shield?" cried the daughter.

Then they came nearer to each other in a fond embrace. The mother's heart beat quickly, and she understood the quickened pulses. "My child!" she exclaimed, "the flower of my heart—my lotus flower of the deep water!" and she embraced her child again and wept, and the tears were as a baptism of new life and love for Helga. "In swan's plumage I came here," said the mother, "and here I threw off my feather dress. Then I sank down through the wavering ground, deep into the marsh beneath, which closed like a wall around me; I found myself after a while in fresher water; still a power drew me down deeper and deeper. I felt the weight of sleep upon my eyelids. Then I slept, and dreams hovered round me. It seemed to me as if I were again in the pyramids of Egypt, and yet the waving elder trunk that had frightened me on the moor stood ever before me. I observed the clefts and wrinkles in the stem; they shone forth in strange colors, and took the form of hieroglyphics. It was the mummy case on which I gazed. At last it burst, and forth stepped the thousand years' old king, the mummy form, black as pitch, black as the shining wood snail, or the slimy mud of the swamp. Whether it was really the mummy or the Marsh King I know not. He seized me in his arms, and I felt as if I must die. When I recovered myself, I found in my bosom a little bird, flapping its wings, twittering and fluttering. The bird flew away from my bosom, upwards towards the dark, heavy canopy above me, but a long, green band kept it fastened to me. I heard and understood the tenor of its longings. Freedom! sunlight! to my father! Then I thought of my father, and the sunny land of my birth, my life, and my love. Then I loosened the band, and let the bird fly away to its home—to a father. Since that hour I have ceased to dream; my sleep has been long and heavy, till in this very hour, harmony and fragrance awoke me, and set me free."

The green band which fastened the wings of the bird to the mother's heart, where did it flutter now? whither had it been wafted? The stork only had seen it. The band was the green stalk, the cup of the flower the cradle in which lay the child, that now in blooming beauty had been folded to the mother's heart.

And while the two were resting in each other's arms, the old stork flew round and round them in narrowing circles, till at length he flew away swiftly to his nest, and fetched away the two suits of swan's feathers, which he had preserved there for many years. Then he returned to the mother and daughter, and threw the swan's plumage over them; the feathers immediately closed around them, and they rose up from the earth in the form of two white swans.

"And now we can converse with pleasure," said the stork-papa; "we can understand one another, although the beaks of birds are so different in shape. It is very fortunate that you came tonight. Tomorrow we should have been gone. The mother, myself and the little ones, we're about to fly to the south. Look at me now: I am an old friend from the Nile, and a mother's heart contains more than her beak. She always said that the princess would know how to help herself. I and the young ones carried the swan's feathers over here, and I am glad of it now, and how lucky it is that I am here still. When the day dawns we shall start with a great company of other storks. We'll fly first, and you can follow in our track, so that you cannot miss your way. I and the young ones will have an eye upon you."

"And the lotus flower which I was to take with me," said the Egyptian princess, "is flying here by my side, clothed in swan's feathers. The flower of my heart will travel with me; and so the riddle is solved. Now for home! now for home!"

But Helga said she could not leave the Danish land without once more seeing her foster mother, the loving wife of the Viking. Each pleasing recollection, each kind word, every tear from the heart which her foster mother had wept for her, rose in her mind, and at that moment she felt as if she loved this mother the best.

"Yes, we must go to the Viking's castle," said the stork; "mother and the young ones are waiting for me there. How they will open their eyes and flap their wings! My wife, you see, does not say much; she is short and abrupt in her manner; but she means well, for all that. I will flap my wings at once, that they may hear us coming." Then stork-papa flapped his wings in first-rate style, and he and the swans flew away to the Viking's castle.

In the castle, everyone was in a deep sleep. It had been late in the evening before the Viking's wife retired to rest. She was anxious about Helga, who, three days before, had vanished with the Christian priest. Helga must have helped him in his flight, for it was her horse that was missed from the stable; but by what power had all this been accomplished? The Viking's wife thought of it with wonder, thought on the miracles which they said could be performed by those who believed in the Christian faith, and followed its teachings. These passing thoughts formed themselves into a vivid dream, and it seemed to her that she was still lying awake on her couch, while without darkness reigned. A storm arose; she heard the lake dashing and rolling from east and west, like the waves of the North Sea or the Cattegat. The monstrous snake which, it is said, surrounds the earth in the depths of the ocean, was trembling in spasmodic convulsions. The night of the fall of the gods was come, "Ragnorock," as the heathens call the judgment day, when everything shall pass away, even the high gods themselves. The war trumpet sounded; riding upon the rainbow, came the gods, clad in steel, to fight their last battle on the last battlefield. Before them flew the winged vampires, and the dead warriors closed up the train. The whole firmament was ablaze with the northern lights, and yet the darkness triumphed. It was a terrible hour. And, close to the terrified woman, Helga seemed to be seated on the floor, in the hideous form of a frog, yet trembling, and clinging to her foster mother, who took her on her lap, and lovingly caressed her, hideous and froglike as she was. The air was filled with the clashing of arms and the hissing of arrows, as if a storm of hail was descending upon the earth. It seemed to her the hour when earth and sky would burst asunder, and all things be swallowed up in Saturn's fiery lake; but she knew that a new heaven and a new earth would arise, and that cornfields would wave where now the lake rolled over desolate sands, and the ineffable God reigns. Then she saw rising from the region of the dead, Baldur the gentle, the loving, and as the Viking's wife gazed upon him, she recognized his countenance. It was the captive Christian priest. "White Christian!" she exclaimed aloud, and with the words, she pressed a kiss on the forehead of the hideous frog child. Then the frog skin fell off, and Helga stood before her in all her beauty, more lovely and gentle-looking, and with eyes beaming with love. She kissed the hands of her foster mother, blessed her for all her fostering love and care during the days of her trial and misery, for the thoughts she had suggested and awoke in her heart, and for naming the Name which she now repeated. Then beautiful Helga rose as a mighty swan, and spread her wings with the rushing sound of troops of birds of passage flying through the air.

Then the Viking's wife awoke, but she still heard the rushing sound without. She knew it was the time for the storks to depart, and that it must be their wings which she heard. She felt she should like to see them once more, and bid them farewell. She rose from her couch, stepped out on the threshold, and beheld, on the ridge of the roof, a party of storks ranged side by side. Troops of the birds were flying in circles over the castle and the highest trees; but just before her, as she stood on the threshold and close to the well where Helga had so often sat and alarmed her with her wildness, now stood two swans, gazing at her with intelligent eyes. Then she remembered her dream, which still appeared to her as a reality. She thought of Helga in the form of a swan. She thought of a Christian priest, and suddenly a wonderful joy arose in her heart. The swans flapped their wings and arched their necks as if to offer her a greeting, and the Viking's wife spread out her arms towards them, as if she accepted it, and smiled through her tears. She was roused from deep thought by a rustling of wings and snapping of beaks; all the storks arose, and started on their journey towards the south.

"We will not wait for the swans," said the mamma stork; "if they want to go with us, let them come now; we can't sit here till the plovers start. It is a fine thing after all to travel in families, not like the finches and the partridges. There the male and the female birds fly in separate flocks, which, to speak candidly, I consider very unbecoming."

"What are those swans flapping their wings for?"

"Well, everyone flies in his own fashion," said the papa stork. "The swans fly in an oblique line; the cranes, in the form of a triangle; and the plovers, in a curved line like a snake."

"Don't talk about snakes while we are flying up here," said stork-mamma. "It puts ideas into the children's heads that cannot be realized."

"Are those the high mountains I have heard spoken of?" asked Helga, in the swan's plumage.

"They are storm clouds driving along beneath us," replied her mother.

"What are yonder white clouds that rise so high?" again inquired Helga.

"Those are mountains covered with perpetual snows, that you see yonder," said her mother. And then they flew across the Alps towards the blue Mediterranean.

"Africa's land! Egyptia's strand!" sang the daughter of the Nile, in her swan's plumage, as from the upper air she caught sight of her native land, a narrow, golden, wavy strip on the shores of the Nile; the other birds espied it also and hastened their flight.

"I can smell the Nile mud and the wet frogs," said the stork-mamma, "and I begin to feel quite hungry. Yes, now you shall taste something nice, and you will see the marabout bird, and the ibis, and the crane. They all belong to our family, but they are not nearly so handsome as we are. They give themselves great airs, especially the ibis. The Egyptians have spoilt him. They make a mummy of him, and stuff him with spices. I would rather be stuffed with live frogs, and so would you, and so you shall. Better have something in your inside while you are alive, than to be made a parade of after you are dead. That is my opinion, and I am always right."

"The storks are come," was said in the great house on the banks of the Nile, where the lord lay in the hall on his downy cushions, covered with a leopard skin, scarcely alive, yet not dead, waiting and hoping for the lotus flower from the deep moorland in the far north. Relatives and servants were standing by his couch, when the two beautiful swans who had come with the storks flew into the hall. They threw off their soft white plumage, and two lovely female forms approached the pale, sick old man, and threw back their long hair, and when Helga bent over her grandfather, redness came back to his cheeks, his eyes brightened, and life returned to his benumbed limbs. The old man rose up with health and energy renewed; daughter and grandchild welcomed him as joyfully as if with a morning greeting after a long and troubled dream.

Joy reigned through the whole house, as well as in the stork's nest; although there the chief cause was really the good food, especially the quantities of frogs, which seemed to spring out of the ground in swarms.

Then the learned men hastened to note down, in flying characters, the story of the two princesses, and spoke of the arrival of the health-giving flower as a mighty event, which had been a blessing to the house and the land. Meanwhile, the stork-papa told the story to his family in his own way; but not till they had eaten and were satisfied; otherwise they would have had something else to do than to listen to stories.

"Well," said the stork-mamma, when she had heard it, "you will be made something of at last; I suppose they can do nothing less."

"What could I be made?" said stork-papa; "what have I done? Just nothing."

"You have done more than all the rest," she replied. "But for you and the youngsters the two young princesses would never have seen Egypt again, and the recovery of the old man would not have been affected. You will become something. They must certainly give you a doctor's hood, and our young ones will inherit it, and their children after them, and so on. You already look like an Egyptian doctor, at least in my eyes."

"I cannot quite remember the words I heard when I listened on the roof," said stork-papa, while relating the story to his family; "all I know is, that what the wise men said was so complicated and so learned, that they received not only rank, but presents; even the head cook at the great house was honored with a mark of distinction, most likely for the soup."

"And what did you receive?" said the stork-mamma. "They certainly ought not to forget the most important person in the affair, as you really are. The learned men have done nothing at all but use their tongues. Surely they will not overlook you."

Late in the night, while the gentle sleep of peace rested on the now happy house, there was still one watcher. It was not stork-papa, who, although he stood on guard on one leg, could sleep soundly. Helga alone was awake. She leaned over the balcony, gazing at the sparkling stars that shone clearer and brighter in the pure air than they had done in the north, and yet they were the same stars. She thought of the Viking's wife in the wild moorland, of the gentle eyes of her foster mother, and of the tears she had shed over the poor frog child that now lived in splendor and starry beauty by the waters of the Nile, with air balmy and sweet as spring. She thought of the love that dwelt in the breast of the heathen woman, love that had been shown to a wretched creature, hateful as a human being, and hideous when in the form of an animal. She looked at the glittering stars, and thought of the radiance that had shone forth on the forehead of the dead man, as she had fled with him over the woodland and moor. Tones were awakened in her memory; words which she had heard him speak as they rode onward, when she was carried, wondering and trembling, through the air; words from the great Fountain of love, the highest love that embraces all the human race. What had not been won and achieved by this love?

Day and night beautiful Helga was absorbed in the contemplation of the great amount of her happiness, and lost herself in the contemplation, like a child who turns hurriedly from the giver to examine the beautiful gifts. She was overpowered with her good fortune, which seemed always increasing, and therefore what might it become in the future? Had she not been brought by a wonderful miracle to all this joy and happiness? And in these thoughts she indulged, until at last she thought no more of the Giver. It was the overabundance of youthful spirits unfolding its wings for a daring flight. Her eyes sparkled with energy, when suddenly arose a loud noise in the court below, and the daring thought vanished. She looked down, and saw two large ostriches running round quickly in narrow circles; she had never seen these creatures before—great, coarse, clumsy-looking birds with curious wings that looked as if they had been clipped, and the birds themselves had the appearance of having been roughly used. She inquired about them, and for the first time heard the legend which the Egyptians relate respecting the ostrich.

Once, say they, the ostriches were a beautiful and glorious race of birds, with large, strong wings. One evening the other large birds of the forest said to the ostrich, "Brother, shall we fly to the river tomorrow morning to drink, God willing?" and the ostrich answered, "I will."

With the break of day, therefore, they commenced their flight; first rising high in the air, towards the sun, which is the eye of God; still higher and higher the ostrich flew, far above the other birds, proudly approaching the light, trusting in its own strength, and thinking not of the Giver, or saying, "if God will." When suddenly the avenging angel drew back the veil from the flaming ocean of sunlight, and in a moment the wings of the proud bird were scorched and shrivelled, and they sunk miserably to the earth. Since that time the ostrich and his race have never been able to rise in the air; they can only fly terror-stricken along the ground, or run round and round in narrow circles. It is a warning to mankind, that in all our thoughts and schemes, and in every action we undertake, we should say, "if God will."

Then Helga bowed her head thoughtfully and seriously, and looked at the circling ostrich, as with timid fear and simple pleasure it glanced at its own great shadow on the sunlit walls. And the story of the ostrich sunk deeply into the heart and mind of Helga: a life of happiness, both in the present and in the future, seemed secure for her, and what was yet to come might be the best of all, God willing.

Early in the spring, when the storks were again about to journey northward, beautiful Helga took off her golden bracelets, scratched her name on them, and beckoned to the stork-father. He came to her, and she placed the golden circlet round his neck, and begged him to deliver it safely to the Viking's wife, so that she might know that her foster daughter still lived, was happy, and had not forgotten her.

"It is rather heavy to carry," thought stork-papa, when he had it on his neck; "but gold and honor are not to be flung into the street. The stork brings good fortune—they'll be obliged to acknowledge that at last."

"You lay gold, and I lay eggs," said stork mamma; "with you it is only once in a way, I lay eggs every year. But no one appreciates what we do; I call it very mortifying."

"But then we have a consciousness of our own worth, mother," replied stork papa.

"What good will that do you?" retorted stork mamma; "it will neither bring you a fair wind, nor a good meal."

"The little nightingale, who is singing yonder in the tamarind grove, will soon be going north, too." Helga said she had often heard her singing on the wild moor, so she determined to send a message by her. While flying in the swan's plumage she had learnt the bird language; she had often conversed with the stork and the swallow, and she knew that the nightingale would understand. So she begged the nightingale to fly to the beechwood, on the peninsula of Jutland, where a mound of stone and twigs had been raised to form the grave, and she begged the nightingale to persuade all the other little birds to build their nests round the place, so that evermore should resound over that grave music and song. And the nightingale flew away, and time flew away also.

In the autumn, an eagle, standing upon a pyramid, saw a stately train of richly laden camels, and men attired in armor on foaming Arabian steeds, whose glossy skins shone like silver, their nostrils were pink, and their thick, flowing manes hung almost to their slender legs. A royal prince of Arabia, handsome as a prince should be, and accompanied by distinguished guests, was on his way to the stately house, on the roof of which the storks' empty nests might be seen. They were away now in the far north, but expected to return very soon. And, indeed, they returned on a day that was rich in joy and gladness.

A marriage was being celebrated, in which the beautiful Helga, glittering in silk and jewels, was the bride, and the bridegroom the young Arab prince. Bride and bridegroom sat at the upper end of the table, between the bride's mother and grandfather. But her gaze was not on the bridegroom, with his manly, sunburnt face, round which curled a black beard, and whose dark fiery eyes were fixed upon her; but away from him, at a twinkling star, that shone down upon her from the sky. Then was heard the sound of rushing wings beating the air. The storks were coming home; and the old stork pair, although tired with the journey and requiring rest, did not fail to fly down at once to the balustrades of the verandah, for they knew already what feast was being celebrated. They had heard of it on the borders of the land, and also that Helga had caused their figures to be represented on the walls, for they belonged to her history.

"I call that very sensible and pretty," said stork-papa.

"Yes, but it is very little," said mamma stork; "they could not possibly have done less."

But, when Helga saw them, she rose and went out into the verandah to stroke the backs of the storks. The old stork pair bowed their heads, and curved their necks, and even the youngest among the young ones felt honored by this reception.

Helga continued to gaze upon the glittering star, which seemed to glow brighter and purer in its light; then between herself and the star floated a form, purer than the air, and visible through it. It floated quite near to her, and she saw that it was the dead Christian priest, who also was coming to her wedding feast—coming from the heavenly kingdom.

"The glory and brightness, yonder, outshines all that is known on earth," said he.

Then Helga the fair prayed more gently, and more earnestly, than she had ever prayed in her life before, that she might be permitted to gaze, if only for a single moment, at the glory and brightness of the heavenly kingdom. Then she felt herself lifted up, as it were, above the earth, through a sea of sound and thought; not only around her, but within her, was there light and song, such as words cannot express.

"Now we must return," he said. "You will be missed."

"Only one more look," she begged; "but one short moment more."

"We must return to earth; the guests will have all departed. Only one more look—the last!"

Then Helga stood again in the verandah. But the marriage lamps in the festive hall had been all extinguished, and the torches outside had vanished. The storks were gone; not a guest could be seen; no bridegroom—all in those few short moments seemed to have died. Then a great dread fell upon her. She stepped from the verandah through the empty hall into the next chamber, where slept strange warriors. She opened a side door, which once led into her own apartment, but now, as she passed through, she found herself suddenly in a garden which she had never before seen here, the sky blushed red, it was the dawn of morning. Three minutes only in heaven, and a whole night on earth had passed away! Then she saw the storks, and called to them in their own language.

Then stork-papa turned his head towards here, listened to her words, and drew near. "You speak our language," said he, "what do you wish? Why do you appear—you—a strange woman?"

"It is I—it is Helga! Dost thou not know me? Three minutes ago we were speaking together yonder in the verandah."

"That is a mistake," said the stork, "you must have dreamed all this."

"No, no," she exclaimed. Then she reminded him of the Viking's castle, of the great lake, and of the journey across the ocean.

Then stork-papa winked his eyes, and said, "Why that's an old story which happened in the time of my grandfather. There certainly was a princess of that kind here in Egypt once, who came from the Danish land, but she vanished on the evening of her wedding day, many hundred years ago, and never came back. You may read about it yourself yonder, on a monument in the garden. There you will find swans and storks sculptured, and on the top is a figure of the princess Helga, in marble."

And so it was; Helga understood it all now, and sank on her knees. The sun burst forth in all its glory, and, as in olden times, the form of the frog vanished in his beams, and the beautiful form stood forth in all its loveliness; so now, bathed in light, rose a beautiful form, purer, clearer than air—a ray of brightness—from the Source of light Himself. The body crumbled into dust, and a faded lotus flower lay on the spot on which Helga had stood.

"Now that is a new ending to the story," said stork-papa; "I really never expected it would end in this way, but it seems a very good ending."

"And what will the young ones say to it, I wonder?" said stork-mamma.

"Ah, that is a very important question," replied the stork.

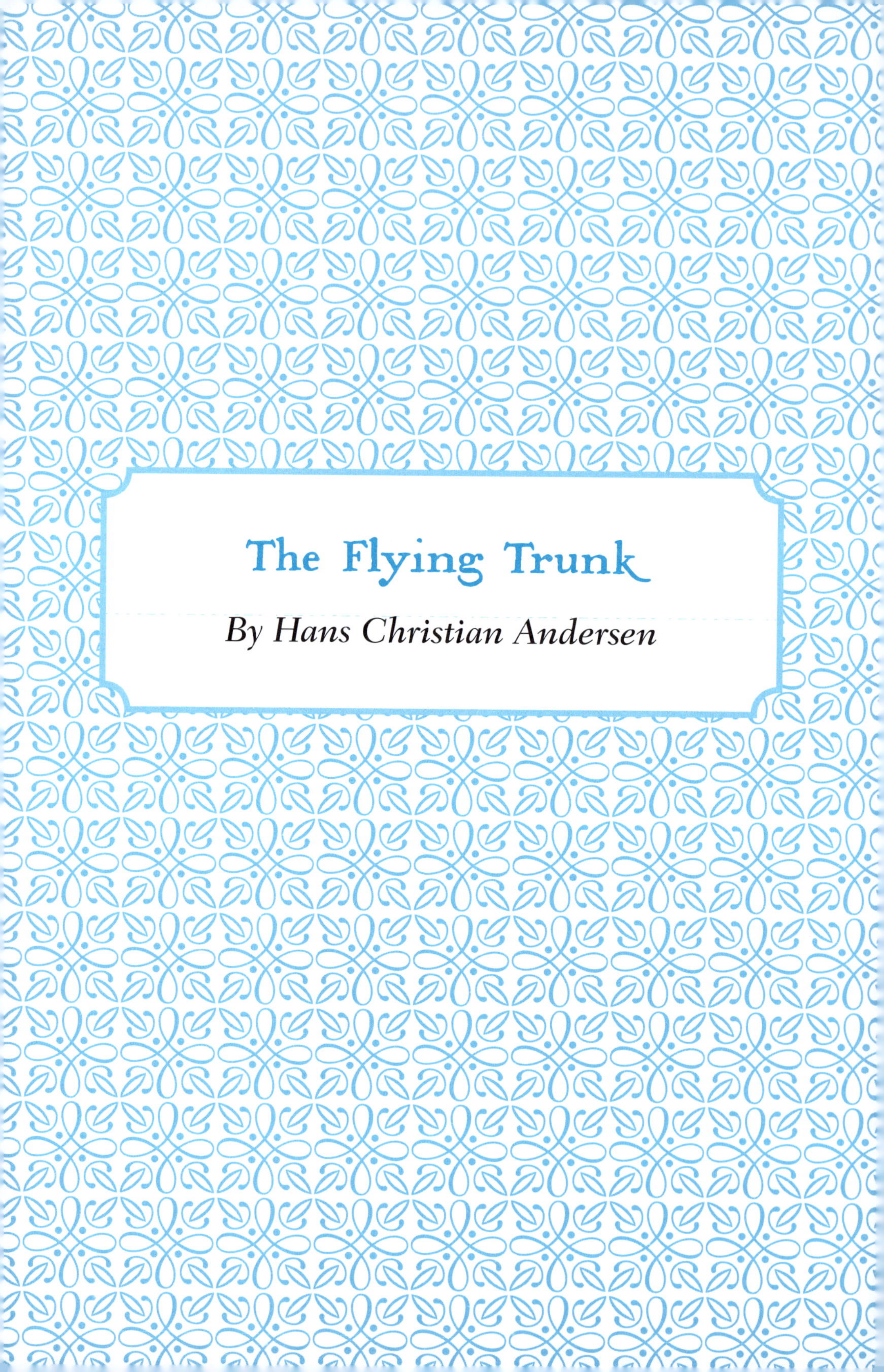

The Flying Trunk

By Hans Christian Andersen

There was once a merchant who was so rich that he could have paved the whole street with gold, and would even then have had enough for a small alley. But he did not do so; he knew the value of money better than to use it in this way. So clever was he, that every shilling he put out brought him a crown; and so he continued till he died. His son inherited his wealth, and he lived a merry life with it; he went to a masquerade every night, made kites out of five pound notes, and threw pieces of gold into the sea instead of stones, making ducks and drakes of them. In this manner he soon lost all his money. At last he had nothing left but a pair of slippers, an old dressing gown, and four shillings. And now all his friends deserted him, they could not walk with him in the streets; but one of them, who was very good-natured, sent him an old trunk with this message, "Pack up!" "Yes," he said, "it is all very well to say, 'pack up,'" but he had nothing left to pack up, therefore he seated himself in the trunk.

It was a very wonderful trunk; no sooner did any one press on the lock than the trunk could fly. He shut the lid and pressed the lock, when away flew the trunk up the chimney with the merchant's son in it, right up into the clouds. Whenever the bottom of the trunk cracked, he was in a great fright, for if the trunk fell to pieces he would have made a tremendous somerset over the trees. However, he got safely in his trunk to the land of Turkey. He hid the trunk in the wood under some dry leaves, and then went into the town: he could do this very well, for the Turks always go about dressed in dressing gowns and slippers, as he was himself. He happened to meet a nurse with a little child. "I say, you Turkish nurse," cried he, "what castle is that near the town, with the windows placed so high?"

"The king's daughter lives there," she replied, "it has been prophesied that she will be very unhappy about a lover, and therefore no one is allowed to visit her, unless the king and queen are present."

"Thank you," said the merchant's son. So he went back to the wood, seated himself in his trunk, flew up to the roof of the castle, and crept through the window into the princess's room. She lay on the sofa asleep, and she was so beautiful that the merchant's son could not help kissing her. Then she awoke, and was very much frightened; but he told her he was a Turkish angel, who had come down through the air to see her, which pleased her very much. He sat down by her side and talked to her: he said her eyes were like beautiful dark lakes, in which the thoughts swam about like little mermaids, and he told her that her forehead was a snowy mountain, which contained splendid halls full of pictures. And then he related to her about the stork who brings the beautiful children from the rivers. These were delightful stories; and when he asked the princess if she would marry him, she consented immediately.

"But you must come on Saturday," she said; "for then the king and queen will take tea with me. They will be very proud when they find that I am going to marry a Turkish angel; but you must think of some very pretty stories to tell them, for my parents like to hear stories better than anything. My mother prefers one that is deep and moral; but my father likes something funny, to make him laugh."

"Very well," he replied, "I shall bring you no other marriage portion than a story," and so they parted. But the princess gave him a sword which was studded with gold coins, and these he could use.

Then he flew away to the town and bought a new dressing gown, and afterwards returned to the wood, where he composed a story, so as to be ready for Saturday, which was no easy matter. It was ready, however, by Saturday, when he went to see the princess. The king, and queen, and the whole court, were at tea with the princess; and he was received with great politeness.

"Will you tell us a story?" said the queen, "one that is instructive and full of deep learning."

"Yes, but with something in it to laugh at," said the king.

"Certainly," he replied, and commenced at once, asking them to listen attentively.

"There was once a bundle of matches that were exceedingly proud of their high descent. Their genealogical tree, that is, a large pine tree from which they had been cut, was at one time a large, old tree in the wood. The matches now lay between a tinderbox and an old iron saucepan, and were talking about their youthful days. 'Ah! then we grew on the green boughs, and were as green as they; every morning and evening we were fed with diamond drops of dew. Whenever the sun shone, we felt his warm rays, and the little birds would relate stories to us as they sung. We knew that we were rich, for the other trees only wore their green dress in summer, but our family were able to array themselves in green, summer and winter. But the woodcutter came, like a great revolution, and our family fell under the axe. The head of the house obtained a situation as mainmast in a very fine ship, and can sail round the world when he will. The other branches of the family were taken to different places, and our office now is to kindle a light for common people. This is how such high-born people as we came to be in a kitchen.'

"Mine has been a very different fate," said the iron pot, which stood by the matches; "from my first entrance into the world I have been used to cooking and scouring. I am the first in this house, when anything solid or useful is required. My only pleasure is to be made clean and shining after dinner, and to sit in my place and have a little sensible conversation with my neighbors. All of us, excepting the water bucket, which is sometimes taken into the courtyard, live here together within these four walls. We get our news from the market basket, but he sometimes tells us very unpleasant things about the people and the government. Yes, and one day an old pot was so alarmed, that he fell down and was broken to pieces. He was a liberal, I can tell you."

"You are talking too much," said the tinderbox, and the steel struck against the flint till some sparks flew out, crying, "We want a merry evening, don't we?"

"Yes, of course," said the matches, "let us talk about those who are the highest born."

"No, I don't like to be always talking of what we are," remarked the saucepan; "let us think of some other amusement; I will begin. We will tell something that has happened to ourselves; that will be very easy, and interesting as well. On the Baltic Sea, near the Danish shore."

"What a pretty commencement!" said the plates; "we shall all like that story, I am sure."

"Yes; well in my youth, I lived in a quiet family, where the furniture was polished, the floors scoured, and clean curtains put up every fortnight."

"What an interesting way you have of relating a story," said the carpet broom; "it is easy to perceive that you have been a great deal in women's society, there is something so pure runs through what you say."

"That is quite true," said the water bucket; and he made a spring with joy, and splashed some water on the floor.

Then the saucepan went on with his story, and the end was as good as the beginning.

The plates rattled with pleasure, and the carpet broom brought some green parsley out of the dust hole and crowned the saucepan, for he knew it would vex the others; and he thought, "If I crown him today he will crown me tomorrow."

"Now, let us have a dance," said the fire tongs; and then how they danced and stuck up one leg in the air. The chair cushion in the corner burst with laughter when she saw it.

"Shall I be crowned now?" asked the fire tongs; so the broom found another wreath for the tongs.

"They were only common people after all," thought the matches. The tea urn was now asked to sing, but she said she had a cold, and could not sing without boiling heat. They all thought this was affectation, and because she did not wish to sing excepting in the parlor, when on the table with the grand people.

"In the window sat an old quill pen, with which the maid generally wrote. There was nothing remarkable about the pen, excepting that it had been dipped too deeply in the ink, but it was proud of that."

"If the tea urn won't sing," said the pen, "she can leave it alone; there is a nightingale in a cage who can sing; she has not been taught much, certainly, but we need not say anything this evening about that."

"I think it highly improper," said the teakettle, who was kitchen singer, and half-brother to the tea urn, "that a rich foreign bird should be listened to here. Is it patriotic? Let the market basket decide what is right."

"I certainly am vexed," said the basket; "inwardly vexed, more than any one can imagine. Are we spending the evening properly? Would it not be more sensible to put the house in order? If each were in his own place I would lead a game; this would be quite another thing."

"Let us act a play," said they all. At the same moment the door opened, and the maid came in. Then not one stirred; they all remained quite still; yet, at the same time, there was not a single pot amongst them who had not a high opinion of himself, and of what he could do if he chose.

"Yes, if we had chosen," they each thought, "we might have spent a very pleasant evening."

The maid took the matches and lighted them; dear me, how they sputtered and blazed up!

"Now then," they thought, "everyone will see that we are the first. How we shine; what a light we give!" Even while they spoke their light went out.

"What a capital story," said the queen, "I feel as if I were really in the kitchen, and could see the matches; yes, you shall marry our daughter."

"Certainly," said the king, "thou shalt have our daughter." The king said thou to him because he was going to be one of the family. The wedding day was fixed, and, on the evening before, the whole city was illuminated. Cakes and sweetmeats were thrown among the people. The street boys stood on tiptoe and shouted "hurrah," and whistled between their fingers; altogether it was a very splendid affair.

"I will give them another treat," said the merchant's son. So he went and bought rockets and crackers, and all sorts of fireworks that could be thought of, packed them in his trunk, and flew up with it into the air. What a whizzing and popping they made as they went off! The Turks, when they saw such a sight in the air, jumped so high that their slippers flew about their ears. It was easy to believe after this that the princess was really going to marry a Turkish angel.

As soon as the merchant's son had come down in his flying trunk to the wood after the fireworks, he thought, "I will go back into the town now, and hear what they think of the entertainment." It was very natural that he should wish to know. And what strange things people did say, to be sure! Everyone whom he questioned had a different tale to tell, though they all thought it very beautiful.

"I saw the Turkish angel myself," said one; "he had eyes like glittering stars, and a head like foaming water."

"He flew in a mantle of fire," cried another, "and lovely little cherubs peeped out from the folds."

He heard many more fine things about himself, and that the next day he was to be married. After this he went back to the forest to rest himself in his trunk. It had disappeared! A spark from the fireworks which remained had set it on fire; it was burnt to ashes! So the merchant's son could not fly any more, nor go to meet his bride. She stood all day on the roof waiting for him, and most likely she is waiting there still; while he wanders through the world telling fairy tales, but none of them so amusing as the one he related about the matches.

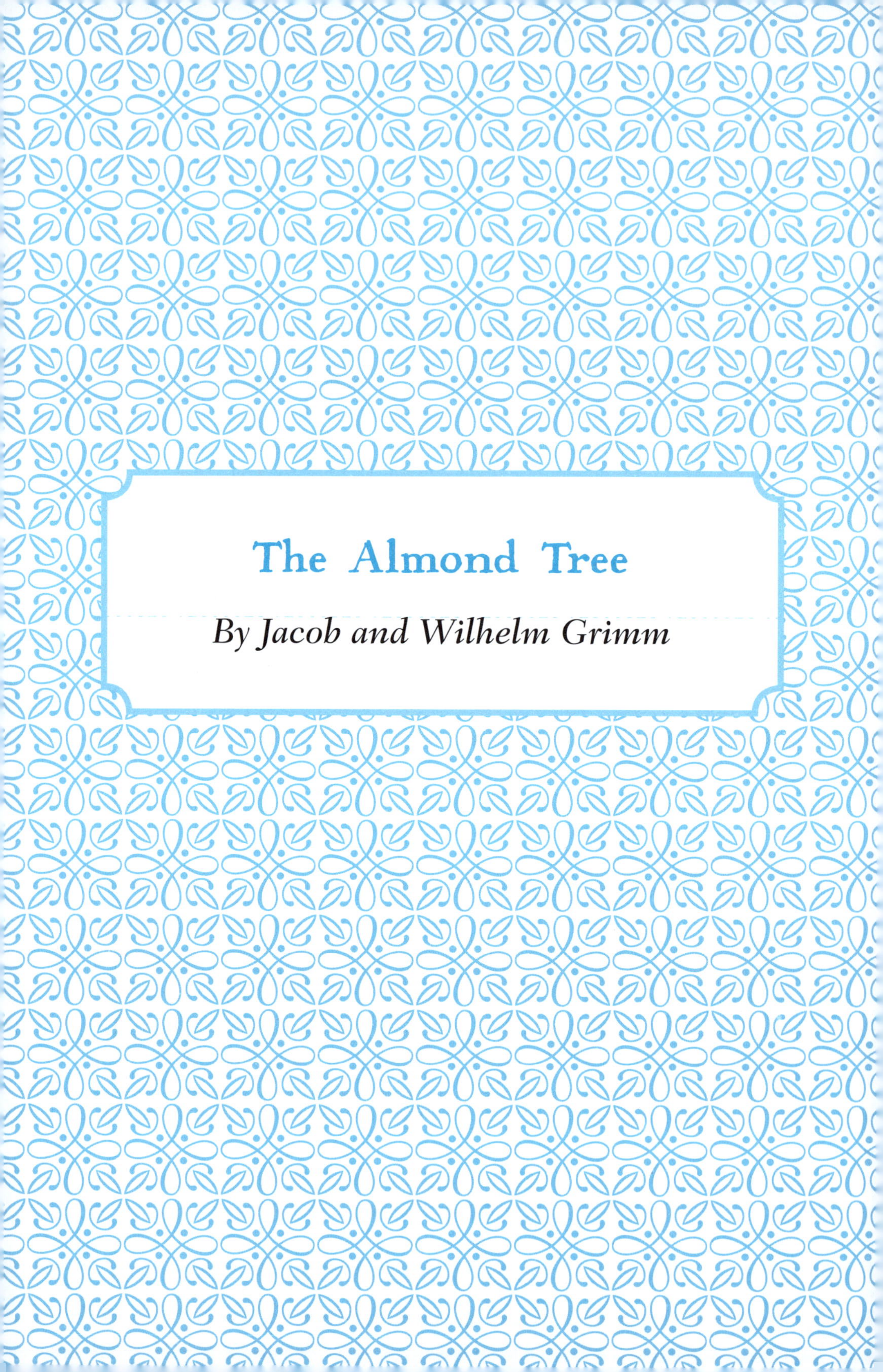

The Almond Tree

By Jacob and Wilhelm Grimm

Long, long ago, some two thousand years or so, there lived a rich man with a good and beautiful wife. They loved each other dearly, but sorrowed much that they had no children. So greatly did they desire to have one, that the wife prayed for it day and night, but still they remained childless.

In front of the house there was a court, in which grew an almond tree. One winter's day the wife stood under the tree to peel some apples, and as she was peeling them, she cut her finger, and the blood fell on the snow.

"Ah," sighed the woman heavily, "if I had but a child, as red as blood and as white as snow," and as she spoke the words, her heart grew light within her, and it seemed to her that her wish was granted, and she returned to the house feeling glad and comforted. A month passed, and the snow had all disappeared; then another month went by, and all the earth was green. So the months followed one another, and first the trees budded in the woods, and soon the green branches grew thickly intertwined, and then the blossoms began to fall. Once again the wife stood under the almond tree, and it was so full of sweet scent that her heart leaped for joy, and she was so overcome with her happiness, that she fell on her knees. Presently the fruit became round and firm, and she was glad and at peace; but when they were fully ripe she picked the berries and ate eagerly of them, and then she grew sad and ill. A little while later she called her husband, and said to him, weeping. "If I die, bury me under the almond tree." Then she felt comforted and happy again, and before another month had passed she had a little child, and when she saw that it was as white as snow and as red as blood, her joy was so great that she died.

Her husband buried her under the almond tree, and wept bitterly for her. By degrees, however, his sorrow grew less, and although at times he still grieved over his loss, he was able to go about as usual, and later on he married again.

He now had a little daughter born to him; the child of his first wife was a boy, who was as red as blood and as white as snow. The mother loved her daughter very much, and when she looked at her and then looked at the boy, it pierced her heart to think that he would always stand in the way of her own child, and she was continually thinking how she could get the whole of the property for her. This evil thought took possession of her more and more, and made her behave very unkindly to the boy. She drove him from place to place with cuffings and buffetings, so that the poor child went about in fear, and had no peace from the time he left school to the time he went back.

One day the little daughter came running to her mother in the store-room, and said, "Mother, give me an apple."

"Yes, my child," said the wife, and she gave her a beautiful apple out of the chest; the chest had a very heavy lid and a large iron lock.

"Mother," said the little daughter again, "may not brother have one too?"

The mother was angry at this, but she answered, "Yes, when he comes out of school."

Just then she looked out of the window and saw him coming, and it seemed as if an evil spirit entered into her, for she snatched the apple out of her little daughter's hand, and said, "You shall not have one before your brother." She threw the apple into the chest and shut it to. The little boy now came in, and the evil spirit in the wife made her say kindly to him, "My son, will you have an apple?" but she gave him a wicked look.

"Mother," said the boy, "how dreadful you look! Yes, give me an apple." The thought came to her that she would kill him.

"Come with me," she said, and she lifted up the lid of the chest; "take one out for yourself." And as he bent over to do so, the evil spirit urged her, and crash! down went the lid, and off went the little boy's head. Then she was overwhelmed with fear at the thought of what she had done. "If only I can prevent anyone knowing that I did it," she thought. So she went upstairs to her room, and took a white handkerchief out of her top drawer; then she set the boy's head again on his shoulders, and bound it with the handkerchief so that nothing could be seen, and placed him on a chair by the door with an apple in his hand.

Soon after this, little Marleen came up to her mother who was stirring a pot of boiling water over the fire, and said, "Mother, brother is sitting by the door with an apple in his hand, and he looks so pale; and when I asked him to give me the apple, he did not answer, and that frightened me."

"Go to him again," said her mother, "and if he does not answer, give him a box on the ear." So little Marleen went, and said, "Brother, give me that apple," but he did not say a word; then she gave him a box on the ear, and his head rolled off. She was so terrified at this, that she ran crying and screaming to her mother. "Oh!" she said, "I have knocked off brother's head," and then she wept and wept, and nothing would stop her.

"What have you done!" said her mother, "but no one must know about it, so you must keep silence; what is done can't be undone; we will make him into puddings." And she took the little boy and cut him up, made him into puddings, and put him in the pot. But Marleen stood looking on, and wept and wept, and her tears fell into the pot, so that there was no need of salt.

Presently the father came home and sat down to his dinner; he asked, "Where is my son?" The mother said nothing, but gave him a large dish of black pudding, and Marleen still wept without ceasing.

The father again asked, "Where is my son?"

"Oh," answered the wife, "he is gone into the country to his mother's great uncle; he is going to stay there some time."

"What has he gone there for, and he never even said goodbye to me!"

"Well, he likes being there, and he told me he should be away quite six weeks; he is well looked after there."

"I feel very unhappy about it," said the husband, "in case it should not be all right, and he ought to have said goodbye to me."

With this he went on with his dinner, and said, "Little Marleen, why do you weep? Brother will soon be back." Then he asked his wife for more pudding, and as he ate, he threw the bones under the table.

Little Marleen went upstairs and took her best silk handkerchief out of her bottom drawer, and in it she wrapped all the bones from under the table and carried them outside, and all the time she did nothing but weep. Then she laid them in the green grass under the almond tree, and she had no sooner done so, then all her sadness seemed to leave her, and she wept no more. And now the almond tree began to move, and the branches waved backwards and forwards, first away from one another, and then together again, as it might be someone clapping their hands for joy. After this a mist came round the tree, and in the midst of it there was a burning as of fire, and out of the fire there flew a beautiful bird, that rose high into the air, singing magnificently, and when it could no more be seen, the almond tree stood there as before, and the silk handkerchief and the bones were gone.

Little Marleen now felt as lighthearted and happy as if her brother were still alive, and she went back to the house and sat down cheerfully to the table and ate.

The bird flew away and alighted on the house of a goldsmith and began to sing:

"My mother killed her little son;
My father grieved when I was gone;
My sister loved me best of all;
She laid her kerchief over me,
And took my bones that they might lie
Underneath the almond tree
Kywitt, Kywitt, what a beautiful bird am I!"

The goldsmith was in his workshop making a gold chain, when he heard the song of the bird on his roof. He thought it so beautiful that he got up and ran out, and as he crossed the threshold he lost one of his slippers. But he ran on into the middle of the street, with a slipper on one foot and a sock on the other; he still had on his apron, and still held the gold chain and the pincers in his hands, and so he stood gazing up at the bird, while the sun came shining brightly down on the street.

"Bird," he said, "how beautifully you sing! Sing me that song again."

"Nay," said the bird, "I do not sing twice for nothing. Give that gold chain, and I will sing it you again."

"Here is the chain, take it," said the goldsmith. "Only sing me that again."

The bird flew down and took the gold chain in his right claw, and then he alighted again in front of the goldsmith and sang:

"My mother killed her little son;
My father grieved when I was gone;
My sister loved me best of all;
She laid her kerchief over me,
And took my bones that they might lie
Underneath the almond tree
Kywitt, Kywitt, what a beautiful bird am I!"

Then he flew away, and settled on the roof of a shoemaker's house and sang:

"My mother killed her little son;
My father grieved when I was gone;
My sister loved me best of all;
She laid her kerchief over me,
And took my bones that they might lie
Underneath the almond tree
Kywitt, Kywitt, what a beautiful bird am I!"

The shoemaker heard him, and he jumped up and ran out in his shirt sleeves, and stood looking up at the bird on the roof with his hand over his eyes to keep himself from being blinded by the sun.

"Bird," he said, "how beautifully you sing!" Then he called through the door to his wife: "Wife, come out; here is a bird, come and look at it and hear how beautifully it sings." Then he called his daughter and the children, then the apprentices, girls and boys, and they all ran up the street to look at the bird, and saw how splendid it was with its red and green feathers, and its neck like burnished gold, and eyes like two bright stars in its head.

"Bird," said the shoemaker, "sing me that song again."

"Nay," answered the bird, "I do not sing twice for nothing; you must give me something."

"Wife," said the man, "go into the garret; on the upper shelf you will see a pair of red shoes; bring them to me." The wife went in and fetched the shoes.

"There, bird," said the shoemaker, "now sing me that song again."

The bird flew down and took the red shoes in his left claw, and then he went back to the roof and sang:

"My mother killed her little son;
My father grieved when I was gone;
My sister loved me best of all;
She laid her kerchief over me,
And took my bones that they might lie
Underneath the almond tree
Kywitt, Kywitt, what a beautiful bird am I!"

When he had finished, he flew away. He had the chain in his right claw and the shoes in his left, and he flew right away to a mill, and the mill went "Click clack, click clack, click clack." Inside the mill were twenty of the miller's men hewing a stone, and as they went "Hick hack, hick hack, hick hack," the mill went "Click clack, click clack, click clack."

The bird settled on a lime tree in front of the mill and sang:

"My mother killed her little son;
then one of the men left off,
My father grieved when I was gone;
two more men left off and listened,
My sister loved me best of all;
then four more left off,
She laid her kerchief over me,
And took my bones that they might lie
Now there were only eight at work,
Underneath,
and now only five,
the almond tree.
and now only one,
Kywitt, Kywitt, what a beautiful bird am I!"

then he looked up and the last one had left off work.

"Bird," he said, "what a beautiful song that is you sing! Let me hear it too; sing it again."

"Nay," answered the bird, "I do not sing twice for nothing; give me that millstone, and I will sing it again."

"If it belonged to me alone," said the man, "you should have it."

"Yes, yes," said the others: "if he will sing again, he can have it."

The bird came down, and all the twenty millers set to and lifted up the stone with a beam; then the bird put his head through the hole and took the stone round his neck like a collar, and flew back with it to the tree and sang:

"My mother killed her little son;
My father grieved when I was gone;
My sister loved me best of all;
She laid her kerchief over me,
And took my bones that they might lie

Underneath the almond tree
Kywitt, Kywitt, what a beautiful bird am I!"

And when he had finished his song, he spread his wings, and with the chain in his right claw, the shoes in his left, and the millstone round his neck, he flew right away to his father's house.

The father, the mother, and little Marleen were having their dinner.

"How lighthearted I feel," said the father, "so pleased and cheerful."

"And I," said the mother, "I feel so uneasy, as if a heavy thunderstorm were coming."

But little Marleen sat and wept and wept.

Then the bird came flying towards the house and settled on the roof.

"I do feel so happy," said the father, "and how beautifully the sun shines; I feel just as if I were going to see an old friend again."

"Ah!" said the wife, "and I am so full of distress and uneasiness that my teeth chatter, and I feel as if there were a fire in my veins," and she tore open her dress; and all the while little Marleen sat in the corner and wept, and the plate on her knees was wet with her tears.

The bird now flew to the almond tree and began singing:

"My mother killed her little son;

the mother shut her eyes and her ears, that she might see and hear nothing, but there was a roaring sound in her ears like that of a violent storm, and in her eyes a burning and flashing like lightning:

My father grieved when I was gone;

"Look, mother," said the man, "at the beautiful bird that is singing so magnificently; and how warm and bright the sun is, and what a delicious scent of spice in the air!"

My sister loved me best of all;

then little Marleen laid her head down on her knees and sobbed.

"I must go outside and see the bird nearer," said the man.

"Ah, do not go!" cried the wife. "I feel as if the whole house were in flames!"

But the man went out and looked at the bird.

She laid her kerchief over me,
And took my bones that they might lie
Underneath the almond tree
Kywitt, Kywitt, what a beautiful bird am I!"

With that the bird let fall the gold chain, and it fell just round the man's neck, so that it fitted him exactly.

He went inside, and said, "See, what a splendid bird that is; he has given me this beautiful gold chain, and looks so beautiful himself."

But the wife was in such fear and trouble, that she fell on the floor, and her cap fell from her head.

Then the bird began again:

"My mother killed her little son;

"Ah me!" cried the wife, "if I were but a thousand feet beneath the earth, that I might not hear that song."

My father grieved when I was gone;

then the woman fell down again as if dead.

My sister loved me best of all;

"Well," said little Marleen, "I will go out too and see if the bird will give me anything."

So she went out.

She laid her kerchief over me,
And took my bones that they might lie

and he threw down the shoes to her,

Underneath the almond tree
Kywitt, Kywitt, what a beautiful bird am I!"

And she now felt quite happy and lighthearted; she put on the shoes and danced and jumped about in them. "I was so miserable," she said, "when I came out, but that has all passed away; that is indeed a splendid bird, and he has given me a pair of red shoes."

The wife sprang up, with her hair standing out from her head like flames of fire. "Then I will go out too," she said, "and see if it will lighten my misery, for I feel as if the world were coming to an end."

But as she crossed the threshold, crash! the bird threw the millstone down on her head, and she was crushed to death.

The father and little Marleen heard the sound and ran out, but they only saw mist and flame and fire rising from the spot, and when these had passed, there stood the little brother, and he took the father and little Marleen by the hand; then they all three rejoiced, and went inside together and sat down to their dinners and ate.